Under
the
Lemon Trees

Under
the
Lemon Trees

Bhira Backhaus

THOMAS DUNNE BOOKS
ST. MARTIN'S PRESS · NEW YORK

THOMAS DUNNE BOOKS.

An imprint of St. Martin's Press.

UNDER THE LEMON TREES. Copyright © 2009 by Bhira Backhaus. All rights reserved. Printed in the United States of America. For information, address St. Martin's Press, 175 Fifth Avenue, New York, N.Y. 10010.

www.thomasdunnebooks.com

www.stmartins.com

Library of Congress Cataloging-in-Publication Data

Backhaus, Bhira.
    Umder the lemon trees / Bhira Backhaus.—1st ed.
        p. cm.
    "Thomas Dunne books."
    ISBN-13: 978-0-312-37953-7
    ISBN-10: 0-312-37953-6
    1. East Indians—California—Fiction. 2. Teenage girls—Fiction. 3. Identity (Psychology)—Fiction. 4. Assimilation (Sociology)—Fiction. 5. Domestic fiction.
    I. Title.
    PS3602.A345U53   2009
    813'.6—dc22   2008035779

First Edition: March 2009

10   9   8   7   6   5   4   3   2   1

For my
mother and father

Acknowledgments

I would like to express my gratitude to my agent, Molly Lyons, and to my editors, Erin Brown and Katie Gilligan, for their faith in this book. Also, a sincere thanks to T. M. Mc-Nally for his guidance and the occasional reality check; to Laura Wynne, Patricia Hays, and Marylee MacDonald for reading the manuscript and for their friendship; and to my family—my husband, Andrew, for his unwavering enthusiasm and support, and my children, Jaclyn and Ben, for joy in my life.

Under
the
Lemon Trees

Onε

The chance to love comes to all of us. We listen for its sound beneath our footsteps, seek it down the improbable paths that we roam. Sometimes we choose to turn away from it, or must. Or we fail to see it at all and it vanishes like a feather on air, leaving only the flicker of a shadow as it passes. By the time she married, my sister, Neelam, had surrendered herself to a fate dictated not by desire or foolish dreams but by the positions of the stars and planets. She was engaged to a man whom she had never met, whom she knew merely by the fuzzy image in a photograph, but whose destiny was clearly aligned with hers. Over cups of scalding tea, my mother watched Charan Kaur as she pored over the creased pages of her astrological charts, settling on the twenty-first of February that year, 1976, as an auspicious day for her daughter's wedding. Thus were Neelam's shame and misfortune to be swept away, forgotten altogether if memory were charitable.

The same Charan Kaur had arranged the match. My mother had developed an unfaltering faith in the woman to whom she had turned to ensure her third child would be a boy. This action troubled me when I learned of it: Had Charan Kaur merely consulted her charts, or was she present in some magical way the fated night my mother and father had, no doubt, so joyously made love, believing a son would soon bless our family? The cherished birth of my younger brother, Prem, nearly a year later only affirmed my mother's instincts. Charan Kaur had become in the interim a much-sought-after matchmaker. Those who took interest in such matters could tell you of her successes: She managed to join the feuding Gill and Thiara families, joining Oak Grove's most eligible Indian bachelor with the starchy, morose eldest daughter of the Thiaras, thereby doubling the land holdings of each. Convinced of the woman's unique and supple talents, my mother eagerly enlisted her to find a suitable boy for her troubled daughter.

My mother, after all, was not one to leave things to chance. In her own way, she was a generous woman, with a blind faith in most things working out in the end. Over the dusty-blue damask sofa in our living room hung portraits of Guru Nanak, Jesus, and John Kennedy, as if she were hedging her bets. Nothing in life is a coincidence, she'd always told us as a preface to some exemplary tale. A favorite of hers: "There was my Uncle Dev, who once took the wrong train from Jalandhar to New Delhi and wound up in a small village in the highlands. At a lunch stand, he encountered a former colleague from the postal service who had retired there with his two daughters. At dinner at this man's home that very evening, Uncle Dev was particularly taken with the eldest daughter, Seema, a ravishing beauty ever so reluctant to marry, though she was nearing twenty years of age. That night, Uncle Dev, unable to sleep because of his thoughts of desire, roamed the dark village streets, when a holy man dressed in mere rags approached him. This holy man looked deep into Uncle's fevered eyes and instructed him to drink at dawn from the spring at the hill beyond to purify himself against such injurious thoughts. Uncle Dev did so the following morning, but then collapsed, exhausted, against a rock nearby. Along came Seema, the lovely daughter, her slender arms embracing a ceramic pot to collect drinking water. She revived him, and soon they were married and produced seven excellent children. Coincidence that he took the wrong train?" my mother would ask, her hands clasped triumphantly. "Impossible!"

We lived on Fremont Road in a three-bedroom house on the outskirts of the small northern California town of Oak Grove. Surrounding the town in every direction, orchards had supplanted a fertile landscape once lush with grasses and dotted with sprawling oaks. The broad domes of Sikh temples competed in the skyline with the lean spires of Christian churches. Since the immigration laws had changed, the town pulsed to the exotic beat of tablas and the sound tracks of the most recent Indian films to hit American shores. The all-white city council members learned to publish their campaign literature in Punjabi, as though each tumultuous decision made at City Hall had some great bearing on our tight little universe. My uncle Avtar, my father's older brother and the first in my family to settle in America, had taken advantage of cheap land prices following World War II to begin securing his holdings. He'd offered my father, Mohinder Singh Rai, a small share of it when he emigrated from India in 1957, seeing that my mother was already expecting her first child.

A young woman scarcely had time to weave the fragile fabric of her dreams in our town. All too soon the hazy faces and soft mouths of imagined lovers were replaced by hard, real ones. Neelam married Davinder Mahal when she was eighteen; I was fifteen then. It was a hasty affair that left all involved a bit breathless and stunned as she exited the front door carrying the last of her bags. In the days following the wedding, my mother roamed the house with a light, buoyant step, as one who is certain of victory.

I hurried off the school bus into a full, slanted wind one fall afternoon, months after Neelam's wedding, the sycamore leaves tossing around me like many brown hands. I was attending Oak Grove High School, and afternoons, I would return home to a living room where my mother, sister, and aunts sat like fleshy fixtures drinking tea. Inside the house, the air felt stiff and dry. Aunt Teji, my uncle Avtar's wife and the eldest among us, greeted me when I entered the living room and tapped the sofa seat next to her lightly with an open hand before pushing her smudged glasses back on her nose. I settled back beside her, taking in the sandalwood scent of her wool shawl. My mother's attention was focused on her sister, my aunt Manjit, who perched at the edge of her chair in her erect and ever-alert way.

"If it worked once, why shouldn't it again?" my mother said, casually flicking crumbs from her kameez. Her voice had a slightly ragged edge to it, and I recognized that, with my presence, the conversation had shifted into what I called "code talk"—matters urgent and unavoidable that required immediate discussion. For I had learned that the women who surrounded me did far more than drink tea on these balmy afternoons; they gave shape to fortune and destiny. I looked from face to face for clues. Neelam turned toward the wall in one long sweep of her lashes and a streak of crimson rose along the side of her neck.

"There's an ointment that can be rubbed into the feet each night. Santi was telling me," Aunt Manjit said. She had a closet shelf stuffed with ointments and ingredients for salves—tattered paper bags filled with old walnut husks, dried pomegranate skins and ajuwan seeds— the woody scent mixing with that of shoe leather from the scuffed collection of boots and sneakers piled on the floor. She was my mother's younger sister and they were perhaps as different from each other as Neelam and I. Only twenty-eight, her body hadn't softened and spread after three children, but had sharpened into the pointed, bony angles of her chin, shoulders, and hips, a body turning in on itself.

"I think the young bride and groom can handle these matters on their own." Aunt Teji shifted her soft, pliant weight on the sofa and playfully slapped Neelam's thigh. Neelam, who had thus far displayed no emotion other than visible agony, stirred and languidly peeled herself from the sofa back, sitting upright.

My brother, Prem, burst into the room with a basketball hooked under one arm and, without any greeting, plunged a dusty hand into the platter of pakoras.

"As many as you like, son," my mother said. "Here, take some for Deepa, too." She handed him the entire platter. Deepa was Aunt Teji's son. The two boys attended junior high together, and for a seemingly endless stretch of their lives, they likened themselves to twin Indian Kareem Abdul-Jabbars, despite their delayed growth spurts.

Neelam rose, collected teacups, and disappeared into the kitchen. The door creaked as it swung shut behind her. I wanted to follow her in, but I remained helplessly sunk into the soft cushions next to Aunt Teji. The sofa rose and fell with Aunt Teji's momentous sigh, and the others joined in a round of sighing and silent assessing. A fly buzzed and skittered against the window.

"It's all in the Lord's hands anyway," Aunt Manjit said. She flung her bony elbows in the air for emphasis. How could something that a moment ago was to be assuaged with an ointment now be in the Lord's hands? I wondered.

"Jeeto, put on another pot of tea." With a snap of her head, my mother motioned me toward the kitchen, from where I heard Neelam running the water and the clinking of cups. There was something she wished to say to the others, something dark and secretive, I was certain, that required my absence. I will miss it, I thought as I plunged past the kitchen door. I'd been unable to decipher entirely the discussion to this point. I knew it had something to do with Neelam, that after eight months of marriage, she had yet to announce any news of an imminent child.

Eight months of marriage had not healed her heart, but perhaps steeled it in some other way. I had lain awake myself those weeks before the wedding, listening to her broken, troubled sleep. Neelam had married so suddenly, married a boy she didn't know, but whom someone—Charan Kaur, apparently—had deemed appropriate. She'd abandoned her plans for secretarial school, and I had watched it all happen, though I was banned from the late-night discussions behind closed doors, when I mostly heard my mother's muffled and pleading voice. Neelam had confided little in me, but suffered in a silent, stoic way. Not that there was anything dreadful about her husband, Davinder, who liked to call himself David, since he'd now lived in the States awhile. Marriage had already softened him a bit about the edges, and around Neelam he couldn't resist the sighing and simpering. Neelam had inherited the best of my parents physically—my father's wide almond eyes, which registered the barest flicker of emotion, my mother's sumptuous curves. One couldn't say that Davinder was inattentive. But before him, I knew, there had been Hari.

In the kitchen, I filled a pot with cold bubbling water from the tap to brew a fresh pot of tea for the women. Neelam's hands were immersed in the basin of soapy water and her arms appeared as though they had been lopped off at the wrists. Her thick blue-black braid hung forward over one shoulder, snaking down her chest.

"More tea? Aren't they ready to leave yet?" She spoke as though this were still her home, that after the others left, she would remain with us, where she belonged. Though Neelam still visited the house nearly daily after her wedding, I missed her constant presence, the slow sway of her shoulders and hips ahead of me in the hallway as I would try to bolt past. She possessed an inherent grace that had bloomed at an early age, that brought approving nods and smiles from the older women and, I had noticed, not a few men. Prem missed her, too. She had been motherly to him, fussing over him, plying him with treats and favors, shielding him with her body if need be when things got rough and heated between him and me.

I cracked the kitchen door open a few inches and peered out at the ladies. Aunt Teji sprawled against the back of the sofa, her eyes shut and her chest heaving with each deep, rhythmic breath. "Aunt Teji's snoring," I said, dashing Neelam's hopes that the afternoon's gathering might soon break up. No one dared to wake Aunt Teji whenever she fell asleep, until she'd had a fitful nap replete with gruff snorts and odd mutterings.

Neelam rolled her eyes and shook the cups under the steaming stream of water. She vigorously dried them with a white cotton towel and set them on the counter. The sleeve of her kameez slipped off one shoulder, exposing the shell-shaped birthmark that kissed her collarbone. "How's driver's ed going?"

"Well, I know what it feels like to hit a curb at five miles an hour. Parallel parking." I added milk to the tea and turned down the flame. "I don't know. Mr. Ronin keeps his eyes shut most of the time when I'm driving."

"He did that with me, too. He must know we're Mrs. Rai's daughters," Neelam said, laughing. "I was so relieved to get my license and that Mom didn't have to drive us around anymore."

I nodded, though I was still regular prey to my mother's herky-jerky, foot-on-the-pedal method of getting across town. She had practically opened a driving school for newly arrived Indian women at one point, toting the three of us along for perilous, bumpy rides crammed in backseats with other children.

"Jeet." Neelam pronounced it in two slow, urgent syllables: Jee-*eet*. She was looking down, nervously stroking her braid as if it were an appendage, an arm with plump, dark flesh. When she lifted her eyes to me, my breath must have stopped momentarily. I knew what she was about to say, and dreaded hearing the words. "You're still checking the mail every day yourself?"

I nodded, feeling my blood slow within me. I knew of whom she spoke.

"But nothing comes for me? You'd tell me first, wouldn't you?"

"Of course. You're still getting notices for senior-class rings, that's all."

Her chin trembled faintly. I'd yet to experience that kind of love. All last semester, Joey Kaminsky and I had exchanged long, burning glances in the back of the classroom in U.S. Government, but then I had seen him the final week of school behind the crab apples planted against the wall of the gym, his mouth hovering around Cynthia Wold's neck. The memory felt dim and paltry as I stared into Neelam's warm, glistening eyes.

She gripped the edge of the sink with both hands and gazed out the window. A row of red, blue, and purple smoked-glass dishes, earned for our mother in fervent coin tosses at the county fair, lined the deep windowsill. Outside, the gnarled fruit trees stood like old men tired of stretching their limbs. In winter, with their leaves long fallen and matted copper and rust against the muddy ground, you could just make out Aunt Teji's house through the dense crisscross of branches.

"I don't think he'd try to get in touch with you here. Do you know where he is now?" I asked. The thrill of these secrets fluttered through my body.

Neelam shook her head. "Don't mention it to anyone. I wanted to ask you before, but it seemed ridiculous, in a way. I guess it still does."

My mother burst through the door with all the finesse of an invading army tank. "How long does it take to brew a pot of tea? You're standing around while the ladies are waiting." Her face turned from mine to Neelam's.

"Just sisters talking," Neelam said.

"Look, you've cooked it too long." My mother pulled the pot off the burner. The tea had boiled away to half its original volume.

"Aunt Teji was sleeping anyway," I protested.

"Well, she's wide-awake and quite thirsty. Neelam, bring out more sweets."

In the living room, Aunt Manjit was back on the topic of old Mrs. Sidhu, a favorite of hers. "Did you see what she wore to the Soba wedding? That orchid pink? You'd think she was trying to steal the groom."

"So the poor old thing wants to turn a few heads. There's plenty of lonely widowers to take notice," Aunt Teji said, waving a hand. My mother wore a poorly feigned expression of disapproval.

The air hung like sticky, thick molasses in the room. I tapped the tip of my sandal repeatedly against the worn wooden leg of the coffee table, earning another stern look from my mother. Such toe tapping was considered a brazen, wanton gesture for a woman, and all my life my mother had sought ways to keep my restless legs still. As the women finally rose to depart, Aunt Manjit sneezed—twice. Everyone retreated to the sofas again for the customary half hour it would take for bad luck to charitably exit our household.

I walked Aunt Teji home later. Neelam had left quietly, nudging me to indicate that we would talk more tomorrow. Aunt Teji and I set off down the dirt road that cut through to the other side of the property. The door on my father's shop was padlocked, as he was away making deliveries for the afternoon. My cousin Deepa followed behind us or scurried ahead, climbing a branch and hopping down every so often. The late-afternoon light had a way of flattering everything at that time of day. Aunt Teji's face looked blushed and radiant in the bronze light, and I could clearly imagine her as the vigorous and willful young woman who had come from India many years ago as Uncle Avtar's bride. Even now, her carriage was strong and erect, and I had trouble at times keeping up with her on these walks, stopping to linger over things as I often did. I rolled up my pant legs and slipped the sandals off my feet, letting my toes curl into the dust. It sifted like fine flour around my ankles, the dust, my skin, one color, so that my legs looked like golden stems rising from the ground.

We approached the big white house, a patchwork of extensions and add-ons constructed as the Rai family grew. Aunt Teji often invited me in, though my father didn't like me spending much time there, since he and Uncle Avtar for years now had spoken to each other only at weddings and funerals (and the women found they could tolerate their stubbornness, since such events came around often enough). When I did go in, Aunt Teji would stop in the shaded yard and provide detailed updates on the menagerie of plants that were like quarrelsome family to her—the fig tree that overproduced each year, attracting swarms of blackbirds, the weak roses that never saw enough sun. The Algerian ivy was overtaking the lawn by the front door. Behind the garage stood the goat pen, where Uncle Avtar spent a good deal of his spare time. A small corrugated-metal shed that he generously called his office was behind the house. Inside, the room was spare, with a concrete pad for a floor. In its center, a shiny black Smith Corona typewriter sat on the old scarred wooden table I'd watched him butcher goats on, though as far as I knew, he couldn't tell an *a* from an *e,* for he'd never learned to read or write. A white family had once owned the land and the house, and I imagined it must've looked quite different—tidy and tamed, not the hodgepodge of life Aunt Teji had accumulated around her even as she strived for some order. Uncle's blue Ford pickup truck pulled into the gravel driveway, and I stopped where I was, just short of the once-prolific bed of cilantro that Aunt Teji was about to tell me had gone to seed and was dying out. She disappeared into the house without so much as a wave to her husband.

My uncle hopped out of the cab. "Jeeto," he called to me, waving with his fedora in his hand. He moved in long strides across the lawn, trampling the sycamore leaves scattered in his wake. "Come help me feed the goats," he said, half-teasing. "You used to like that when you were a little girl." He wiped his brow, which was gleaming with perspiration, with his denim shirtsleeve. His hair, once his hat had been removed, lay sweaty and flat over his head; the occasional gray flecks in the day's growth of beard glinted against his dark skin. He smiled, the soft lines around his mouth and eyes in sudden relief as he squinted into the sun. When I looked at him this way, I could still imagine the young man he had once been. His face was as familiar to me as my father's.

"I'm sorry, Chacha. I can't today. I've got to get back."

He nodded, understanding in his own way how things were.

My mother must've waited that night, watched for the crack of light under my bedroom door to disappear before she came in. She rarely interrupted as I did schoolwork, yet she made certain that I wouldn't get to it until well after dinner, after the dishes were washed, dried, and put away. In this way, my education became a source of tension, a wall between us. If I wished to distance myself from her, I would merely recite theorems from my geometry book, or comment on the Louisiana Purchase, and she would grow silent. "Hoshaar, smart," she would say to the others, referring to me. I had to believe a thread of pride existed somewhere in that statement, just as there can be a vein of silver in stone, although it takes the smashing to find it. My education frightened her, for she knew one day it would take me away from her.

"Jeeto," she called to me, pushing the door open. Her long, wavy hair, loosened from its dignified bun, cascaded well past her shoulders. In the shadowy light, she appeared as a young woman, as though it were Neelam coming to bed when we shared our room.

I sat up cross-legged on the bed and flipped on a light. She wandered into the room and inspected a page in my geometry book, which lay open on my desk.

"We're learning the Pythagorean theorem, how to find the lengths on the sides of a triangle."

"Acha," she replied, "okay," as if she had gotten the essence of it. At such times, she would nonchalantly leaf through a book, and I'd see a wonder seep through her, a guarded amazement that there was a system, a body of logic beyond her gods and goddesses. This from a woman who had lived in the States nearly twenty years now, whose husband was a heavy-equipment mechanic. She smoothed my cotton blankets and rested one hip at the edge of the bed. The lamp on the nightstand cast a bright arc of light over her green kameez and the pink covers on my bed. Her full, unlined face remained in a shadow. "So what were you and Neelam talking about today?" she asked casually.

"Nothing, really. She might go shopping in Berkeley on Saturday. Can I go with her?"

"With all the clothes she has? She hasn't even worn every outfit once yet."

I shrugged. "She has those empty closets to fill in that new house." Neelam and Davinder had bought a house in a subdivision on the west end of town called Stonebrook Heights, though as far as I could tell, its elevation was no different from the dull flatness of the rest of Oak Grove.

"Now that I think of it, you could use something for the festival. But I won't pay the prices in Berkeley. I'll have Balwant Kaur make you another one."

I sat forward, resting my chin in my palm and picking at the loose weave of the blanket with my other hand. "She'll make something ugly, like she always does. I think she wants me to look ugly on purpose. Last time, I had to wear that beige thing with huge light blue roses. I felt like I was walking around in someone's awful curtains."

She took my arm and patted it. "When you marry, you can have nice things to wear, like Neelam." I didn't want to look at her then, though she watched carefully for some positive reaction from me. "If Neelam's going anyway, you can go along," she continued. "Davinder's going, too, isn't he?"

"I don't know."

"Well, they had some beautiful chunis at Sardar's. You can pick up one or two for me," she said, though she owned veils of every color imaginable.

Later in the dark and quiet, I could hear a faint humming in the walls of the house. A branch on the walnut tree outside my window creaked against the eaves, as though its burden was greater now that it was shedding its oily leaves and hard, wrinkled nuts. I could imagine Neelam lying in the bed against the other wall, in the grip of a fevered slumber. As I settled back into my pillow, I felt my pulse roaring into its cushiony fibers, and I knew that I would lie to her again.

Two

The letter lay on my mother's dresser among the unopened amber bottles of cologne that she collected like a precious cache of jewels. Tucked inside the envelope was the black-and-white photograph of Davinder Mahal, a corner of it already beginning to crease from the many hands that had handled it and the few that would handle it many times. Sitting against the dark mahogany wood and the glittering glass, it became a small planetary object, the three of us—Neelam, my mother, and I—revolving about it like moons held fast by its gravity. I had passed the half-opened bedroom door late one night, to see my mother leaning against the headboard, the letter in her hands as she mouthed the words silently in her usual fashion. I used pretenses myself to enter her bedroom— the retrieval of her shawl before an outing, the stowing of folded laundry—to glimpse again the features of my future brother-in-law's face. A thick flush of wavy black hair dominated his head, as if impatiently awaiting the remainder of his features to catch up and balance the whole. His expression bore the somber quality so common in Indian photographs, the avoidance of any display of overt joy or satisfaction that might look undignified, so that the viewer had to depend on the eyes for any useful clues at all about the subject. Yet I saw in the corners of his mouth the rudiments of a smile about to bloom, even if the eyes remained serious, wet-looking, as though he was waiting to blink. He wore a black suit and tie, the white collar of his shirt slightly loose about his neck.

It had arrived on a chilly December afternoon in the hands of Charan Kaur. It was hardly a day to be out, with a dull, creeping fog coating everything like pewter. Charan Kaur stood shivering in the doorway, with only her sea green eyes and delicate nose peeking out from under a russet-colored shawl. Inside, she reached into a large canvas bag. She would not surrender the letter to me, but kept it pinched between her fingers. "Your mother will be pleased with the news I have for her," she told me. I led her across the patchy winter lawn and down the gravel driveway toward my father's shop.

The old wooden structure had once housed the assorted equipment required for the running of the farm—tractors, trailers, sprayers, rows of wooden ladders used in the harvest leaning against the walls on all sides. During marathon games of hide-and-seek as a child, I would slip inside there and crouch among the metal flanks, which I imagined belonging to giant insects or horses, listening for small footsteps as the dusty air and diesel burned at my nose. The first change my father made when he converted it into an auto shop was to pour a concrete floor, and those earthy odors, along with a trivial slice of history, were sealed away under the hard surface. The entire family had assisted one warm and breezy afternoon in coating the parrot green exterior a neutral gray-blue, with fine mists of paint bandying through the air and pelting our faces and arms. We hacked back the tangled branches of the mulberry trees that clung to its walls and roof, then stood back to survey the appalling outcome of our efforts.

I unlatched the cold metal lock and heaved the sliding door open far enough to let Charan Kaur enter the shop. A bright apron of light leaked onto the floor from a bulb slung on an axle beneath a truck. The '65 flatbed Chevy belonged to the Sidhus, and my father had been working on it the better part of the week. His booted feet jutted out from beneath its front end. A small space heater buzzed and rattled a few yards away.

"Jeeto, bring me the long needle-nose pliers in the second drawer," he said, his voice escaping into the hollow metal channels under the truck. He'd learned to recognize his children as much by the sounds of their footsteps on that concrete slab as by their voices or faces.

"Masi Charan Kaur is here," I said. My father slid out on his dolly and stood up.

Her neck tilted at a demure angle, Charan Kaur brought her palms together in greeting. "Sat Sri Akal." She covered her head once, then again with her shawl, fussing mightily with each fold before clasping her hands at her waist. "Bhaji, we've finally received word on the question of Neelam."

My father scrubbed his hands at the sink a long minute. His coveralls were grayed and faded along the back areas that pressed for hours at a time against the dolly. The sound of Neelam's name coming from this woman's mouth appeared unsettling to him, as well. He'd argued with my mother over her unreasonable rush to marry Neelam. I could see the tendons working in his neck and pulling at his jaw as he silently dried his hands on a towel. "What question of Neelam?"

"The boy's family has written from India. They sound amenable to the marriage. Here, they've sent a photo for your approval." The photo slipped off the crisp pages of the letter as she unfolded it and then fluttered to the floor. The remote and solemn face stared back from the grimy surface and across thousands of miles. What would Neelam say to it? She was away visiting a friend for the afternoon. She's relinquished everything, I thought, for a few words exchanged between my mother and this woman . . . and now this face looking up from the ground. I handed the photo to my father. Charan Kaur watched closely for his reaction. His thick black brows threw a shadow over his eyes, but his face remained placid and steady. My father was handsome, I suppose, in a lean, austere way. Growing up, I'd had a vague notion that it came from having denied himself something essential, but there were the soft, wide eyes, vulnerable, like Neelam's, that demanded consideration and countered the stony set of his jaw as he worked on engine after engine.

"He's quite fair," Charan Kaur said. "And tall, I hear. Of course, you can't tell that from the photo." She stifled a mild giggle with a corner of her shawl, her eyes fixed somewhere past my father's shoulder. I had never seen her so nervous, so at odds with the movement of her own body, the placement of her feet and hands; the faithful protection offered by distant stars and planets had abandoned her temporarily. "The family works in mining. A *top* family in Ludhiana." The "*top,*" spoken in English, made a small uncorking sound.

"We'll go into the house. Jasbir will want to see it. And Neelam, of course."

My mother had returned from the market, and, taking the photograph from my father's hands, her approval was clear and swift. "A fine-looking young man," she announced in a congratulatory tone. Alongside her on the sofa, Charan Kaur basked in the sublime essence of her good deeds. It had grown dark and the low windows reflected back into the room the pale blue walls washed in the yellow lamplight and our silhouettes. We waited for the sound of the pickup truck Neelam had borrowed for the afternoon, and when she came in, her eyes first met Charan Kaur's and she understood.

The engagement was brief then, and not uneventful, with Uncle Avtar insisting on his particular mischievous brand of involvement in such affairs. The Mahals arrived from India in early February and remained most of the three weeks prior to the wedding with relatives in the Bay Area. News of their stay came to us in intermittent and unexpected waves: They'd enjoyed a snowy interlude at Lake Tahoe, taken a tour of Alcatraz. Some mysterious conduit of information had been established to keep us abreast of their whereabouts. Sethi Mahal, an aunt of the groom's who resided in San Jose, had already visited once, plying us with hearsay so that Davinder's stature swelled among the Rai women. He grew yet taller, more clever with each anecdote. His aunt had not seen him since he was a boy in India, but the way he could swing a cricket bat even then! The close of each story brought a choreographed turning of heads in Neelam's direction (the lucky young lady!), and she bravely summoned the expected blush each time and displayed the proper level of coyness.

Davinder's image rose from the photograph and began to take a clearer shape in our minds. My mother began to speak of him as though he had always been a part of the family, constructing the scaffold of a story, a life she hoped to ease her daughter into, which Neelam and her husband would then infuse and fill with their own lines. Hari's name was never to be spoken again within the walls of our home, as if the silence could deconstruct that bit of history. But none of us could see into Neelam's heart. She withstood the scrutiny, the whispering, until it was generally agreed, for the time being at least, that hers was the briefest of falls from grace.

Hari had left town, after all, at the urging of his own family, swiftly dispatched by his grandfather to an unknown location to shield him from the kinds of threats the elder man himself had inflicted upon others. It had seemed a drastic course of action at the time, but one that my family certainly welcomed, since plans for Neelam's engagement were under way.

Hari was someone the Indian girls talked about. He was the grandson of Mohta Singh, one of the Punjabi men who'd emigrated to California early in the twentieth century, whom even Uncle Avtar held in some form of begrudged esteem. Hari was already a second-generation American, which in itself was not interesting to the girls. He simply looked comfortable in his skin, and carried none of the awkwardness that tormented other Indian boys as they watched white girls at school swaying through the hallways clad in miniskirts. When our school bus pulled into the parking lot in the morning, his souped-up Impala would cruise by, filled with Indian boys. He would pass me in the hallway, his skittish glance gliding over me with that curiosity, I realized later, felt for a sibling, one so closely tied to the object of one's fixation. One girl in our group said he dated, or ran around with girls, white or Indian.

So it surprised everyone that Neelam, who still insisted on wearing salwaar kameez to school many days, had caught his eye. Neelam and her band of Indian girlfriends managed to circumvent those rituals, great and small, of high school. They would huddle around a bench as if it were a spontaneous gathering that had nothing to do with academics, and there was little allure among them for events such as homecoming or prom. Neelam had been conceived, after all, in India, my mother would tell me a few years later in a rain of tears, on a rope bed on the rooftop of a brick dwelling on a humid summer night with bats swooping overhead and the air thick with the scent of jasmine.

But no one was more surprised by the whole affair than my mother. She came marching through the corridor at lunch period one October afternoon of my sophomore year, the ends of her veil snapping indignantly in the air behind her. I thought someone had died, the way she plucked me almost wordlessly from the table where I sat with friends, which was a feat for my mother, and guided me to the parking lot. In the car, Neelam was slouched in the backseat, her skin damp and translucent, like the peel of a grape. It had all been found out, apparently, and if my mother felt the once-solid walls of her world crumbling around her, I viewed my sister with a renewed curiosity. Neelam would not discuss the matter in any detail with me, but she had acknowledged that it was Hari whom my mother could only refer to as "*the boy*," "*that boy.*" But how, and when? Like so many issues in my young life, this, too, was left to the furtive workings of my nimble imagination. Neelam would only say that it was for my own good that she left me out of it, and I understood only later, when my mother confronted me. And when I told her truthfully that I had known nothing, she didn't believe me.

The weeks of gloomy weather that had stretched endlessly since early winter broke suddenly in mid-February. Out my window each morning, the sunlight slanted through the trees and lay in ripples over the tufts of grass that had sprouted everywhere. A steady trickle of visitors began to besiege our home, and we welcomed them, for all the bustle and activity was a respite from the pointed accusations and long silences. Neelam's wedding sari and jewelry arrived, and after a day or so of careful handling and admiration, stowed in a closet. My father worked long hours in order to clear up his schedule before and after the twenty-first, the date that had become like a fulcrum for all of us.

The official introduction of bride and groom was to be held at Aunt Teji's, for reasons never entirely clear to me. Uncle Avtar was the patriarchal head of the family, and some last-minute unofficial nod of approval may have been required of him. Having raised three spirited sons, he'd taken to sniffling about with the news that his eldest niece was soon to be wed. He took an exceptional interest in the whole business, it seemed to me, for while he was hardly aloof, he carried himself often in a manner that indicated he was a little too preoccupied to be bothered with those more mundane affairs of everyday family life (it frustrated Aunt Teji no end). But then just as easily, he could take you back behind his house and tell you about his goats for a good hour—about the cysts plaguing the female's udders or some other equally horrific condition—with a few questions about school thrown in to have it all appear constructive and worthwhile.

We were to meet the Mahals on Saturday, the week before the wedding. Aunt Teji suggested a lavish afternoon feast, but my mother insisted that tea and sweets would be appropriate. Aunt Teji bustled around as though she were the mother of the bride; her eldest son, Paul, who worked in the restaurant business in the Bay Area, remained unmarried, so it was the first big wedding among the Rai children. The day before the proposed meeting, the three of us, my mother, Neelam, and I, went into town for some last-minute items we needed. Neelam needed shoes to match the satin shell white salwaar kameez she'd selected to wear to the meeting, and we visited three shoe shops before she found the right pair. Neelam, by this point, seemed resigned to the whole affair, even relieved that the big event was now only a week away, and if she had to do it, she would have the right shoes and bags and matching everything. When we arrived home, Uncle Avtar's blue Ford pickup was parked beside a Caterpillar tractor on the driveway just beyond the house. He had one foot propped on the tread of the tractor and gestured with one hand to a young man next to him, pushing his gray fedora back on his head as he always did when he was excited about something, or felt a question forming in his mind. We stepped out of the car and Neelam called after him. My mother had already started toward the house, seeming too preoccupied to converse at the moment with the man whom she often considered her great nuisance of a brother-in-law. Hearing our greetings, the young man turned first, and it was the silence that followed that caused my mother to stop suddenly and look back. Before us materialized the figure from the image we had been stealing looks at in that photograph. He pulled his hands from his pockets and brought his palms together in greeting, the still, solemn image coming to life. Neelam's hand went instinctively to the strands of hair that, after hours of frantic shopping, had loosened in unruly wisps from her braid, as though she felt suddenly shabby.

"It's him!" I blurted out in something considerably louder than the whisper I had intended.

"I didn't know you ladies were in," Uncle Avtar said, stepping forward and pushing his hat even farther back on his head, so that it barely balanced there. "The shop is locked. I don't know where Mohinder is. I was giving the young man a quick tour of the place. Showing him what all the Rai family has managed in the States." He slapped Davinder playfully on the back, but the young man didn't appear to feel it, or to hear any of that brief conversation, for he had not taken his eyes off Neelam.

Well, the damage was done. Neelam turned sharply and disappeared into the house. My mother attempted the sort of skillful diplomacy required in those delicate moments when murder is really on one's mind. The only worse thing that could have taken place in her view was perhaps the premature death of the groom. "You'll come in for tea?" The exaggerated arch of her brows lent a vaguely threatening tone to her words.

"I've got to get the boy back." Uncle Avtar slung an arm through the open window of the truck, as if prepared to flee.

"Well, we'll meet all of your family tomorrow, then," she said to Davinder. She stormed up the front steps, her minor triumph being that Aunt Teji would hear about this. I had found something unbearably humorous about the situation—the "chance" meeting of the two that my uncle had so deviously managed to arrange—and doubled over each time I recalled the utterly silly and helpless look on the young man's face. Yet, when I closed my eyes to sleep that night, I could not forget that look, and a great urgency swept over me to be regarded in that same desperate, if foolish, way.

A large black Lincoln, followed by a smaller gold sedan, pulled up at Aunt Teji's around two o'clock the following day. We had arrived at noon, to find my cousin Juni, who was a year older than I, tidying up the last of some lawn clippings in the front yard. He greeted my mother in English—"Hello, Auntie"—finding his parents' native tongue largely useless. Also useless to him were the endless hours he'd spent working in the orchards, helping his father. He spent any idle afternoons hurling a baseball at a target he had fastened to the thick trunk of a cottonwood on their lawn. He watched sullenly as Neelam exited the car and adjusted her clothes, the bangles on her arm. The American way was much less complicated.

My uncle's home, like ours, rested back from the main road by several hundred yards, so that you drove over a small dirt lane through the orchard to reach it. The white house looked bright and exposed under the bare-limbed cottonwood trees that arced around the edge of the lawn. A splatter of daffodils nodded in a corner bed, where bearded iris would take over in summer. Inside, the sheer white curtains flared with the breeze at the open windows and a lingering trace of Pine-Sol mingled with the smell of cut grass. Aunt Teji had wiped and polished the furniture and the glassware and photographs, so that everything gleamed with little flecks of light. We set out the sweets—layers of golden ladoo, barfi, and besan—on Aunt Teji's best trays and arranged them on the coffee table. Neelam fussed awhile with a vase of daffodils, then moved them from one surface to another, finally settling on a side table next to the sofa.

It was Prem who alerted us first to the Mahals' arrival with a piercing "They're here!" cried from a front window. We tugged him back from the window, then huddled behind him for a quick peek at the entourage filing toward the house. My father, a bit re-laxed, no doubt, after sharing a shot of whiskey in a back room with his brother (this was one of those occasions where they would speak), opened the door and a crowd of Mahals entered. Davinder swept down and touched my parents' feet with his hands, a custom rarely seen anymore in California, at least among the Sikhs, so that it startled me at first when he dropped to the floor. Prem and Deepa carried in extra chairs from the dining room and everyone took seats. At the far end of the room, Neelam sat in her pearly white satin like a fresh calla lily poised in a slender vase. She rose long enough to quietly greet her new family.

Tea was brought in. There was talk of London, where the Ma-hals had stopped for two weeks on their way to the States. "Ken-sington, actually," Mrs. Mahal clarified in her Indo-British accent. She looked dignified in her royal blue-and-gold sari and with hair that was not streaked, but splotched with silver, as though she were some rare breed of person. Next to her sat a fair-skinned young woman, the wife of Davinder's older brother, in whose lap squirmed a restless baby boy.

"I have cousins in Southhampton," my mother announced proudly. "And Rugby. They visit every few years, always in the summer, when they can complain of the heat."

"Jasbir has family everywhere," my father said. "But the Rais—"

"Only in California and Punjab," Uncle Avtar said, butting in. He sat forward, resting his elbows on his thighs and clasping his palms together between his knees. Over his light blue buttoned shirt, he wore the burgundy wool vest Aunt Teji had knit for him years ago. "It was like a pipeline between Punjab and California for a while. In 1947, when I came over, my first boss—his name was Joe Duncan—he spoke fluent Spanish, and he would come over to me and start rattling off directions in Spanish. This was in the onion fields down in Imperial Valley. He wouldn't believe I was from India, until he finally checked the name on the payroll. So, you see, I had two new languages to learn."

"I hear there are four gurdwaras here in town," Mr. Mahal said, referring to the Sikh temples we attended.

"It's not that we are exceptionally religious people . . ." Uncle Avtar said, to laughter.

"There are factions," my father interjected. "It's inevitable when the population gets large enough."

"And, of course, the newest one must be more lavish than the last," Aunt Teji said.

"Many, many changes," Uncle Avtar said. "There were only a few dozen families in the area when they built the first one in Stockton. That was in 1912. Bring out the photo from 1950," Uncle Avtar said to Aunt Teji.

"They're not interested in those old times." But she rose just the same and left the room.

"We have wonderful festivals . . . Baisakhi, Independence Day," my mother piped in. She had only recently complained to my father that all these events were going downhill, even the weddings, where young couples were beginning to request disco music at the receptions.

"It's encouraging to see the traditions maintained. It's a little different in England, from what I saw," said Mrs. Mahal. The baby arched his back on his mother's lap, eager to be let down. He crawled off and plopped himself in the center of the room, slapping his palms against the glassy veneer of the polished wood floor, then crawled to Neelam's feet. She scooped him up and he sat contentedly with her awhile, wiggling his plump toes in the air.

"Are you in school right now, or working, bhout?" Mrs. Mahal asked Neelam.

"I've finished high school. I worked in a fabric store this summer, but right now, nothing. I help keep my father's books."

"If you start a business, you'll have an excellent accountant," my father said to Davinder.

"Young brides have plenty to occupy themselves with," Aunt Teji said, returning with a large framed photograph. "When I married your uncle, I had no idea how busy he would keep me knitting gloves. It would get cold in the winter and his hands would tighten up working outdoors, so I made him a pair of fingerless gloves. Well, when the other men saw his, they each wanted a pair, too. Even his boss. I must've knit fifty pairs that winter." She held the photograph before Mrs. Mahal. In it, a large group huddled on the steps before the arched doorways of the Stockton temple, the solid and upright bodies of the men clad in suits and turbans or hats gathered at the back, the women and children in front. If you squinted a bit, you could make out Aunt Teji in the second row with baby Paul slung on her hip.

The conversation took its natural course, the men talking loudly in one half of the room while the women gravitated to other topics. Neelam and Davinder barely acknowledged each other, but I suppose that was in keeping with all expectations. And they were spoken of by the others as if they were not even present. I had sat nearly motionless next to Neelam the entire time, playing on occasion with the hem of the sapphire blue kameez she had loaned me for the day. The whole scene seemed distant and unreal to me, these two families brought together—by what? The stars? A photograph? At any rate, here they sat, enchanted with one another's company, or at least making every effort to have it appear so. When the Mahals rose to leave, it was like long-lost relatives once again having to part.

Sangeets were held over the week—celebrations of food, song, and dance in anticipation of the wedding. The sofas in our living room were pushed against the walls so the women could perform their dances ostensibly out of view of the men, though we suspected

Uncle Avtar would be lurking somewhere, for he always found reason to be nearby on these occasions. I blushed as I watched the nimble bodies, young and old, circling the floor, the provocative hip thrusts that told the story of a virgin bride's sexual initiation. Among them was my mother, swirling, clapping, lithe and light on her heels, laughing like a girl. Neelam declined when a married friend of hers clutched her veil and pulled her toward the circle of dancers. Afterward, the room still pulsed with a sweaty odor and the echo of songs as I swept up paper plates and rumpled napkins.

The gurdwara we attended, where Neelam's wedding would be, was the first to be built in Oak Grove. It was rather simple in design, though anyone passing by would immediately recognize it was something other than a Christian church because of the single gold-painted minaret that towered over it and the fine latticework and scalloped edging at the entryway. The others had tried to outdo one another in ostentation and poorly attempted authenticity. One had a courtyard with shallow reflecting pools running the length of it—which had already had to be drained due to faulty plumbing. Another had three grand minarets, one at each corner, but the fourth had been forgone when funding suddenly dried up. Ours was not the grandest, but it had a dignity earned with the struggles to have the first one built. The oak trees that framed the building were beginning to spread and mature, and if the other temples were glaring in their newness and grandness, ours looked as if it had come to belong in that site.

On her wedding day, we whisked Neelam through the back entrance of the gurdwara into a small dressing room. She had dressed at home, a process requiring hours before the last gold bangle was fitted over her wrist. She swayed and shimmered with the weight of the gold and the gold thread woven through the fabric of her red silk sari. A throng of women and girls—those young enough to regard her with envy—gathered around her. Her friend Mani stood like a sentry by her side, viewing all others with that pinched, flat mouth of hers, as if they were rude intruders. My mother soon chased us all out, all but two of my aunts, who would escort Neelam into the cavernous main hall.

The room swelled with a swarming tide of people. Their voices rose in a collective din above them toward the high carved ceiling. On the women's side, Mrs. Mahal and her daughter-in-law sat on the floor next to Aunt Teji and Aunt Manjit. Across the aisle, crouched rather uncomfortably, were my father, Prem, and Uncle Avtar and his sons, with the Mahals flanking them on the far side. My cousin Surinder and I squeezed next to each other on the floor behind Aunt Teji. She was a cousin of sorts, meaning that we were not related by blood, but through some convoluted system of kinship. Surinder was the kind of girl who made the most of her looks, despite her longish nose and small, narrow eyes. Part of her jet black hair was gathered up in a twist at the back, and the rest fell well past her shoulders. Her mother allowed that. Surinder had called Neelam the night before to offer assistance with makeup, jewelry, and other details ("beauty treatment karenge," she had said gaily over the phone). We shuffled on the floor to make room for my mother. As the groom was seated, the crowd inched forward in a final push, so that my knees were scrunched against my face. A knee repeatedly grazed my back, and I turned, to see Charan Kaur wedged close behind me. We waited some moments—Davinder ahead of us, with his head bowed in a saffron-colored turban—before Neelam was led out. Only then did the crowd quiet down.

"She looks beautiful," Surinder whispered.

"You can't even see her," I said, for Neelam was covered head to toe in that glimmer of red and gold. The granthi appeared, dressed in white kurta pajamas and a charcoal-colored vest. His long beard swung like a silver curtain over his chest as he lowered himself before the low lectern on which the holy book, the Guru Granth

Sahib, lay under layers of brocade. A group of musicians, also dressed in white kurta pajamas, took up their instruments—a harmonia, and dhol, or tabla—and began to play. The harmonia player, a sunken-faced man whom I recognized from earlier performances, stretched his long hands over the bellowslike portion of the instrument and summoned the most aching and plaintive notes. Soon, Aunt Teji was pressing the backs of her hands against her cheeks, and among the married women, heads were bowed in communal reverence. An outsider, at least, would not have regarded it as a joyous celebration at that moment. All of us, together, seemed to be yielding to something, submitting quietly and seriously to that which had to be. I had attended countless weddings already in my fifteen years, but I felt the shape of something indistinct but hard and quiet lodge within me just as the music faded and the granthi began to pray.

Soon, Neelam and her new husband were circling the Guru Granth Sahib, their wrists tied together with a band of white cloth. There had been a moment of laughter before when the two rose and turned in our direction, suddenly paralyzed, and Mrs. Mahal made a clockwise gesture with her arm as if to propel them into motion around the holy book. Aunt Teji silently mouthed the words the granthi spoke as the couple circled the Guru Granth Sahib: "Ek Jot Doe Murti," one spirit in two bodies. After they sat, we circled bills and coins over their heads and laid them in their laps, a wish for prosperity, then showered them with rose petals.

Only relatives and close friends, a small portion of the humanity streaming out the temple doors, were invited to Aunt Teji's for the reception. The decision to hold it there had required little discussion. Her house was larger—with two bathrooms, Aunt Manjit mentioned several times—and the large expanse of lawn would hold the numerous picnic tables where the men would convene. Uncle Avtar had stopped by one evening a few nights earlier to discuss preparations for the reception, but by the way he stood in the doorway, spinning his hat in his hands, we all recognized it was really a kind of apology to my mother for the unexpected meeting of bride and groom. He spoke mournfully of the goat he would slaughter and curry for the feast following the wedding, probably wishing to arouse a kernel of sympathy for his sacrifice from my mother. It was one of Regina's sons—Regina being his favorite, now-aged goat, whom Aunt Teji had muttered unfavorable things about, at least as to the possible source of her name. I occupied him with idle questions for a while at the doorway, but my mother hovered just barely within earshot with a broom in her hand, though she couldn't quite bring herself to sweep anything (it was evening and that was bad luck).

Aunt Teji's place appeared deceptively quiet, almost sleepy in the strong, hazy light of midafternoon. A few children ran among the wooden tables and benches lining the front lawn, their laughter scattered and absorbed into the large open space. Small plumes of smoke threaded toward the sky on the north side of the house by a grove of citrus trees, and there a group of men gathered around a fire with a large iron pot pitched over it. My mother offered some parting words on moderation to my father as he headed off, and he laughed in his mild way and told her not to worry. Prem ran off with his basketball clutched under one arm, in search of Deepa and his other male cousins.

I passed from the cool sunlight into the dusky shadows of Aunt Teji's living room, aware of those four pale walls that contained a sea of faces. They looked at Neelam first, but I knew their scrutiny would next turn to me. For if the circumstances of Neelam's life had changed that day, mine had also.

Mrs. Mahal rose and engulfed my mother and Neelam in lengthy embraces. Neelam had changed into a light peach-colored salwaar kameez and looked remarkably refreshed and rested, though she had snarled at me twice for coming into the bedroom earlier while she attempted to nap.

"Your husband is resting," Mrs. Mahal said to her, tapping her lightly on the thigh. "Teji hid him away somewhere. He'll be up soon. If not, I'll go tell him myself that his bride has arrived." Her earlier disappointment, when Neelam declined to go with Davinder straightaway to Aunt Teji's, seemed to have disappeared. I was standing against the wall with my hands pressed behind me at the small of my back. Mrs. Mahal motioned me over, and as I sat next to her, she took my chin in her hand and smiled approvingly.

I felt other eyes on me, dozens of pairs of brown eyes (and that pair of green ones) blinking and flashing in my direction. I was being appraised in a new light—as a woman, as marriage material— now that Neelam's future had been settled; I couldn't be sure their assessment was entirely agreeable. My toes turned fat under their close gaze, bulging over the tips of my sandals, my ankles knobby, my neck long and spindly, barely able to support my head. I longed for something clever to say, to put them all at ease, to show them I was Neelam's equal and more, but all I could manage was that Aunt Teji's samosas were the best.

"Serjit, you've grown taller than Neelam and your mother," Charan Kaur said to me. The other women nodded at this milestone, which I assumed was a compliment of some sort. "But quite thin," she added severely.

I was relieved to hear a male voice behind me. Davinder appeared under a ruffled crown of hair, which he attempted to smooth with one hand as he greeted Neelam. His face still wore the dreamy languor of sleep. "You've had some rest yourself, I hope?" Davinder asked, leaning down toward her.

Neelam threw her elbow over the back of the chair and faced him. "A little. There was still some packing to do." She couldn't quite bring her eyes to meet his.

Taking her nephew by the sleeve, Sethi Mahal guided him toward the door. "It's time for you to join the men outside. You'll see
plenty of her later," she said, to laughter. She was a petite woman
with an energetic, high-pitched voice that always attracted attention. Davinder threw up his hands as if in surrender and left.

The thrill engendered by that brief exchange receded like
floodwaters from a low plain. Hunger brought on by the wafts of
curry and masala coming from the kitchen began to dull our
moods and an acute torpor settled over us. Someone brought up
the Mann wedding that was coming up in April. Not even Charan
Kaur's information about the groom, a boy from Fresno, could
pique much interest. "The older son or the younger?" someone
asked. "The one with his eyes too close together," another replied,
putting to rest that little mystery. I picked away at the decorative
silver leaf covering a piece of barfi. Neelam traced with one finger
the delicate henna pattern scrolled on the back of her hands. These
parties could be miserable affairs. The men always congregated
outdoors, while the women remained sequestered inside, where the
walls could barely contain the mix of cooking smells and the hot,
slightly acid breathed-in air. The children ran freely, weaving back
and forth among the two camps. An irritable old woman encamped
in a gray armchair by the door waved her cane at the unruly band
each time they burst in.

Surinder and her family arrived, and the two of us were mercifully called into the kitchen. Neelam shot a desperate glance at me
not to abandon her, but I had sat and listened to the satin folds of
my salwaar rustling long enough. In the kitchen, my mother was
still rolling out rounds of wheat-flour dough for roti and slapping
them on the griddle. Surinder and I ladled out bowls of chana dal,
saffron rice with almonds and raisins, and yogurt kutha with small
pakoras floating in it and specked with small grains of masala and
cayenne pepper. Surinder had fixed her hair differently, wearing it in

a high ponytail at the back, while her bangs were curled and teased to frame her face. She was an only child, a rarity among Indian families, and her parents doted on her as though she were a boy. We were inseparable at these parties; at school, there was at least the luxury of other distractions, but at these affairs, we hunkered down together and got each other through. She nudged me sharply with an elbow to my side as we worked. "Did you see who's back? I saw him when I came in."

"Who?"

Uncle Avtar poked his head through the back entrance. "Ladies, my goat is waiting," he said, waggling his head. "I've refined my recipe. You'll all be clamoring for more." He was renowned for his fiery cooking.

"Acha, we'll see. Last time, you gave your uncle Sodhi a gall-bladder attack," Aunt Teji said. She whisked a stick of butter over a roti, leaving creamy pools that splattered as she tossed it onto a mounting pile.

Outside, under the cluster of orange and lemon trees, Uncle Avtar lifted the heavy charred pot from the platform onto a wooden table. The fire still smoldered under a fine layer of gray ash. A phalanx of ribs jutted out as he stirred the thick golden sauce. I thought of him standing at our door, spinning his hat in his hands and talking somberly of Regina's boys as though they were his own. He ladled the curry into bowls with great care. Cream-colored buds were forming along the spiked, leafy branches of the citrus trees overhead, and my nose filled with their expected, but as yet absent, fragrance.

The house, facing east, cast a wide shadow over the lawn as the sun lowered in the sky. Surinder and I spread the bowls of dal among the long rows of tables, and the sight of food enticed the men to take seats. The place had the feel of countless other parties my aunt and uncle had thrown here. A maze of lightbulbs strung over the tables had not yet been lighted and bobbed in the light breeze. Small glasses filled with Aunt Teji's purple violets decorated the tables. A few rusted metal drums, the kind Uncle Avtar burned trash in, were scattered around the grounds. Later, when it grew colder, he would light fires in them so the men could huddle there and keep warm; it was his way of extending a night's festivities.

From the head table, my father's eyes followed me as Surinder and I moved about the tables serving food, the warning implicit in his watchful gaze. Davinder appeared a bit droopy and sullen, propped as he was amid an impassioned conversation between my father and his. The lights in the house went on just then, and his face swept toward the window, beyond which Neelam sat inside, in the same chair, a soft bank of light spreading across her back. Her veil fell from her head, caressing her shoulders, exposing the smooth alabaster nape of her neck. She pulled the veil over her head a moment later and Davinder turned away.

"You never told me," I said to Surinder when we had finished serving the food. "Who's back?" We walked together to a corner of the house, near the citrus trees, and she pointed her chin in the direction of the large cottonwood at the far edge of the lawn. A group of boys slouched against its trunk—Juni and the other cousins, I had assumed. I could hear their laughing and teasing the entire time but hadn't paid much attention. It was dusk by then, but even with the shadows growing deeper, I could make out his profile, the thick, waxy black locks of hair perpetually falling over the forehead, as he looked off toward the main road. It was Pritam, Charan Kaur's son, who had been sent away a year earlier to live with an uncle in Stockton.

THREE

The hallways at Oak Grove High clattered with the sounds of heels scraping against the cement floor, the tinny echo of voices, and lockers creaking open and shut. Fourth period had just let out and I waited outside my English class, as I did each morning, for Surinder to join me for lunch. I focused on the telescopic glare of light that spilled in from the end of the hallway where bodies illuminated by the March sun were suddenly submerged in the shadows as they entered the tunnel-like space, then gradually assumed form and color again as they fell under the pallid green of the fluorescent lights overhead. A few couples walked past, hand in hand, followed by the odd student quietly shuffling by with his or her head down. It was spring of my junior year, and having to wait for anything seemed an eternity. The week had been windy, which irritated me, for it gave me the false sensation of being rushed and pushed at, though I could think of nothing in my external world that would have me feel so. My classes were going well; the expected challenge in chemistry surfaced, then waned as we moved from covalent bonds to the periodic table. Daily, it seemed, I awaited something that might leap off a page, blow in through a cracked door or window, and seize me in some new way.

Surinder emerged amid the knot of bodies, her familiar lope accented by a pair of high brown boots. Her heavily kohled eyes scanned the hallway until they met mine. She'd slathered herself with Jean Naté after PE, skipping her shower, as usual, to cross the campus from the gym at its south end to the main classrooms on the north side, the lemon-sweaty, sweet-and-sour smell advancing ahead of her like a sharp warning as she approached. It was not me she rushed daily to see after fourth period, but Pritam, who was in my English class this year.

"You just missed him," I told her, peeling my shoulder blades away from the cool, slippery wall. She crossed her arms at her chest with a pronounced heave of her shoulders. That made two days in a row; three would be utterly unbearable. I would have to stall him tomorrow after class, I decided, or fall prey to one of Surinder's distraught, mean-spirited moods. It had all happened during fall semester, not gradually—a flower unfolding its reticent petals—but in a sudden and alarming way, like an umbrella snapping open too close to one's head. Pritam seemed oblivious to Surinder's overtures, her daily pilgrimage from the south end of campus in hopes of a glimpse, a word.

Under the shady ramada at the outdoor snack bar, the tables were filling with students according to some regimented seating plan adopted over the course of the year. A coterie of scrawny second-string baseball players dominated the center tables, their knotty elbows jutting out in a series of V's that linked to form a fence forbidding trespassing. The Davermeyer twins, Phil and Dave, occupied their usual spot on the fringe, where they silently nibbled on ham sandwiches, blinking their long white eyelashes. On the far end of the open quadrangle in the center of campus was a bench under two stout weeping eucalyptus, where the other Indian girls congregated. Surinder avoided that bunch assiduously, embarrassed by the soggy roti unwrapped from cheesecloth and dipped into soupy bowls of dal, and the steaming thermoses of tea passed around. Young women who had already grown old like their mothers, Surinder would say.

At our corner table, Surinder squirted a slurry of catsup on her napkin and slathered her corn dog in it. "So what happened in English today?" I knew she was really asking about Pritam, expecting me to make the enormous leap from Hemingway to the color of the shirt he was wearing that day.

"We're still going over 'The Snows of Kilimanjaro.' Mr. Iverson asked Pritam what he thought the mountain represented."

Surinder's shoulders snapped back, her mouth arrested mid-chew and her half-eaten corn dog poised in the air like a small missile. "What did he say?"

"He shrugged and looked out the window. He never talks in class." Pritam had slouched indifferently the entire class period, a habit typical for him lately. Something in Surinder's flattened expression, her disappointment, pleased me. She had never taken an interest in him until he returned from his uncle's, bolstered by that year away, following an incident with the police and a brief arrest. He and I had been friends as children, herded together with packs of kids—his siblings and mine, assorted cousins—whenever Charan Kaur visited. Amid the complicated weave of allegiances that would emerge in a game of hide-and-seek or kickball, he and I would ultimately band together against those older and younger than we were. Lately, though, we could manage little more than shy nods or brief, tortured hellos.

"He seems changed since he moved back from his uncle's. I don't think he's happy living with his mother again." A look of pain flashed across Surinder's face. There was something nearly lovely about her in moments like that, when her narrow, dark eyes softened their focus and she seemed genuine, unaware of how her skirt grazed her knee or the way the prodigious waves in her hair tumbled across her shoulders. "Who understands Hemingway anyway?" she said, smiling at herself for finding a way to defend Pritam. She let out a full, contented sigh, dreaming of his hazel eyes again.

"Would you want to live with that Charan Kaur?" I asked. "It's like she knows everything you're doing and thinking, even if she's in the next room." I shuddered, thinking of her sea green eyes, which seemingly penetrated physical surfaces into the essence of things. Sitting at tea once, I'd complained of a headache and she'd remarked on the delicate strain of a young woman's menstrual cycle; that evening, scraping the peel from a squash for a sabji, I felt the blood beginning to drip between my legs, and myself powerless against her.

"It must be horrible for him," Surinder said. The trace of sincere concern in her voice always surprised me. I had to remind myself now and then that even she had her contemplative moments; I was more accustomed to the searing retorts that she normally tossed about like a sharp-bladed knife.

Mani Singh, a friend of Neelam, approached, balancing a tray loaded with french fries and a large strawberry milk shake. She usually preferred the company of the girls on the bench, piously enjoying her sabji, dals, and roti until she could no longer hold out and caved in to her weakness for more exotic fare. This happened predictably, every five to eight days, and always with the pretense that she had something terribly significant to tell us (which she would, loudly, in Punjabi). She slid next to Surinder, across from me, the slack weight of her body falling and spreading over the concrete bench. Taking a fistful of fries, she began poring over a pamphlet. "Community college schedule," she said when we didn't bother to ask. "I'm enrolling in the fall."

Surinder and I exchanged glances. Mani had never struck us as particularly ambitious that way. She was the eldest of five children, and after helping her ill mother raise the younger siblings, she had already developed a cloying maternal outlook. I expected the traditional path of marriage and children for her, especially since Neelam, whom she idolized, had done so.

"These marketing classes look interesting." Mani bit gingerly into a french fry, savoring it as if it were sweet gulab jamun. "Neelam's thinking of going, too."

"I think she wants to have a baby," I said. "She can't go to college if she has a baby. At least not yet."

She glanced once behind the table, then jutted her head toward me. "*He* wants it, not her." Her thin lips vanished into a vacant smile.

"If Neelam wants to go to college, Davinder wouldn't stop her."

Mani enjoyed this kind of game of one-upmanship with me, especially when Neelam was involved. Staring from her heavy, lazy lids into her inert brown eyes, I was unsure what could have inspired such loyalty on my sister's part. She leaned toward me once more, her mouth exaggerating the words. "She told me she's using birth control."

Surinder pulled at an earlobe and pretended not to hear. That bit of information would not have alarmed me, but for my mother's singular devotion as of late to my sister's condition, or lack of one. My mother's face bore countless expressions of love and exasperation on any given day, but there was the one that strafed our bodies intermittently, tagging them with their sexual capabilities. "Has your period come this month?" she would ask Neelam over a cup of tea. And Neelam would nod yes, ashamed, like a child who hadn't washed her hands before eating.

"Besides, why would she want a baby so soon after—" Mani stopped, her mouth collapsing around the words designed to incite our curiosity. Her eyes dropped once more to the pamphlet and her lips pursed around the straw as she sucked noisily at the milk shake. "—after everything that happened," she added.

The peculiar restlessness that had ushered in the week remained with me. Mani's words and her smug, puggish visage revisited me often in my idle moments. I would speak with Neelam myself about her, I decided, but I knew already that love was not dictated by the truth. It was during the weekend, when Neelam visited, that I realized what Mani was so coyly suggesting, and what my mother and sister had kept from me all these months.

It was late March, and the peach trees that surrounded our house had shed their lacy pink blossoms. Thick clumps of grass blanketed the orchard floor, and sporadically among the grass grew tufts of mustard plants with their broad, puckered leaves, which we harvested each year to cook saag. My mother had been out scouting and discovered a large patch about halfway to Aunt Teji's. She suggested we gather some to prepare an enormous batch of saag, which we could divide among the households.

Neelam looked well as she breezed into the kitchen early Saturday morning. She was wearing no makeup, and her face looked clean and warm, like a plate of pearls set in the sun. Davinder followed behind, enjoying a leisurely pace, his hands tucked deep into the pockets of his brown wool trousers. He worked as an accountant for one of the canning companies, and though he was very bright, he lacked a certain intensity and drive, which I attributed curiously to his education and rather privileged background in India. (The childhood musical training and equestrian classes were strictly summer pastimes, however, under the tutelage of a rich uncle with an estate in the highlands.) I privately wondered if the conversations with my father about machinery and local politics didn't bore him completely, and how he could manage in an insular place like Oak Grove. He was attractive in a conscious and pampered way, and I imagined a number of girls in India—the kind whose parents held lavish birthday parties for them—wanted to marry him. He must've seen the photo of Neelam then, Neelam when she refused to smile even slightly as she sat in a high-backed chair, a vase of roses on the floor by her feet, wearing a pale open-necked kameez, the pale chuni draped over her slightly tilted head and her hands clasped on her lap. It must have all changed for him then. It could happen just like that. They stood side by side in the kitchen now, he a head taller, lanky and congenial next to her soft, fluid form. He murmured something to her, and her chin grazed his shoulder when she turned and looked into his face, nodding.

"An extra pair of hands!" my mother called from the next room when she spotted her son-in-law. A brisk breeze accompanied her quick footsteps into the room. Mustard collecting never failed to buoy her spirits. She said it reminded her of harvesting wheat kernels outside her village in India. Winter through spring, she was known to drag everyone from Aunt Teji to the granthi's mother on her pilgrimages into the orchards. Davinder declined, saying he would accompany us only as far as the shop, where he intended to spend time with his father-in-law.

Outside, I fell into step alongside Davinder, behind Neelam and my mother, who were tangled already in one of their inextricable conversations. He strolled easily along in a pair of sandals, squinting up through the shadows of the trees into the sky. The sound of a hammer pounding on steel vibrated through the air.

"I hope your father doesn't mind me dropping in."

"He'll like the distraction. He's spent the whole week working on a Caterpillar."

"He's a very talented fellow. Very sharp." He tapped his skull with a forefinger. "I watched him change the engine on a flatbed truck in one afternoon. It was impressive."

My father would laugh at such words: *sharp, talented*. He saw it simply as seeing things from the inside out, at least if they were mechanical things with smooth, predictable gears and bolts. Other, more unpredictable and mortal things—daughters, for instance— were an eternal mystery to him. "I guess he has his talents," I acknowledged at last.

The pounding from the shop resumed and we paused along the dirt road. "And what about you?" Davinder asked. "Keeping up your grades? Neelam tells me you have plans for college."

"Yes. I mean, I'd love to go." I shrugged, watching as Neelam and my mother gained distance ahead. I was flattered that he would acknowledge the appeal of my simple dream to attend college away from home. Davinder spoke to me in a different way than most Indian men, who seemed dismissive, impatient with my opinions, if not my presence.

"You'll be the first in the Rai family to get a college degree. That'll be quite an accomplishment."

"Not everyone thinks so."

"Your mother . . ." he said, nodding. "How can I criticize her when she's my biggest fan? Sometimes it seems it's places like Oak Grove that are behind the times. In India, we have many young women attending college. What will you study?"

I paused to think. Few people had asked me that question, among them Mrs. Hanover, my school counselor, who had checked off boxes on a yellow form in a standard, perfunctory manner during our interview, recommending textile sciences when I mentioned I liked to sew. "Biology. Maybe history. I haven't figured out that part yet."

"You will. And that'll be the easy part, won't it?"

Davinder ran his fingers over his head, further mussing the unruly pile of hair on his head. "You remind me of my cousin Suthi . . . Sumeth. She's seventeen. Very independent. I spent my summers at her father's place. She was an excellent shot." He noticed my look of disbelief. "Oh, yes, her father permitted her to go on hunting trips when she turned twelve or so. I hated them, but she wouldn't sleep nights in anticipation; she'd come padding into my bedroom in the middle of the night and poke her head through the mosquito netting and jostle me awake." He smiled and shook his head at the memory. "She plans to study law at Delhi University."

I didn't know how I could remind him of this Suthi. I was aware of my own inclination toward stubbornness, but the hunting and shooting—there was something infinitely more glamorous in that style of independence.

Prem, who had taken refuge inside my father's shop, briefly appeared outside the door, clutching a hammer. The mustard harvest was women's work and these days he preferred the company, the graver duties of men. The knuckles of his hands bore a row of black smudges as proof. "Bhaji, you can help us pull the engine out. Daddy's sliding the winch over," he said to Davinder.

"Put me to work, sahib."

I caught up with Neelam and my mother, who were still entrenched in their kind of merciless examination of some trivial event. A warm breeze picked up and licked at my face and hair. Over the tops of the trees, a bank of clouds massed in the western sky, funneling above me in a narrow stem along the sun's path. We soon veered left into the orchard over wet ground, the soft grass grazing our ankles. The bare branches threw a sharp lattice of shadows, which crawled over us as we moved ahead. Clusters of delicate lemon yellow mustard blossoms came into view. My mother preferred the mustard before it bloomed; she could detect a slight bitterness in the saag once the plants began to flower, even after hours of cooking it into a thick pulp. She rustled the paper bags open and handed us several each and we set to work. The crisp stems snapped easily, leaving a watery nub at the base. For a few moments, it was the only sound other than our exhaled breath each time we bent forward.

"We're picking extra for your Aunt Manjit," my mother said when she noticed me slow, then stand in a weary slump. I had filled roughly half of my bags. "Don't forget the saag cooks down to nothing. We'll need as much as we can pick."

My arms began to ache and my shirt, soaked, was sticking to my back. "Why doesn't she come out and help us?" I asked.

My mother straightened, as though willing herself to ignore my question, then leaned over and quickly trimmed a circular swath around herself. "She's not feeling well," she replied finally.

I looked to Neelam, who was smearing sweat from her neck with her chuni. When Aunt Manjit felt ill, it could mean only one thing. "She's having a baby," Neelam confirmed, her tone mechanical. It would be her fourth in seven years, I calculated; she was not yet thirty. The novelty had surely worn off, but there was the other thing, the secrecy that always accompanied such news. None of the congratulatory hoopla and joyous embraces, just a stern, embarrassed "She's not feeling well."

"Again?" I said. My mother gave me a sharp look. Neelam squatted on her haunches, tugging wearily at a stubborn stem. I remembered what Mani had told me at lunch, that Neelam was on birth control, not wanting a baby. Still adjusting to her marriage perhaps. And there was Aunt Manjit nonchalantly producing children as though she were growing a new fingernail. There was no easy way to broach that sort of off-limits topic, however.

A chlorophyllous scent of broken stems and crushed grass filled the air. I stood, paralyzed by my own ignorance, mustard leaves bunched in my fingers as I watched the women work silently, their backs facing each other. The sky had turned dark, a solid sheet of indistinguishable gray clouds. I thought it would rain. As we gathered up the bags in our arms, a few promising pellets began to fall, but they stopped before we reached the dusty road back to the house.

"We'll be eating saag all week," Neelam said a little breathlessly. She set several bags on the tiled countertop in the kitchen. We fell wordlessly into a rhythm of work. I began washing the mustard, tugging at the edges of the rough leaves to let the water run over the veins and fissures that crisscrossed their surface like deep valleys. The kitchen warmed as the gas stove was lighted. I began to hum a tune from a childhood game, cheered by the thick, yolky light in the room. Neelam joined me. The butter sizzled in two enormous silver pots on the stove. My mother added onions and spices, then tossed in handfuls of the pungent leaves, and finally a bit of water. She set the lids on the pots, instructing me to stir the saag every so often before she left the room.

"Can you believe Masi Manjit is pregnant again?" I asked Neelam when we were alone.

"Poor woman already has that wild bunch on her hands."

"Why doesn't she do something about it?"

"What can she do?" she asked. "Sometimes . . . it just happens." She was mumbling, pushing hairpins back into her bun. Sounding more and more like the women we had always vilified in private: stoic, resigned to their predetermined fates. Was this what happened with marriage?

"I don't know how she can stay with Uncle Girpal. The way he—"

"Look, there are some things you don't know yet. You think she can just leave him and go do whatever she wants? Where will she go? Tell me. Tell me, Jeeto." Her voice was a low, squeaky snarl by then. Her hand moved to the slight rise in her belly, below her navel.

She was right. There was much I didn't know. I watched her hand drop lifelessly to her side. Neelam wiped her moist eyes with her chuni, leaving a long streak of surma, a black line smearing its fine cotton weave.

Davinder returned from his visit with my father, lifting the lids on the pots and peering into the clouds of fragrant steam. "A very efficient operation. You should open a restaurant."

"And who would go to eat there? Indians never go out," Neelam replied. Davinder took her hands, covered with leafy green flecks, in his. He turned them over, inspecting her palms. In India, he seemed to be thinking, a maid would be doing this work, and my wife's lovely hands would be spared. His grip tightened around her wrists. Neelam lowered her eyes. I wondered what Davinder knew, if anything, about Hari. He must know, I thought, the way people talked. He gently released her arms, as though it were futile to ask any more of her. I felt certain then that he did know, sinking a little as I recalled the kindness he had shown me earlier. Davinder traced a finger along the gold chain around her neck, then lifted the oval ruby-encrusted pendant from where it lay against her breastbone. "Is it the one my mother gave you?"

"Of course. I've only been wearing it the last six months."

"And I thought I had every part of you memorized," he said, nuzzling closer, ignoring—or forgetting—my presence.

"Haat!" Neelam cried. She slapped his chest playfully with the end of her chuni as he recoiled.

Davinder straightened into a businesslike posture, as though bitterly rebuked. "I can see it's time for me to rejoin Father." Neelam draped the chuni back over her shoulders and smoothed her kameez.

"It needs more water," I said, pouring a pitcherful into each pot and watching the saag rumble and hiss.

Neelam took the spoon from my hand and replaced the lids. "Best not to stir it too much."

"I had lunch with Mani last week," I said. "She said you might take classes with her in the fall."

"We were just talking. I think she's more serious about it than I am."

"It might be good for you." It would get her out, circulating in the world; Neelam tended to brood alone within the stark walls of her new home.

"Why does everyone seem to have an opinion about what is good for me? I thought you at least would give me more credit." She tossed a dish towel into the sink.

"I didn't mean it that way."

"What did you mean?"

"Just . . . I wish you were happier."

Her high-pitched, mocking laugh made my comment seem ludicrous. "Come with me." She took my hand in hers and led me out the back door to a wooden bench propped against the wall of the house. The sky was still overcast. I looked off into the orchard, the trees fixed in perfect lines viewed from any direction.

"Maybe you've never been in love. You haven't, have you?" She nudged my wrist with a pointed finger.

I thought of Pritam then, as I had increasingly during the last week. But I didn't know what it was, that feeling. So many things had gone unsaid, unspoken already in my life, that I would wake up nights, perspiring and longing for something I was not allowed to name. I needed to know now, from Neelam. . . . There had been Hari and now there was Davinder, the way they were in the kitchen, the things Mani had said, other things implied. It made no sense to me. I slumped against the wall, feeling Neelam's gaze on me.

"I promised Mother, but I think you're old enough to understand," she said. "Remember the day she picked you up at school and I stayed in the car? We went to a clinic that morning because I was pregnant."

It was the time my mother had come for me at lunch, and Neelam lay in the backseat, pale and damp. I thought she had just been upset that everyone had learned about Hari, their poisonous tongues whispering lies. I'd known nothing, misunderstood everything. "I'm so sorry, Neelam," I said. My face burned with the indignity of my own ignorance and the hurt I felt for her. That afternoon, I'd felt little more than inconvenience and humiliation when my mother burst onto campus to fetch me. Hari had already been sent away; the vacant look on my sister's face in the backseat that day, I realized now, was that of someone staring into a vast void. Neelam clutched my shoulder as though she understood, then released me, retreating under a protective veil of silence. The citrus trees and the privets seemed to shudder around me, but it was only a sudden breeze rustling their waxy, dark foliage. In this way I learned, before Pritam ever touched me, the danger that lay in the path to love.

Four

Bhajan Singh might have called it a chosen place, but he was given to polemics and teary, long-winded sermons at the Grove Road gurdwara. Others imagined the winds of fate blowing across the pinched midsection of California, eastward from the bays on the Pacific, inland along the channels of rivers, near the confluence of the Sacramento and Feather rivers, where they spawned a western outpost of the Punjab. It was simply a run-down brick red bus that guided Uncle Avtar to Oak Grove in early 1948. Back then, the town retained only remnants of its former gold rush glory—the once-elegant Placer Hotel with its glum, chipped exterior, a handful of saloons silenced for eternity behind the plywood boards where windows had once been.

Mohta Singh, Hari's grandfather, had leased a large tract of land southeast of town by then, a few miles west of the river, where the soil was rich and loamy. The promise of steady work had already lured a healthy band of Indian men to his ranch. My uncle arrived with a sense of relief, a guarded hope after rooting around the state for many months. The way he told it, the mere sight of Mohta Singh's farmhouse—the windows lighted in the early evening with an amber glow, for it was a damp, dreary day—had livened his spirits. Others felt that relief, as well. Amid the sprawling oaks, an optimism welled from man to man that some kind of home had been discovered. At the conclusion of World War II, many of them departed for India to collect the wives they had left behind, returning to this rare enclave to start families. Some would return to claim wives for the first time.

It was that history, those humble beginnings, that compelled Mohta Singh to suggest a special celebration marking the tenth anniversary of the opening of the Grove Road gurdwara. The suggestion immediately seized the interest of the Indian-American Association and the community as a whole; the clergy at the temple felt especially gratified by this unexpected honor. The town's white citizens, however, viewed this sort of unabashed civic and cultural pride as peculiar, if not bizarre. They would boast loudly for the benefit of anyone within hearing distance of their weekend shopping trips to San Francisco and beyond (the Schmeidermeiers and Dr. and Mrs. Holcomb would return with breathy commentary on performances of *La Bohème* or *Turandot*). There were the ski trips to Alpine Meadows at Lake Tahoe, occasional jaunts to Europe; words, the names of places such as London and Paris would drip from their mouths like the juice of some exotic fruit.

Our own Gold Rush Days and the Prune Festival, after all, were not the sort of cultural fare one admitted attending. Those who tried to counter Oak Grove's reputation as a gas station– and burger joint–infested town overrun with Indians did so cautiously, apologetically. It wasn't far from the coast; it wasn't far from the Sierra Nevada. It was merely a place lacking a soul of its own. So this strutting and posturing by the Indians for a weeklong celebration— a mela to be held in the fall—puzzled the town leaders. The *Oak Grove Republican* ran an editorial praising the contributions of the Indian community, but one could sense the head scratching and throat clearing in the background.

My uncle demanded his rightful place in the unfurling of that piece of history. He would trot it out like a worn, discarded garment; a little recutting and shaping and a few ribbons and bows added in the right places would revive the thing, transform it into something not quite new, but altered in imperceptible ways. He appeared in our kitchen one morning with his hair boyishly parted at the side, removing his boots in deference to my mother and padding across the linoleum floor in his stocking feet.

At the kitchen table, my mother quickly covered her head with her chuni and set down the blue aerogram, a letter she was writing to my grandmother in India, whom she had last seen seven years ago on our trip there. It was a Saturday, and I waited beside her with a pen in my hand to write the lengthy address I had memorized long ago in English. I started with my grandfather's name—Jagjit Singh—recalling the surly white-bearded man who had lifted me by the waist from the ground when he first saw me and held me high over his shoulders, as if he were offering me to the sky.

"Hai. You look as shiny as the new set of platters Chindhi brought back from India for me," my mother said to my uncle, whose hair gleamed in the opalescent light cast through the window by a muggy, gray day.

"I'm here on an official duty," he replied.

"Keri duty? What duty?" she asked.

"Mohta Singh has appointed me to head the historical committee for the festival." My uncle spoke in an earnest tone, as though he wished to solicit my mother's respect for once.

She folded the aerogram, licked and sealed it in silence.

"I actually came to ask for Jeeto's help." He looked at me and shuffled on his feet, waiting for permission to sit. He bowed to her imperious style for his own amusement, I think, and on they would continue, prodding each other, as though they knew terrible things about each other.

"Behto, Chacha," I said, rising and pulling a chair for him.

"He's not your chacha; he's your thaiya! How many times do I have to remind you?" my mother said.

Uncle Avtar chuckled. "Actually, I prefer chacha. It makes me the younger uncle."

My mother eyed my uncle and then me as if we were a pair of lunatics and certainly closely related. "How could Jeeto possibly help you?"

"I'm putting together a historical display—photos of the old days, some stories, how the gurdwara was built. Jeeto could help me with the writing. It's one of her talents, I think."

I returned my uncle's generous smile, flattered that he had recognized in me qualities that my mother never would. He had admired my penmanship on several occasions, the careful, even script, slanted as if windblown across the page, so unlike the stout, upright letters of his own language. He could narrate the stories, feel their embryonic stirring rise from his diaphragm like a song, but he was no good at these other practical applications.

"Jeeto won't have anything to do with whatever that man is involved in. Even if *you* do."

My uncle set the tip of his elbow daringly on the edge of the table and faced my mother squarely. "Maybe we can show the portrait of you and Teji wearing those fancy skirts," he said.

"That was the professional photographer's idea. When have you ever seen me running around in skirts since?"

He looked deflated that his attempt at humor had not succeeded as it occasionally did with her. She had seemed melancholy earlier as she wrote the letter, then stiffened, as if her spine had gone cold when Uncle Avtar mentioned Mohta Singh's name. I thought my uncle might remind her again, as he once had, that it was Mohta Singh's charity that had rescued him when his luck had run out.

And if his own fortunes hadn't turned, she would be languishing yet in that ramshackle village in India without the washing machine she had wept over the day it was purchased. But my mother had been reminded of that other thing, a lingering shame that had burrowed and spawned within her, and would never leave her as long as she lived. I now understood those obscure references at tea to Neelam's condition, the urgent pleas that she should have a child as soon as possible, as though that could erase the memory of the one snatched from her. After Neelam had confided in me that afternoon we cooked saag, I realized the score was far greater than Neelam loving Hari, Hari loving her back. My mother would have banished all of us back to my father's village in India had modern medical practices not intervened. My uncle had managed to dredge up all of this with a mere mention of a name.

I spoke up, wanting to shatter the awkward quiet filling the room. "I'd love to help you, Chacha. Let me do it, Mummy," I insisted.

I had never tired of his stories, never outgrown their sense of adventure and discovery, nor the razor's edge dividing their truths and exaggerations. History had to be lived, breathed, spoken, not merely perused in flat, unwieldy textbooks, he would tell me, a ring and charge in his voice. The lucky ones got through the trying times—wars, poverty, natural disaster—he would say to the children gathered around long after the grown-ups had retired. He spoke of the woman on the fishing boat the first time he had sailed from India, who had thrown herself overboard because the nights were so black, or of the foreman in a ten-gallon hat on the farm in El Centro who spoke only Spanish to him, but it hadn't mattered, because my uncle didn't understand English yet, either. What it was like seeing his brother Mohinder again, not in their village in India, but stepping ashore in San Francisco in that ill-fitting jacket with its stiff, peaked shoulders like the gables of a building. The tall woman next to him, proud even with the coils of black hair whipping across her face in the steady breeze off the bay, gripping her swollen belly, where Neelam lay curled inside.

I had never thought of history in these terms, as a chronicle of ordinary lives. My books at school were filled with events that gave birth to nations; charts and maps bore the evidence of migration, invasion, and battle. I watched my uncle sip water from a glass, annoyed with my mother that she would refuse him tea. Did his tales, too, constitute a history of sorts? Did it count when, as children weary of outdoor play at day's end, we would gather on the linoleum floor by his feet and watch his hands spread wide, as though trying to encompass the world of his story, to feel its edges and incongruous shapes; hear the voice rising and falling and the words vibrating for these moments in our ears, then escaping like a thread of smoke into the still blue air. My mother had always dismissed these stories. They apparently lacked that mythological dimension that so captivated her. No Ramas rescuing Sitas. And who was Uncle Avtar, this man with a refined historical sense, other than a ruffian in a crumpled fedora who sometimes drank too much? she would ask.

My father came in and hung his wool red-and-black-checked coat on a hook on the wall. Curiosity and a familiar wariness, I think, drove him from his shop when he saw his brother's truck parked in front of the house.

"Mohinder," my uncle said, swinging around. "I may have found some new customers for you. Gardner Brothers. They're looking for a good mechanic."

My father removed his cap, revealing a matted, sweaty dome of hair. He had been laboring for hours already in his shop. "Since when do goras come to us for repairs?" he asked, sinking heavily into a chair beside me.

"Does it make a difference who owns the equipment parked in your shop? A job is a job." Uncle Avtar shifted in his chair, turning to my mother, who was half-visible behind a cabinet door, where she busily jostled items. "I've always looked out for my younger brother, haven't I, Jasbir? Didn't I put him to work right away his second day in the States?"

"Sure, hauling equipment in that old '47 jalopy you called a truck. The front window was missing and I had flies in my teeth," my father said.

"And when had you ever driven a truck, or anything, window or not, before that? Anyway, we all took any work we could find."

My father gazed directly into his brother's eyes. "We all have debts we can never repay."

"I wasn't referring to debts. I'm trying to help you—"

"You needn't come by every other day to remind me that the house is yours, the land yours. In fact, I'm not sure it was ever truly *yours* in the first place."

The lingering resentment in my father's words surprised Uncle Avtar. I had heard these vague accusations from my father before. My uncle had given him the piece of land, a wedge-shaped corner of his own property with the house and the garage my father had converted to his mechanic's shop, while Neelam was still in diapers. He was not in a position then to deny that kind of generosity, but his acceptance, that taking of what wasn't his, had seemed to torment him ever since. I don't know that he ever tried to repay my uncle. My uncle would've refused him, I think; I learned later that he was bound by his own complicated transactions, the columns of debits and credits never entirely balancing out.

Uncle Avtar retrieved his boots by the door. The subject of the festival had been forgotten entirely.

"When can we get started, Chacha? The project for the festival?" I reminded him

"Oh, yes. Very soon." Then, turning to my father, he said, "If you'd like, I can contact the Gardners tomorrow."

"All right, but I won't charge them any less than they're accustomed to paying."

"Take it, Mohinder," my mother said. "We need the money. We'll have another daughter to marry off in a year's time."

It was the first time I'd heard her speak of it so directly, nonchalantly, as if I were not present. I was no more than a shadow in their presence, lurking at the edges of the dreams and worries that shaped their minds. I heard the door shut behind Uncle Avtar, and set off to my room without a word.

We stayed in my grandfather's two-room brick house on that summer trip to India when I was nine. He didn't speak to my mother the first six days. His own sister had arranged my parents' marriage, but he never imagined his daughter would follow her husband across an ocean to live on another continent. The village children gathered at the doorway each day to witness who had come from America. They pointed at our patent-leather belts and rubbery sandals and smiled their toothy grins behind balled fists, and followed Neelam and me whenever we ventured out on the dusty path to the nearby well, or to my cousin Rani's house a few doors away. Neelam was never allowed very far from my mother's watch; she was twelve, and it seemed that overnight the small cones of her breasts had begun to push against her thin cotton kameez. At night, in my rope bed on the rooftop, I could smell the rain approaching from miles away. First there was the mud scent, the air stirring and gathering as if preparing for an assault, and finally the thunder ripping through the sky like an angry whip. And when the sheets of water descended, we would rise and scramble from our beds indoors. We did this every night for a month, squealing as the rain soaked through our garments in seconds, as if its coming each time were a surprise.

FIVε

Mr. Iverson paced the width of the linty gray carpet in front of the blackboard. The signature plaid bow tie—blocky chunks of blue and red today—hung like a placard beneath his broad chin and the matted frizzle of gray hair ringing his face. Our books were open to the final section, twentieth-century American drama. He had scribbled some terms on the board—*dramatic structure, hero, conflict,* and the like—ones we had grappled with through Hawthorne, Twain, and Steinbeck. Mr. Iverson was attempting to ignite a discussion on the week's reading, Wilder's *Our Town.* "Wilder says he created Grover's Corners out of frustration with the dull, hackneyed theater often produced during the Depression era. He wanted to offer a human drama that . . ." His words faded in and out of my consciousness and I scarcely heard the question he posed to the class. ". . . So why does Emily Webb choose to relive the day of her twelfth birthday?"

Even the fidgeting stopped among the students and the room fell silent. I was sharply aware of Pritam sitting behind me, near the back of the room, where he had taken refuge with other apathetic souls in the waning days of the school year. I had ceased slumping at my desk; now I was unfurling and straightening my spine, smoothing, twisting my hair, thinking he was watching. He wore a red corduroy shirt, his dark hair brushing the top of its collar. Tomorrow, it might be a plaid one, or a T-shirt with stripes. I absorbed these details morning after morning, for Surinder, I thought. But I had begun to be drawn myself to the mystery of Pritam: the same fingers that had idly rubbed an itchy nose when he was a child, now grown long, drumming on a book, his shoulders moving with a latent power under the fabric of his shirt.

Mr. Iverson paced anew. He pointed a finger in the air, jutted a flabby lower lip as he struggled to extricate a grain of interest from his lethargic pupils. He grazed the aisles of the classroom, it seemed, for an eternity, like an animal foraging, waiting for someone to offer even a nibble of wisdom. He stopped at the head of my aisle to survey the figures before him, slumping and hunched at their desks, dreaming of the promises the approaching languid days of summer would hold for them. In the next aisle, Debbie Harper was checking her makeup in her mirrored compact, swiveling her neck at various angles to get a complete view. Behind her, Gil Schuyer's legs were stretched like giant sausages across the aisle.

Had anyone bothered to read the play? Mr. Iverson asked the class. There was no response. Even Jenny Holcomb, one of our star pupils, seemed distracted as she examined a swatch of her hair for split ends. I stiffened as his pleated gray trousers brushed past me. Heads turned to the back of the room and students had already begun to snicker. Pritam braced for his approach with his arms crossed over his desk. Mr. Iverson was not an unkind man. It may have been no more than a nagging curiosity that propelled his attention occasionally toward Pritam, who attended class many days without his textbook, and devised other means to test his instructor's sympathetic ideologies about the immigrant experience. His other Indian students had been mostly pleasant, compliant, occasionally brilliant. Then there was the rare incorrigible type. A vein bulged from his temple to his jaw as he repeated the question to Pritam: "Why does Emily choose to relive the day of her twelfth birthday? It's not a difficult question."

Pritam dropped his eyes to the bare desktop in front of him. I recognized that tendency in him to shut everyone, everything out, usually the result of the humiliating sort of discipline his mother imposed on her children. His eyes began to search the floor, stopping at the pair of gray-trousered legs in his direct view. For a brief second, I was afraid he might lunge at Mr. Iverson, tackle him to the floor, and begin pummeling him with his fists.

"Because she wants another chance . . . to experience the happiest day of her life and . . . to appreciate life," I blurted out.

Mr. Iverson stepped back. His dull blue eyes looked defeated. "Kind of you to rescue your friend here, Serjit. But I was waiting for *Pritam's* response." Some hoots and whistles went up around the room as Mr. Iverson retreated to the familiar sanctuary of his lectern at the front. "And what does Emily learn from this experience?"

The sound of the bell injected life back into the students and they pressed in a flurry toward the door, trapping me behind them. Jenny Holcomb put her hand on my shoulder as she passed. "Thanks for rescuing *all* of us." Pritam stalked off ahead.

As I dialed the combination to my locker in the hallway, I was uncertain whether it was Mr. Iverson or I who had humiliated Pritam more. I stuffed my books inside, then rushed to the end of the hallway and stepped outdoors, where the heat radiated off the brick walls with a steady hiss. Pritam had already fled, but Surinder came around a corner and her face lighted up. "Hey, lunch buddy!"

The summer unfolded in its usual manner, with its own impossible set of demands and directives. *Don't wander past the workers;*

don't stay in the sun too long, or your skin will darken like a peasant's. . . .
Before any boredom or lassitude could settle too comfortably in my
limbs, the summer harvest would resume. Few went unscathed. The
roadways clogged with a jumbled parade of trucks old and new,
loaded down with produce, peaches going south, tomatoes heading
north, as if even fruits and vegetables had the good sense to leave
town. Someone like Jenny Holcomb, whose father was a physician,
might elect to accompany her parents to London or Paris for a few
weeks, avoiding the sweltering cauldron Oak Grove became during
the hot months. If she stayed, we would hear in the fall about the
wild pool parties, the summer romances, and who had passed out
beneath the cotoneaster hedge by the kitchen window.

My father's business would double by midsummer as rotted
axles buckled under the strain of work. Many nights, the advancing
darkness would be pierced by the pale rectangles of light coming
from his shop as he worked late into the evening. My mother
would carry his dinner to him in a large fine-woven basket those
nights, a task she always insisted on performing alone. If I were to
burst in on them with some urgent message, a phone call or an
unannounced guest who had dropped by, I would find them sitting
side by side in bowed metal chairs and staring up at me as if it were
the most inexcusable invasion. They were like most Indian couples
of their generation, their affection private and sacrosanct. Their ar-
guments, too, were clipped and contained, like things in boxes that
could be neatly packed away and stored on some inaccessible internal shelf. My mother could sense well ahead of time when she had
gained the upper hand, my father when to quit, and that would be
that.

By midseason, the fruit ripened into globes, clinging to the trees
like bright lanterns. The workers moved into the orchards around
our house, with shouts in Punjabi and Spanish volleying back and
forth all day. Like a siege, they arrived at daybreak, spilling out of

trucks with canvas picking bags draped over their shoulders and scurrying under the weight of the ten-foot ladders stretched over their heads. Uncle Avtar roared about in his pickup truck—they were his orchards, after all—stirring up massive clouds of dust. (Aunt Teji would complain to him if she had left the windows of her home open at an inopportune time: One's importance in this world was directly equivalent to the tonnage of dust one could manage to unleash into the atmosphere.) She dropped in occasionally, worried that a truckload of fruit had been rejected by the canneries and would have to be dumped. My mother would ask her to sit awhile and would serve her a proper lunch. Even my cousin Juni rose early each morning, loading the bins of fruit with the forklift onto the flatbed, climbing into the cab of the truck to deliver the fruit to the inspection stations. As for me, I was forbidden to go out on my early-evening walks, when there was a glimmer of a breeze, though the workers had long since departed for the day.

I attended gurdwara regularly that summer. I met Surinder there each Saturday evening. We sat cross-legged on the floor in the shadows at the back of the hall, a massive room whose peculiar acoustics in the absence of its normal capacity crowd could cause even the barest of whispers to echo across its expanse, or descend mysteriously from the ceiling as some heavenly message. As soon as the musicians gathered their instruments to begin playing the *kirtans* and the voices of the congregation rose, Surinder and I would abandon our trite concerns about boys and fashion and meddling mothers.

The temple continued its other vital role as a gathering place where news and hearsay vaulted through the air as freely as blossoms in a spring breeze. It was here we learned of Charan Kaur's latest venture. Surrounded by her own loyal circle of devotees, she preened and puffed as though a press conference were about to take place. Then, elongating her neck and clasping her hands at her waist, she delicately cleared her throat and announced that she was set to purchase India Bazaar from Dilip Singh and his wife, who had moved to join extended family in Vancouver. "July fifteen. Grand opening," she said to Surinder and me as we passed by, demonstrating that her dubious command of English would be a most valuable asset for conducting business. She returned once more to her flock of admirers. "Of course, my son Pritam will be helping me out in the store. I can rely on that boy for anything."

India Bazaar's rebirth under Charan Kaur's ownership constituted a victory for both merchant and customer. The place had deteriorated in recent years, inspiring woeful tales of rats scurrying in the storeroom, muddy footprints from farmer's boots left to cake for days on its wood floors. Curiosity, and a dwindling supply of wheat flour, could no longer keep my mother from its desmudged, pristine glass doors. I agreed to accompany her on her first visit; for me, it simply meant that Pritam would be there.

The atmosphere around the shop was like a mela, with bright, plastic banners streaming from its eaves, gold tinsel draped along the windows, and the constant flow of customers in and out of its doors. The neon orange blocked letters on the window read GRAND OPENING, NEW OWNERS.

Inside, shelves were crammed with items that bore no particular relation to one another, the henna and beauty products stacked beside oily jars of mango pickle and jalebi mix, brass incense holders and votives perched over sacks of atta. Along the wall behind the main counter, pale-skinned Indian starlets pouted from movie posters. Charan Kaur's aura and chaotic sense of order permeated the place. But order was not what drew customers to her door; they wished to imbue themselves with the good fortune that clung to Charan Kaur like honey as of late.

She was soon by our side, jovially complaining that business was good, too good. "The secret is to keep inventory in stock," she revealed in a raspy, worn voice, pushing her fists into her tired back. "Never leave your customers wanting."

My mother seemed too distracted to appreciate her plainspoken wisdom. She rustled open a yellow square of paper with a list of items scribbled in Punjabi. Charan Kaur's face puckered as she examined it. "Take this to Pritam," she said to me, motioning to the back of the store, where a lime green curtain separated the main floor from the storage area.

Charan Kaur lowered her voice again as she spoke to my mother. "Bhainji, I've something to tell you."

At the back of the store, I pushed the curtain aside, allowing a shaft of light to fall across the concrete floor littered with cardboard boxes filled with canned goods. In the shadows, Pritam shoved a box onto a stack against the cinder-block wall, then emerged from the dusty room onto the main floor. He muttered hello while trying to catch his breath, then took the slip of paper from my hand. He frowned when he tried to read it. "In English, please?"

He seemed neither pleased nor displeased to see me. A gold pendant with a lion's face hung from his neck.

"Sack of atta, moongi dal, chana dal . . ." I said, pointing to the individual words. He held the list tentatively in his palm, as though it were some delicate creature his hand could easily crush. "Don't you remember your Punjabi lessons from Ram Singh?" I asked.

A broad smile brightened his face, and I felt something shift inside me. When we were little, Ram Singh had denounced the younger generation's preference for English in a series of lectures at the gurdwara. With the overwhelming support of parents, he initiated a popular Saturday-morning class to teach his young students to read and write Punjabi. Pritam and I had sat weekly in rows on the hard concrete floor in a side room of the temple, reciting along with the other children the uncomplicated Punjabi words for *boy* and *good*. The words were inscribed on large rattling sheets of butcher paper that were curled at their edges, and Ram Singh would tap his wooden cane on one word, then the next, like a doctor checking a heartbeat with a stethoscope.

Pritam wiped his chin against the sleeve of his navy blue T-shirt. "I still mix up my Punjabi with English."

"All the kids do that."

"Not you. Ram Singh always said your Punjabi was perfect. And that you were too smart for your own good." His eyes slid down the length of my body, as though he was impressed by more than my language skills. He disappeared into the storage room, then emerged pushing a new bright red dolly. He was the eldest of four sons and seemed inured already to the careful plans that his mother laid before him like a bright, summoning path. I vaguely remembered his father as an unassuming man who spent a lot of time at home with his boys during the day, when other fathers were at work; he slumped over in his chair and died from a stroke after dinner one evening when Pritam was six. Charan Kaur's bidding thus fell on Pritam's shoulders.

He appeared resigned and somber, watching the wheels of the dolly scrape along the floor. I caught a glimpse of my mother and Charan Kaur by the cash register, still engrossed in conversation, their veils swaying behind them like shadows of their every movement and gesture. We slipped behind the shelves piled with pillowy paper sacks of atta—wheat, corn, and gram. A fine dusting of flour coated the floor and sweetened the air.

"How do you like working here?" I asked.

He eased his grip on the handgrips. "It doesn't really matter if I like it or not. I just do it."

"I know." One did things simply because one had to. Still, it seemed out of character for someone who could try the patience of even Mr. Iverson. Growing up, Pritam and I had managed regularly to kindle a sense of mischief in each other. Once, during a particularly lengthy and dull service at the gurdwara, we had retreated to the mahogany-paneled lobby and mixed up the pairs of shoes worshipers had dutifully removed before entering the main prayer hall. After the service, we watched from behind a door as women and men rummaged through the mismatched piles, alerting one another about a brown tasseled loafer or a white sandal in a size seven.

"Well, it looks like the store's going to be a success," I said.

"Sure. It couldn't be anything less with my mother running the place. Anyway, I'll always have a job if law school doesn't work out."

"Law school?"

"Just something I tease my mother about. When she starts in on what my father would've wanted for me—she never does that with my brothers."

"The favorite son."

"Sure," he said dubiously. He lifted the fifty-pound sack onto the dolly, the ligaments flexing in his arms as he did so. "You'll never guess who came in this morning." He paused. "Your sister might be interested to know."

"Hari? When did he come back?"

"He said his grandfather had a stroke. He's here to help out for a few days."

Bhainji, I've something to tell you. It explained my mother's lengthy deliberations with Charan Kaur at the moment. "Neelam's married. She's not interested in him anymore," I said. The words sounded rehearsed, and I didn't know if they were true.

"Is that how it works? She just gives up and someone finds her a decent guy to marry and it's all over with?"

"Someone, yes. *Your* mother," I said, balling my hands into fists. "It's not as if Neelam had a say in anything."

A harried-looking Rachan Kaur marched into the aisle, accusation booming in each pounding footstep. "Pritam! Pritam! Where have you put the fenugreek? And the cardamom? The big black ones. Everything's been moved. I can't find a thing," she complained, one furry eyebrow cocked in a sharp inverted V.

"In the last aisle, Auntie," he replied calmly. "Where they've always been," he whispered to me in English.

Rachan Kaur looked disappointed that her request had been handled in such a smooth and facile manner. I moved aside as she flew past, a flurry of purple paisley. When she turned the corner, we burst out laughing. "Good customer skills," I said.

Pritam shook his head. "These people amaze me. You don't see them for three months and they come up to you like that. 'Where's the okra?' No 'Hello, how are you?'"

Standing by Pritam, I saw just how much taller he had grown than I had; my forehead just reached his neck. I studied the lion's miniature gold face, bright as a sun, and its expression of serene power gleaming against his T-shirt. I forgot where I was in that moment. Everything else shrank away as my eyes fixed on the hollow of his throat, then met his. His face softened. He stepped closer and smoothed the hair from my ponytail back off my shoulder, letting his hand rest on my back.

That was how my mother found me. She managed a smile, trying to blink away the fear erupting like a wave of tremors across her face. "Jeeto . . . ? I've been waiting for you at the counter." She ignored Pritam, as if doing so would erase his presence.

"You were talking to Masi." I reluctantly followed her to the counter, listening to the wheels of the dolly squeal behind me.

Pritam stowed the sack of flour in the trunk. My mother drove away from the store in silence, Charan Kaur's news that Hari had returned pulling on the flesh and bones of her face. It was news she must have hoped she wouldn't hear for a very long time. At a traffic stop, she turned to me. "I won't have you behaving like your sister. I won't have that kind of shame in my house again. I'd sooner cut my throat. And yours."

The summer passed, its heat crackling like a slow, indifferent thaw. I visited Surinder often and attended gurdwara every Saturday night. Sometimes I would take a detour along Kenton Avenue, where the legions of high school kids gathered around picnic tables at the burger joints, the girls laughing and flushed with that other kind of tan—golden-pink—while the boys slouched around them scratching their muscled arms. And my mother kept watching me, always watching.

Six

As she bent over a wooden trunk with rusting copper hinges, a tide of sweat broke over Aunt Teji's forehead. We had pulled it from its shadowy berth at the back of her bedroom closet and wiped the dust from its cracked surface. It was painted a lacquered green, with two fans of peacock feathers on either side of the front latch.

"This one here," Aunt Teji said, pulling a photograph from a packet. "That's your uncle on Mohta Singh's ranch. Look, there's Mohta Singh standing next to him. The poor man's been ill lately." Mohta Singh, with his almond eyes, had always looked a bit Oriental, like an old Tibetan warrior. My aunt squinted at the photo through her glasses, her warm, milky breath on me as she spoke. "I know there's one of your father here somewhere." She regarded each photo carefully, holding it up into the creamy light, away from the shadow of her own body. She clutched one to her bosom as it began to heave and shake with spasms of laughter. "I once thought it would be easy to be an American." She stood in the photo, wearing a pale calf-length skirt and a matching fitted jacket with shoulder pads over a white blouse, and stockings and loafers. She was unrecognizable but for the heart-shaped face accented with dark-rimmed glasses and the familiar stance, hardly demure, with her feet set well apart, as if captured in motion. Was this the same Aunt Teji who'd shown me how to stitch the hem on a salwaar? Uncle Avtar, in a dark suit with a wide, bold-patterned tie, had one hand on his son Paul's shoulder; the other held the ubiquitous fedora. His hair was thick, shiny with tonic and cresting upward from his side part, only to tumble down over the other side of his head.

"He kept his hat constantly within reach even in those days, when he had a nice head of hair," Aunt Teji said, as if reading my thoughts.

"Did uncle like you dressing like this?" I asked.

"He liked the modern things back then. But it was uncomfortable for me. People stared . . . whether I wore Indian clothes or American." She snapped her hand impatiently in the air, as if shooing a fly. She removed an ivory jewelry box from the trunk, then a cardboard shelf, exposing stacks of rubber-banded letters, aerograms from India, old passports and documents piled in the bottom. "Your uncle's a great one for delegating, rushing off to that meeting this morning. He wanted to look through these items himself. He likes to relive the old days—at least the good ones."

The festival was three weeks away. With the harvests completed, Uncle Avtar had time finally to embrace his coveted role as community historian. He continuously sought ways to display the ingenuity that had always compensated for his lack of education. Here was an opportunity to participate in a distinguished civic project, a refreshing departure from the usual bailing out of quarreling or drunken relatives and third cousins of friends. His stature would be elevated once again in new and unforeseen ways. When I'd last spoken to him, he'd promised a story-filled evening and a display that would impress even the most cynical viewers.

The task seemed both to absorb and repel Aunt Teji. Maybe grown-ups felt that way about their lives; even I knew that things couldn't be easily swept aside, forgotten by will. She looked hesitant before she reached down and retrieved a packet bound with blue silk cloth and tied with a rough string. "Show him these. They should jog a few memories."

I sorted through the photographs of people I didn't recognize, studying the young faces filled with anticipation or those waiting for that great thing to come along and happen to *them*; the few old ones would be dead by now. In one, my uncle stood beside two Mexican men in front of an old Hudson. He appeared even younger here. I pressed my thumb along his image, as if the motion would make him come magically alive. Unspoken promises lighted their expressions, lifted their square shoulders. I retied the string over the cloth and placed the packet in a canvas sack. A musty sandalwood scent lingered on my fingers. It was the same scent my mother wore, and before her, the grandmother I had met only once.

Aunt Teji shuffled through a pile of papers on her lap, faded documents of various kinds that were curled in one corner or another. It was quiet, with just a whisper of a breeze swelling the base of the curtains.

"Are you looking for something, Auntie?" I asked. She didn't answer immediately, licking her bottom lip as she glanced over a legal-size sheet with a gold seal stamped in a bottom corner. I could just make out the words *Declaration of* . . . across its top when she filed it behind the other papers on her lap. She picked up another sheet and held it close to her face, as if with that proximity, the words would come to life for her. She seemed to be searching for some particular thing. Her eyes scanned the page for some larger meaning that might be gleaned from the experience itself, even if the words were indecipherable to her. I was witnessing a private act, I realized, and came to believe that it was not the first time she had rummaged through these contents.

I leaned closer to examine the legal document. The name Sammy Gill was typed along the bottom, along with an illegible signature. Gill was a retired attorney who had mostly represented Indians during his long, successful career. "Should I read something for you?" I asked.

"No, no. Just some of your uncle's old papers. Strange how one's life can be reduced to mere words and numbers written on a page." Perhaps she had absorbed something of their content, but she looked neither pleased nor displeased. "You must be ready for something to drink." She set the papers in the bottom of the trunk, next to an old cigar box. "Soda, or should I put on some tea?"

"Soda," I replied, reaching for the smooth cedar box the color of honey, the words COHIBA, LA HABANA, CUBA burnished over its face. "What's this?"

"More things your uncle can't bear to part with."

I opened the lid, releasing a smoky, ancient scent from its interior, then snapped it shut as though I had violated some sacred agreement. In these brief seconds, my mind had already recorded a picture of its contents: a lottery ticket stamped with Chinese characters in red ink, a pair of dice, some old newspaper clippings, and, lying along the edge of the box, a scarlet fan made of silk and balsa wood, with Chinese characters printed along its base.

"Come, let's get a drink," Aunt Teji said, pulling the box from my fingers. Her bare heels slapped down the wood floors of the hallway ahead of me. The impressions of memories remained with her—she prepared a float with 7 Up and vanilla ice cream, something I'd enjoyed as a little girl, then started a pot of tea for herself. It was late afternoon by then, the western windows dimming as the sun fell behind the trees. Aunt Teji rattled about the kitchen, assembling an assortment of sweets. When she came to the table finally, I knew better than to inquire further about the box; I think she trusted me not to. I would never forget that about her. With a steaming cup of tea fogging her lenses, she wondered where her boys could be.

At a time when I might have looked to the future—those early weeks of my senior year—I felt drawn inescapably to the riddles of the past. Perhaps it was my mother's warning, which alternately dulled or fueled my thoughts of Pritam or attending college or any other thing I wished badly for, because to want something had become risky, frightening even. The future promised only the burden of choices with their certain consequences. But the past was safe, immutable. And were they truly our choices to make? All my life, I'd heard of events, whether joyous or supremely tragic, that elicited the same numbing response: Whatever happened was already written, predetermined.

We gathered around the kitchen table one evening to work on the history project. My father retreated to his desk for some book-keeping; my mother picked up an abandoned knitting project of some sort. Everyone understood these activities were a way to avoid the kind of unpleasant scene that had erupted the last time my uncle had spent a measurable amount of time in the house. He seemed to have forgotten the incident and now produced a shiny brown vinyl briefcase, whose latches he snapped open very officially, like an attorney preparing for a case. Arranged neatly inside were a fresh pad of paper, a Mont Blanc pen, two newly sharpened pencils, and a wooden ruler.

"A good place to begin," he said, lifting the pad and pulling a sepia photograph of the Stockton gurdwara, the one he had shown the Mahals, from the briefcase. "If you want to know about the early families, they're all here."

"Did you know most of these people, Chacha?" I asked.

"Oh yes. Most of them. The services at the gurdwara, they were like big melas for us. Catching up on news, gossip." He scratched at his temple with a thumbnail. "Oh, and prayer, too, of course."

I retrieved the photos I had collected from Aunt Teji and presented them one by one, recording the names and places Uncle Avtar recalled. They were mostly of families in Oak Grove, beginning with that one of Mohta Singh and him. "What was it like working for him?" I asked.

"He worked everyone hard. There were no half days. No one argued. You could leave, but where would you go? Indians were flocking from all over, looking for jobs, and if a job could be had working for your own kind, all the better."

"He doesn't look like a rich, important man in this photo."

Uncle Avtar's jaw puffed at the notion. "Rich? No, not yet. You couldn't really own land if you were Asian until the early fifties. And he was a lonely man after his wife passed away. He lived only with his daughter, Hari's mother. She was a teenager then, a real beauty. She's somewhere in that photo of the gurdwara."

In the photograph, the two men stood side by side, not like a boss and his employee, but more like . . . brothers. "You look like you were good friends."

"Well, friendship was something different in those days, too. You helped one another out. Everyone needed help from time to time. And he helped me when I had some difficult times."

"And you helped him, too?"

My uncle paused, as though my question caused him to reevaluate matters. "Yes, I did. I did in my own way."

There was a period in his life before that, his first days in the States, before he married Aunt Teji. "What about before you worked for Mohta Singh?" I asked. I was intrigued by the contents of the cigar box, the lottery ticket with the Chinese characters, and the red fan.

"I've told you that story many times . . . the days in the river district, the old bus I rode in on from the delta. . . ." He managed to route the conversation back to other families—the Sahotas, the Garewals—and how their fortunes had grown or withered over the years. By the end of our visit, I had filled several pages with notes. After my uncle departed, I scoured the gurdwara photo again, searching for Hari's mother, the teenage beauty. Perhaps I would show it to Neelam.

In between my studies, I spent time sorting through the photos, attaching simple captions to them—names, dates. My mother added Punjabi translations. I arranged them over the oval braided rug on my bedroom floor like they were a deck of cards, shifting their order as if I were master of their fates. A few suggested a more complex story. In one, for example, a man named Kirpal Singh sat next to his wife, Dorotea Ramos Singh, and their two sons, Ramon and Jimmy; the names had been marked on the back. When I showed it to my mother, she explained that Doro sometimes visited the temple when I was little. "But I wouldn't use that photo," she said.

My father cobbled together a freestanding structure from spare plywood (it was Uncle Avtar who was delegating again). He stood over me as I glued the photos to the poster-board backing, suggesting an alternate arrangement, one that offered his own version of the story. My mother penned in "Waheguru ji ki khalsa, Waheguru ji ki fateh" across the bottom; even historical displays required proper blessings bestowed upon them. I found Neelam appraising it coolly by the living room window, saying only, "Mohta Singh, everywhere." I covered it with a sheet thereafter and, with my brother's help, carried it into a corner of the garage, where it stood ghostlike until the closing day of the festival.

The festivities commenced with a special prayer session at the gurdwara. The aim of the festival, after all, was to commemorate the tenth anniversary of its opening in 1967. An overflow crowd (that is to say, more overflow than the usual overflow) attended the Saturday-evening ceremony, in which the granthi prayed for special blessings for the events of the coming week. Factions from the Morgan Avenue and Tannet Road gurdwaras laid aside their kirpans to celebrate an Oak Grove original. The temple hall was unbearably packed with bodies by the time the rhythmic chanting of the kirtans began. It was an ordinary ceremony otherwise, painfully long, with my mother tugging at my chuni ends whenever my eyes began to wander.

Despite the blessings, there were assorted late-hour crises to be averted. A venerated musical trio from Chandigarh had taken a wrong turn from San Francisco and mysteriously turned up at the Lions Club in Santa Rosa demanding overtime pay. The members of our own Lions Club, who rented us their hall each year for the Independence Day festival, nearly caused a last-minute reversal when a member complained anew of the mysterious damage inflicted upon the men's rest room the previous year. And there was the news of Mohta Singh's worsening health, which cast a humorless pall over the events.

But still the thing went on, carried by the inertia of years past. Anyone with a pickup truck or an extra-large karahi frying pan deemed themselves indispensable, so how could it not? I waited all week for the parade with its bright, unwieldy floats bearing kurta-clad men with megaphones tottering away from the gurdwara toward the main streets of Oak Grove. The spectacle would elicit a derisive curiosity from many of the white townsfolk, and in the end, its garishness and lack of any subtlety would embarrass me. Then why did I enjoy it so? I imagined unveiling the display at the final ceremony to a hushed and enthralled audience beaming with renewed pride.

At home, I examined the outfits hanging in my closet, rejecting them one by one for a host of reasons—the wrong print or color, a baggy salwaar that hung like ballooning curtains over my legs, a high, suffocating collar. I called Neelam finally to borrow something. Balwant Kaur had sewn her a new suit, she chirped over the phone, the kameez with thin black irises on a white background, over a black salwaar. Strappy black sandals. Black or white chuni? she wanted to know. Either way, I thought as I hung up the phone, she will look stunning. Since Hari would be there, as surely she, and the entire community, was aware of by then.

The parade was late getting off that morning. Mother and I wandered among the crowds gathered to see the floats strewn like giant insects in the parking lot of the gurdwara. It was a clear day with a cool, persistent breeze ruffling through the trees and snapping at the loose bits of our clothing. Tika Singh, a barrel-chested man in a yellow turban, boarded the Oak Grove Community College Indian Students Association float and boomed through his megaphone that all floats should begin lining up per the orange instruction sheet. And that the crowd should keep moving along the parade route, especially in the downtown area, so the event would appear well attended. We'd heard the mayor himself—no doubt anticipating the flood of campaign contributions in return—would be riding in the parade. His sky blue Cadillac turned off Grove Road well past the scheduled hour. After some hearty hand shaking, he boarded the lead float, the official Oak Grove Indian American Association contribution, which was a wooden trailer sporting Sikh and American flags, pulled by a pickup truck and overflowing with men beyond reasonable capacity. The floats lighted off down Grove Road, a ragtag line of crepe, tinsel, and the pounding of dhols. A popped clutch nearly sent one man dressed in full Sikh regalia, with a steel kirpan hanging from his side, overboard. Someone had contacted a television station in Sacramento. A blond woman in a cream-colored pantsuit had gotten hold of Charan Kaur, who was smiling into the cameras but couldn't muster much more English than "Happy day!"

The Lions Club building was remarkably plain, austere even. The squat chocolate brown rectangle was located on Rand Road, a few blocks past India Bazaar. Inside, rows of paper-covered tables lined the length of the hall. At the far end was a low stage draped at either end with blue curtains. Above the stage hung a giant banner displaying the Sikh emblem—the Khanda with its ring and swords, which represented God's unity, power, and justice. We arrived while the parade was still winding through town, and before the crowds, so the women could fulfill their duties in the kitchen. Both my mother and Aunt Manjit had earned reputations as formidable cooks, though my aunt, her belly round as a ladoo, was slowed by the late term of her pregnancy. We scattered our purses and sweaters at a table at the front center of the room. My mother appraised the wine-colored salwaar-kameez with silver piping I had borrowed from Neelam, not entirely pleased that I had selected one that made me look a bit more mature. Worried that I would remain idle and, worse, alone for the time being, she urged me to help with the food preparation.

"But the women always criticize everything I do," I protested. Even the most menial tasks were subject to their ridicule; there was too much butter slathered on the rotis, one would crow, while the next would surely complain of their dryness.

My mother sighed with sympathy, she herself a veteran who had worked her way through the inordinate ranks and hierarchies imposed by the older women. "Acha. When Neelam arrives, send her back to the kitchen immediately. And don't go wandering about like a lost chicken," she ordered. "Find Surinder."

A shuffling, scraping noise came from the entrance. Uncle Avtar and Juni carried in the display still covered with the white sheet and set it by the front door. "Where does it go?" my uncle asked, out of breath as I approached.

I glanced around the hall. "Right here, I think. Everyone will be sure to see it."

He nodded, making some minor adjustments in its position, then stood back to admire it. The sepia eyes in the photos stared back into mine as though aware of being seized from their usual cozy shelves and scrapbooks and placed in this more public context. They appeared self-conscious, wary of the exposure.

More people began trickling in. Surinder soon joined me, her narrow eyes lost under heavy coats of mascara. "Oh, nice" was her only comment about the display; the stream of bodies filing in held infinitely more interest for her. One can only share parts of oneself, I thought, a different part for every person, so that in the end, you're a million different, jumbled pieces.

The Gills arrived, then the Garewals in a grand entourage of four generations. The entrance was like a funnel, constricting everyone in close quarters before they fanned off in separate directions according to gender. Charan Kaur's diminutive frame did not detract from the overpowering sense of command she carried into the room. Trailing behind her with his younger brothers, Pritam acknowledged us with a seminod and halfhearted wave. It seemed odd, impossible even, that he could have sprung from her. I'd heard more than one woman remark that he was lucky to have inherited his father's looks. Surinder's gaze followed him until he disappeared amid the throngs of men gathered among the tables. I focused again on the display, pretending to smooth a corner of a photograph.

I heard metal wheels creaking against the wood floor behind the display. I should have realized that the photographs would have most interested one of their principal subjects. I poked my head around, to find Mohta Singh approaching in his wheelchair, Hari pushing him. So he *had* returned. He recognized me right away, of course. Again, I felt his slow appraisal, his eyes sweeping over me once, as if by looking at me, he would learn something of Neelam. I was being presumptuous, of course. He might have begun an entirely new life, even fallen in love with someone else. Yet, standing there, it seemed no time had passed since he and Neelam had been discovered, and then, her wedding.

Mohta Singh struggled from his wheelchair toward the photos that had captured his attention.

"Chacha Avtar Singh's niece," Hari said to Mohta Singh when he turned to face me.

"Oh, yes," he said in English. "Is your uncle here?"

My eyes raked the length of the hall. "He was here just awhile ago." I stepped forward, drawn to the old man, who appeared unsteady and vulnerable, as I'd never seen him before. I pointed to the photo Aunt Teji had given me. "I like this one of Chacha and you."

Mohta Singh leaned close to the photo. He lifted his hand in midair, as though he were about to reach for it, then turned his watery gray eyes on Hari. "Is she the oldest daughter or the younger one?" he asked of me.

"The younger one. Serjit." Hari stepped away from the wheelchair. "She's grown up a bit," he added in English. He gazed out the open double doors, a flicker in his amber eyes once, as though he'd recognized someone. His face and shoulders had broadened, giving him the stony, somber look of one uneasily settling into manhood. "Grandfather," he said, taking the wheelchair. Mohta Singh eased back into it and they moved on.

I felt a blast of hot air in my left ear. "What do you think Neelam will say?" Surinder whispered as soon as we were alone. "Does she know . . . you know, that he's back?"

"Of course, she knows." I pretended that her question was ridiculous, offensive even. I shrugged off her wide, inquisitive stare to show that all that was finished between them. We returned to our seats, glum, mournful, purged of the romantic notions we so carefully nurtured each lunch hour at school; it was as though we had witnessed the death of something.

Neelam arrived just as Tika Singh, who had surrendered his megaphone, only to seize the microphone, welcomed guests and promised a delightful afternoon of song, story, and dance. I couldn't hear what Aunt Teji was saying to my sister over the clattery echo in the hall before she led her back to the kitchen. Tika Singh launched into a long announcement of sponsors and contributors, among them Mohta Singh, five hundred dollars; Avtar Rai, two hundred dollars; India Bazaar, ten sacks of wheat flour and twenty pounds of moongi dal. . . . The list droned on. The musical group from Chandigarh mercifully took the stage. The female vocalist, a Miss Anita from Bombay, opened with a ballad from a recent hit movie. She looked fortyish, her black hair cut in an ear-length bob. She wore a purple sari, a ribbon of flesh exuding at the waist, and thanked the crowd in Hindi between songs in a mellow voice that seemed practiced from years of performing. The more upbeat song she followed with failed to lift the veiled sorrow she seemed enveloped in.

The door leading to the kitchen swung open as the group paused between numbers. Neelam, my mother, Aunt Teji, and Aunt Manjit trailed out like a small militia unit. Neelam smiled at acquaintances, mouthed Sat Sri Akal a few times. My mother followed behind, her mouth pinched in defiance. What one has to bear in a lifetime! she seemed to be thinking. Even I could feel Hari's eyes on Neelam as she wound her way among the tables to ours. He was leaning against the opposite wall with his arms crossed. Mohta Singh, in his wheelchair, was by his side.

Seated, Neelam readjusted her chuni on her head, not looking up, certain that she had been seen by him, even if she was prohibited from scanning the room to seek him out. The women at our table shifted and straightened in their chairs. It was awkward, humiliating, but they'd endured this sort of abuse before and had always managed the shifting and straightening afterward. It was all they expected of Neelam now.

A dour-looking man who often lectured at the gurdwara then took the stage, reminding one and all of the serious nature of the celebration. "Hard work and devotion have brought us together today, nothing less," he cried, wagging an accusing finger. "He could squeeze the fun out of a wet rag," Aunt Teji whispered. The granthi himself hurried him offstage. The curtains were drawn and the crowd broke into a restive commotion.

"Go find your father and Prem. We're leaving." My mother was beside me, her purse straps anchored inside her elbow, her shoulders squared.

"But . . ." I looked around helplessly. I hadn't had a chance to speak with Neelam, who sat quietly, blinking from beneath her dark chuni. And worse, I'd barely gotten a glimpse of Pritam before he disappeared.

The curtains reopened just then, revealing a small flock of children scrambling to their places onstage, one dressed as Guru Nanak in a flowing green robe, white turban, and long silver beard.

Aunt Manjit appeared offended by my mother's sudden plans for departure. "But, bhainji, you can't leave before seeing the story of our dear Guru."

My mother plunked her purse down. "Of course not."

"This is the story of Guru Nanak and Bhai Lalo. Guru Nanak liked to visit his friend Bhai Lalo, a carpenter who lived in a small village," the young narrator began, pointing to a child dressed in rags and clutching a hammer. "Bhago was a rich man who lived in the same village." Another boy wearing loose pajamas and an embroidered vest stepped front and center, setting his hands on his hips. "One night, Bhago held a great feast, hoping that the Guru would join him also."

Children garbed in chunis and turbans passed silver platters of food around a small wooden table. "I wish Guru Nanak would come to my house and enjoy a real feast instead of always staying with that no-good Lalo," little Bhago said. "I know, I'll go to Lalo's and fetch the Guru myself." He marched to a sheet of plywood standing on end, a brown door painted on it, and knocked. The Guru and Lalo emerged from one side.

"Bhago, why have you come to my humble home?" Lalo asked.

"I've come to invite the Guru to a great feast tonight at my home."

The Guru hooked his forefinger at his chin, obviously in deep reflection. Finally, he said, "I will come only if I am permitted to bring food from Lalo's."

Lalo and Bhago stared at each other, puzzled. "Please, take some of this bread. It's all I can offer you." Lalo gave the piece of bread to the Guru, who then departed with Bhago for the feast.

The narrator stepped forward. "The Guru accepted food at Bhago's. With the guests gathered around, he held the food from Bhago's in one hand, the coarse bread from Lalo's in the other. As he squeezed the food in either hand, blood dripped from Bhago's food, and milk from Lalo's." Red liquid splattered to the stage floor from one boy's hand, white from that of the other boy. The guests at the feast gasped, pressing their palms to their cheeks. "Guru Nanak taught us the value of honesty is greater than the mere accumulation of goods and wealth." The narrator bowed as everyone applauded. "Waheguru" was uttered earnestly by all those at our table, and my mother reached for her purse again.

"But the karah is about to be served," Aunt Manjit protested anew to my mother. Skipping the karah parshad, a communal sharing of food, would be an even greater offense than missing the Guru's story. My mother lowered herself slowly into her chair, willing to withstand a bit longer the barrage of gossip and stares

she imagined was directed at her defenseless family. Or perhaps she
sensed that things would deteriorate after this point.

A great clanging of chairs erupted as people rose to move
about. Peering through the stream of bodies, I spotted Pritam. His
head was covered with a white ramal, or kerchief, the prescribed
head cover in lieu of a turban when serving karah parshad. He
scooped the buttery, farina-like mixture with both hands from a
large karahi held by an assistant, then deposited it into the pairs of
palms opened before him like the beaks of hungry birds.

"Our own Pritam serving karah!" my mother exclaimed when
he approached. "Your mother will be so proud."

His devout, servile expression remained unchanged. I felt his
smooth, warm fingers slide along mine as he pressed the dollop of
karah into my hands. But I didn't dare look up. I brought my cupped
hands to my face, saying "Waheguru" once before dipping my fingers
into the mixture and tasting its puddinglike texture.

Surinder jammed two fingers in her mouth and removed a large
wad of chewing gum. "Thank you, Pritam," she crowed when he
dropped a lump of karah in her hands. Aunt Manjit's brow
bunched disapprovingly. She had already consumed her portion of
parshad and now got busy rubbing the buttery remnants over her
hands, arms, and face, a kind of holy anointment. It was a habit of
many devotees at the gurdwara, and Surinder and I had passed
through a phase where we would wickedly imitate them by pretending to rub our skin lavishly, as if we were enjoying a bubble
bath, or dab behind our ears as though applying expensive perfume. It didn't seem funny now as I watched Pritam's figure recede
among the guests until I could see only the white ramal covering
his head. My mother dabbed at a trickle of butter dribbling down
her chin. I squeezed my fingers where he had touched them.

We gathered our belongings once again. The remaining scheduled event was the bhangara dance, and Aunt Teji felt she might

spare herself this time from the sight of her husband scrambling onto the stage wearing an ill-fitting dhoti and turban, banging away on some godforsaken dhol as he leaped wildly about. Neelam decided she, too, had seen enough. My mother invited them all for tea.

Across the hall, Mohta Singh must have also tired of the event. Or perhaps Hari had decided it was time to wheel his grandfather out to the car. It was soon apparent that the two parties would arrive at the entrance at the same time, an unfortuitous collision my mother wished to avoid at all costs. She quickened her pace, horrified, but behind her, Neelam faltered. Ahead of us, Aunt Manjit muffled a remark with a corner of her maroon shawl. Her husband, my uncle Girpal, swaggered by the doorway, his face shadowed by a navy blue trucker's cap. A muddy vomit stain trailed down the front of his plaid cowboy shirt. We were accustomed to his frequent drinking binges, though everyone, his wife in particular, dreaded the unpredictable behavior that accompanied them. In another moment, his intentions became clear as he volleyed a loud curse at Mohta Singh and his grandson.

"Son of a whore," he called out to Hari, teetering as he blocked his path.

Aunt Manjit seized her swollen belly as if the baby had kicked hard inside. My mother shielded Neelam with her body, her arms spread wide. Neelam's hand covered her mouth.

"Let us pass through, bhaji," Hari said calmly. When he glanced in our direction once, the women reeled back as if someone had fired buckshot at us. In front of him, Mohta Singh appeared shrunken and confused in his wheelchair.

"I'm not your bhaji, you son of a whore. You've shamed my entire family." Spittle flew from Uncle Girpal's mouth and his face twisted like a wrung rag.

"That's enough, Girpal. Not here," my mother said. She looked around wildly, mortified that the commotion was attracting attention. Pockets of curious folk gathered along the fringes, inching closer. I felt my ankles sink into the floor.

"Whore . . . that's what they called your mother," my uncle continued, speaking even louder, heartened by his growing audience. "And you take our little bibi, Neelam, and make her—"

Aunt Teji swung him around with surprising agility. Uncle Girpal bobbled on his feet and swatted his stringy arms. "Don't make a fool of yourself," Uncle Avtar said seconds later as he struggled to hook Girpal's arms behind him. The two men scuffled around the display in an out-of-control tap dance. Hari tried once more to pass through during a brief lull in the action. But the sight of him enraged Uncle Girpal anew. He charged toward some imaginary target, catching his foot on one leg of the display, which swayed uncertainly, then spun in a half circle before it toppled over in a massive heap.

"Look what you've done," I shouted, stomping toward the limp figure sprawled on the floor, muttering to himself. I knelt down and reached for the photos and scraps of paper that had scattered like confetti everywhere.

"Jeeto, take Neelam and go out to the car," my mother ordered, lifting and lowering her brows to indicate it would be the end of me if I made a further scene. Uncle Avtar escorted Hari and Mohta Singh outside.

I stashed the photos in my purse. "Let's go," I said to Neelam. I tugged on her sleeve, but she felt leaden, paralyzed. Finally, she began to take little, minced steps toward the door. Outside, Hari was helping his grandfather into the backseat of the black Lincoln parked by the entrance. He nodded slightly to Neelam in acknowledgment, looking sorry she had to endure the pathetic scene her uncle had created.

Uncle Avtar intervened. "Girls, I'm sorry you have to miss the bhangara," he said goodnaturedly. "You'd better run along before your mother comes."

In the car, I thought my mother would pull the steering wheel from the dash as she swerved onto Rand Road. "The nerve of that husband of yours. Defending that boy after what he did to Neelam."

Aunt Teji appeared stunned by my mother's angry tone. She was older than my mother and so loved by us all. "He wasn't defending anyone. He was only trying to stop Girpal from making things worse."

"Girpal is a fool. Everyone knows that. Avtar doesn't have to cozy up to Mohta Singh's kind every time he gets an opportunity. Whose side is he on?"

"Their friendship goes back a long way, Jasbir."

"Friendship? He should choose family over friendship." She made a strange gargling noise in her throat. "Or maybe that is precisely what he's doing."

Aunt Teji said nothing. We rode the remaining five miles home in silence, the air churning with old, private grief, each of their separate stories about to converge, then glancing off one another like atoms colliding. With no stories of my own, I felt childish sitting among them. Neelam simply stared out the side window, her face blotched red where the tears had dried.

Tea soothed us. Aunt Teji's disappointment registered as an exaggerated politeness: The tea was sweetened just right; the koa simply melted in one's mouth. My mother wondered when the men would return, thought of dinner, fell back into the rhythm of her life. Later, Neelam and I lay on the beds in my room, talking.

"Well, I'm glad they had their little bit of fun. What will D think of me now?" she asked, fretting about her husband. She turned from her side to her back and stared up at the white ceiling.

"I had a chance to speak with him," I said carefully.

Neelam knew I meant Hari. She turned onto her stomach, facing away. "Hari . . ." she started to say, her voice faltering. She lay still, only her shoulders heaving and falling with each breath. "I wish D would come."

Uncle Avtar

The plywood display board lay on its side, relegated to a dusty back corner of my father's shop, awaiting its reincarnation and role in some future folly. The jagged points of one leg clawed the air where it had snapped off. The photos had been returned to their normal resting places, yet somehow their stories lingered, thrumming quietly beneath a thick stratum of silence. I imagined the photo that never existed: one of my uncle standing on a dock. Behind him, the *Mariposa* looms like a large white bird, its breast succulent, beckoning. He wears pressed gray trousers, and a wool jacket hangs on his arm; would it be cool that evening as he disembarked up the river?

My uncle would never tell me this particular story. Oh, he told me plenty of them, but not this one—at least not the whole of it. He merely circled its edges, as though it were a raging fire threatening to jump the line. He wished to contain it in the end, I suppose, so he could define his life in some way. I imagined that photo only because another man, one who came to know him better than his own sons, told me of a journey he took up the river, of many journeys he took. And when he spoke, it was as if my uncle himself were sitting before me telling me in his own rich, clear voice. There was a romance to it that charmed me; it spoke to me and filled those quiet moments in my life when little else made sense, and I came to know the story well enough that I vowed I would tell it myself one day.

He roomed then with a Filipino man named Leandro in a small bunkhouse at the camp north of town. Sloping down the levee, the street turned into a gravel lane at a battered and irrelevant stop sign, then branched out amid the scatter of small clapboard structures. Someone had bothered to plant roses on the grounds, and they flourished in the summer in a rage of neglect, their bowers sagging under the weight of extravagant blossoms.

Uncle Avtar felt fortunate to have the place. Leandro had shown it to him one rainy night after they'd gone to a tavern. It was a spare, dim room in the night, with two bunks stretched from opposite ends over the wood floor. He had flipped the mattress, which smelled of piss, over to the less stained side and decided he would stay.

In the daylight, he would notice it had many windows. Awakened by the strong light early one morning, Avtar boiled a pot of water on the hot plate for a cup of coffee. The smoky blue scent of cigarette lingered in the air as he poured the hot water into a mug. Leandro had already risen and gone off to the job at the cannery— the day shift. Avtar wouldn't start his job at the packing plant until three o'clock. Then he'd walk the half mile back along the levee road close to midnight, moving through mists of pink-and-blue light shed over the roadway by an occasional neon sign. The week before, someone in a passing car had heaved an empty liquor bottle at him and, in the headlights, he'd watched the glass splinter, the shards scattering across the asphalt, before he ducked behind a bush. He was lucky to have the work. He hadn't lasted more than two weeks picking pears, the work promised him when he left the Imperial Valley to try his luck north.

He liked to have his coffee on the stoop, leaving the door open behind him to let in the cooling breeze. It carried a damp algal smell that morning, bred along the marshy fringes of the river. The air itself had a different texture—palpable, nearly always stirring— than in the Imperial Valley, where the sun was so intense that he felt its dry, astringent taste in his mouth all day. He'd spent the better part of a harvest season there, until a Mexican named Armando had told him of work up north. He'd ridden as far as Merced with him and four other Mexican laborers. Green fields stretched as far as the eye could see on either side of the road going north: alfalfa, beans, cotton plants frosted with white bolls, orange groves sequestered in the more sheltered valleys. What had blessed this land, this soil, to make it so bountiful? At Merced, he took up with another group bound for Stockton. The hours spent squeezed in the backs of trucks with strangers made him think the land, and the work required to farm it, extended beyond the horizon, limitless. But the guarded look on these strangers' faces, men who had spent a portion of their lives traveling up and down the state, following one crop to the next, told him otherwise.

The barracks looked abandoned already, the workers toiling since early dawn in the fields or canneries. Only Ping Zhang remained. The sound of his sesame oil sizzling in a pan would soon carry across the way. In the afternoon, on his way to work, Avtar could expect to see Zhang returning from his daily trip to Lee's for fresh supplies for supper, something leafy and green dangling from his shopping sack. Avtar poured the remainder of his coffee over a weed struggling out of the ground beside the stoop. He would make tea that afternoon, a thermosful he could savor at his meal break that evening beside the wooden ramp leading down to the dock.

How to occupy oneself: The hours before work suspended before him like a vast, open trough. He felt himself becoming restless thinking of it. Time had a different dimension in America. It had never troubled him in India to idle away an afternoon, to wander among the thickets outside the village with his friend Gishi until dark. Those carefree days of youth are behind me, he thought. He focused his attention on the day ahead. There were always odds and ends to buy at the market—milk, cigarettes for Leandro, though he tried to spend frugally. He would walk to Lee's in Locke, stroll down Main Street. Plenty to distract oneself with there. Leandro had shown him around that first night, guiding him through the weave of streets and alleys, the peculiar noises of their life sharpened in the darkness. In El Centro, he'd circulated among the Punjabi-Mexican families already established in the area. He'd been welcomed into their homes, played games of hide-and-seek with the children. Here, the signs on the streets, the gesturing and shouting were Chinese dialects. He'd entered yet another land, with another set of rules.

By eleven o'clock, Avtar had bathed and dressed. He set off on the gravel road toward the levee. Zhang was on his haunches, his toes splayed over the black dirt, plucking weeds from a patch of bitter melon. Avtar nodded to him and received the usual verbal barrage, which left him uncertain if it was in greeting or meant as an insult. He stamped his booted feet on the paved section of road, releasing fine clouds of gray silt that clung to every surface. It was that same cursed dark soil that the foreman at the pear orchards had grasped in his chubby fingers and declared to be gold. "Peat dirt!" he had shouted at Avtar, perhaps that he might understand more clearly.

Near the top of the levee, he could hear the water swirling south in eddies in the river. The breeze had ceased; the quiet heat descended in its absence, and Avtar welcomed the dappled shade of a cottonwood or sycamore. He crossed the road at the top of the levee to walk along the tree-lined waterway. Below, the gray water rippled through tule marshes, snagged along low-hanging limbs.

It was 1947; he was twenty-three, a young man reminded occasionally by odd chance and circumstance to take some measure of his life. The brick and mud village in India flickered as a grainy yellow image in his mind. He'd crawled up through a hollow passageway far enough to see the wide funnel of the world flaring open above him, a buoyant sea that bore him safely away from the carnage that would soon rip apart his homeland in the Punjab. The train ride from Velhi to Aligarh memorable with its singing schoolchildren, the phalanx of British troops gathered along a street in Kanpur. The rusted bucket of a fishing vessel churning off into the milky green Bay of Bengal. Chittagong, Rangoon, Hong Kong. The six weeks in the hold, where others retched the meager contents in their gut. Land again, the hills burnished gold at midday.

Along the road, the cluster of rooftops became visible ahead, the buildings huddled against the levee wall and connected to it by a row of wooden gangplanks. A black Packard crawled up from the town like a giant bug and turned south onto the main road. The bustle of the little place beckoned and he quickened his steps in anticipation. He'd been in the country long enough to know that this place was different from the manicured towns of Germans and the Swiss that had dotted the Central Valley on his way north. Locke was exclusively Chinese. People preferred to stick to their own kind; it was as simple as that. And what was he doing here, in this foreign among foreign places? He was earning a living, learning to make his way, he reminded himself. Every other paycheck, he would send back to his father and brothers in India.

The Southern Pacific Railroad wharf lined the riverbank opposite the town. Beyond was the drawbridge, the water below it speckled with beads of silver in the sunlight. He took the paved road down the levee into town, listening to the gravel grind under his boots. Main Street ran north and south, parallel to the river. Two-storied shops lined the road, many of them with covered second-story balconies hovering over it. By midday, a line of cars crowded the short length of the street. He passed Dai Loi, the gambling hall Leandro had dragged him into that first night. He had been introduced around as the Hindu, what all Indians were called regardless if they were Hindu, Sikh, or Muslim. He'd refrained from gambling, preferring to watch Leandro play the lottery, and wary of the pointed, sizing-up stares of others. And he'd gotten a good look at the iron knuckles lying on the front table and reputedly used on cheats and trouble-makers. He wanted no part of that kind of discipline. The Chinese could be as clannish as Punjabis; he realized that much.

The wooden walkway thumped with passing footsteps. Ahead of him, a slow, stooped woman chased a frantic rooster into a nar-row, shaded alley. In the market, he quibbled over carrots or squash. He had in mind a sabji; Leandro had enjoyed the last one with long beans. He'd brought packets of turmeric and masala from the Im-perial Valley, and indulged in a curry dish occasionally. Otherwise, it was beans and bread or tortilla—roti, as he knew it. At the counter, the cashier spoke to him, as Zhang had earlier, in an unbroken chain of sentences while he piled the purchases into a wood crate, as though Avtar understood, if not the words themselves, then the meaning of their rhythm. Avtar dropped thirty cents on the counter and went out.

The old-timers were crowding the benches along the shops by then, talking and reading Chinese-language newspapers. Men who had survived the Depression, some who had lost fortunes. He didn't return their mild glances; after a month or so in the area, he still considered himself an outsider, though no longer an object of their curiosity. More and more Indian men worked the fields and orchards beside the Chinese, Filipinos, and Mexicans. He knew of the Sikh Temple in Stockton, though he'd had no chance yet to visit. He'd travel a bit once he had some money saved up. He'd take one of those steamboats to Sacramento or someplace up the river.

A few children played on a second-story balcony across the street. A young woman with pigtails, probably the mother, paced back and forth, carrying her bare-bottomed youngest in her arms. He passed a hardware store, then the barbershop, the lively epicenter of local gossip. Soon he was heading back up the levee road to the camp.

The freight ship's scheduled arrival at the packing plant was delayed that evening. The captain had radioed: They were detained downriver, some sort of passenger mix-up, no mechanical troubles, fortunately. It pulled up at 7:45, over an hour late, with its whistle blasting and the steam engine cutting and whishing. Avtar heard the call from the foreman to start the conveyer belt. The crates were stacked six, eight deep, and as soon as the thing lurched into motion, he began to shift them onto the conveyer belt. The metal chains crunched under the weight and movement as they slowly bore the crates out an opening in the tin wall and down the bank to the ship. There, several men would unload the crates into a hold. That wasn't such bad duty. One could at least leave the musty, dark air in the plant, get a glimpse of the passengers, the women so elegantly dressed in hats, and the crew and the feel of the boat swaying over the water. He'd wait his turn. He'd been on the job for only two weeks, but he was eager to show the foreman, Mr. Bingham, that he could be trusted with duties beyond the packing and stacking of crates within the plant. He was strong enough for any of the jobs; the months of field work in the south had bulked up his upper body. He was not a big man, but he worked hard, ate reasonably well, and took care of himself. Avtar watched the last of the crates for that day's shipment crawl away from the plant toward the ship. He peered out the four-by-four-foot opening in the wall where the belt cranked through, gaining a triangular view of a section of the boat where the young bearded captain strolled the deck in a white jacket with blue trim and brass buttons.

The supper bell rang as the boat pushed off upriver. Avtar collected his lunch pail and thermos of tea, walked out to the riverbank, and sat beside a meandering sycamore with one errant branch dipping low over the water. He preferred that spot to the open deck where the Chinese workers gathered to share their food and animated stories. It was nearly dark. The violet-pink of passing clouds reflected off the water. He unrolled two rotis from their cheesecloth wrapping and plunged them piece by piece into the sabji he'd prepared earlier. Even out in the fresh air, with the curry before him, the scent of pears bit at his nose. When he closed his eyes to sleep at night, a hail of green orbs flooded his vision before they fell away, and he could dream.

It was Wednesday, he reminded himself. Leandro had promised some sort of outing the following Sunday. He knew someone with a car. He was a talker, that Leandro, a restless sort. Still, Avtar found himself relieved and grateful for the offer. He hadn't come halfway around the world to spend every waking hour toiling. He was entitled to find some pleasure now and then. In America, he had come to learn, one could find paid work, and one always looked forward to Sundays.

Leandro woke him early that Sunday. In his bed, Avtar blinked sleep from his eyes, to find his friend's pox-scarred brown face leaning over him, urging him to get up. The car would arrive in an hour or so, and then they would be off. "*¿A dónde?*" Avtar asked. He sometimes found it easier to speak the little Spanish he knew with Leandro.

"Wherever we want to." Leandro made flourishing circles with the cigarette in one hand. "Eddie, he has a friend in Sacramento he wants to see. After that, he'll take us around."

"I've always wanted to go to San Francisco," Avtar said, rising up on one elbow.

"That's in the other direction. Haven't you ever looked at a map?"

"Of course it's in the other direction. I just meant I'd like to go there sometime, maybe take one of those freight ships."

"Yes, hide yourself in one of those pear crates," Leandro said, laughing and taking a puff. Avtar suspected something childish about the man at times. He claimed to be twenty-six, but with the slightly fleshy, shadowed pouches under his eyes, he appeared a bit older, early thirties perhaps. It wasn't lack of experience in itself. Leandro was all too eager to relate his experiences, the winding sphere of paths he'd traveled—like a ball of yarn—small jobs he'd taken along the way, the women. Somehow, the experiences didn't stack up with the man, or perhaps the man, even as he relished telling them, seemed to resist their lessons. Strange that you could trust implicitly someone you'd caught in a lie, albeit a small one, but he felt this way about his friend. They'd met in town one evening when Avtar had first arrived. He'd heard there was work picking pears, he told a group of men gathered outside the market. Leandro overheard him and said he knew where he could find out, and where he could stay.

They waited until well past noon before the hunter green 1946 Hudson pulled up. Leandro's friend was a slim, energetic fellow in his twenties, big on slapping one's shoulders or back. He'd been raised in the area, but worked now at a service station in Stockton. Avtar recognized from Leandro's easy teasing way with Eddie that they had been friends for some time.

They drove north on River Road, the road itself, like the river beside it, lolling and curving, the car swaying over it in a smooth, un-hurried motion. The dry side of the levee fell away to pear orchards and the elegant homes and expansive lawns of white landowners tucked amid them. Steel drawbridges with honeycombed metal-grated roadways linked the two sides of the river. He'd watched them groan and split open like giant metal jaws to allow the freight ships past. The river channeled off in a dozen places into a sleepy network of sloughs that wound through the valley, so one was never far from the water. The Chinese, perhaps the grandfathers of the men who lined the benches along Main Street each day in Locke, had constructed these waterways to reclaim marshy backwaters for agriculture. They'd proceeded to plant orchards, working the rich black peat for the prized green goods it could yield.

"It's my uncle Ernie's," Eddie said, looking through the rearview mirror. Avtar seemed confused, as if he had dropped into the middle of some conversation. "The car," Eddie added. "It's my uncle Ernie's. He's letting me borrow it for the day."

"Yes, very nice."

Eddie drummed his fingers on the steering wheel. "So, you Hindu," he said, turning briefly toward Avtar, who was in the back-seat. Hindu, Hindu, he repeated like a mantra. "Lots of Hindus coming out here now."

"Yes." Avtar didn't bother explaining the difference between a Sikh and a Hindu. He'd sat in a coffee shop in El Centro next to a young farmhand once, a white boy with a stubby scar next to his right eye, trying to tell him just what a Sikh was, if such a thing could be explained. He'd shorn his hair and shaved his beard be-fore boarding the boat from India. What difference did it make now?

"I'm hungry, Eddie. Let's stop at Lupe's," Leandro said.

"You're always hungry. Anyway, my friends have some kind of picnic planned. You like hot dogs?" Eddie shouted back to Avtar. "You guys don't eat meat, right?"

He had a face like a pony's, Avtar decided, with a long jawline extending toward a narrow chin, and a nose to match. Friendly eyes. "I'll eat anything if I'm hungry enough."

Eddie punched Leandro's shoulder. "You got a smart friend here."

Leandro carried the plate with the hot dog over with both hands, elbows jutting out and shoulders rounded, as if it were a priceless delicacy. They were gathered on wooden dining room chairs spread over a spiky, overgrown lawn under drooping mulberries in the front yard. They had turned off River Road somewhere south of Sacramento and sped past velvety yellow wheat fields into a loose cluster of homes. Eddie's friend Michael exited the screen door, shedding a red-and-white-checked apron. "How you like those hot dogs, Eddie?" A friendly round of shoulder punching followed.

Avtar bit into the bland, textureless meat. He watched as a petite woman joined Michael and slipped her arm behind his back. Her auburn hair was cut short, to her ears, and had been curled, then fastened with a small butterfly clip. Michael's expression softened in her company. He clapped his hands together. "How about some horseshoes. Ever play horseshoes, Avtar?"

"No."

"What kind of games you play in your country?"

Avtar barely stifled a laugh. "I wrestled a pig in my village." A traveling troupe of entertainers had stopped there when he was sixteen, and Rami had been standing in the crowd, her bare toes scrunched in the red dust, so he'd stepped forward. "They give it something, you know, to make it angry." The others were laughing. "I chased it in the mud; then it chase me."

He joined in the game of horseshoes, watching the girl squeal each time she took her turn, tossing the thing in the direction of the metal stake as if she were blindfolded. Leandro, playing with his left hand, as his right one held a succession of beer bottles, still managed to win. Afterward, he went off toward the road for a smoke. The others scattered off in small groups. Michael and his girlfriend wandered off hand in hand toward the house. By the front door, he stopped and leaned over her, his hands on her hips. She tilted her face up to his, and what Avtar saw in her clear brown eyes made his heart crack. Avtar turned abruptly, the way one might from some unbearable, even tragic scene. He sank into a chair under the drooping trees, unable in his thoughts to evade that pair of eyes and the intention implicit in their gaze. He heard the screen door slam behind him. And so went another Sunday.

"That Michael, he's got a nice girl," Leandro said on the drive home.

"Oh, Eliana? She's got a different guy every month."

Leandro deflated against the back of the seat. Avtar stared out at the river, at the shadowy figure of a man bent over, pulling the day's catch of catfish from the hull of a small fishing boat. Leandro's enduring bachelorhood seemed to confirm his own. Following a dip and curve in the road, Leandro's face lightened. "Lupe's is coming up. We stopping?"

How come a guy like you stays so skinny but eats so much? Eddie asked.

It was dark by then. A warm, buttery light seeped out the front glass windows of the building onto the sidewalk. The café was small and crowded, a jumble of wooden tables crisscrossed with the brawny forearms of farmhands. A row of red vinyl bar stools lined the side counter. Avtar studied a painting on black velvet cloth of some sort of chieftain or warrior with an eagle perched on his shoulder, tacked on the wall behind Eddie's head. A waitress hurriedly deposited menus on the table, then dashed back toward the kitchen. He'd seen only the back of her, the flared brown cotton skirt swishing off and the red heels, the color of those bar stools. Leandro recommended the Swiss steaks. "Three Swiss steaks," he told the waitress when she returned.

"All three of you?" She made a little triangle in the air with her pencil. "The special is meat loaf. Comes with braised carrots." She arched her dark brows and began scribbling on a pad.

"I'll take meat loaf," Avtar said. He had no idea what it might be, but it was enough to get the girl to look directly at him for a second. She scribbled again on her pad and was soon at the next table of customers, beaming her pearly straight teeth and the pink of her gums in a smile. She trotted off in the heels like a young girl playing grown-up. How many tips did she save up to buy those? he wondered.

"That's Lupe's daughter." Leandro had noticed him staring. "Olivia."

The food arrived, the same pasty beige gravy covering the meat loaf and the Swiss steak. A small gold cross dangled from the girl's neck where the collar of her white shirt flared open. He thought he detected a scent, a trace of perfume, when she leaned over him with his plate, but it was only the warm olive scent of skin, he realized. He ate in silence, the meat drenched in its thick sauce curdling in his throat, the flurry of the brown skirt in his peripheral vision.

Outside after the meal, his eyes traced the curved lines of the car, the hemispherical rear hold gleaming and marbled under the streetlamp. "What does a car like this cost?" he asked Eddie.

"My uncle paid about twelve hundred bucks."

"Bucks," Avtar repeated, trying out the word. Where would he get money like that? It would take years. He climbed into the padded backseat, an odd notion stirring within him, a premonition perhaps that he would somehow. He had been grateful for the string of steady, if only temporary, jobs that had come his way, always looking ahead when the lettuce or tomatoes had been harvested to the next crop down the road. The money he wired back to his family in India was a healthy supplement to their meager earnings as sharecroppers for a greedy landlord. Yet he was convinced there had to be a better way and that he would find it. Because he knew now that he wanted things.

George Bingham leaned against a wooden post and ran his hand over the tight rust-colored curls on his head. Gathered around him in the packing shed were men already prepared for the foreman's inevitable news. The men had been grumbling for days, watching the shipments coming into the plant dwindle after a late-August surge. Avtar tossed a packing crate on the packed-dirt floor and collapsed onto it. Strange that he felt winded, when he'd handled only half the normal quantity of crates that morning. He attributed the fatigue dawning in his limbs to the general anxiety stirring among the workers. Even the one they called Chen, the muscled veteran who refused to relinquish his slot as the top packer, sucked furiously nearby on a hand-rolled cigarette.

Bingham raised his hand to silence the last bit of murmuring. Stepping forward, he tucked his thumbs in the waist of his khakis. "I suppose you men know why I've called this meeting. Most of you are used to hearing this kind of speech, and you know the boats are coming in twice a day, tops. As of this week, we're eliminating the night shift. That means some of you'll want to move on. You might want to try the canneries, or there's tomatoes, and the grape harvest will be under way soon. For those of you who stay on, we'll last another ten days or so on pears, and we'll pick up another couple of weeks at the tail end of tomato season. That takes us into the third week of September." He paused. "Then we shut down for the season."

Avtar noticed the men around him, even those who barely understood a word of English, nodding. Bingham's gaze moved quickly from one man to the next, as though he was mentally noting each one of them. He had a way of making a man feel counted—Avtar granted him that—while still holding himself apart, sufficiently insulated from the uncertainties that marked the lives of the men who worked under his watch. A fresh crease ran the length of his khakis. Avtar imagined he owned several pairs of them and slipped on fresh ones each day.

The men worked with added zeal that evening. Damaged or rotting fruit was quickly removed and discarded. As soon as the packing was done, the unused crates were hauled off to the towering stacks along the far wall. The packed-dirt floor was swept, then reswept. The few remarks among the men were good-natured jabs or inquiries about one's future status. At the end of his shift that night, Avtar stopped Bingham as he was stepping into his car.

"Mr. Bingham?"

The foreman turned slowly, his hand clasping the rim of the car door. The tension had drained from his face, leaving the skin slack and spongy, and Avtar got a glimpse of the man retreating into his private world.

"I want to stay on the day shift. I'm a hard worker."

"Yes, you're a good worker, Ray."

Avtar had ceased insisting on the correct pronunciation of his name; "Rai, like *bye*," he would say, waving his hand. But the English name had stuck out of convenience, a casual disregard, and soon he had begun to introduce himself to his coworkers simply as Ray.

Bingham ran a thumb and forefinger over his slim mustache. "I'll see what I can do. I'd like to keep you on. But I'd start looking if I were you. Can't postpone the inevitable." He slid onto the seat and started the ignition as if suddenly remembering an urgent task. Perhaps it was just that there was someplace else he wanted to be, and Avtar wondered what that place might be like. Bingham's wife drove out occasionally at meal breaks, fluttering her slender hand like a white handkerchief out the car window to wave her husband over while a passel of blond children bounced in the backseat. He recalled the time Bingham, visibly agitated, had reprimanded Chen for an errant pile of crates before heading over to meet his wife. One couldn't truly tell about other people's lives.

Avtar lay nearly dozing on the mattress, which felt like a thin, doughy wafer beneath him. A block of sunlight from an open window fell over his chest and the gathering warmth roused him from a half dream; he'd been lolling under a favorite sprawling tree on the outskirts of his village in India, evading duties with a small cadre of fellow dawdlers. He had seen his father walk by—if one could only freeze those fleeting frames of dreams!—clutching a sack of wheat, his back bowed by its weight, and the currents of water in the river had been lapping all the while at the edges of his mind.

Avtar had showered after returning from work, and now he used the towel that covered his naked body to sop up the sheet of sweat on his skin. That pleasant dream reminded him of a letter from his brother that he'd tucked, half-read, under his bed the previous night. He pulled the aerogram from a blue silk case where he stored the few mementos he possessed from India—earlier letters, an English text of his brother's titled *A Welsh Boyhood,* which he had parted with tearfully, and the single photograph of his mother taken at a festival and paid for with a large tin of fresh goat's milk. Avtar squinted at the image, trying to make out her vivacious eyes, what he remembered most about her. She hadn't been much older than he was now when the photograph was taken. She had demanded to stand alone in it, leaving his one-year-old brother, Lal, wailing by his feet next to an oxcart. It pleased him now that she had had her moments like that, moments of self-appreciation, vanity even, for she was gone all too soon.

The letter had been written by that youngest brother, Lal. Oh, Mohinder, the middle child, included an occasional anecdote, some mischief at the hands of the village boys, scrawled in a hasty, obligatory fashion. But in Lal's lush, careful script Avtar sensed pleasure and purpose; he could imagine Lal's pen point dipping into the inkwell and heard the initial scratch of a line on paper, from which the letters descended artfully in bows and curves. Neighbors in their village often requested Lal's services, and he would at first push the tip of his pen into his bottom lip, perhaps elevating their words and desires as he finally began to compose them on paper.

> *Dearest brother,*
>
> *We've once again received your generous gift, twenty-five dollars. A month's pay, you say. You can imagine the difference these payments have made in our lives. Father is, of course, reluctant to boast about this income to others, though our neighbors continue to behave curiously toward us, as if some special fortune has befallen us. They regularly inquire if letters have come from America, and what astonishing feats our mischievous Tari has accomplished lately. I read a portion of your last letter—brief as it was—to a small herd of them gathered eagerly by the door. Your talk of freighters and cities of glass and steel left them silent, and you know how difficult that is to do!*
>
> *I myself have purchased an old bicycle that allows me to ride the four kilometers to Kitri to attend a class. It is a blend of history, politics, and mathematics, held in Gian Singh's home. He has just returned from Jalandhar, where he served as a political liaison in the independence movement, and has*

many interesting perspectives on India's future course. Father
still haggles regularly with the wheat farmer to the south.
And Mohinder—well, he is Mohinder, enigmatic as ever.
Keep safe and don't let the months pass before we hear again
from you.

> *Your fond brother always,*
> *La!*

His youngest brother, a budding scholar! It didn't surprise him.
The meager pay from long hours at the packing plant was doing
someone good after all. He glanced again over the letter, ruing his
own shoddy writing abilities, gleaned under a lean-to, where old
Dev Kaur seemed more fond of rubbing the children's faces in her
scant bosom than teaching them letters and numbers. He placed the
letter in the cloth case with the others and retied the string. Leandro
hasn't returned, Avtar thought, and he smiled, thinking he might be
up to his tricks, stopping in town for a drink or to see a girl.

Bingham had managed to keep Avtar on the day shift after all.
The new schedule provided both opportunities and minor incon-
veniences for Avtar. Working regular hours provided him little time
to himself. He hadn't realized that privacy was something he coveted until he began returning home afternoons, to find Leandro
humming one of his show tunes as he brewed a cup of coffee, or
chatting outdoors with neighboring laborers. There, too, were the
nights such as the previous Saturday, when Leandro would insist on
his company for a little jaunt into town. The place was transformed
on weekend evenings, when out-of-towners flooded the streets and
packed the gambling hall in Locke. He'd noticed that Leandro was
well acquainted with a couple of the ladies regularly seen around
the various establishments. The big blond one, Ingrid, had frightened him a little and, by contrast, called to mind a more refined nature he had observed in Olivia.

Lying there thinking of her now only reminded him of his uncertain future and how foolish he was to entertain the notion that
she would be included in it. She came to mind erratically. He might
not recall her face for what seemed like days; then its clean oval
would appear in his vision, as if taunting him, and he would begin
anew counting the days and weeks since he'd first seen her. It had
been four weeks now. Surely he would get back to Lupe's soon. He
sprang from his bed—he would not return as one of those penni-
less drifters he'd seen carrying bedrolls on their backs.

Awhile later, he found himself swaying down the wooden gangplank at the dock where the *Mariposa* stopped to unload and pick
up passengers and supplies each afternoon. A man in a gray cap and
blue overalls touched the bill of his cap and nodded to Avtar. He
padlocked the door to a windowed ticket station at one end of a
small boathouse, then headed up the gangplank, whistling a jaunty
tune that belied his slow, measured steps. A stooped, wiry fellow paced
the length of the dock, securing sections of thick rope around the
posts. "Boat's come and gone for the day," he cried out, his back to
Avtar. When Avtar didn't respond, the man turned, stiff and hunched.
A pair of deep furrows ran the length of his ruddy, chapped cheeks,
but his gray eyes looked alert and focused.

"I said the boat's come and gone. Are you looking for someone?"

"I'm looking for work."

The man stepped onto a lower platform that encased a large
winch. He began to tussle with a crank seemingly rusted and frozen
in place.

"How much weight will that pull?" Avtar asked, kneeling next
to the winch. The man's face reddened and his jaw trembled as he
thrust his weight against the crank. Conversation, or company of
any kind, seemed unwelcome to him. Avtar feared the bones in the
old man's wrists might splinter with the effort. He watched another moment as the man pushed against the crank, then eased it

from his grip. Taking a deep breath, Avtar applied all the force he could muster. On the third try, the crank began to free up, a centimeter, then an inch. He could feel its grinding movement vibrate to his elbows. Soon the cables reeled up out of the water, humming and squeaking as they wound around the drum. When the twenty-pound hooks emerged from the water, it seemed the drum would continue rolling, but it halted suddenly with a painful screech. Momentum, Avtat thought. The basic law of motion. Afterward, he shook off the fatigue that ran like steel strips through his arms.

"Pearson's name," the man said. "Boss—the real boss—he lives in a big place on a hill near San Francisco. Owns a bank, couple of boats, hundreds of acres around here. Sailed up here a couple of months ago on the *Mariposa* with the wife on his arm. I heard he was on his way up the river to see the governor." Pearson gazed disdainfully to the north, as though unspeakable acts were the norm in the vicinity of the state's capital.

Avtar couldn't make out the corrugated tin walls of the packing plant, which sat a mile or so upstream, where the river curved gently toward the northwest. He felt the light breeze ruffling his hair and shirt collar, the moist air expanding his lungs. As he turned to leave, Pearson acknowledged his assistance with a stiff nod. "Come by around noon tomorrow and ask for Charlie."

Thin slats of sunlight reflected off the tall reeds growing along the gangplank, which creaked and swayed as Avtar climbed to the top of the bank. Purple, inky pools of water, the first shadows of the evening, crept along near the opposite bank. Below, Pearson's figure scrambled up and down the dock like a bewildered crab seeking shelter.

He had not waited for the whistle ending his shift. Avtar had discovered the one thing possibly worse than the grinding work required when the plant was in full swing, and this was the idle chunks of time when he tried to appear occupied as the shipments gradually came to a halt. His boss spent much of the day cleaning out the contents of his desk in a makeshift office set up in a corner of the plant. Earlier, Avtar had wandered over and asked what plans he had for the off-season, and Bingham had swung around in his chair as though alarmed by the question. "I'm a year-round employee of Hayes and Company, Ray," he replied. "They always find something for me to do." He fumbled with a stack of shipping records that covered his lap, making a perfunctory check here and there. Aware of the young man's lingering presence, Bingham checked his watch. "Why don't you take the rest of the afternoon off?" he said to Avtar.

At the dock, Avtar discovered that Charlie was the tall man he had seen locking the ticket station the previous day. He wore the same blue coveralls and gray cap and stood on the dock in the mid-afternoon like a massive pillar, shouting instructions to Pearson and the other men. The sight of passengers shuffling about the vicinity of the ticket booth heartened Avtar. The freight ship was evidently expected at any moment. He had jogged the last quarter mile from the packing plant in hopes of catching sight of it and the general commotion of arrivals and departures.

A young woman and her two children appeared at the ticket booth, bearing a trio of leather bags, which they set on the platform. The woman searched in a handbag as the children stood around her, bunching the folds of her skirt in their fingers. Avtar stepped from the gangplank toward the ticket booth, where Charlie was stamping the woman's ticket and taking bills from her white-gloved hand. He threw a gruff warning glance at Avtar when he approached too close, and Avtar promptly backed away until the young family had gathered by the others in the departure area. Determined to ignore the young intruder, Charlie proceeded to shout orders at the handful of men on duty. Pearson, too, failed to notice him as he directed the stacking of supplies on a landing adjacent to the passenger loading area.

The *Mariposa* could not have arrived at a more convenient time. Avtar watched the small stern-wheeler chug in under the acrid charcoal plumes of smoke. As it slipped beside the landing, the onboard crew tossed over ropes thick as his wrists and Pearson's men secured them to posts. A crewman opened the doors of the hold and Pearson's men disappeared into the dark chambers, emerging with luggage, trunks, and crates. Avtar joined Pearson, who was enjoying a rare moment of inactivity by the loading area.

"This here's my favorite," Pearson said to him, his gaze trained on the boat. "Built in 1903. The owner got her out of a salvage yard and had her rebuilt. Don't find any like her on the river these days."

"Why not?"

Pearson motioned toward the Southern Pacific wharf upriver. "Trains, cars, bridges—progress. Fifteen, twenty years ago, there were dozens of 'em going up and down the rivers, even into the sloughs. They could go as far as Fresno when the water was high enough."

He had a perpetually chapped look wherever his skin was exposed; even his broad stubbled chin looked calloused. He was obviously a man who had spent his life on or near the water. "Can't imagine the owner makes any money on her anymore. About breaks even, at best."

"Where does it go?" Avtar asked.

"Sacramento. Oh, it stops for passengers at about every little landing along the way. The big steamers are gone for good. The *Delta Queen*'s running on the Mississippi these days."

It was the last of the small steamers to still traverse the waters of the San Joaquin Delta, Pearson told him. One hundred and six feet of history. Pearson spat into the water. "Did you talk to Charlie?"

Avtar watched as the last of the passengers disembarked. "No, I haven't."

"Come on. Let's see if we can catch that old weasel in a good moment."

Avtar held a five-dollar bill in the air. "My first tip."

Leandro lay on his bunk reading a magazine. "What for?"

"Carrying a fine lady's bags." He studied the image of the grave bearded man on its face. A large bill deserved to display such a dignified man as that. "Let's celebrate. Let's go into town."

Leandro cocked his head, as if he hadn't heard his habitually cautious roommate correctly. "All right. I'm always ready for a night in town."

On a Thursday evening, the streets of Locke hummed with a noticeable surge of activity, due, in part, to the early arrival of revelers from San Francisco and other towns in the region. By the following day, Main Street would be humming with tourists eager to try their luck at fan-tan or pai gow in the gambling hall or visit its other, more illicit attractions. It reminded Avtar that the dock would be teeming with passengers the next day. With a little luck (and Charlie looking the other way), he might earn another tip. They passed a trio of young men, two white men and a Chinese fellow, wandering along the street, peering through the windows of various establishments. "San Franciscans," Leandro said to Avtar before scurrying across the street toward the Dai Loi Gambling Hall.

The smoke was thick inside the hall. Avtar suppressed the urge to cough. He stuck close to Leandro, who seemed familiar with various patrons and employees. The gaming tables were full and the two friends were left standing amid the other men waiting for a turn. The gambling room was a large open area with a high ceiling and a couple of storage rooms and a toilet in the back. A gruff man at the fan-tan table raised his voice; he seemed to be trading insults with another man at the table, but they both erupted into laughter seconds later. When they rose to leave, Leandro slipped into one of the chairs.

Avtar noticed an iron teakettle set on a burner on a side table along the wall, where the patrons helped themselves to warm cups of tea. It felt like a boiling kettle inside the room, with everything sealed and churning with activity. Leandro had told him the windows had been covered up so wives couldn't look in on their husbands. Many of these men looked too young to be married, or at least displayed a kind of bravura he associated with bachelors. Leandro was already placing bets on a second game, his face ruddy with concentration. The dealer collected buttons under a brass bowl. He lifted the bowl and separated the buttons in piles of four. Three buttons remained. Leandro apparently bet on two; he pounded his fist once on the table. Everyday items were used in these games, Leandro had explained to him, in case the place was raided.

The line forming in front of the lottery window intrigued Avtar. There was something in the pure chance involved, submitting oneself coolly to it, with none of the nervousness he observed in Leandro's face. He passed one of the domino tables, stopping to watch the banker shake the dice and spill them onto the table. The player who got first turn struck a match over a sandpaper strip attached to the leg of the table and lighted a cigarette before drawing his dominoes. The five-dollar bill beckoned from his wallet. He thought the lavish tip might bring him luck with the lottery. Perhaps he could double at least part of this small fortune. He obtained change in one-dollar bills, recalling the woman who had placed it icily into his hands; she'd clutched a Bible in one arm, and her gaunt face had looked ahead of him, never at him, as she'd pressed the bill firmly in his palm.

The line before the metal-screened ticket window had grown longer in anticipation of the eight o'clock drawing. Looking behind the window, Avtar could see the lottery cage holding the Ping-Pong balls painted with Arabic numerals.

Leandro joined him in front of the lottery window; the exhilaration had drained from his face and he looked drawn.

"Any luck with fan-tan?" Avtar asked.

"Not today."

"How do you play this lottery?"

"Just pick some numbers . . . up to twenty. The clerk'll mark them for you."

"You want to play, too?"

Leandro shook his head. "Not enough excitement."

At the ticket window, Avtar set a dollar bill on the counter. "One ticket." The clerk squinted at him through wire-rimmed glasses and placed a ticket before him. The numbers one through eighty were listed backward in rows on the sheet. He tried to recall the ages of his family members; how old would his brothers be now? With a pencil, Avtar marked nine numbers in all. The clerk examined the numbers and blotted each one with black ink. He duplicated the numbers on a second copy, then stamped them both. With a copy of his ticket in hand, Avtar wandered over to the vestibule by the front entrance. The gambling hall had grown noisier, smokier. Leandro was haggling with a dealer at a domino table.

The drawing was announced at eight sharp and the players surged toward the counter, the paper sheets flapping in their fingers. The clerk turned the handle and the balls in the wire lottery cage began to spin and tumble. He pulled out the balls one by one, calling out the numbers before placing them in a wooden rack. Avtar glanced from the crumpled sheet in his fingers to the clerk with mounting excitement. When the twenty numbers had been called, he counted six winning numbers on his ticket.

He collected his winnings at the ticket window—$169 on a dollar bet. He smiled to himself. He remembered his mother and what she would say. Gathered by the well, the women in his village regularly repeated the same tired refrain: It was written already that it would happen; it was karma, they would claim of fortune and tragedy alike. Karma nothing! his mother would insist the moment she was out of their earshot. It was luck.

Leandro rushed up and whistled. Six out of nine! Avtar placed the winning ticket and bills in his pocket and the two headed back to the camp.

How much for a ticket to Courtland?" he asked Charlie one day.

Charlie appraised him, from the crisp points of his new taupe-colored fedora down to the secondhand chocolate brown loafers he had picked up at the general store. "You gotta ride in the hold. No fancy views down there."

"I know." Not even a winning lottery ticket could erase the fact of his origins. He set forty cents on the counter and headed to the boat, then climbed into the cramped space belowdecks, which was filled with luggage and assorted boxes. When the passageway was sealed shut, he could no longer smell the water, whose forceful currents guided him these days wherever he went. Avtar reclined uncomfortably against a stack of suitcases. The engines struck up with an earsplitting blast and vibration. The boat rocked into motion, but the overwhelming noise made it impossible to perceive any sense of direction. He could have taken the train north those several miles, but a ride on the refurbished *Mariposa,* even in its confined, womblike hold, held a certain charm and appeal. A Chinese couple seated nearby held on closely to their young daughter. Farther back, an old man with a long braid down his back clutched a cloth sack. Avtar studied the worn map of his hands, the long, knobby fingers spread out like tributaries leading nowhere. He must have some stories to tell, he thought.

He emerged again to the world awhile later, the breeze chilling his damp skin. It was a brief journey, as Lupe's was located only a few miles north of the camp, but it was the notion of traveling once again by water that had seized him. He walked a quarter mile north on River Road before spotting the familiar lights of the restaurant. He stopped to pull a handkerchief from his pocket and mop the sweat on his face and neck; he had been perspiring now, despite the cool air wafting up from the river. He felt his stomach drop as he approached the small restaurant. What would he say to her? She with her flawless English and a tiny frame that hoisted trays laden with meat loaf and enchiladas as if they were mere cushions. Avtar hesitated by the entrance, but he was forced to enter when two men approached behind him from the parking lot.

An unfamiliar waitress slapped a menu on the table he had taken in the center of the room. The same lively atmosphere he had noticed on his first visit permeated the restaurant. He felt conspicuous sitting there alone while those around him conducted friendly, animated conversations. He regretted coming now. Not even the boat ride had been the experience he had romanticized it to be. When the waitress returned, he asked what the special was, managing to circumvent the problem of being unable to read the menu. She gave him a harried look; work seemed an unwelcome distraction from whatever chaos she was experiencing in her private life.

"Chicken. Pot. Pie." She pronounced the words slowly, as if the daily special constituted three separate items.

Avtar nodded, unsure what to expect when the food arrived. He imagined chicken in a pot, with a serving of pie for dessert. Having ordered such a lavish meal, he suddenly felt famished. Only then did he notice Olivia behind the lunch counter; she was handing change to a young male customer leaning over a red bar stool.

Her dark hair was pulled back with a pink bow. Would she remember him? "Meat loaf" had been the only words he had spoken to her previously, the only instant their eyes had met directly. The customer shoved the change in his pocket and lingered over the bar stool, talking to her. An acquaintance, evidently. He wasn't surprised that she had other admirers.

A bowl covered with a steaming, fragrant crust was placed before him. He poked at the flaky layers with a fork, releasing more steam, revealing the creamy chunks of chicken, peas, and carrots swimming underneath. The warm crust quickly melted in his mouth as he chewed, but the vegetables and meat tasted bland, like most American food. He finished it anyway, watching as Olivia came and went to her post behind the counter. When it became clear to him the pie would never arrive, that, in fact, the single dish before him that he had consumed in a few short minutes was chicken, pot, and pie, he craved the sweet dessert he had anticipated. He paid the bill and, rather than exiting the restaurant, seated himself at a bar stool at the counter.

Olivia swung around to face him. "Hello. What can I get for you?"

"Pie, please." He removed his hat and straightened his hair.

"Lemon meringue, apple, peach cobbler, blackberry, or cherry?"

"Peach," he replied.

"A la mode?"

His quizzical expression made her laugh.

"With ice cream?" she asked.

"Oh, yes." A-la-mode; he would have to remember that. She turned away, swinging her hair and her skirt; the lights and everything in the room seemed to twirl with her. He watched as she removed the pie from a glass case and cut a slice. She scooped vanilla ice cream from a bin in a refrigerator, then set the plate before him.

A husky, balding customer at the end of the counter requested his check, then, frowning, pointed to the yellow square of paper. "You charged me for four beers, Olivia."

"Well, you've *had* four beers, Frank," Olivia said, waggling her head.

The man spread his hands before him, appearing dumbfounded, as though accused of a monstrous crime. "Wouldn't be the first time, Frank," someone yelled from a nearby table.

When she returned, she set her elbows on the counter and folded her fingers under her chin, her mouth drooping a little in exasperation. If he never saw her again, he would remember her that way, Avtar decided.

"How's the pie?" she asked.

His mouth full, Avtar pointed to the orange-and-white slurry flooding the remaining bits of crust on his plate. "Very good."

Olivia nodded. "Irene Apodaca makes them special for us." She leaned back against a metal cart and pushed the bangs off her forehead with the back of her wrist. "You're not Mexican, are you? You have a different accent."

"I'm Hindu."

"Hindu. I thought so. There's more and more Hindus coming to America."

"Just looking for work."

"There was one guy who used to come in here often. He showed me a picture of his wife and son once. Said he was waiting for the time he would be allowed to go to India and bring them back here." She picked up a damp cloth and pretended to wipe a section of the counter. "How long have you been in this country?"

Avtar noticed he was her only customer at the moment. Saat mahine, he wanted to say. He looked at his fingers and counted silently. "Seven. Months." He was speaking like the other waitress now.

"Well, I've lived here all my life. My father nearly moved us all

back to Sonora—that's in Mexico—but my mother had this idea
to open a restaurant. I started working here when I was twelve,
cleaning tables after school or helping in the kitchen, peeling potatoes or making tortillas."

"It's a good place to live."

Olivia wrinkled her nose. "A little dull. Unless you go to Sacramento to a dance or see a movie." She lifted the salt and pepper
shakers and swabbed them with the cloth, then moved on to stacking a tray of glasses the dishwasher had set before her.

Avtar felt his hands begin to perspire. Her slight hint of displeasure only magnified the seemingly insurmountable distance that
separated their worlds. It was a hallmark of youth, of course, not to
be too satisfied with one's lot; his own father had told him that. He
himself had crossed an ocean. Still, he longed to know her dreams
and passions, what her heart held beneath the green-and-white-
striped apron and the gold cross hanging at her throat.

"I'll take my check," he said.

"Thirty-five cents. I won't charge you for the ice cream."

Avtar left some change on the counter. "I'll come back next
Saturday," he said, climbing off the stool. The smile vanished from
Olivia's face. He put his hat on his head and left.

Pearson claimed he had felt it coming in his bones for days.
When Avtar woke to it that morning, he momentarily feared the
world had been altered permanently. An intractable silence filled
his ears. Looking out the window, he could scarcely make out
Zhang's bunkhouse, a mere twenty-five feet across the way. He had
never witnessed anything like it. In time, he came to know the various hues and textures of the tule fogs, some days a dry, chalky
white, on others gray, laden with a heavy mist. At the dock, grim
tales of the fog resurfaced, as they did each year—tugboats that had

collided with freighters midday on the water, a woman who had let go of her child's hand for an instant, never to see him again.

He negotiated the wooden planks along the dock carefully that morning; one wrong step could send him tumbling into the frigid water. Muffled voices reached him as though traveling over vast distances. He heard Pearson calling his name. The crew's shadowy figures gradually revealed themselves as he trudged through the damp, pillowy pockets of air. Pearson was kneeling at the south end of the dock, where a boat had scraped its hull and sheared away a section of wood. A lanky young hand named Howard squatted next to him and assessed the damage.

Avtar heard something splash, perhaps a bird or fish thrashing against the inhospitable climate in the small patch of tules beyond the dock. It was a kind of blindness, this unbreachable fog, where every sound was heightened, its meaning magnified. And nothing had permanence.

Pearson scrambled to his feet, his jowls puffing and swaying briefly like sails in a breeze. "I don't think we'll see any boats coming through today. Might as well send you home for the day, Ray. Sometimes the fog doesn't clear up for a week or more."

Two days passed. Avtar stretched on his bed for hours at a time, reread letters from his brother and cleaned his boots. He purchased an aerogram from the post office in Locke, but only stared at the blank blue page, unable to form his thoughts clearly. The inactivity, the fog circling at the windows had muddled his mind, sapped his limbs, and he settled into a restless lethargy. He recalled the string of days in his youth in the village that he'd spent waffling aimlessly about. Then, time had been like a bottomless well that he could draw from as he pleased. He had watched his father struggle against the traitorous whims of the landowner Gurdev Singh, who himself had succumbed to the tyrannical ways of the British. He'd been angry with his father on those days when he returned from the fields, cursing some fresh, impossible demand from Gurdev Singh. The portly, overfed man would stroke his beard, then spike a finger in the air as he made his outlandish claims: The paltry wheat crop had nothing to do with the village's misbegotten fate or the months of rainless skies, but with ill management, which required certain penance. "Our own people are learning too well their masters' ways," his father would reply. He despised his father more and more as he dreaded the cursed future that would mold his own manhood. And there were the stories wafting back from a different continent. He imagined that place where the light and shadows fell crisply, benevolently over the land. Increasingly, the images pulled at him, inhabited his mind, until he could endure their distant promise no longer.

When Avtar awoke the third day to an unfamiliar brightness, his eyes throbbed, but his spirits lifted. Leandro snored extravagantly in the bed across the room, his feet uncovered and his toes spiking the air. Avtar washed and drank a cup of coffee, then whistled a tune, a jazz piece he had heard somewhere, as he closed the door behind him and set off toward the dock. The sun crawled upward over the trees, tracking along its lower arc in the sky. Half the week's wages had been lost, but he consoled himself that the workweek was nearly finished and in two days, Saturday, he would board the boat to Lupe's to see Olivia again.

The scene at the dock was like a painting, once still and silent, that had suddenly come to life. The trucks had arrived from the canneries and a small crew unloaded the boxes.

Pearson led Avtar to the damaged section at an inner corner of the T-shaped dock where the smaller fishing boats stopped for supplies. The same young man he had seen three days earlier, whom Pearson introduced as Howard, crouched on the deck, clutching a claw hammer. Howard looked up; a toothy grin spread across his face, causing his small eyes to shrink back into their sockets. He removed a work glove and extended his hand to Avtar in a hearty handshake.

They got busy dissembling the damaged planks. The wood had grown brittle from years of exposure and sheared easily in places. Avtar accompanied the two men to the top of the bank, where the fresh lumber lay in the long bed of a truck. They carried the sixteen-foot planks to a worktable behind the boathouse, where they sawed the boards to ten-foot lengths.

The ringing sound of a woman's laughter came from the top of the bank. The first boat of the day was due at 10:45 and passengers were beginning to huddle in the vicinity of the ticket booth. Avtar could see only the back of the petite woman, who wore a brown wool suit and a fur over her shoulders.

"You got a girl?" Howard asked.

Avtar twirled the bolt in his fingers, feeling its sharp threads rake his skin. He wanted to say, Yes, I have. He felt Howard's eyes inspecting him as the fellow waited for a response. Part of his assessment of Avtar, the man, would naturally be his experiences with women. Avtar was not a virgin, but he did not choose to dwell on his early sexual experiences. He was young enough still to recall the woman with the torch with a mixture of revulsion and acute pleasure. She carried the flame day and night in a tribute of sorts, the villagers conjectured, to the two husbands she had lost, both of them drowned in the nearby river. Others said she carried the torch to protect herself from animals when she wandered daily out of the village. Avtar had encountered her in a small patch of woods the first time, when he was fourteen. It was dusk and she had guided him back to the squalid hut in the outskirts of the village, where she promptly put her hand inside his pajamas. She cackled at his awkward thrashing and thrusting and doubled over in laughter when he returned two days later wanting more.

No, he replied to Howard. His mouth went dry as he sifted

through a wooden crate for nine-inch nails. Sharp peals of laughter erupted once more. Avtar looked up. He didn't recognize the couple right away; she wore an opulent hat with a curved brim punctuated with a pheasant plume. He recognized the man only when he briefly removed his gray fedora and ran his hand through a thinning crop of rust-colored curls. It was Bingham, his former boss.

Without thinking, Avtar was on his feet, rushing to the top of the bank to meet them. He grabbed Bingham's hand and shook it vigorously. "Mr. Bingham."

"Ray!" He seemed genuinely glad to see his former employee. "Working down here, or waiting for the boat?"

"Working. Lucky to get a job here."

"I've got some business up in Sacramento, but Sallie didn't want to take the car." Bingham looked down at his wife, whose arm was hooked in his, with a feigned expression of exasperation.

"A little change does us all some good now and then," she said in a silky voice.

Avtar had never seen her up close, only as she delivered lunch or a message to her husband at the packing plant from her car. Her skin was ghostly pale, made more so by a fine layer of face powder. A swarm of blond ringlets framed her face and wiggled like coiled springs when she spoke. "My husband thinks it's a nuisance to take me along on these trips. Don't worry, darling, I won't infringe on any of your business. I've plenty of shopping to do."

"Now there's a comforting thought." Bingham laughed.

"The packing plant?" Avtar asked.

"The packing plant is shut down for the winter. Come around again in March, April. We'll have something for you to do."

Pearson was back working beside Howard, Avtar noticed. "I'll go back to work now. Good-bye, Mr. Bingham. Good luck on your business." Avtar circled around the other passengers gathered on the dock and headed toward the corner where Howard was hammering another board into place.

"Say, Ray." Bingham left his wife's side and walked swiftly toward Avtar, taking his shoulder in a firm grip. "I may have some extra work for you. You interested?"

Extra work? Avtar nodded. "Yes, sure."

"Good. I'll be in touch."

The sun's rays burned off the last of the mist swirling above the water. The sun! As he walked along the deck, Avtar was swept along by the feeling he had had so many times in his life, of being saved just before he was swallowed by the world.

Seven

Winter drifted down from the sky early that year, not as snow or rain, what might alight on a bare patch of skin and tingle or tease, but with a fog that settled into the bottoms and hollows of the town and countryside. I fumbled through its diaphanous haze on my way to the bus in the mornings, pulled its smoky shape around me like a silver shroud before stepping into the house in the afternoon. A certain treachery clung to the walls of that house like a dull coat of paint. Within them, my mother's toneless humming and my father's silence were ceaseless reminders of the difficult journey that not remembering could be.

I brought a letter home from school one November afternoon to show my mother. It was from Mrs. Hanover, the counselor, concerning a meeting advising students on college and scholarship applications. The humiliating incident with my uncle at the festival had only fueled my determination to attend a good college away from home, but it made it no easier to approach my parents on the matter. I found my mother seated before the small altar in a corner of her bedroom, a miniature replica of the dais at the temple, with the holy book cradled among the satin ramals that normally covered it. Sticks of black incense wafted a smoky sandalwood scent from a brass cup. Her infinite search for well-being and fortune had brought her back to the Guru Granth Sahib. Growing up, I had thought of faith as an absolute thing, solid as a stone; by a certain stage of one's life, one either subscribed passionately to it or did not. My own wavering belief I attributed yet to my youth and the disturbing portraits, for example, of Guru Gobind Singh, whom I considered the most dashing and handsome of the ten gurus, seated on the ground and holding his own head, dripping with blood, in one hand. It occurred to me then that even my mother must have had lapses. That there were different kinds of faith, the "Waheguru" that she uttered in muted exasperation, or the kind that escaped her lips like a gasp when Prem had fallen from a tree when he was six.

I turned the envelope over and over; it rattled in my unsteady hand, its sound immense, grating in the otherwise-silent room. I waited as she quietly chanted her prayer, knowing the words in the letter were no match for the calligraphic flourish of the script on the fragile pages before her. She closed the holy book and ceremoniously draped the ramals one by one over it, smoothing and tucking their embroidered edges.

I knelt on the floor beside her. "Mummy, I have this letter from school. . . ."

She motioned with her hand that I not speak yet. She remained seated on the floor, with the flowery folds of her salwaar billowing around her, snared in the thralls of some mystical moment. Her eyes were shut, the lids oily, the surma lining her eyes smudged from spiritual effort. When I was little, I would sit next to her before the holy book and shut my eyes in the same manner. I wished to be transported to that same distant place that called to her daily and I would ask her what we were praying for. "Many things," she would reply solemnly. "Many things."

Now, her voice punctured the stillness. "My citizenship test is coming up in the spring. I really have to study harder if I'm going to pass it. Why don't you show that letter to your father?" She pushed herself off the floor, slipped her feet into chappals, and left the room.

The conference room at the high school was nearly at capacity when I arrived for the meeting. Rows of metal chairs were filled with eager students sitting beside parents clutching college brochures and applications. At the front of the room, Mrs. Hanover recited a litany of extracurricular activities to list on applications—key club, ski club, marching band, French club—a separate realm of the school I had never participated in. I found a seat in the back row, behind Jenny Holcomb, whose fingers were entwined with Brian Schlamm's. Jenny's mother crept quietly to the seat beside me, the same restless blue eyes as her daughter's roaming and scanning the room, seeking the next thing. "Hi, hon," she whispered, jangling her thick gold bracelets as she leaned toward Jenny. Jenny acknowledged her with a curt smile.

"And now on to scholarships," Mrs. Hanover continued. A pounding began in my head. Mrs. Hanover's mouth moved in its exaggerated fashion, but I could perceive no sound, only the motion of her mouth gaping and closing over her starched gray pantsuit. Parents scribbled notes on corners of papers; futures were at stake. I imagined showing the forms to my own parents, my mother's warning eyes moving to my father. A year or two at community college would be plenty for a girl, they would say.

The meeting concluded. A bevy of concerned parents swarmed around Mrs. Hanover with urgent questions. Mrs. Holcomb rose, smoothing her navy blue Chanel two-piece. When I asked Jenny what schools she was applying to, she blew her bangs off her forehead, considering the multitude of possibilities. A trace of the golden-pink tan she had cultivated all summer long still bloomed on her high cheekbones. "I'm thinking about UC Santa Barbara or San Diego. Pepperdine, maybe?" She arched her brows at her mother.

"Anywhere there's a beach close by," Mrs. Holcomb said to me. "I keep telling her she's good enough for Stanford. And what are your plans, dear?"

"I'm trying for Berkeley."

Mrs. Holcomb perked. "Excellent choice. A little closer, though they did have all those riots awhile back. Maybe you should think about Berkeley, too, Jenny."

Jenny slumped, the wealth of choices and alternatives weighing on her pink-sweatered shoulders. We wished one another luck. "Good to see you, Serjit." The principal nodded at the door, incorrectly rhyming my name, as he always did, with *turgid*.

$\mathfrak{m}$y mother called from the hospital when I got home; Aunt Manjit had gone into labor. "It's a girl," my mother said mournfully, as if the appalling finality of the baby's gender was just beginning to dawn on her. "There's no sign of your uncle Girpal. I hope he's not off on one of his binges again."

We named her Lakshmi. Aunt Manjit had offered the name shyly, the dark hollow of her mouth forming the shape of the word as she lay in the white hospital bed. My mother chimed in with her predictable objections—it wasn't a typical Punjabi name—but we silenced her. Lakshmi. I said the name out loud, hearing the crash of its consonants, picturing the face of the goddess of fortune, the golden coins that spilled from her tentative grasp. Aunt Manjit folded her hands in her lap, pleased.

We brought them home with us for a period of recuperation, though Aunt Manjit claimed the delivery of her fourth baby was as smooth as spitting out a melon seed. My room became the quiet place where Lakshmi curled and slept in her wicker bassinet. I would slip in to feel the soft wisp of her breath against my wrist, her hand unfolding like a small fan in the tender surprise of some dream. "She's dreaming something from her past life," Aunt Manjit whispered to me once when a smile spread on the sleeping infant's face. Her skin was the color of milk, dewy and fragrant. Occasionally, when I visited my room, I might find my cousin Minder, Aunt Manjit's eldest, sorting through my jewelry box and lining up pairs of earrings along the bedspread or wrapping a silk scarf around her neck or waist, and she would turn her black eyes on me with a guilty but unflinching stare and say nothing. Mostly, my aunt's children ran in a pack through the rooms and the hall, then out into the circling breeze, where their shouts and wails crackled off and away with the air currents.

Aunt Manjit never mentioned her husband's name during her ten-day stay. Uncle Avtar found him the day after she had given birth, sitting along a curb in the east end of town and clutching a paper bag. He stood in the entrance of our home a few days later, his hands hanging like two large sacks at his sides. His children regarded him cautiously at first, then rumbled toward him and climbed onto his limbs. Aunt Manjit sat in my father's blue armchair, one hand rocking the bassinet. She did not look up at her husband, though he glanced regularly in her direction, rubbing one wrist, then the other. Uncle Avtar finally nudged him toward his wife and newborn, and Uncle Girpal, the ridges in his brow melting, looked into his daughter's angelic face for the first time.

During dessert one evening, Aunt Manjit proclaimed that it was time for her and her children to return home. "You and the children are all I have," she said as she sniffled into a damp and rumpled corner of her chuni. My brother, Prem, paused long enough to digest the welcome news, then proceeded to wolf down the last piece of spice cake. It wasn't exactly a look of relief that crossed my mother's face, but a familiar discomfort, perhaps, that everything would change all over again: a course of events to be added to all the accumulated episodes in our collective lives, their steady accretion like a slowly dripping tap forming an unfathomable pool.

"Family must look out for one another," my mother said.

We packed up Lakshmi and the other children's belongings and, in a small caravan of cars that included Aunt Teji, Neelam, and Davinder, delivered them home. Aunt Manjit's place was the pumpkin orange one among the row of houses along Orchard Road, flanked at the rear by Chima Ranch. The children dashed off over the stubble of grass and the network of roots fanning away from the base of a large ash tree. Inside, the house smelled stale and slightly moldy, as though it had been closed up for weeks. The front door led into a small kitchen and living area, where a rumpled pile of my uncle's work clothes lay on the table. Aunt Manjit relinquished Lakshmi into Neelam's arms and carried the clothes to a back room, urging her guests inside. My mother rummaged through a stack of dirty coffee cups piled by the sink, but otherwise she did not comment on the general untidiness of the place. We set Lakshmi's bassinet in the back bedroom. A sliver of sunlight sliced through the part in the brown poplin curtains. Neelam had slipped a white eyelet bonnet over the baby's head, and the little one somehow seemed too grand and regal for her shabby surroundings. My sister paced the floor, rocking Lakshmi lightly in her arms, cooing at her, coaxing her to sleep.

"Sit, sit," my aunt insisted after Davinder carried in the last of the luggage, offering up the one sofa draped with a cream-colored chenille cover, and several mismatched wooden chairs. She opened a can of evaporated milk. "There's always the makings for tea, if nothing else," she said.

Settling into our chairs, we could hear the children rooting around in the corners of the house like small animals reestablishing their territory. Aunt Teji rubbed one knee and complained of rheumatism.

Aunt Manjit's ears perked at the news of physical discomfort. "Try the pomegranate husks; they'll help with circulation."

There was a brief tapping on the door; it flew open as Charan Kaur burst in, carrying a package wrapped in lavender paper. Her unannounced visit seemed to surprise no one; we were accustomed to the radarlike ability she possessed to harness the random signals of joy and distress roaming the airwaves in the community. Aunt Manjit, suddenly radiant and honored by her visit, abandoned her kitchen tasks and helped Charan Kaur into a chair.

"Bring the child to me." Charan Kaur spoke solemnly, like the member of an imperial court about to pass sentence.

"She's just fallen asleep," I said.

Aunt Manjit balked. "Nonsense! She's been sleeping the entire day. Why does she need another nap? She'll be up all night."

I collected the baby from the bassinet, feeling the warmth of her rousing body spread across my chest. I placed her warily in Charan Kaur's outstretched arms. The baby was alert now, aware of some strange musky scent other than her mother's, her mouth a little O where her satin pink tongue pushed through like a flower bud.

Charan Kaur squinted into the tiny face. "My vision isn't what it used to be." Her green eyes, however, looked as clear and sharp as ever. The women scooted to the edge of their chairs, eager for her pronouncements. She commented authoritatively on the shape of the baby's head, cautious, though, not to blurt out anything that might be perceived as an outright compliment, which could have compromised the newborn's luck. I wanted to snatch Lakshmi away, out of the woman's peculiar influence, something indelible I saw in her bright stare.

"Her birth date is a lucky one. And anyone can see in the child's disposition that she is strong-willed. That should present you with some challenges, bhainji." Her husky voice was filled with certitude.

Aunt Manjit's shoulders puffed with gratitude and, beside her, my mother smoothed the folds in her kameez as though spreading a cloth over a grand table. The believers wanted to believe; as for myself, I imagined the fierce net Charan Kaur cast over all who surrounded her, the tangle of it that snared her son Pritam.

"Well, I mustn't stay long. I can't leave Pritam on his own at the store all afternoon."

The sound of his name, even coming from her mouth, quickened my breathing.

"I look forward to the day I can turn it over to him and his bride. But he tells me he wants to live a little first. That's how children say it these days—they want to live a little. As if marriage is the beginning of one's death."

"Even these days, in this country, children have certain obligations," my mother said. "Our Jeeto would be perfectly happy going to school for the rest of her life."

Aunt Manjit gave me a pitying glance; what a misguided young creature her niece was! "Biyaa kerala, bhout—Get married first. Your mother wishes so for it. There's plenty of time for college. Look at your sister here, how happy she looks, how nicely dressed."

"Look what a fine husband I found for her," Charan Kaur chimed in.

Neelam shrank on the sofa next to Davinder, curling her nose as though someone had made the most inappropriate, even offensive comments about her.

Davinder bit into an apple he pulled from his pocket. "Be sure to get your college applications filled out, just in case Mr. Dreamboat doesn't come along." He winked at me, aware that he was defying the reigning opinion of what my future should be. Perhaps he was thinking of his cousin Suthi, of saving her as well in some remote, karmic fashion.

Aunt Manjit remained emboldened; this was her territory, however rumpled and disheveled. "College? Hai ha! She'll be staying right here. A seed has to be buried awhile before it can sprout and blossom." She reached under her kameez and retied the naala—drawstring—on her salwaar. Davinder looked away.

It was useless trying to argue with them. What could my aunt know about sprouting and blossoming? I wondered. She was someone who seemed to have grown overnight from an awkward girl to an old, spent woman. Her blinking, uncomprehending face bore no imprint of regret, of dreams unfulfilled. I stared at the drab taupe-colored walls, a rust-colored stain the shape of a flower in one corner of the ceiling, then at the women around the room. My mother's gaze emphatically avoided mine. It was clear the women had settled on my future already. Their dispassionate tone, as if none of this concerned me, angered me. I was no more than a knot in that net, and if I unraveled, there were plenty more to take up the weight. Aunt Manjit was on her haunches, sweeping up a pile of bread crumbs by the stove. Aunt Teji apologetically examined the weave of her muslin kameez. My mother, as though feeling a sudden chill, pulled a wool shawl close about her shoulders and, for reassurance, patted the thick bun at the back of her head. Charan Kaur made a great rustling motion as she rose from her chair and squished her fleshy toes into a pointed pair of jutti. They were my possible futures, these women with their black hair gleaming with fragrant oils, who in their youth had offered up their fates to the wisdom of others as coolly as passing a plate of sweets.

It grew dark, and over the voices and clatter of teacups, our ears were expectantly trained to the sound of a pickup truck entering the driveway at any moment. It never came. Our home felt chilly, vacuous when my mother and I returned. I rearranged my room, yet the space no longer seemed mine, not entirely. In the silence, I continued to hear the pattering of quick feet on the linoleum and bony elbows bumping along the walls. I sat down at my desk, pulled the college applications from their folder and in the first blank printed in solid black lines my name: Rai, Serjit Singh.

But that gesture did little to offset a gathering momentum, spurred, I believed, by my aunt's words. Soon thereafter, I found my parents convened around the dining table with Uncle Avtar and Aunt Teji, in the midst of negotiations. I overheard the mention of a doctor, a well-respected family. An uncomfortable silence filled the room as I rummaged in the fridge for a cold drink. My uncle dropped his eyes to the table, as though wanting no part in this betrayal.

At the dinner table, my mother announced that Hardeep Gill was engaged, her restrained tone a perfect alchemy of defeat and hope. A wedding date had been set for the summer in India. Hardeep, a fellow senior, was rather plain physically, and if she had any real passions or interests in life, she seemed to take great pains to conceal them from the world. Marriage must have sounded unbearably romantic to someone like her. She would return from India, as I'd witnessed many young brides do, entirely transformed, with a trunk full of bright silks and heaps of gold jewelry, and a man of some semirespectable profession who might mistreat her occasionally, who, even if she grew one day to despise him, would never leave her.

Surinder assaulted me with questions when I told her. "Who is he? When? You can't! What will you do?" But her mournful "I may be next" expression lifted suddenly. "What if your doctor is good-looking, with lots of money?"

"What are the chances of that?" I imagined the legions of mismatched couples who seemed to demand our wry commentary as they filed into the gurdwara before services: bristly, short men with elegant, statuesque wives; smiling, affable men followed by stern, unforgiving women. Our hearts had been broken a few years past when the dreamily handsome Rajinder Singh returned from India with a dour, bearded woman who proceeded to bear him three sons. And then, of course, there were the elder widowers who grieved briefly for their deceased wives, then appeared in the shadows of the massive gurdwara doors one day with shy, bewildered teenage brides trailing behiind.

Still, an unsettling question—one I didn't dare to ask Surinder—occasionally prodded some corner of my mind: What if Hardeep was the one who had it right?

Eight

Later that week, Pritam waited outside the wood-shop building where Surinder and I caught the bus each afternoon. His head snapped in the other direction, toward the street, when he noticed me. In the same instant, I re-collected the stack of books threatening to spill from my arms and resumed a more dignified pace. He proceeded to act as though he hadn't, in fact, seen me at all, craning his neck left and right at cars passing on the street. I was struck again by how forlorn he could look with his hair tumbling over his forehead and his slightly slumped posture. The tails of his plaid shirt hung out over his jeans and a book dangled from his hand like some unfamiliar object. The title *Business Management Skills* was printed in grave blocky letters along the glossy spine of the book.

"Test tomorrow?" I asked.

He nodded wearily. "Ratio and cost analysis."

It was finals week. The sun had come out in the late afternoon in an indifferent sort of way, a weak and colorless band of light against the horizon. Pritam pushed his hands in his pockets, hunched and shivering in the chilly air. "Where's your friend?' he asked.

"Surinder? Probably just late."

"I've got the afternoon off from the store." He licked his lips and swallowed, as if he had suffered unduly waiting for this opportunity to tell me. Still, his shivery, nervous manner encouraged me in some way.

I realized what he was asking me in his indirect manner. "Don't you usually park on the other side of campus?" I asked.

"I'm parked on Brown." He pointed his chin toward a small leafy side street that led off campus, an area where smokers and couples congregated after hours.

A crowd of bus riders swarmed around us. Karan Singh, the designated valedictorian of the senior class, passed us once, then twice, his mug-size eyes focused on us disapprovingly. No matter which direction I turned, I was unable to avoid his salmon pink turban bobbing and weaving in and out of my peripheral vision, like a flag borne by a restless cavalry member. I searched for Surinder, trying to spot her waist-length black hair among the roving bodies. The buses began filing into the parking lot.

"Come on. I'll give you a ride."

I trotted off after him across the street, looking back once more for Surinder, seeing a flash of the tyrannical bit of salmon pink hovering over the crowd. I gave no real thought to what I was doing at that moment. My movements felt involuntary, like an irrepressible shiver on a calm, warm day. I was swept along by an inertia gathering within him that I could not resist. I ran up alongside Pritam on the far end of the sidewalk, trying to match his quick, long-legged gait. I recalled how my mother always dutifully followed several steps behind my father. And, too, how Jenny Holcomb strode confidently hand in hand with Brian, as if she wanted to, needed to be there beside him.

My mind was seized by a jumble of thoughts as we reached Pritam's car. I'd have to return to the school office to call my mother and tell her I'd missed the bus—say there was an experiment in biology I'd had to redo, that Mr. Steemer had held most of the class late because our *E. coli* cultures had gotten contaminated. The bus carrying Surinder and Karan Singh rumbled past. Surinder, too, would be wondering where I was; she would call the house later as she smeared acetone over her nails to remove last week's fading polish, exhaling one of her prolonged sighs into the phone, an indication that her young life was not quite measuring up to her grand expectations. I will lie to her, too, I thought, watching Pritam fumble with the key in the passenger door. It was his mother's old Ford Galaxy, barely large enough to contain the clamor of four growing boys, now relegated to high school carpools and grocery deliveries.

I still could've gone to the office and called my mother for a ride home. I remembered as I stepped into Pritam's car that she had gone to Aunt Manjit's for the afternoon to help paint her bedrooms. I would've told her about the moldy, contaminated petri dishes we'd had to discard carefully in biology lab, the fresh ones with pearly agar we had only begun to swab with resterilized metal hoops dipped in pure bacterial cultures after the last bell rang. The details would unfurl before me like a curtain parting to reveal an elaborate theatrical set—the Bunsen burners flaring to life with a simultaneous *whoof,* the smell of ethanol, Mr. Steemer polishing the smudged lenses of his glasses with a rumpled handkerchief as he paced from table to table. I would tell my mother all of this as I poured dressing from a bottle into the salad I was preparing for dinner, and she would answer with her standard "Acha," meaning she was worried that Aunt Manjit's family might not make rent this month and that her feet ached, but that she believed me in that dismissive way parents do when other problems overwhelm them.

How easily these thoughts fell into place as I stepped into Pritam's car. We drove off in some direction that had no bearing, it seemed, to the poles or the farthest longitudinal reaches of the planet. Street after shadowy street swept by, transfigured and unrecognizable from the tattered front seat of the car. The sharp outlines of shops and office buildings turned soft and foamy as the sky darkened.

"Where are we going?' I asked when we approached the outskirts of town.

Pritam seemed to drive aimlessly, with no particular destination in mind. He shrugged. "Where should we go?" His voice lacked the nervousness I'd noticed in him earlier. I wanted to feel the old wordless trust that had forged our childhood friendship. But it was different now. We were seventeen; we'd known each other too long; that was the problem. He would be different with another girl, I thought. He would have devised a definite plan, mulled it over carefully, settled on some exclusive destination, wishing to impress her. I wondered where Neelam and Hari had gone all those times, which inhospitable corners of town or country had sheltered them and nurtured their love.

He drove another two or three miles, sloppily steering the car with one wrist, as though he was killing time and had never imagined this kind of moment between us. "I've got a place I want to show you," he said, snapping his fingers. He pulled onto the shoulder of the road, then swung the car around, heading south toward town.

"Where? I've always wanted to see the Gold Room at the Placer Hotel." Jenny had described the room once, now a distinguished dining hall with glittery chandeliers and a large circular rose velvet sofa with a swan gilded with real gold rising from its center. It had been an elegant gambling establishment during the gold rush and its second-floor rooms an upscale brothel. "I've got to get back, actually," I said to Pritam. "I'm going to be in trouble, you know."

"It's just after five. It won't take long."

North of town, Pritam turned onto Richmond Road, which

headed east over the Feather River and wound eventually through the foothills as State Route 35 and into the Sierra Nevada. We crossed over the river, a black sliver below, flanked on both sides by dense brush. Ahead, the roadside was dotted with auto shops and gas stations and the odd restaurant that had been boarded up. The general character of the area changed dramatically as you traveled in this direction. One had a sense of being connected to other towns and destinations going north, south, or west. But going east, the road dipped into a lengthy stretch of bottomlands where cows wouldn't even graze, where one lifted one's gaze high from its sunken depths to locate the horizon. Beyond, when the road finally ascended, it continued like a faint scratch mark through hills that looked dry as dunes in the summer.

It was getting late and dark as he pulled off onto a dirt road heading south toward the river. We'll be there in a minute, Pritam said, reassuring me. The road became increasingly muddy and rough, and the low-slung Galaxy scraped along the many ruts gouging it like small craters. The headlights illuminated a silver gate that closed off the road just before it climbed the levee. Pritam stopped the car and turned off the headlights.

"So, what is this place?" I asked.

"It's just a place I come to sometimes. Too bad the gate's closed. There's a great swimming hole and an island in the middle where the river splits off. You've never been out here?"

"Indian girls aren't exactly encouraged to hang out at swimming holes," I replied. "It's a different story for Indian boys, of course." The whiff of anger in my voice seemed to please him.

"Yes, we boys can do whatever we please. We can jump one of those gates and get arrested for trespassing."

"Is that what happened? When your mother sent you to your uncle's?"

Pritam nodded. "She said she didn't know what to do with me

anymore, that she couldn't control me." He scratched his chin thoughtfully, deliberately, as though expecting me to console him.

"Well, don't expect me to feel sorry for you." I crossed my arms in mock indignation. It was black outside and so quiet, I thought I could hear our voices reverberating from some distant place. There was nothing to distract us from each other.

Pritam stretched his arm over the back of the seat and I slumped against it, feeling his wrist against my hair. My eyes followed the outline of his shoulders and his neck, still trying to adjust to the growing darkness. I heard him swallow and, even in the dank humid air, I detected a faint scent on his shirt, smoky and slightly sweet, as though he'd been outdoors all day. Pritam's face moved closer to mine; his eyes shone with a soft rim of light, something tender and pleading in them. I could feel his breath on me. Nothing in my life—not a lifetime of my mother's warnings nor Neelam's rapt, secretive smiles—had prepared me for this. He leaned down and we kissed lightly, then harder. Pritam's hands slipped from my shoulder to my waist, then under my sweater, finding the cup of my bra.

"Pritam," I said, pulling his hand away but holding on to it. "Pritam, I've got to get back."

He kissed me once more, then moved away, resting his head on the seat back; the disappointment seeping into his face sliced through me like a knife. I began to tremble, the chill wrapping like a reptilian skin around me and a new kind of regret rising like a sad song in my throat. He started the car and it rocked slowly over the bumps and ruts toward the main road.

I slid closer to him on the vinyl seat. "Don't be mad, Pritam."

He shook his head as if it hadn't mattered. "There's a river that runs along the back of my uncle's property. Maybe it's why I like this spot so much." His voice was quiet, weighted in a familiar and intimate way.

"Would you ever go back there?"

"Sure. It's different there. I can forget about certain things."

I wondered if he would forget about me there, my clumsy inexperience. An Indian boy has to understand how it was with an Indian girl, I thought; I was seventeen and it was my first kiss.

We crossed the bridge over the river, and at a bait and tackle shop just on the other side, Pritam bought two sodas. I made a phone call to Neelam, who answered in a faint and sleepy voice. "Can you pick me up?" I asked her.

"Where are you?"

"At the bait shop by the Richmond Bridge." I heard her suck her breath in. She didn't ask what I was up to, but something of my predicament—what I didn't tell her just then—must have sounded familiar to her.

"I'll be right over."

"One more thing," I told her. "Call Mom and tell her I've been with you."

Pritam and I sipped on our sodas in the car, waiting for Neelam. He had parked around the side of the shop, where the light from the lone streetlamp fell through the bare branches of an elm tree in silvery streams onto the hood of the car. "I really would like to see that place sometime," I told him.

"Sure," he said, holding the soda bottle up guardedly between us.

When Neelam pulled alongside, she stared straight ahead, not looking toward us at all. Her hands were clutched tight around the steering wheel, as if she was determined to keep her bearings.

"What did Mom say?" was my first question to her.

"Well, she was worried. She wanted to know why we waited so long to call. Why don't you stop by my place anyway? Just in case she asks which towels I had hanging in the bathroom."

Neelam's home smelled warm, like she had just prepared atta, wheat-flour dough. I felt grateful not to have to face my mother's prying questions just yet.

"I've got some carrot sabji. You can tell Mother we had carrot sabji for dinner." She went about like that, garnering the necessary pieces of evidence like a bird gathering bits of fluff to build a nest. The ease of her complicity frightened me a little, but I was grateful for that, too. In the kitchen, she heated the sabji and a roti, then sat beside me at the table to watch me eat, yawning repeatedly as I fed a ravenous appetite stoked by the events of the evening and the chilly night air. Afterward, she quickly cleaned the dishes, returning her kitchen to its previously immaculate and undisturbed state. She flopped into an armchair, her body slack and drooping, like a garden gone untended. Davinder was working late hours again this week, she explained. "So naturally I would've been inclined to spend time with you." She smiled sympathetically. Her mouth crinkled at its corners, but her eyes remained remote and dull.

"It must be lonely for you. You should come by the house more," I said.

"Oh, I have tons of projects here to keep me busy." She waved her hands about, a gesture that implied walls that needed painting, chairs that required recovering, sweaters that went unknitted. "So, what were you doing all the way out there with Pritam?"

"He wanted to show me a place on the river. He goes there a lot, I guess. We're just . . . friends." I wasn't sure where I'd left things with Pritam, but I felt a warmth surge through me, lift me just then as I spoke of him.

"Careful, or you'll end up with that Charan Kaur for a mother-in-law," she said, shuddering. She shifted on the chair and propped her legs beneath her. "You do have to be careful, Jeeto. Don't make the same mistakes I've made." Her words sounded halfhearted, obligatory, what one was expected to say to a younger sister only beginning to navigate her way through the tortuous maze so endearingly termed "love."

"Do you mean it wasn't worth it?" I looked at Neelam and saw, in the color that suddenly flooded her face and the bloom that was her mouth, that she regretted nothing. I was stunned, awed by the power of what she had felt and done in her love for Hari. Then I saw a look of envy flash like a harsh spotlight across her face, the color draining from it as rapidly as it had appeared. So it's your turn now, she seemed to be thinking. I've had mine. Mine has come and gone.

"Come," she said. "I'll take you home."

My mother was waiting at the house for me with her hand stiff and poised to strike; she pushed Neelam aside as we stepped inside, and I felt her palm smack hard against my cheek, throwing me off balance a little. "You'll learn that you can't go running off by your-self whenever you like." I crouched behind Neelam, frozen, my hand on my burning cheek, feeling a well of tears starting. My mother turned back to the table, where my father and Prem sat eat-ing dinner. My father's head hung over his plate, as if he had wit-nessed the worst sort of carnage. Even Prem, who banged around our house daily as though denied of the princely station he truly deserved in life, appeared stunned.

"She should've called," my mother muttered, taking her seat. "She didn't call."

From my room, I could hear Neelam talking brightly, chattering on about the inordinate mundaneness of her life, couching it all in the terms of a pampered young wife for whom life had turned out to be quite all right, blessed even. "Davinder has taken new respon-sibilities with his accounting position and works so many hours. I so enjoyed my sister's company this afternoon." Later, I heard my mother's voice through the wall, a low ache in it, punctured with oc-casional muffled sobs. My cheek still stung against the coarse fabric of the pillowcase. She had no idea where I'd been, what had taken place, but it was just in case—she had come after me just in case I had done something, or in case I'd only imagined doing it, tonight, or in the last week or month, or anytime in what she foresaw as my certainly troubled future.

Nine

We tread around each other as if one were the dynamite, the other the fuse, my mother and I. She carried her suspicions about her like a grave wound, feeling its fresh stabs of pain at regular intervals during the course of her day. I arrived home from school promptly on the bus each afternoon, reasoning to myself that the winds would change one day soon, if the usual course of my family's history was any indication. And so overnight, it seemed, my mother's attention shifted almost effortlessly from one daughter to the other. It was difficult this time for Neelam to conceal her pregnancy as she might have wished, watchful as my mother was for any signs a child was on the way. The fatigue I had noticed in her the night she picked me up by the bridge had been more than a simple listlessness. The inopportune bouts of morning sickness, followed by a doctor's visit, heralded the certain news that Neelam was indeed expecting. Davinder hovered with extraordinary concern each time she excused herself, fleeing the room with her hand over her mouth at the sight of the most ordinary things—eggs, onions, and such. My mother's usual vigor eluded her and she managed little more than a whimper when she confirmed the news to my aunts.

"God has answered our prayers," they took turns saying. A great cloud had mercifully swept off to some distant horizon to darken someone else's days. From within the womb, the tiny embryo already exuded its redemptive powers.

How differently this pregnancy was received by the family. Sanctioned by marriage, it was also the perceived antidote to Neelam's long days alone in her pristine modern home. Neelam herself seemed heartened by the prospect of sharing her days with an infant, for whom she would be the sole connection to a larger world. She began to take the requisite interest in all things maternal: books on what to expect during pregnancy and motherhood, burping and bottles and bibs.

No one appreciated Neelam's news more than her own husband. Had he understood up until then how fragile his marriage had been? He carried on around our family as a bemused but interested bystander, regarding our quaint provincial dramas with humor and a healthy detachment. They seemed a relatively content couple by all outward appearances, forgoing some of the strict traditions of our parents' generation, one or the other openly touching an arm or resting a hand on a leg. But no one could say for certain what had happened within the walls of their bedroom, what wounding accusations had been left like stains on their sheets. Uncle Girpal's scene at the festival had confirmed the talk that had gone around, had linked his wife and Hari in Davinder's mind once and for all. He concealed his pain well, but the burden of knowing would distort his face now and then, cleaving it in two anguished halves, like a cliff shearing down its center. Just as swiftly, it seemed, he would push from his mind the possibility— cruel and staggering as it was—that his wife had loved another man more than she did him. For his devotion to her now seemed as strong as that first day Uncle Avtar had brought him to our place, that first time he had laid eyes on her, struck by her frank, unvarnished beauty. Already awash in his good fortune, he had watched as she fled into the house, smoothing the unruly strands of her hair.

An unsettling sense of normalcy pervaded our home during the next weeks. There was the tentative hope of things gained, despite those that had been lost, an optimism enforced on the household by my mother as she padded around the house coaxing smiles from the rest of us, the cowering victims of all her unreasonable demands.

Encouraged by the amicable atmosphere, I stood outside my father's shop one day, shivering, my breath fogging against the metal door. I glanced at the application I had carefully filled in, the one blank remaining on the final page.

"You'd be so far away from your mother," he said after scanning the papers. "She would never forgive me."

An hour and a half isn't so far, I thought, but I knew that wasn't what he meant. He meant that without her influence over me, she would wither and shrink away like fruit left to perish on a vine. If not her, then at least a husband would watch over me, protect me; it was what they believed with all their hearts.

Outside the shop, the Gardner Brothers' half-ton truck rumbled to a stop. Jeff Gardner, the backup quarterback of the varsity football team a few years back, jumped out of the pea green cab, removed his work gloves, and hitched them in his back pocket. My father greeted him at the door like an old friend, sounding grateful there were things other than daughters to occupy one's mind.

In my room, an old permission slip to participate in volleyball that fall lay on the corner of my desk. My mother had signed it, then decided against allowing me to play. I had kept the note as a means to indulge my frequent anger toward her. But what caught my attention just then was her signature at the bottom of the slip, the chubby childlike letters spelling Jasbir Rai. It was an easy signature to forge, and though it was not the first time I'd attempted it, my hand had never shaken so.

Spring semester started, the seniors breathless with talk of the future—careers, colleges, plans. A grave urgency tinged our voices; any misstep at this crucial juncture in our lives could ruin things forever. Pritam and I stole time together when we could, in the hallways between class, or near the end of the lunch hour. There was always that moment when his eyes probed my face and a question hung in the air like a faint echo. We would linger like that those extra moments, until he would pull me close, his hand fitting perfectly along the curve of my hip. Other days, he detected a certain caution when he moved toward me, and I would stiffen or step slightly out of the warm field of his shadow, though I waited for him to ask me again to go to the place along the river, even if I had to decline. I never told him how my mother had raised her hand to me that evening, not merely in warning. I feared it might discourage him and that he would discover what I sometimes suspected of myself—that I was unremarkable, nothing more than a typical Indian girl, confused and paralyzed by my sexuality. Too petrified to step outside the bounds carved into my consciousness as a young girl.

During this time, my mother indulged in what could best be described as a final cram session for her citizenship test. To my relief, my father volunteered to coach my mother in a last-minute review of the U.S. government and the Constitution. His patient instruction kindled her interest for a brief period in the Bill of Rights and the separation of powers. She practiced pronouncing key words and phrases ("prez-ee-dhent," "joo-dhish-ull") out loud, a peculiar conversation with herself as she rolled out roti or embroidered her tablecloths. This new lexicon of possibilities, Neelam's pregnancy, and the rains that arrived late in the winter preoccupied my mother's already-anxious mind. Beneath that frenzied exterior lurked that other matter of my engagement, which she, preoccupied or not, had put off mentioning to me. Perhaps she believed a hefty dose of prayer would fortify her position, for I found her often sitting before the Granth Sahib with her forehead resting on her clasped hands, the citizenship pamphlet tossed on the floor beside her.

The sweet, medicinal aroma of banaksha filled our home one morning. My mother had returned from a visit to Aunt Teji's the previous day, speaking of her bikaar, a fever of 101 degrees. In the kitchen, she strained the boiled herbs from the brown liquid, which she poured into two tall stainless-steel thermoses. "I'll take them to her," I said, grabbing the thermoses from the counter. My mother hesitated before handing me the car keys; she had rarely allowed me to drive alone since the evening I had returned home late from school. On the short drive to my aunt's, I pictured her pale figure lying prostrate in bed, wrapped in wool blankets. I found her instead crouched by the tulip bed in her front yard, bundled in a gray shawl and tugging at the seedling crop of dandelions sprouting in profusion.

"And what elixir has your mother prepared for me today?" she asked. "Yesterday, she brought semiya. Probably what brought my strength back."

"Chacha scared us when he told us how sick you were."

She managed a weary, knowing laugh. "You know how your uncle likes to run about stirring things up. Well, it gives me a chance to visit with my busy young niece."

Inside, she peeled away the shawl and wound a sheer white chuni about her neck, appearing youthful and refreshed by the change. "Let me tell you something about your uncle." She set a tall glass of milk in front of me, hitched up the sides of her kameez, and sank into a chair. "He wasn't always the rascal we all have to keep one eye on. He was quite a serious fellow when he returned to India—when we got married. He was a little afraid of me, like a wounded animal. He wouldn't touch me at first." Aunt Teji paused, aware that she had been unusually frank with me. She pressed her lips together and attempted a different tone. "The very first time I saw him, he was sitting cross-legged on the dirt floor at my uncle's place, with my uncle's cow swatting its tail just inches above his head. He was wearing a brown suit and he kept hunching down and raising one arm over his head to keep that tail off him. He must've forgotten what an Indian household could be like. I wasn't supposed to be there," she said, wagging her finger. "My cousin sneaked me into their home and we'd moved an old wooden trunk by a back doorway. I lay on the floor behind it, the dust in my nose, covered in a blanket, and I would crawl out a little from behind the trunk every so often to look at him. I might see his back, or his legs, or get a glimpse of his face, but I wanted to see who it was that had come such a long distance for me."

"That's not the version Uncle told me. He said he lifted your veil and saw the most beautiful creature he had ever laid his eyes on." He'd told me that when I was much younger—eight or so—and the words were reassuring, gratifying then, as if my uncle had found the person he was truly meant to spend his life with.

Aunt Teji cupped her hand over her mouth and we laughed together, her chest heaving with open pleasure. She stared quietly at the walls. "When he lifted my veil, it was my heart that stopped. Your uncle's had already been broken.

"And how is your sister?" she asked, rising from the table and rousing herself from the immutable past. She began shifting pots and pans about the kitchen in a great burst of domestic energy.

"She's feeling much better. Eating more."

"Good. Actually, they say that morning sickness is the sign of a healthy pregnancy. But tell that to a woman who can't hold down a tablespoon of dal. *Baas!* Enough! You won't have these worries for a while yet."

"It may be very soon—if my mother has her way."

Aunt Teji spun around, as if astonished by my comment. I sometimes had the feeling I could talk to her about things the way I couldn't with my mother or other married women. But it was difficult to tell exactly where her sympathies lay. "You should've come to me," she'd quietly told Neelam after her first pregnancy was discovered. But she was close to my mother, too. How did she reconcile the two—acknowledge the passions of a young woman, as she had with Neelam, then turn in the next instant to align herself with the old traditional ways, congratulating an acquaintance on the engagement of a daughter or the birth of a son? She had been sitting at the dining table that afternoon alongside my uncle and parents as they planned my future. Perhaps a look had been enough for her, but I needed more than that. I had mailed off my college application a few days earlier with a forged signature. If I were to leave in the fall, I needed to know exactly what I was running from.

I unsealed one of the thermoses and handed it to her. "Here. Mummy would be angry if she thought her banaksha went untouched."

Her glasses fogged as she held the thermos to her nose and inhaled. "Even the aroma clears the head."

I lingered beside her at the counter; my reason for coming, after all, extended beyond a natural concern for my aunt's health. "Is it true they've picked a boy for me?" I asked.

Aunt Teji scratched at her elbow, glanced at the clock on the wall. "He's well educated, studying to be a doctor. From a good family."

"When is he coming?"

"You should ask your mother."

"I can't ask her. That's why I'm asking you. Tell me!"

Aunt Teji picked up a stainless-steel stockpot from the counter to admire its luster. "The plans are that he'll come in the fall. Your mother hasn't told you?" she asked, blinking, as though she had already revealed too much.

"No. So when Chacha came for you, you were willing. No questions."

"I was terrified at first, like most brides. I hadn't set foot beyond the neighboring village. I think my burning wish at the time was to have a sparkling pair of jutti like Amina brought back from Lahore." She flexed her toes and they retreated beneath the hem of her salwaar. "You'll see, Jeeto. . . ."

Even she, Aunt Teji, I thought, disappointed. I wondered when exactly it was that grown-ups relinquished their chosen dreams, as though they were nothing more than childish clothing long outgrown. Aunt Teji, sensing my resistance, provided her version of an acceptable response. She walked me to the car later, and as I swung the door open, she stopped me. "The truth is, Jeeto, you think you can manage it, trying for the one thing that you think you must have. You cry, you scream, but a few years go by and it's all the same in the end, whether you have it or not."

I left her standing by the edge of the lawn, her hand up in a halfhearted wave, and started home, then stopped the car on the dirt lane that cut through the orchard. A mist was forming over the carpet of grass under the trees. I put my hand out the window and felt the tiny pellets of water settle on my skin. I thought of Aunt Teji's words—vague and startling. If only I, her niece, could be spared the heartache that befell every human being who ever walked the earth, she seemed to plead. How deftly Neelam had been corralled into her safe, silent corner. And now they wanted to do the same for me.

Ten

Eight miles southeast of town, a dirt road veered off Howard Lane and into a verdant, shadowy orchard at the back of Mohta Singh's property. Somewhere beneath that leafy stretch of canopy, Neelam squatted by the gummy, blackened trunk of a peach tree and vowed she would never do so again. It was the most brazen meeting place she had agreed to thus far, but Hari had been unable to get away from the house earlier. His family had since departed en masse, taking all the cars, he had insisted two hours earlier over the phone, and he wanted to see her. Neelam had taken care of the errand that had conveniently arisen, a trip to the market for some greens, which now sat wilting in the passenger seat of the car parked well into the orchard. Neelam's eyes followed the dirt lane through the orchard to a block of homes in the distance, visible by the little squares of light leaking from their windows. In the gathering darkness, she could make out the house he lived in—the small pink-and-white bungalow next to his grandfather's grander two-story brick home. She strained to hear a screen door slamming shut or footsteps crunching over the rocky soil so she could anticipate his approach. Cars occasionally passed on Howard Lane, each set of headlights like a pair of searching eyes.

Before leaving for the market, she had changed into a navy-colored kameez, telling her mother that the one she had worn all day was dripping in sweat from the unrelenting heat, reasoning to herself that the dark colors would conceal her in the orchard. It was a warm May evening, and the fabric of her kameez clung to the damp skin on her back. She felt an irritation rising in her that he would make her wait this way. A moment later, she felt a hand on her shoulder, its steady, insistent pressure familiar to her, and she jumped to her feet. She began beating a limp fist against Hari's chest, scolding him that he shouldn't frighten her this way, though he hadn't at all. It was merely a way of assuring herself that it was Hari standing before her, his body she felt under the white cotton T-shirt (he had made no efforts himself at camouflage), the certainty of him the reason she was here. She had seen a look of mild surprise in his smile that she had managed to come after all, following her vocal protests over the phone that she couldn't get away. Later, he would tell her he'd grown nearly frantic when he hadn't found her immediately—she'd concealed herself so well amid the grass and trees—chiding himself for asking her to meet like that. He drew her close in an embrace she felt would swallow her, then pulled her down onto the ground so they would be hidden from view. She lay back, feeling the warm earth cradle her, as if molding to the curves of her body.

"So they've all gone?" she asked, needing reassurance.

Hari nodded, drawing his mouth close to hers. "To gurdwara. Except for Thiara Singh, who, as you know, loves his evening strolls." Neelam's head shot up, jerking from one side to the other in the hope that the old man had chosen to forgo his evening ritual just this one time. "He's been in bed all week with a chest cold," Hari said, easing her down beside him. He pulled her long black braid off the ground, where it had trailed into the clumps of grass like a snake, holding the tip and regarding it inquisitively, as though it were the hose end of some bewildering contraption.

"And you didn't want to go with them?" she asked, teasing.

"I don't believe in all that anymore. Besides, I wanted to see you." He took the tip of her braid and brushed it across her face, like a painter bringing a face stroke by stroke to life. He was looking at her differently now, his gaze intent on her face and the fingers of one hand beginning to fumble with the folds of her salwaar until they found the naala, its tie knotted against her soft belly. He tugged at the stubborn knot, but she stopped him even as her body willed him on, entwining her fingers in his. Not here. The words caught in her throat, unintelligible, a stifled sound more like a gasp. She'd grown up running and playing chase through orchards like these, shouting into their silent branches; the dirt felt as natural under her as a bed might have. She struggled from her clothes, her underclothes. She arched her hips up toward him as she cushioned her backside with his shirt, then spread her legs for him, a dark flower opening, taking him in. She buried her mouth against his salty neck, feeling her body surrender to a rhythm she had learned from him. They clung to each other like tangled vines when they made love. It was that sensation of feeling both lost and so completely entwined with him that she would crave the rest of her life.

He wiped her brow with the palm of his hand afterward, easing a crease of worry (I've got to go) he might have seen forming there. Neelam was already on her knees, scrambling for her clothes, preparing for the unpleasant business of returning home. Hari took her arm and she turned, almost startled by his look, his unspoken demand that she remain another moment this way, with her hair loosening from its braid, her nipples like a purple stain on her breasts, the color of her mouth.

"Don't leave yet. They won't be back till after dark."

Neelam slipped her kameez over her head, then settled on her side, facing him, her head propped on an elbow. "I remember when you used to come to gurdwara with your aunt Shindo. I didn't like you much then. You threw rocks at me once," she said with a cross look.

Hari drew up his arms, clasping his hands on the ground beneath his head and gazing up toward the indigo sheet of sky visible through the lattice of branches. "I was after you even then. I said to myself, That one there, she'll grow up to be a fine-looking woman."

"After women at such a young age?" She made a reproachful clucking sound with her tongue.

"It must run in the family." He had shut his eyes, and spoke, Neelam thought, as if from a dream.

"Then what took you so long to find me again?" Neelam pressed her face against his chest. His skin felt warm and alive against her cheek. She could hear his heart thrumming against his ribs; to her, it sounded as if the ground itself were beating.

"I guess I like to save the best for last."

"The last? Am I to be the last?"

"That's up to you."

"Up to me?" she repeated with a baffled expression, as though it couldn't possibly be true.

Hari sat up. It wasn't like him to brood during their short time together. More likely, it would be she who pouted in the moments before they parted. Neelam stared at his brown back, the shoulders rising with each breath, and the waves of black hair that curled at his neck when it grew a bit long. She thought it odd that he could feel more familiar to her than those she had known all her life.

"You should come to gurdwara with your grandfather. At least I could see you there."

"He's getting old, losing his health." He smiled, forgiving her for clinging to beliefs that struck him as simplistic, unsatisfactory as a measure against his own life. Even his grandfather had attended services out of an obligation to the community rather than from true faith. Only his failing health had brought him reluctantly back into the fold. Hari resisted that kind of convenient faith; it was a crutch for the weak and old, and he had no patience for the long sermons he had suffered through as a child. A merciful God would not have taken his mother from him as he breathed his first breaths in this world. He was no longer bitter; he stood to inherit all of Mohta Singh's land one day. His grandfather had told him so on many occasions, wishing to steer the boy away from the rocky paths he seemed naturally inclined toward. Hari had regarded those lectures as plodding and burdensome, but he realized now, admiring Neelam's profile beside him in the fleeting light, that his offer had its advantages.

Neelam gathered her belongings. Her mind was consumed now by the prospect of walking through the front door of her home, tossing the wilted greens on the kitchen counter before she could flee to her bedroom and the prying stare of her younger, uncomprehending sister. They stood a moment face-to-face without speaking, and he brushed bits of grass and dust from her hair and clothing. She would drive home feeling the dull ache of him still inside her. As for Hari, he would remember this spot, the very tree they had lain under, some years later when the entire orchard was uprooted, the trees chained and dragged to funereal piles, where they were set aflame in a massive bonfire to make way for new, more productive saplings.

There were other times—in his pickup truck during lunch hours at the back lot of Sarnoff's lumberyard; at the Sodhis' sprawling dinner party, where they had nearly been discovered behind a shed, locked in an embrace, by a wayward pack of children playing hide-and-seek among the rubble of rusted machinery and old tires. The memory of each episode ran constantly through her mind like a song whose cherished melody lingers, not easily expunged, maddening at times. In those days, she fancied herself a woman transformed by love, unshackled from an unreasonable bond that denied what her own body was demanding of her. The shame that had burned within after the first time they made love had dissolved, then recrystallized into a sharp and brighter light. She had been wary of Hari at first, even as she was drawn to him; she had heard plenty about him with other women. But he was tender with her, only mildly teasing her for her lack of experience, her wonder at his ability to elicit sensation in her body. She wanted to believe that he was this way with her because it was different and new for him, too.

He'd hung around long enough with that Margo Venutti, the skinny one who wore eyeshadow as blue as the sky and ghostly white lipstick. She'd seen the two of them draped all over each other plenty of times in the parking lot after school. And there were the few Indian girls, unafraid, willing to be seen around town with him. Then what had made him turn to her, his long, anxious gaze burrowing into her? That final image of him as she drifted off to sleep at night like a fever in her mind. Him. Mohta Singh's grandson. The one they said wouldn't outlive his venerated grandfather, but who lived within her each passing day.

We'd heard little of Hari in the months since we'd seen him at the festival. He had come into India Bazaar twice during that time and Pritam had waited on him. But neither the ordinary items he purchased nor his polite but aloof nature on those occasions revealed his state of mind. He had been transformed in the course of a few months from a fixture in the high school and community to someone mysterious, flagged by the marriage of the one woman he would ever truly love to another man. Apparently, he was managing a parcel of Mohta Singh's property near Merced, and came and went from Oak Grove as his grandfather's health and his own managerial duties dictated, but no one in town saw much of him. Still, there lurked that possibility, which was my mother's greatest fear and Neelam's secret, dormant hope, that something would bring him back to our town for good.

It was early spring when we learned of Mohta Singh's death. The air was sweet with the pale aroma of peach blossoms, late in blooming that year. The Baisakhi Festival was under way, a commemoration of Guru Gobind Singh's establishment of the Sikh brotherhood of Khalsa. The gurdwara parking lot filled with cars; from each tumbled its own bounty of humanity, the old and the young eager to move out of one another's way.

Charan Kaur hustled like a scrappy goat across the parking lot toward my mother, breathless with the news that would consume the community for weeks. Her sons lagged behind—Pritam and his three brothers—and one of their younger cousins.

"Did you hear, bhainji?" she asked, her gums showing red from the walnut bark she'd chewed that morning. "Did you hear that Mohta Singh died in his sleep overnight?" My mother stiffened, as though prodded by a sharp stick. "He died peacefully in his sleep; that's what I heard from Rachan Kaur." Charan Kaur dabbed her eyes with the back of her slim, weathered hands. "He suffered enough, the poor fellow." She regarded her succession of sons sorrowfully; they were growing, all of them, growing away from her.

Whenever I heard Mohta Singh's name, I thought of Hari. I was at a self-centered age, where I believed the true, consuming passions in life centered around youth. Mohta Singh's passing, for me, had everything to do with Hari and Neelam, little else. I remembered him in odd ways: the sword collection he displayed in his living room, the time he unsheathed a Japanese one in front of the children and whipped his wrist with Zorro-like dexterity.

My mother, at a rare loss for words, snapped open her purse and milled through its contents as though the trace of retribution she had been seeking lay among its dark recesses. "My brother-in-law will certainly miss him," she said, snapping the purse shut. Charan Kaur appeared baffled by my mother's cold reaction. She squinted into my mother's face, trying to read some gauge whose numbers suddenly appeared inexplicably wrong.

The general feeling among the congregation that day was that a giant in our community had passed on. Uncle Avtar was too distraught to attend the festivities. The atmosphere was subdued and the service rife with miscues; at one point, a visibly tipsy Gunda Singh rose to sing a premature rendition of the ardas before he was pulled down by others to the floor.

When Lakshmi began to fuss later, Aunt Manjit hoisted her into my arms and I carried her outside. Pritam leaned against a column in the entryway, framed by the scalloped arch overhead.

"Pritam?"

He turned, startled by my voice and the infant I carried in my arms. "Too bad about Mohta Singh."

"Yes. My uncle was good friends with him."

"More like a son, from what I hear."

"What do you mean?" I knew some of that story, but the rest of it was guarded carefully by the Rai family. I didn't wait for an answer. I was tired of stories I didn't know the endings of, if they had endings at all. But I was fooling myself if I thought they had no bearing on me, or the young man standing before me.

Keyed up by the general commotion of the day, Lakshmi spun around and swatted a small fist at Pritam; it was that motion, I think— her reaching helplessly toward him—that caused me to imagine what I did, that we were a family, that she was ours and that at any moment

Pritam would step into the car and we would drive off to some dilapidated household whose walls stood solely by virtue of the love garnered there. Lakshmi clapped her hands together once as if in approval and I blushed at my adolescent dreams.

Pritam's long fingers tapped lightly on the column. Thoughts of Mohta Singh's death seemed to have evaporated from his mind. We had talked the previous week at school about the senior class trip, planned later in the month, to Strawberry Canyon, a recreation area fifty miles east, at the base of the Sierra Nevada. Two separate dates had been set to accommodate the large senior class. "So which day are you signing up for?" I asked.

"You mean the picnic?" He stroked his chin, suddenly pensive, as though he had forgotten the entire matter. "Probably the fourteenth. What about you?"

"The fourteenth works for me."

Mohta Singh's memorial service and cremation were scheduled for the following Saturday at one in the afternoon. My father yielded to Uncle Avtar's badgering and, despite my mother's protests, agreed in the end to attend. Perhaps he had decided that the past, insofar as it concerned Neelam and her indiscretions, should be laid to rest. After downing a bolstering shot of whiskey, the two of them set off in their finest black suits on a crisp and cloudless day. Uncle Avtar had patted my shoulder before departing, resting his hand there a few seconds. I felt the grief boxed in his stubby fingers drain into me, saturating my own blood. We watched them leave from the front door, so rare was it to see them together in that kind of sustained, close proximity. Neelam and I lingered by the window, as though something were drawing us through the glass toward the somber white building several miles away where Mohta Singh's body lay.

I'd been permitted to attend only one service of this kind, three years earlier, when a cousin of Uncle Girpal's had been killed in an auto crash. He was eighteen and had smashed his car into a burly sycamore along Route 26. It was a horrible affair, the mother tearing at her chuni, beseeching Raab to take her, too, and draping herself over her son's body. The women of the family gathered around her, wailing, screaming, willing themselves to faint and collapse like rag dolls on the floor.

My mother called us for lunch, and we sat for an excruciating length of time, pretending to enjoy the dal and kutta. She ignored the gloomy nature of the occasion, doting on my sister's nutritional needs, inquiring in every manner about her future grandchild. What did the doctor say at her last visit? Had she felt any movement yet? Neelam replied with enthusiasm, but her eyes drifted frequently to the clock on the wall, which showed that the service was just beginning . . . was well under way . . . would soon wrap up when the body was placed in the incinerator in the back room of the mortuary and it was left to Hari as the only male heir to push the button that would reduce his beloved grandfather to a heap of ashes.

I stared down at the dark beads of moongi dal swimming in the bowl, then pushed the food away and stated to my mother that I needed to go to the store, speaking in a way that signaled menstrual pads or Midol were immediately required. She waved me off, as though relieved to be freed of my irritating demands.

The Oak Grove Mortuary had once sat amid a grove of towering oaks, flanked themselves by a large walnut orchard. The bucolic setting had since been violated by a gas station on one end and a sprawling set of office buildings on the other. We'd passed the place many times on our way to Sacramento. When I was a child, I would brace myself as we approached, then peer out with my nose pressed against the window at the hearses like gleaming black bullets parked in its drive and the women in black dresses and hats. Someone was always dying, a thought that still struck me as impossibly cruel. I had once thought the row of white striated columns that lined the front of the building to be elegant and grand, but that day as I drove up, they appeared pretentious, a poor facade for the dreadful business indoors.

The parking lot was filled with cars and some had pulled into the orchard behind the mortuary and parked in a jumble, at odd angles under the walnut trees, as if some joyous harvest festival were taking place. Every Indian family, excepting my own, had come to pay their respects to the man who, in ways both obvious and unseen, had touched their lives. I abandoned my mother's sedan at some distance along the shoulder of the road and spotted Uncle Avtar's blue pickup truck as I entered the lot and headed toward the mortuary. As I drew closer, a low rumbling noise emanated from the building. Its walls seemed to hum and strain from the collective grief building inside.

It was more than morbid curiosity that had brought me there. Uncle Avtar's hand on my shoulder had triggered a dormant nerve in me, but it went back further than that. As I reached for the brass doorknob, I realized nothing could've kept me away from the memorial service for Mohta Singh. I had scarcely spoken to the man, but that didn't matter. I could not resist whatever had taken hold of me, its fierce centripetal spin pulling me into its center. When I opened the door, a piercing wall of sound nearly knocked me backward. It was a chaotic scene, with people milling about as if they were attending a sporting event. The half a dozen women collected at the front stretched their arms toward the coffin, which was being lifted off its stand and carried to the crematory, their shrill screams audible as a single cry. I caught a glimpse of the stony, dark profile lying in the satin-lined coffin. In the second row, Uncle Avtar's back and shoulders trembled, his hat crumpled in his hands. My father bowed his head.

Hari stood by the coffin. He looked changed since I had seen him at the festival; his hair was cut short and the sleeves of his jacket hung over his hands, which were gripped in tight fists by his side. He looked boyish, yet aged, unprepared for the grim duty that lay ahead.

Uncle Avtar joined the small procession out of the room. A pale, sandy-haired man held the doors open as the coffin passed, then pulled them shut, as if wanting to barricade himself from the restive crowd. The sound shuddered through the suddenly silent room. The stark quiet was eerie, more unsettling than the wailing of the women; all had ceased, it seemed, along with the beating of Mohta Singh's heart. The shrill cries still reverberated in my ears and Mohta Singh's body seemed to suck the air from the room as it was carried away, and I found myself gasping for a breath.

Around me, the mass of still bodies slowly began to stir. The older citizens struggling from their chairs remained dry-eyed, as though reconciled to the inevitable after witnessing a lifetime of it. The group of grieving women, suddenly animated and purged of their sorrow, filled their arms with shawls and bags and helped themselves to the potted white lilies lining the front. I didn't recognize any of them and had the disturbing notion that someone might have hired them to perform.

The room gradually emptied, until only my father remained, slumped forward in his chair, waiting for Uncle Avtar to return.

"Jeeto," he said when he saw me. My name sounded like a scratching in his throat. He took my hand the way he would have when I was a little girl. His eyes looked cloudy and sad; I had never seen him cry, and now he was crying for a man I thought he despised. I squeezed his fingers gently, a way of thanking him for not asking me why I had come.

Eleven

It was Mohta Singh's death I still think of as unleashing the chain of events that followed. Perhaps it was their clustered timing, or the way the momentum of one swept along in its path the gathering force of others, like the currents in a river: water spilling over banks, carving fresh tributaries, whose sudden power would carry them lashing ahead into new lands, only to converge again and mingle at some distant point.

There were the misgivings of the community itself, which grew morose and sullen following his death, prodded like a misbehaving child toward some long-overdue self-examination. His absence raised the perplexing question of who precisely Mohta Singh had been and what he had meant to our community. The *Oak Grove Republican* ran a gracious article tracing his roots in the area, praising his keen business sense and fine civic contributions (he was the only Indian ever to be a member of the chamber of commerce). But it read, all in all, much like a standard obituary, with the blanks thoughtfully filled in. With his short stature and fine woolen suits, he had been the most recognizable Indian citizen in town. Yet he maintained, cultivated even, an aura of mystery about him, like a fine aroma whose essence one cannot immediately locate. His demise only heightened a dormant need to define the man. Why had he borne only one child—a tempestuous daughter at that—during his long and privileged life? Where had he actually disappeared to those months purportedly spent tending business interests in Vancouver and Toronto? These issues haunted those quarters of society most removed from the man himself. Among them, there was talk of the graying but taut and curvaceous professional dancer, a Miss Rani, who had launched herself sobbing onto his cold prostrate body in the mortuary. In the end, as always, the question of Mohta Singh's identity remained mired in conjecture and hearsay.

His absence was sorely felt at the following meeting of the Indian Association, when members delayed elections, which set off a round of fisticuffs that resulted in a late-night caravan to the emergency room to have Sher Singh's jaw wired shut. For others, it was simply the reassuring sight of his black Lincoln sedan crawling down the road toward an urgent business appointment—he had been an inordinately cautious driver—that would be greatly missed.

No one expected Hari to step into the role his grandfather had labored for decades to create for himself, that of a father figure to a community constantly replenished by a stream of new faces that settled in its midst, all bearing the same burdens of how to live and eat. Hari moved more or less permanently into the brick home off Howard Lane, transforming the character of the place for good. I drove by one evening, to see the lights on in every room, a merry illusion that the house bustled with family and good cheer, though he lived there alone. His red Chevy pickup was the only vehicle parked in the curved gravel driveway once crowded with the vehicles of those seeking his grandfather's counsel. A dim shadow fell briefly across an upstairs window, a swift reflection of movement, of a presence.

Shortly after I attended the memorial service, I received the letter I had been anticipating for weeks, an offer of acceptance to

Berkeley. I tore at the envelope, then read its impossible words of congratulation, their tone cool and restrained. Dashing from the mailbox to the house, a feeling of terror swept over me as I recalled the forged signature on the application. I buried the letter deep in my desk drawer, where I would retrieve it late at night from its tangled nest of school papers. The words typed in clear English concealed a hidden message, and if I gazed at them long enough, I told myself, they would recede, revealing an image of what my future held, like a photograph bathed in developer solution coming bit by bit into view.

Over school lunch in the courtyard, Surinder threw her arms around my neck. Suffocating in her Jean Naté, I pleaded with her not to tell anyone yet about the letter. A perplexing inverse proportion had taken root in my head: The fewer people who knew, the greater were my chances of going.

"I promise not to start any scandalous rumors about you," she said in a mocking tone. "Going off to a top college—can't get much worse than that."

Neelam's reaction was more tempered: Davinder would be thrilled I had been accepted. Her flat tone suggested that my leaving was more of an idea than a real possibility to her. I couldn't muster the energy to become angry with her, only mildly disappointed. She was pregnant, after all, vulnerable that way. The changes imminent in her life, the demands that would be placed on her body and affections consumed her already. I knew, too, that she'd set her private hopes aside for the duration, like a quaint artifact placed among other cherished treasures on a shelf, to be admired at infrequent intervals for its odd charm, mostly gathering dust.

In the hallway of the language building, Jenny Holcomb caught up with me, perspiring in a baby-blue V-necked sweater. At Mr. Iverson's prodding earlier in English class, she had announced her intentions to attend Berkeley, then acknowledged her classmates' words of encouragement with a bleak smile, as if her decision had been a sacrifice of something dear to her.

"Have you gotten your letter, Serjit?" she asked me after class.

I nodded. "Last week."

"Who knows, maybe we can room together," she said half-heartedly. She swiveled in her high leather heels, as though uncertain of which direction to pursue next. "A school back east would've been fun." Just for the record, she felt obligated to express a certain level of dissatisfaction for the opportunity afforded her. Her brows arched mischievously over her bright eyes when she saw Pritam approaching; she approved, apparently. Her expression clouded when she spotted her boyfriend, Brian, at the other end of the hallway, the sculpted square of his shoulders proudly sporting his letter jacket. She puffed her cheeks and blew her bangs off her forehead. What to do about him now that the world had opened up for her?

The day of the senior class trip, Pritam stopped me in the parking lot, delivering a "See you there" look at close range. Surinder noted the greeting with a protective curl of one shoulder toward her neck. I had thought of the trip for weeks, devising various scenarios in my mind where the entire class would disappear mysteriously, stranding Pritam and me fatefully alone to navigate the perilous mountain trails. As the chirpy mass of students squeezed toward the bus doors, I couldn't shake the feeling that it would be a momentous day, that everything now was a slow unfurling of the path toward our futures. It was a clear day, the sky a sheer, glassy blue as the sun climbed over the treetops. I settled into my seat on the bus next to Surinder, who fussed with a strap on her sandal and generally shifted and strained to find a comfortable position. Again the feeling gathered in my chest—a knot coiling itself there—that something would happen this day. By the end of the day, I would recognize it had been no less than a premonition.

The line of school buses wound through town; their jangling and squeaking, the little plumes of smoke trailing from their exhaust pipes caused the town's citizens to turn and take notice as they went about their daily business. Oh, yes, the seniors are taking their class trip today. We lumbered past Morton's Bait and Tackle Shop, then over the Richmond Bridge before the road flattened in the bottomlands east of Oak Grove. On the bus, the patches of silence where some struggled for a brief nap were broken by a few overly chatty groups whose conversations wafted to the rear. From eight seats ahead, I could hear chubby Jimmy Waebel's monotonous recitation of the items he'd enjoyed for dinner the previous evening: string beans and this neat kind of meat loaf his mother made from three varieties of ground meat, and apple cobbler with vanilla ice cream.

Next to me, Surinder dozed, or at least pretended to. Her head bobbed limply to the side, hovering close to my shoulder, her eyelids shut tightly, fluttering from the effort, as though she was trying to flush some image from her mind. She was overdressed for the occasion, in full makeup and wearing a purple knit shell and a short beige cotton skirt and the most impractical sort of high-heeled sandals. One wrist gleamed with a band of multicolored glass bangles that would never do for a game of volleyball.

We passed the dirt road on the right side where Pritam had taken me that night weeks ago. It stretched like a gold sash toward the scrubby undergrowth and, finally, the towering fence of trees along the river. The soft, gauzy focus of the place in daylight somehow refuted my memory of what had occurred that night in the cover of darkness. The events of that night struck me then in much the same way as that dirt road, glittering in the light, but then stopping suddenly and going nowhere. I wondered at times why, for all

of Surinder's stylish bravado and overt attention to Pritam, he preferred me to her. That willingness she demonstrated in his presence
could not have escaped him. I relaxed back in my seat, recalling
the minty shampoo smell of him and his scrubbed face inches from
mine just moments earlier in the parking lot. Surinder stirred next
to me, stretching her arms ahead of her with a feline indifference.
She would never have panicked in the car that night with Pritam;
she would've wound her arms about his neck and pulled him to
her the second he had cut the engine.

The oak-studded grasslands of the foothills receded as massive
walls of granite rose abruptly from the ground like a colossal foreign outpost. By late morning, the buses pulled into a dense grove
of ponderosa pines at the base of the cliffs. Dusty shafts of light descended through the treetops, mottling the floor of the shaded
parking area. Mrs. Krieger hopped out of the lead bus, armed with
a clipboard, wearing a whistle strung around her neck, and sporting
a military-style cap that warned she would be doling out the fun in
measured doses like a bitter medicine.

Wooden picnic tables were scattered among the trees beyond
the parking lot. Two volleyball courts and a horseshoe pit dominated a grassy clearing. Numerous trails spoked off from the clearing, leading toward a creek and off through the slender canyons
and backwoods.

At lunch, Surinder scoffed at the idea of sitting with the other
Indian girls until she noticed Pritam at a nearby table with the
other Indian boys. She sniffed at her salwaar-clad neighbors and
their simple pleasure of unsealing their usual dishes of curry as
they hummed tunes from recent Indian films. She bit into her sub
sandwich with satisfaction, savoring the knowledge that her own
life was open to a limitless array of choices, including a turkey and
ham club. At the next table, the Indian boys prodded and teased
one another. The tantalizingly close proximity of females, of their

own kind, with minimal supervision, emboldened their talk and swagger. It was a brave prelude to the next big step, where one day Indian boys and girls would actually sit together at the same table, but we were a generation away from that kind of bold experimentation.

Pritam's gaze from the next table was unremitting, demanding. His hair lay in damp waves, streaked blue in the sunlight after a forbidden plunge into the nearby creek. It was an open display of disregard for Mrs. Krieger's unyielding authority. He wouldn't have hesitated walking by her and shaking the water loose from his soggy locks, watching her lips purse as the will to reprimand him fled her temporarily. The trespassing charge had branded him, not as a true threat, but as troublesome.

Surinder grew increasingly sullen with each glance I exchanged with Pritam. She was accustomed, as an only child, to her parents offering her, if not the world on a platter, then at least the modest reapings of her father's career as a construction worker. But this unnameable thing that involved Pritam defied logic; it would require a dose of cleverness, foolishness even.

I smiled at Pritam, who listened distractedly to some joke Gian Singh was sharing with him. Gian was a tall, muscled boy with sleepy eyes, whose fair complexion was subject to the ravages of puberty. Neelam's friend Mani had once claimed his families were Gypsies, not upper-caste Jats like us. The family had moved up and down the Central Valley regularly when he was a child, the latest stretch of three years spent in Oak Grove the most settled of his life. Surinder summoned a sudden fascination for the young man, his mumbled elocution and thick biceps. She traded her bag of ruffled potato chips for his plain ones, her sinuous reach crossing over Pritam's shoulder.

"I saw you at the community college orientation," she said to Gian. "Taking classes there in the fall?"

Gian shrugged "My mother made me go."

Surinder cocked one hip, determined not to allow his lack of ambition to discourage her. "Well, I hope some fun people decide to go there." She stood there long after their smoldering exchange was complete, nimble and statuesque, allowing Gian's full appraisal before settling again beside me on the bench.

"I thought you were going to beauty school in the fall," I said to her.

"Well, we can't all go to schools like Berkeley, can we?" she said to Pritam. She played with the straw in her soda, avoiding the obvious spark of anger flaring on my cheeks.

Pritam set his sandwich down and wiped his hands on his jeans. "Gian, what year Cougar is that you're driving?"

Gian's arms puffed with pride. "Sixty-eight." He grinned at Pritam. "Four on the floor."

Surinder smiled appreciatively; that four on the floor, whatever it meant, added immeasurably to his appeal.

The shrill ring of Mrs. Krieger's whistle signaled the end of lunch and the start of the volleyball tournament. Using an old megaphone battered by years of dry announcements and harsh reprimands, Mrs. Krieger called out the first teams to participate. A crowd of students soon assembled around her, listening for their garbled names to be announced. Mr. Iverson pushed himself up from his lawn chair to join them, his legs, in denim cutoffs, like two pieces of white chalk moving stiffly beneath him. The girls at our table, led by petite Hardeep, gathered their stainless-steel dishes and dashed off toward the volleyball courts with their veils streaming gaily behind them. "You've got to be kidding," Surinder groaned, shuddering at their unbridled enthusiasm.

The mood had shifted at the table, with Pritam smarting that I had kept a secret from him; I was furious with Surinder for having told him before I had had a chance. I started down the path to the courts, where the teams were taking sides, but heard Pritam call me from behind as I emerged into the clearing.

"Let's skip the game," he said, pulling me back under the trees. "There's a great waterfall about a quarter mile upstream."

Showing me places again, I thought. It was the chance I had been waiting for. I looked back at Surinder. She rose from the table, brushing crumbs from her purple knit shell and stopping with one hand on her chest as she caught sight of us. Gian was hovering beside her, looking pleased by the fortuitous turn of events.

I quickly followed Pritam along a path that dipped away from the picnic area into a thicket of willows and toward the stream. A cool blast of air met us as we reached the stream bank. The water spilled in silvery sheets over rocks embedded in the stream, its crisp sound like fine glass shattering. We could no longer hear the frenzied shrieks of athletic competition or the regular blast of Mrs. Krieger's whistle. It was as if a curtain had parted and we had stepped onto a different stage, the light and shadows, the mosaic shapes and textures of leaf and bark in bold relief—velvety mosses clinging to rocks, spiky reeds, feathery grasses swaying rhythmically at the stream's edge to the movement of water.

The ringing sound of the water, the padding of our footsteps on the slightly muddy ground echoed along the steep granite walls. We soon turned at the sound that was half shriek, half laughter, a playful cry for help. At the spot where we had started along the stream, about thirty yards back, Surinder teetered on a boulder in the middle of the water, shaking a wet ankle. She grabbed Gian by his waist when he comically leaped onto the boulder beside her. They waved their arms wildly about, trying to regain their balance. Surinder squatted down, her skirt pulling to the tops of her thighs as she scooped up handfuls of water, which she hurled at Gian's chest. It sent him reeling backward, an exaggerated effort, plunging him knee-deep into a shallow pool. There were more shrieks of laughter and accusation. Gian's hands cupped her shoulders in mock retaliation and she stopped, looking squarely at us, flicking the water from her open hands. Gian waved unwittingly at us— what a good time we were all having!

Weary of Surinder's pathetic display, I impatiently took Pritam's arm and we moved off. The path narrowed amid a grove of alders. My irritation with her soon fell away as I savored the feel of my hand in Pritam's, the little bumps of our shoulders as we moved through the dappled shade. We stepped swiftly along a slight incline toward the shadowy origins of the stream in the narrow canyon ahead. The path curved at the point where it bisected a steep granite cliff and the stream. I stopped, catching a glint in Pritam's eye: We were alone again.

He pushed me back against the granite face, his hands at my waist, then my neck as he kissed me hard. His skin smelled like water, a clean metallic scent. We pulled away, surprised at each other, then slid down onto the sandy bank. The gold lion pendant shimmered faintly against his chest and his hazel eyes played that trick of becoming pale in the shadowy light. I pulled my knees to my chest and felt his thumb and forefinger slip around my bare ankle, the ring of pressure there tender and exhilarating. He didn't understand at first when I moved his hand, linking my fingers in his, that I wanted more. We fell back against the sand. He brushed the hair from my face, the small lion face hanging between us. I watched his face move closer, waiting to taste his mouth again, His weight pushed against the length of my body. I felt myself sinking away into the sand as our bodies ground against each other, our faces sticky-wet. He slid his hand under my shirt and bra and began to circle his palm over my breast. "Pritam," I began to mumble, pushing back at his arms.

He rolled away from me. I sat up and adjusted my shirt, then brushed the grainy bits of sand from my hair. He looked downcast with his face drawn into a pout and his hair pointing in stiff peaks on his head. He reached into his back pocket and offered me half of a chocolate bar that had flattened to a gooey wafer. For a few moments, the only sounds were our smacking and chewing, the water trickling through a shallow portion of the stream, and a couple of jays thrashing for seeds in a nearby bush.

Pritam mussed his hair with his fingers, a kind of hopeless gesture.

"I wonder what happened to those two," I said, pointing my chin downstream.

"Gian and Surinder? Why are you worried about them?" He idly poked a slender branch at a small beetle struggling along his appointed route.

"I'm not worried. I just never imagined them together."

"Gian's all right. His family's a little strange. I'm more afraid of her, actually."

"Surinder? She's harmless," I said, frowning as I pondered her bizarre behavior earlier.

He watched as the beetle shuffled away, making a temporary retreat toward the water. "You could've told me yourself that you got accepted."

"I meant to, but . . . I haven't even mentioned it to my parents."

"Sure. They'll book the first flight to India. Can't have two wayward daughters in the same family."

I buried my hand in the sand, bringing up a fistful, which I watched sift slowly through my fingers into a powdery mound. "You know, I think my mother never expected all that from Neelam. She might expect it from me, but Neelam was always so obedient . . . so . . . good." The clipped monosyllable bore no relation to the vast implausibility of that final word.

"But then she gazed into Hari's eyes and everything changed," he said, affecting a silly, dreamy tone, but there was a mocking quality in it that suddenly made me uncomfortable. I leaned back against the pewter slab of rock beside Pritam and stretched my legs across the sand. There is no simple way to measure one's feelings for another, I later recalled thinking. One couldn't simply fill a jar with sand and say, "Look, I love you this much." What if my jar was bigger than his jar? I wanted Pritam to look at me just then, to pull me against him once more. Was that love? We sat instead like two scared kids, unable even to bear the sight of each other.

"My mother was looking through pictures the other night," he said. "She was sitting at the table one night with the pictures spread in front of her and she picked up this one and said, 'Look, wouldn't he be nice for Jeeto Rai?'"

We had often joked about the photos of eligible young bachelors his mother would ritualistically trot out; the store brought her success and stature in the community, but her true passion still lay with this meddling, this so-called joining of souls. I had an image of Charan Kaur playing with a deck of cards and, after careful deliberation, selecting the one she would bet on. And now she was consulting her son—Pritam—for matchmaking advice!

"You're lying." I waited for him to crack a smile, to indicate he was only teasing, needling me the way he had that beetle. "What does he look like?"

"Very handsome. Big ears, though. A mechanical engineer. Studied in London."

"He's going to be a doctor, actually. At least that's what I heard." I crossed my arms in a huff, ignoring Pritam's look of surprise. "Maybe your mother should find you someone. She can help you manage the store."

He smiled, as if welcoming the bitterness in my voice. "Not me. I've got other plans." He tossed the stick aside, as if it were the source of animosity surfacing in him, then leaned over and retrieved it, twirling it in his hand and reexamining its usefulness. "Don't you want to go off to school? I think you should."

I felt my stomach begin to tremble, hating that he was being generous like this. Stepping aside, making room for me, though he may have considered it noble. I realized he would resent me if I stayed or left. If I stayed, I would become ordinary, one of the lunch girls, waiting for the right photograph clutched in Charan Kaur's fingers, one that might stir a vague feeling in me, no more. And if I left? I imagined seeing Pritam a few years from now, the two of us exchanging the blank stares of strangers, indulging briefly in figuring out who the other had become, but finding the effort too strenuous. Even now, we could no more than look past a shoulder, at lips that parted to speak, but couldn't. The beetle returned, treading stodgily like an overburdened old man in Pritam's direction for another round of tortured prodding. By some unconscious, Pavlovian urge, Pritam lifted the stick toward the poor creature and plunged it into the sand in its direct path.

"Leave it alone!" I seized the stick from his hand, but he resisted and it snapped in half. He stared at its frayed edges as though fragile tendons had been severed.

"I'm going back," I said. I jumped to my feet; the streambed, the boulders piled along its edges thrust upward at a sharp angle. Pritam didn't prevent me from leaving. He must have started off upstream, toward the waterfall, because when I stopped along the path and looked back a moment later, there remained only the bumps and ridges of disturbed sand where we'd sat together. And what if I had stayed there beside him? If, hand in hand, we had retraced our path along the stream back to the picnic grounds together? I've often wondered over the years—would it have changed everything? That swelling of anger, the synapse that surged through my legs and propelled me onto my feet, would always seem an irrevocable act. I fled down the path along the stream, flinching at snatches of phrases that seemed suspended like savage knots in the air: "Don't you want to . . . You could've told me . . ." The shadows had diminished under the advance of the sun's sharp white light directly overhead. In the harsh brightness, I could no longer hide from the realization that had struck Pritam and me with equal bitterness: We both knew what my choice would be, and so he would never ask me to stay.

I emerged through the willow thicket by the picnic grounds, panting, then running toward Mrs. Krieger and the ridiculous safety of her whistle. The teams were just changing on the volleyball courts. I stepped into the back line of players just as the ball was being served. After a point was scored on our team, there was some wrangling about too many players on our side. A beet-faced Marjorie Crimshaw gladly slunk off toward a less strenuous game of horseshoes. My eyes briefly met Mrs. Krieger's as she patrolled the sidelines between the courts. Noticing me, she began furiously flipping through the pages on her clipboard, consulting her schedule, until Mr. Iverson intervened with a fresh crisis. A ball flew past and I mustered enough reflex to get a hand on it. It fell just out of bounds, a point scored for the opposing team, to the groans of my teammates. I paid attention after that, trying to avert my eyes from the path that led back onto the picnic grounds from the stream.

The path remained undisturbed in its deep shadows. At the barrel-shaped orange cooler, I filled a paper cup with water, drank it down, then carried another to a shaded picnic table. The games had broken up by then, the nets taken down from their posts and the balls stored away in their canvas sacks. The cleanup committee scavenged the area for soda cans, napkins, and other debris scattered over the trampled grass; there was a general shift toward packing things up, preparing to leave. I glanced toward the path again when the call came to board the buses.

The crowds converged from all directions into the parking lot, separating and filing onto the buses as names were crossed off checklists. I took the same seat I had ridden over in and braced for an unpleasant scene with Surinder. I had not seen her since her theatrics with Gian at the creek. When the last of the stragglers had boarded the buses some time later, she still had not shown up. Outside, the aides were convening around Mrs. Krieger and Mr. Iverson, who were thumbing through pages of checklists. Mrs. Krieger placed her fists squarely on the shelves that were her hips and swiveled her small head from left to right, scanning the grounds.

The din on our bus quieted when she boarded. I could hear each row of students exhale a collective breath of relief as she slowly passed by. She paused when she recognized me near the back of the bus. She stooped over me, glowering at the sheer inconvenience this trouble was causing her. I knew she was looking for Surinder.

"Serjit," she said, placing a spongy hand behind me on the back of the seat, "do you know where Surinder is?"

I looked up, finding only the broad swath of her neck. "I haven't seen her since lunch."

Mrs. Krieger pressed her chin doubtingly toward her chest. "Come now, you two are always joined at the hip."

I didn't know that expression, "joined at the hip," and paused a few seconds to form the image in my mind. "We had lunch together, but I didn't see her after that. I was playing volleyball." I felt a tic beginning to vibrate in my right cheek.

Mrs. Krieger's pale sage green eyes narrowed in concentration. "Yes, I do remember you on the courts."

We were asked to descend into the parking lot once again, where we stood in uncertain, wavering lines along the orange flanks of the rows of buses. A weary impatience had set in among the students, a listless shifting of weight from leg to leg. The once-palpable magic of the place had vanished as the dusky shadows of midafternoon crept eastward. Next to me, Jimmy Waebel scratched longingly at his belly; an unabiding hunger had set in.

I searched the grounds for Pritam, Surinder . . . Pritam again. It was like him to set off on his own and disappear for stretches at a time. He was finally making his way back, having beaten his anger out along the winding trails; I was certain of it. But then I spotted Gian's tall figure, the multicolored striped T-shirt, at bus 56, Pritam's bus. The air rushed out of me. The faded white microphone flashed like a bright beam from the opposite end of the lot. I heard Surinder's name called once, and, seconds later, Pritam's. The other students were grinning around me, elbowing one another, embracing the obvious conclusion that I could not.

TWELVE

Surinder showed up two days later, a Saturday, at the Denny's at the corner of Fifth and Burgess. At the scratched Plexiglas counter, she ordered a chocolate shake and fries with the money Pritam had left her, then called her mother from the pay phone located by the restaurant entrance. The police had launched a search spanning several counties for her by then. Her senior class photo had been splashed across newspapers and television stations as far away as Eureka. She was described as tall, with long dark hair, wearing a purple top and short skirt, and having a pale crescent-shaped scar like a single parenthesis by the left corner of her mouth. I had forgotten about the scar; it had faded into a permanent but delicate feature of her face, received in a precipitous tumble from the jungle gym onto the buckled asphalt playground in third grade.

I clipped the article with her photo from the newspaper; there was a brief mention of Pritam, how the two were suspected of running off together, his misdemeanor charge for trespassing, and the parents' pleas for their safe return. In the forty-plus hours they had been missing, I imagined them together in ways that made my flesh ache. I could still feel the pressure of Pritam's body against mine, and now he was with her.

The news of their disappearance had beaten me home the evening of the class trip. Our green sedan was parked illegally in the bus-loading area when we returned, and my mother emerged from the car, a flour-dusted blue-and-white-checked apron tied around her purple kameez. I could tell she knew; she stood by the car, an unlikely sentinel, shading her eyes with one hand as she scanned the windows of the buses in her forgotten apron, her salwaar flapping noticeably in the breeze.

"Can you believe it, Mohinder, that those two would disappear like that?" my mother asked at the dinner table. "Ramesh was out of her mind when I spoke to her." She seized Prem's hand as he dipped a finger into the bowl of chutney. "Jeeto, when was the last time you saw either of them?" she asked for the third time.

I stirred the bits of rice floating in the bowl of curry in front of me. "I told you. At lunch. I didn't see them after that."

"There's got to be a logical explanation," my father said. "We'll learn more tomorrow." He swept a curry-stained napkin across his mouth, as if he were eager to let the matter rest. But my mother pushed on.

"Well, the family can only endure so much. . . ." Her clouded gaze drifted toward the window; I knew she was thinking of Neelam again. "Ramesh has always complained that she's too independent. And now look what's happened. That girl's karma has already been written," she said, her voice cracking. It was the standard line that always got my father patting her hand. "Now, Jasbir . . ."

Wasting no time, Charan Kaur encamped herself in our living room the following day. How could that worthless girl have led her son astray in this manner? she asked over and over. Her shawl was spun tightly around her shoulders, giving her a stiff, mummified look.

I tried to muster the confusion and sadness expected of me as they questioned me repeatedly. It was not difficult to summon tears, but they were tears of anger that burned as they welled in my eyes. Earlier, I had been interrogated in the principal's office by the principal himself, and then a police officer who chewed on the insides of his cheek as I repeated the story that I had had lunch with Surinder and Pritam but had not seen them afterward. I prayed that Gian would slink off somewhere, out of sight and hearing range, as was often his nature, and that my lie would remain undiscovered. I was lying not for those two, but for myself. It was the only way to preserve what was left, what hadn't been stripped from me when I stood by the buses in Strawberry Canyon, and the fact of their deceit seeped slowly into me. Sitting next to Charan Kaur, listening to her damp, mucousy noises, I fixed on the moment when Pritam would have assented—the look, the reach. Neither Pritam nor Gian would have noticed what passed between Surinder and me that afternoon, standing some thirty yards apart along the stream as I took Pritam's arm and pulled him toward the narrow, shaded canyon where he would kiss me over and over. I realized then how I had wounded her.

But it was not enough to coax me to visit her when my mother insisted she owed her support to Ramesh despite her daughter's abominable actions. She made it clear she was not condoning such deplorable behavior and she clasped my cheek in her palm at one stage in appreciation of her younger daughter's display of good sense.

"But she might not want visitors just yet," I protested, trying to mask the true source of my anxiety.

She lowered her voice, though we were alone in the house. "When Neelam had her difficulties, I wanted to barricade myself inside these walls. Not see anyone. Every pair of eyes directed toward me was an accusation. At such times, one sets aside notions of propriety to aid a friend. Ramesh and I were such girlfriends in India. Her father and mine shared a pair of water buffalo, if that gives you any idea."

I distrusted my mother's nascent sense of compassion, but even more, I wanted to avoid arousing her suspicions, so I yielded finally to her wishes and we departed for Surinder's. She lived just south of the town limits, where the homes sat on spacious one-acre lots with neatly trimmed geometric borders of boxwood and pittosporum. A sprinkler twirled on a square of lawn in front of her house, flinging silvery chains of water in crazy patterns across the grass. My mother commented enviously on the hollyhocks, whose fleshy, bud-laden stalks grazed the front windows of the home.

I hesitated when Mrs. Singh, her heavy brow drooping over her dark, deep-set eyes, slowly opened the door and invited us in. "Surinder's in her room," she said, expecting me to rush to her daughter's side. As my eyes adjusted to the cool dark of the living room, I realized that confronting Surinder was going to be far more difficult than I had imagined. I hung around the kitchen, where Mrs. Singh began uncovering various tins with a pronounced clatter and concern, apologizing beforehand that the muttis had become rather stale and crumbly. Surinder came in and flipped one hand up in a short greeting. Her hair was pulled back in a ponytail and her face looked puffy from excessive sleep.

Mother and daughter circled each other, the troubled gap of space between them never diminishing. One could detect that the initial luster of their ecstatic reunion had worn considerably to a dull glimmer. Surinder settled on the sofa, sitting painfully upright and demonstrating little residual harm to her self-pride, or her spine. We remained silent until my mother gently took her hand and inquired if she was feeling well. The question made me simmer, as it implied that she had suffered at Pritam's behest. A muffled wheeze escaped Surinder's straining throat, and I couldn't tell if it was genuine regret or if she was playing along with the sympathy. We avoided each other's gaze. She seemed to be avidly studying the portraits of the gurus lining the wall opposite her, which had festive, gold-tinseled haar hanging about the frames, what normally embarrassed her about her home.

Mrs. Singh approached with a tray of teacups. "You girls should go off and talk like you always do."

"Yes, go," my mother insisted. "No use sitting here being glum all afternoon."

I followed Surinder to her bedroom. She opened the door to the bright apricot light drenching her room. In the doorway, we listened to the low murmurs of our mothers' voices in the living room. It was the boldness of Surinder's deceit that left the two women agape, nearly speechless. Neelam had at least attempted to carry on her affair discreetly, but Surinder—she had managed to have her news blared over television screens across the whole of northern California.

"There's only one topic of conversation around this house these days." Surinder sprawled luxuriantly atop her satin rose bedcovers; perhaps there were some things worth returning home for.

I lingered by the vanity across the room, examining the bottles of nail polish, the cases of eye shadow and blush, and the bangles and earrings accumulated there. "What did you expect?"

"I didn't expect anything. I didn't think about anything. I just did it."

"Where did you go?" With Pritam, I wanted to say. Why did you go with him? "Well, you must have had a good time, wherever you went."

"Look, I ran into him on the trail. We hiked up over the ridge. There was a view of the valley from up there. We lost track of time, and when we got back, the buses had already left."

"Lost track of time? And then what?" I moved closer, perching myself stiffly at the corner of her bed. I wanted to know, but I didn't.

Surinder smiled, a new knowledge lurking behind the pallid stretched lips, which made her look changed, hardened. She removed the band that tied her hair and flung it across the room. "It was a stupid thing I did. And now my uncle Bindi is threatening to go find him and teach him a lesson." The trembling in her face told me it was not all regret she was feeling; her drama had come to a premature end, played out too quickly, and here she sat within the same four baby blue walls that had cradled her most of her life. "My parents think I was forced into the situation, that Pritam is to blame. Do you know what I told my mother? That it was my idea. It was, in a way. After I dumped that Gian up there, I went looking for you two." She glanced sideways at me. "I could tell something had happened. He was all red-faced, mad. And that made me so angry with you. . . ."

"But how could you run off with him when . . ."

Surinder crawled onto her knees, lunging toward me on the bed. "How could *you*? *I* liked him! But I could tell after we . . . I could go out there and tell your mom what you were doing up there. Then see if you get to go off to your big college."

I heard the front door open and close, then Neelam's voice, the ring of it soothing to the grinding noises in my skull. Soon she was at Surinder's doorway, poking her head apologetically through. "They're in the front room sniffling, so I thought I'd rather join you two." She planted a kiss on Surinder's forehead and waved the ladoo in her hand in greeting at me. "You gave us all a big scare." Neelam squinted at Surinder when she smiled and her eyes were moist and shiny. She bit into the ladoo; she seemed to care nothing for the circumstances of Surinder's disappearance, or perhaps had understood right away.

"You look well," Surinder responded with mock contempt.

"Me? I'm turning into a whale. Look at these!" she cried, cupping her breasts with both hands. "I feel like a cow." She laughed. She had entered her second trimester and the contours of her body were shifting, realigning, like a house preparing for company.

Surinder was called into the principal's office during first pe-

riod on Monday. Mrs. Krieger had been present, she told me tearfully over the phone that evening, expecting our friendship to resume at her convenience. Had she realized the chaos her carelessness
had set into motion? Mrs. Krieger had asked. Her voice shaking,
then choking, Surinder told me not to look for her on the bus in the
morning; she had been expelled from school. Pritam was expelled,
as well. Neither of them would be attending the graduation ceremonies in June. "Don't worry," she assured me in a flat tone. "Nobody knows that you were with him that afternoon."

I washed the last of the dinner dishes that evening, a disheveled
heap constantly replenishing itself, as Aunt Manjit and her brood
had decided late in the day to join us for supper, then proceeded to
drag the meal on with various requests for dessert: besan, cookies,
ice cream, milk. I hadn't truly minded. The pretext of appearing
occupied with these small tasks postponed further questioning.
Earlier, I had encountered my mother and aunt whispering in the
kitchen about Surinder. Well, a customary whisper for my mother
was a few decibels below a shout. I had caught most of the conversation while standing by a bookshelf in the next room, pretending
to be absorbed in a travel book.

"Running off with a boy like that. I don't know who was more
upset . . . poor Ramesh or Charan Kaur."

"Hare ram!"

"Gone for two days! Where do children get these ideas?" my
mother had continued. "One can only imagine . . ."

"Our Jeeto wouldn't have wandered off that way," Aunt Manjit
had said.

"Jeeto was playing volleyball at the time. Ramesh told me herself
that her daughter should've followed our Jeeto's example and participated in more sanctioned activities." I had heard the rolling pin slap
sharply on the counter. "She would've made the volleyball team this
year." Considering the unsavory alternatives, volleyball suddenly had

a wholesome appeal for my mother, though she forbade me to play when the season started. I had slammed the book shut.

"Jeeto, is that you?" she had called. "Come set the table, bhout."

After the dishes were done, I settled on the carpet in front of the television to watch an old *Gidget* movie. It was one I had seen a few years before with Neelam. My sister had sat rapt, recognizing in some single molten glance the thrilling promise of what her future years could hold for her.

My mother called my aunt into the living room. "Gidget di movie dek lo."

"Oh, darling, you're in love!" Gidget's mother cried with sympathy as she held her sobbing daughter in her arms. Moondoggie had jilted the poor girl once again, preferring the flat, waxen-hard company of his surfboard to her soft curves. Aunt Manjit watched with her half-bitten samosa held in one hand, agape at the wounded stripe of Gidget's pouty mouth. Fidgeting in the armchair with her embroidery work, my mother struggled to locate the appropriate emotion; there was an excess of triumph and celebration in Gidget's mother's tone (my daughter, in love at last!), but even she succumbed to a short sniffle.

When the movie concluded, I languished on the carpet, my cheek flat against its stubbly terrain, thinking of Pritam. He wouldn't be at school tomorrow, or the next day. I felt worse with each loving smile from my mother, aware that I had gained her good graces falsely. Earlier, I had welcomed the company of my aunts and cousins, the noisy distraction they provided. But now I wanted them all gone. I wanted silence so I could release the hurt twisting and bumping like a trapped animal inside me.

Those next weeks at school, I would round a corner in the crowded hallway, still expecting to get a glimpse of those narrow, slouching shoulders before the sober face would emerge, the eyes that would lift in recognition to meet mine. Then I would feel angry with myself, and with him, that I still wanted him there walking toward me in the hallway. Surinder I missed in more complicated ways; that she had gone off with Pritam, done things with him still hurt me, but she also had tried to protect me when she explained the events to her mother and the principal.

I ate lunch sometimes with the lunch girls, Hardeep and the others who maintained their insulated routines. Once, Jenny Holcomb invited me to sit with her crowd; it was an off day, when one of her friends had been forbidden to leave campus as they usually did. Jenny took my arm and pulled me to the bench beside her. "Serjit and I will be at Berkeley together next year," she announced, conscious of her own generosity. They spent the remainder of the forty-five minutes berating cafeteria food and plotting postgraduation festivities. "How's Surinder?" one of them turned to ask me, her widened eyes barely concealing her pleasure that even strictly raised Indian girls could abandon their will, tangled and lost in the arms of a boy.

Thirteen

It was grayish pink, swimming in the dank water like a little fish, then slowing, floating, spiraling, and sinking to the bottom of the bowl. She had known right away what merciless trick her body had efficiently performed. The clotted tissue tore apart in her fingers when she reached instinctively into the water to retrieve it, to preserve it, patch the bit of life together, but it unraveled there in the tentative grip of her fingers. She took refuge in her bed then, that same idle afternoon she had contemplated crocheting a sunny yellow blanket for the crib. She lay still listening to her own shallow breaths, then startled when she felt the blood gush from within her and seep through her clothing, staining the white sheets. She drove herself to the emergency room without calling Davinder or her mother.

It was painless, Neelam told me that night, too drowsy to appreciate her own irony. She lay in a curtained-off area in the recovery room, shrouded by the whiteness of the bedsheets and drapes and wall. In a chair by the bed, Davinder sat rigid, unblinking, like a dark stone. He had finished scolding Neelam for not calling him immediately, and he seemed to contemplate that earlier impulse in his wife to face this alone. "She lost it," he'd said coolly on the phone, as if relaying the results of a cricket match.

"They could at least put her in a private room," my mother complained. She paced the side of the bed unsteadily, unable to gaze fully at the figure slouched under the sheets before her.

"She won't need one. They'll be releasing her soon."

My mother let out a sharp gasp; she expected a lengthier convalescence, considering the gravity of this abrupt turn of events.

"The bleeding has slowed," Davinder continued without emotion. He consulted his watch. "The doctor should be coming by shortly."

I smoothed the sheets that covered Neelam. "You're staying with us for a few days."

Neelam managed a weak, apologetic smile, which my mother accepted without a further word. Davinder patted her hand, his fingers stretching like tentacles over her balled fist. It was nobody's fault—that was the maddening part, as well. It was unsettling to see my mother in this state, bereft of her quick tongue, her fierce, uncompromising attitude that things happened for a reason, that one event led inexorably on a path to the next. She was already weighing on some internal scale the debts and gains incurred in our family these last years. In the days following the miscarriage, my mother cushioned her grief with the burden of familiar tasks—her needlework, a batch of nimbu chutney prepared from the lemons harvested in our backyard. Despite her efforts at concentration, she lifted her brow now and then, her gaze fixing on some unseen horizon whose amorphous lines suggested the very question: Had she tempted fate in some way when she dragged her pregnant daughter to that clinic several years earlier?

In my room, I cleaned the heaps of clothes off of Neelam's old bed and spread the indigo covers embroidered with a red star pattern over the bed and pulled the stuffed doll with yellow yarn hair from a trunk in the closet. I wanted it to be like it always had been now that she had come to stay with us awhile. She slept noisily at night, as she always had, snorting, murmuring as though some furry nocturnal creature inhabited her body after her eyes shut in slumber. I envied this secret, unconscious life of hers. I would wake in the middle of the night and stare at the two rectangular panes of glass, dulling, brightening as the moon arced higher into the sky. I would listen to her peculiar sounds and think.

There were things I longed to tell Neelam. That I finally understood about Hari and her. But I would look into her long, brooding face and the will would escape me. She never lacked for company at our house. She would sit the bulk of her day on the sofa while the aunts visited and chattered endlessly. A mind occupied with trifling matters is a mind relieved. Aunt Teji's eggplants were sprouting blossoms already; there would be some excellent bharta prepared this summer. It was the warm, rainless days of late, Aunt Manjit counseled before she announced that, regrettably, her migraines had returned. There were plenty of silent rebukes and indelicate elbow jabbing when unintentional but inappropriate comments slipped from their busy mouths: "Did you hear Balwant Kaur is expecting again? What a fertile little thing!"

Neelam tolerated their mostly harmless bantering, twisting her gold wedding band with her fingers, stricken that her womb had twice expelled the life growing within her; numbed by an overwhelming grief for something she had desired most in the moment it sloughed away from its frail mooring. She would match one unborn child against the other in her mind the rest of her days. Which one more clever? Stronger? Strangely, she imagined them both to be boys. Though she had thrilled at the thought of a girl with a dark halo of stubborn curls and her own swollen mouth. That was when her dreams were her own, fed into her heart like a clear subterranean spring.

Davinder visited in the evenings, behaving as if he was finally being awarded a long-awaited opportunity to properly court his bride. He brought bouquets of lilies, roses, heart-shaped boxes of candies, stuffed animals and peculiar little ceramic figurines of dancers, which she propped on the dresser in the bedroom. "Whenever you're strong enough to come home, darling," he would say each time. "I'm feeling better every day," she would reply, lying.

There were afternoons with the women, evenings when Davinder and my father sat mostly silent, swirling empty shot glasses in their fingers, staring into the brassy rings of liquid clinging at the bottom like they were tea leaves divulging fortunes. The last night before Neelam left, Davinder ventured into my bedroom, where Neelam and I had encamped ourselves. Aunt Manjit and her brood had stormed into the house unannounced around dinnertime, an increasingly frequent occurrence as of late. From my room, we could hear the floor thumping under the children's feet. Davinder looked lonely and sullen as he asked if Neelam had prepared her belongings.

'You act as if we're crossing the Sahara Desert," she replied, scooting on the bed to allow room for him. "I have only a few things here. I'll be ready tomorrow morning."

"I've asked Mr. Goodlight for the day off." His gaze turned to me for solace. "She's looking better, isn't she?"

"Of course. We've been doting on her all week. Mom made her kheer and lots of carrot halva. I'm surprised she hasn't turned orange."

"What about you, Jeeto? I heard your saheli was in a little bit of trouble. Ran off with Charan Kaur's boy, wasn't it?"

The words struck me like a blow at the back of my neck. I shifted on the bed, burying my fists into the limp, spongy pillow I cradled in my lap. "Yes. Pritam." His name echoed once inside me. It had felt odd, unnatural to speak it again, though I had thought of him many times.

"Weren't they both expelled from school?" Davinder asked.

"Yes, I already told you all about that." Neelam pulled the hairpins from her bun, clenching them in her teeth as she twisted and rewound her hair into a coil that fell loosely behind her neck.

"It's a shame, so close to graduation," I said, though I felt pity for neither of them. In my softer moments, whatever sympathy I could muster swung wildly like a pendulum between them: I imagined the depths of Surinder's envy as she lured him away, Pritam's willingness—no, eagerness—to rush into what he was certain awaited him. His frustration with me. Then I would become consumed with anger again.

Davinder seemed amused by the incident and the predictable stir it had created in town. "Well, I suppose Oak Grove will survive its latest scandal."

Neelam threw me a hopeless, desperate look; she seemed as impatient as I was to change the topic of conversation. And she recognized how painful the episode had been for me. "What is Pritam doing now?" she asked me, shoving the pins into her bun one by one.

"Helping at India Bazaar full-time. At least that's what I heard."

"What a waste. That shop is like something on a Calcutta back street." Davinder's tongue moved in his mouth, as though he was trying to remedy an unpalatable taste there.

"This isn't exactly the posh section of Jalandhar or Delhi, is it?" Neelam said.

Her tone startled him and he seemed to regret his sarcasm and how he had spoiled the friendly mood in the room. He moved closer to her on the bed and took her hand in his, his voice tender. "There'll be other children, N."

"Do you think so? My track record isn't so great."

"Yes, I'm aware of your track record."

Neelam pulled her hand away and rose abruptly. She fled the

room, one hip grazing the side of the dresser. The audible snap of the chappals on her feet was enough to breed a depthless remorse in her husband. He slouched back on the bed against the wall, as if the weight of a crushing weariness had pinned him there. For a few moments, he seemed unable to move, or to speak.

I found Neelam on the living room floor, engrossed in Lakshmi's antics. She swung the baby onto her hip, fortifying herself against her husband's caresses before he departed. Aunt Manjit attempted to reassure him that his wife was recovering splendidly; the sooner she returned home now, the quicker her transformation would be to her former self. She gathered her own passel of children around her and sent them out the door, then threw her arms around Neelam in a hearty embrace. "Savkosh teekh hai, bhout?" she said, turning to me to ask if everything was well. I saw the fading bruise along her jawline and figured Uncle Girpal was spending more time at home these days. She pressed her palm flat against my belly below the navel, feeling its size and shape before she pulled her hand away. I felt the print of her palm remain there like a branding iron. I had seen the women do that to Neelam often until she married, and I knew what it meant. When the house was quiet and my mother collapsed into a chair, I wondered what she knew about that afternoon in Strawberry Canyon, and if Surinder might have said something after all.

Neelam tied the loose corners of the satin throw in a tight double knot, patting the orange bundle with her sand-colored hands. She hesitated then, as if she might have overlooked something; as if she were journeying to some distant place, when, in fact, it was only Davinder who had come for her to transport her across town to the home that had felt quite barren to him during her absence. She lifted the bundle, which was the size of a large pumpkin, in her arms.

Davinder regarded her oddly. Could she not have found something more practical and sturdy to pack her items in? He must have expected a more modern wife when he came to America. But she had been conceived in India—that was the difference. Her habits and temperament were formed by the shape of another continent, according to my mother. Neelam was holding that orange bundle of clothing as if she were waiting to catch a black-sooted train among the throngs with their bundles, in a faraway Eastern land.

Despite my sister's protests over his fussing, Davinder eased her into the car carefully. The car window reflected a silvery triangle of light, and I could barely make out Neelam's wrist, her hand above it waving good-bye, and the orange bundle on her lap that one day should have been an infant swathed in blankets. My mother lifted a corner of her chuni to her mouth, as she did instinctively when she felt sorrow or shame. As the car turned from the driveway onto Fremont Road, she retreated indoors, where her mourning would unleash in a less private fashion. She was too distraught to ask me about the car keys clutched in my hand, etching grooves into my fingers. "The burden of girls, you've no idea," she would whimper over the phone to Aunt Teji, whom she considered thrice-blessed with sons. With boys, one could loosen the rope. My father disappeared into the shop, where a sharp grating noise, as if something was being sheared in half, soon commenced.

Fourteen

"*Chacha?*" *I called from the doorway of* my uncle's home. My eyes adjusted to the thick purple light that floated like a haze through the living room. From his padded green armchair, Uncle Avtar leaned toward the television, watching an episode of *Soul Train*. His fedora lay mournfully forgotten on the floor by his feet. On the screen, a ring of girls gyrated and shimmied in identical pink hot pants, tossing their luxuriant manes of hair. My uncle's head waggled dissonantly to some separate bhangara beat that must have been playing in his head.

I called to him again. "Chacha?"

He leaped from his chair and shut off the television. "There's some good singing on this program. Excellent talent," he said, rubbing his palms lightly on the sides of his trousers. "Where's your aunt? I saw her wandering around just a moment ago with an empty vase."

"In the garden. She's tidying her flower beds. She said you were in here."

"You've come to see your old uncle?" He extended his arms, exaggerating his surprise. "My own sons don't bother with as much. Even Juni is threatening to leave and find a job somewhere.

Who'll run the place when I'm too old?" He ran his hand through his thinning hair, still more black than gray, looking puzzled that he had entered all too soon this unexpected juncture of his life.

"That won't be for a long time yet, Chacha. I can't imagine you giving up your work, sitting around the house doing nothing." It was true. Aunt Teji had often complained that she had never been quite certain what it was her husband did all day; he could never be easily located at an appointed hour. If he had planned to plow the orchards, he would most certainly be at a meeting in town with Mohta Singh. And yet things got done.

Uncle Avtar glanced at the manila folder in my hands. "So, what have you brought for me today?"

I pulled the papers from the envelope and handed the college materials to him, the letter of acceptance and a form requiring a parent's signature. He recognized the emblem at the top of the page. "Oh, acha," he said. He dropped back onto the sofa and perused the pages in an official manner that belied the fact he couldn't read. He paused at certain paragraphs, sensing intuitively their significance, it seemed. "And what do your parents say about this?"

"They've been so preoccupied with Neelam lately, I haven't brought it up." I avoided his careful gaze. Neelam, of course, was not the only reason I couldn't bring it up: I had never truly gotten their permission.

Uncle Avtar returned the papers to me and clasped his hands in his lap as he seemed to search for the words that he realized would disappoint me. The folded pages felt lighter in my fingers, scant, nearly buoyant, with an unfamiliarity that bordered on irrelevance; it was like rereading an old diary entry and wincing a little at the preposterous dreams so vainly expressed there.

"Your sister has a fragile constitution," he said. He leaned back, his gaze fixing on some distant point, as though his mind latched onto, then struggled with a difficult thought. "Her karma is marked somehow. You might think she's unlucky, but it's more than that. I've seen it before in someone I knew once."

"Who was that, Chacha?"

"Someone I knew a long time ago . . ." he replied in a thin and vaporous voice. He watched Aunt Teji's reflection pass in the gilt-framed mirror on the opposite wall, her hand balancing a bundle of clippings from her garden on her head. I wondered how Neelam might have triggered his memory of this person.

"I can't go against your parents' wishes. If it was only a matter of money, I wouldn't hesitate. You and Neelam are like our own daughters to us."

"Would you at least speak to them on my behalf? You could convince them."

Uncle Avtar's eyes looked moist, weary. "Your father will only say I'm meddling. You know how it is with us."

'I think he's always envied you, actually. Your success."

"My success? A hundred and twenty acres is a modest success. I tried to help him out when he and your mother first arrived from India. Oh, she complained. 'Mohinder, dragging me halfway across the world in my condition!' Your aunt took care of her when Neelam was born. 'Zamin lajo—here, take some of my land to start yourselves off,' I told them. I myself benefited from the sympathy of others when I was struggling. But Mohinder . . . perhaps stubbornness and a keen mind go hand in hand. Why do you think he hides under those machines all day?"

I should have known not to expect a simple, direct response from my uncle. For him, one matter was tied inextricably to the next, all of it harkening back like a net cast into the deep waters of the past; the manila envelope I held was merely a fresh knot in its tattered weave. "Chacha," I said, longing to speak to him in a frank manner my own parents would have found disrespectful, "why should any of that hold me back from what I want?"

He tossed his head back, as though the answer lay somewhere above him. "Because your father is a fine man. You should respect his wishes."

"But you must know what it's like . . . to want something different, something everybody tells you you shouldn't want just because—"

"What you want and what you get are often two different things. When I was a young man, sure, I wanted this, I wanted that, but when I got it, it was something completely different from what I had imagined. You have to be careful, Jeeto, not to give up everything for it."

It was hardly the type of motivational speech we heard at school assemblies, packed into the gym on Friday afternoons, listening to some former winning football coach's tiresome metaphors about the game of life, or a local business tycoon drone on about successful habits. Still, my uncle put it differently than my own parents would have; my mother's native hysteria would always prevent that kind of talk. He shrank back on the sofa, his chin drooping toward his chest, as though sinking under the knowledge that he could never entirely believe his own words himself. He *had* given up everything once. He had forsaken his old life to start a fresh one. I would learn, though, that he had done this more than once in his life.

"What if I never get another chance?"

"Jeeto," he said, leaning forward again, "you're too young to believe this is your only chance. You must promise me that you don't believe this."

I heard a car door slam, boots stomping at the front entrance as though fine clouds of dust spritzed into the air around them, then a knock.

My uncle perked at the sound of the door pushing open. "I'm sorry, Jeeto. My two o'clock business appointment has arrived. Why don't you see what your aunt is up to now with her rattling and banging things in the kitchen?"

"Bhaji?" The voice was familiar, resonant, and when the young man waiting behind the sofa removed the cap from his head, I saw that it was Hari. He seemed equally surprised to see me. "Jeeto?" he said, using the more familiar nickname and greeting me with that sidelong glance, the same slow measuring of what he might learn about Neelam by appraising me. My black hair woven in a single plump braid draping forward over my shoulder, the shape of my mouth, my sudden shyness—did these remind him of her in some way? Or was it that I sat motionless on the sofa, momentarily frozen by his appearance, and so it cemented in his imagination that Neelam, too, would be sitting in a similar room not too far away? I had last seen him at his grandfather's funeral only a few weeks earlier, though it seemed like it had been a year.

"Sit, sit," Uncle Avtar insisted. "Drinks for the children," he called out to Aunt Teji. Hari and I smiled with embarrassment. He fumbled with the dusty khaki cap in his hands.

"I forget, Serjit," he said, remembering to be more formal before my uncle, "are you still in high school?"

"I'm graduating next month."

"Thinning fruit yet?" Uncle Avtar asked interrupting. "Your grandfather always insisted on hiring a massive crew. Just gets the job done faster, he always said, but for those of us who needed steady work, getting the job done too fast was a little risky."

"He was an efficient man, wasn't he?" Hari said. "He had the knack of making it all seem effortless."

"I learned a great deal from him."

Aunt Teji brought a tray of glasses filled with soda and ice. She displayed a certain ambivalence around Hari, as if she were holding back the warmth and openness she normally lavished on guests in her home. She asked me to bring in the platter of snacks, which I understood to mean "You shouldn't be sitting in here with menfolk," so I disappeared into the kitchen for the pakoras and spicy mix. Later, I sat in the kitchen with her, scouring mung beans for the small pebbles and stones that naturally got mixed into the sacks. We poured the small olive-colored beans ladle by ladle over the Formica surface, where they scattered like glass beads. She had closed the kitchen door, and the men's voices buffeted against it like rain pelting wood. We picked out the small stones and set them aside, comparing the sizes of our little piles as if they were coins won in a game. I was expected home shortly, but something kept me in Aunt Teji's kitchen. She spotted the manila envelope lying next to my purse on the counter.

"You had something to discuss with your uncle?"

I hesitated. "Just my college papers," I replied. I felt her studying my face as I worked, attempting to read the wants and needs that lay just beneath the surface of my skin, where I had learned too well to conceal them.

"Everything in its time, bhout."

"But now's the time. Why can't I do it now?"

She held a tiny bean in the air, revolving it in her fingers as she carefully inspected it. "These are dull-colored, dry. You pay top prices for inferior quality."

I pushed my chair away from the table, listening to the legs scrape against the linoleum.

"Jeeto . . . you must get your life settled first. Your mother and father have only the best in mind for you."

"The best for me? Do you have any idea what Neelam feels on a daily basis?"

"Acha," she said, though there was no surprise in her voice. "Just a moment." She rose to her feet and left the room briefly.

The door swung open. Hari leaned with one shoulder against the jamb. One side of his denim work shirt hung untucked over his jeans. "How is your sister doing? I heard she was ill."

I looked up from the table splattered with beans. "She just went home today." I scooped the beans into two small hills, cleaned and uncleaned, whisking the piles of stones into their own banished corner while he waited for me to say more. I pondered whether his question was in the worst of taste or simply mandated by the Indian custom of asking after one's welfare. She had lost another baby, first his, now a second, which was sanctioned and blessed by her marriage. Few who were familiar with her circumstances would view this as mere coincidence. Hari seemed conscious of this, of his role in what Uncle Avtar had so facilely identified as Neelam's "karma." Hari shifted uncomfortably on his feet, as if knowing he could never mourn the loss of the one without thinking of the other.

At the sink, I rinsed the small beans to flush away the film of dust coating them, then submerged them in a pot of water to soften them for cooking later. I gathered my purse and the envelope from the kitchen counter, preparing to leave, but I didn't want to go home, where, it seemed, my own parents conspired against me. Hari stepped into the kitchen, gazing up at the open shelves and cabinets, the corners of the room in Uncle Avtar's home that was lately unfamiliar to him.

"I haven't been in this room for years. I remember Uncle was painting it once and he let me help him. Later, I found him painting over the mess I made." His cap was tucked in the back pocket of his trousers, the hasty gesture of youth. Yet an eternal sadness seemed to lurk beneath his broad smile. It didn't seem possible that this was the same young man I had seen so often at the high school, thrashing through its hallways as if the place belonged to him.

I dropped my keys in my purse. "I saw you at your grandfather's funeral."

'I didn't know you came—"

"I came alone. I'm sure you didn't see me—there were so many people. You must miss him."

"Sure. It's rough running the place myself. My heart isn't really in it."

"You could sell it."

He looked at me from across the room as if it were a ridiculous thought. "I could, but I won't, not right away. It would be removing his imprint from the world altogether. He did so many things, but it was the land he always returned to. 'The land is the very fiber of our being,' he used to say to me. 'If I'm lucky, I'll return in my next life as a simple farmer back in the Punjab.' He said that lately, but I never really believed that last part."

And I had never truly believed the part about souls being reborn; the consequences of a life lived simply seemed too enormous. "One can only wonder what happened in her past life," the women often lamented of some unfortunate soul. But in Mohta Singh's case, it was difficult to imagine his life erased for good; he had been simply too imposing a figure in our community. "I was always scared of your grandfather," I said.

"I was scared of him, too." Hari approached the counter, laying his palms flat over the beige-tiled surface as he studied the row of yellow canisters, arranged from large to small and painted with bright clusters of plums and grapes. "He gave me everything I wanted, in a way. Nice clothes, a car. He was generous like that. Maybe I was just too stupid to want the things that matter." He shrugged, as if none of it was important now.

But it was, still; I could see it in the slope of his shoulders. If I had leaned over and stretched my arm, I could have touched him. We were standing that close. "I wish . . . I wish it was you who had married Neelam." The words bubbled from my mouth even as I felt them betraying Davinder, whom I adored. I heard the firm fall of Aunt Teji's footsteps approaching down the hallway and my eyes locked briefly with Hari's. He was asking something silently of me; I wasn't sure what. "I'll tell Neelam you asked about her."

He nodded.

"What ideas is my husband putting into your head these days?" Aunt Teji asked Hari as she entered the kitchen.

"Just business advice, Auntieji. I've got developers wanting me to sell some acres on Walker Road."

When I left, I turned north instead of south onto Fremont Road, heading into town. I wasn't prepared to face my inconsolable mother so soon after Neelam had gone. I raced toward the center of town, the very place I wanted to escape from. Those who went away often returned to it chastened, as Hari had; others died and the town stirred, buzzed for those brief moments, then lapsed once again into its former torpid state. Not even Hari could break from its implacable hold. How could I hope to? The college forms lay unsigned on the passenger seat. It was only my life; it was only *this* life, someone would say. The outlines of trees and buildings blurred, merging into a single shapeless mass. The best for me? What was that? A portrait of the future crystallized in my mind. I imagined the faceless man, the husband, the doctor they might agree to, whose lean brown hands would reach for patient after patient, but how would they reach for me?

I drove past Surinder's house near the edge of town. The drapes were drawn and the driveway empty of cars. I steered the car through the oppressive silence, the air that was drowsy and thick with the first heat of the year. In town, old blue-and-yellow banners announcing the annual Springfest were stretched from lampposts above the main streets and flapped in the mild breeze. I turned onto Rand and drove past India Bazaar, and when I didn't see Pritam's old Ford Galaxy, I circled around once again.

The entire block along Rand was gorged with cars and pickup trucks, cluttering the parking spaces for the dry cleaner's and shoe-repair shop that flanked India Bazaar. In the lot behind the shop, I spotted the taillights of Rachan Kaur's red Buick lighting up and the car jerking back slowly with several hard punches of the brake. I parked and remained in the car for several minutes. I had neither seen nor heard from Pritam since the picnic. The sickening feeling I had in the bus that afternoon—*Pritam and Surinder*—rose in my throat. Why had I come? It was what my uncle couldn't bear to say to me earlier, something I had seen in Hari's face. I didn't know where else to go, so I had come to see Pritam.

By the back entrance, I said "Sat Sri Akal" to a lady friend of my mother as she negotiated an armful of packages along with a trail of small children lagging behind her. Pritam emerged with a glowering Sher Singh shuffling behind in his cracked leather juttis. The wheels of the dolly creaked from the strain of the old man's exorbitant order, as if mimicking his complaining tone. Pritam lifted his eyes, stiffening when he saw me, but he pushed on, propelled by the momentum of his tedious work and Sher Singh's tirade. I waited by the door as he unloaded the sacks of flour and beans into the bed of a pickup truck. It was a mistake to have come, I told myself. I should've stayed away. Sher Singh widened his stance and crossed his arms in a final bid to convince his captive audience of this latest and most egregious of injustices.

The sun had fallen behind the two-story office building beyond the cramped parking area. Succulent branches of Boston ivy traced the back wall of the building, the pointed leaves suspended like pawprints covering the stone. A sign reading THE LAW OFFICES OF HOLT, FLEMING AND BURKE in brass letters hung over a rear door. It occurred to me that it was the same afternoon that Neelam had left, the orange bundle nestled in her lap, the same day that Uncle Avtar had advised me to abandon, for now, my plans for Berkeley, and that I had seen Hari twirling a dusty khaki cap in his fingers as if it were a toy, not the indelible reminder of what his future would be.

Sher Singh's pickup sped away, leaving in its wake Pritam clutching the red dolly. We walked together to my car.

"Did you need something?" he asked.

"I was just visiting my Uncle Avtar and—" I stepped toward him. "I wanted to come by and say hello."

He shoved his hands in the pockets of his jeans and looked off down the street. Perhaps he was awaiting my tirade.

"I was talking with my uncle. . . . It looks like I won't be going away to school after all. Not just yet."

"I'm sorry." He sounded disappointed, or, worse perhaps, indifferent to my change of plans. "I don't remember you giving up on things so easily."

"I'm not giving up," I replied hotly. "Just postponing things." I leaned back against the car, feeling suddenly sapped by a tumultuous week. "What about you?"

He gestured toward the faded white exterior of his mother's shop, where metal trash bins along the back wall huddled in a failed kind of promise. "I won't need a college degree to run this place. And I can pick up a GED anytime." He had already taken his designated place in his mother's plan for him a bit earlier than expected. He'd spend his days haggling over the phone with unreliable distributors, listening to rude customers rant about the rising price of wheat. Out of a characteristic and stubborn pride, he might even argue it was for the best.

It was nearly dark and I shivered a little in the warm, still air. I wanted to go but managed only to shift the weight on my feet. Pritam pushed a messy clump of hair off his forehead. There. It was Pritam still, I reassured myself. Pritam, with the same slouchy, casual manner, despite what he might be feeling inside. Maybe there was nothing more we could say to each other right then. But I had known him too long to simply walk away.

The car shifted slightly when he leaned back against the trunk next to me. He studied the dolly, the red metal handgrips idly awaiting his grasp, the next sack of rice or wheat flour. Then, as if revolted by its presence, he turned away. It only reminded him, it seemed, of what lay ahead—weeks, months, years perhaps, toiling in the store. The crude embodiment of his destiny. Like Hari's khaki cap.

"I'm thinking of getting out of town myself for a while," he said, facing me. "Helping my uncle on his ranch."

"So, now you're going and I'm the one staying." I paused to consider the sudden change of fortunes. I would have said anything at that moment to get him to stay. "What happened with Surinder . . . it wasn't really anybody's fault. How long will you be gone?"

He turned to me, his steely glance searching my face, his mouth moving for an instant. I knew what he wanted to say: There were no simple answers for anything.

The rear screen door of the shop snapped open and shut. Charan Kaur, draped in a pale gray shawl, called out in the darkness. "Customers are waiting, Preet." She swooped toward us, her shawl spreading around her like the wings of a barn owl.

"Jeeto, I didn't see you in the store. Did your mother send you for something?"

I shook my head. Her polite tone carried the veiled warning that she would do anything to spare her son, her family, from further humiliation. Had she written the letter to India on my mother's behalf? Aja, bhout, she said, taking Pritam's arm and pulling him away.

Uncle Avtar

She was exactly as he had remembered her. On a walk along the river road at dusk, she clasped her hands behind her back, her flared skirt rolling around her calves with each step. A dark boiled-wool jacket covered the plain white waitress blouse she wore each day at the café. Her hair was pinned away from her face and fell to her shoulders in the back, allowing him an unfettered view of her face—her eyes black in the fading light, her small, stubborn chin. It had been only a week since his last visit, but he knew things could change utterly in that space of time.

The lights of the little town receded behind them. To the east of the riverbank, the valley spread away, dotted with lights and dark clusters of homes, the land carved into rectangles of fields and orchards. They walked on the river side of the road, following the gentle bends and curves of the glassy strip of water below them. He pulled her well off the shoulder of the road each time a car passed.

"What did you tell your mother?" Avtar asked Olivia.

"That I had a splitting headache from all the overtime I've been doing lately." An exaggerated frown faded as she broke into a smile.

"She let you go for a headache? She's a kind woman."

"We're open seven days a week. There's nothing kind about that."

"What would she say if she knew?"

Olivia stopped. "She wouldn't like it. I'm the oldest. She never leaves that kitchen, but she seems to know exactly where I am, what I'm doing all the time."

"Your father?"

"He goes back to Mexico this time every year. He has to be there for the Christmas season. We don't celebrate it properly here, he says."

"A religious man."

Olivia burst into laughter. "That's not what I meant by celebrating."

"He doesn't miss his family?"

"He has family in Sonora—brothers, sisters, uncles. And he comes back in February, sometimes March. My mother says she can't complain because he comes back to her every year." Olivia shrugged, as if she had completed some simple calculation whose result didn't quite add up. "Besides, she's so busy herself. The restaurant was always her dream. He gets bored with it."

"What about you?" he asked.

"I don't know. Nobody ever asks. Somehow, everyone expects that I'll follow my mother's path. Some days she comes home rubbing her feet and she tells me, 'Soon you'll have to put away your fancy dresses and take over at the restaurant.' But I have my own dreams. I want to go places, see something besides water and mud before I settle down with some Mexican boy who has to run off to Mexico for Christmas every year."

A heat rose in Olivia's face. The two resumed walking, Avtar watching as the dull tips of his loafers revealed themselves with each step. "I've seen some of the world. It's big and . . . strange."

He felt like an old man telling dreadful old tales; he was grasping for words, trying to extinguish the thought of the Mexican boy. "I met a man in Jalandhar once—this is a town near my village—who could balance all his weight on his small finger." Avtar wiggled his pinkie to clarify. "Insisted it is all in one's mind."

"No!" Olivia gasped in amazement, then puckered her face. "But I want to see those kind of real places. This is a place for drifters. People pass through and you never see them again."

Better than his village, Avtar thought, where time passed only if you wrung it, like drops of water from a barely damp cloth.

"What about you?" Olivia asked. "When the work is finished here, where will you go?"

Avtar didn't reply. It seemed an impossibly absurd question. What about him? All the plans . . . he seemed sure of nothing now. What could he say to her? How did one say all those things? Avtar had not even the words in English to tell her.

She took his arm and guided him across the road to a narrow lane that led down the bank. "My house," she said, pointing to a small white cottage ahead, whose porch and lace-curtained windows were lighted. A low lattice fence edged the porch and a row of pillars seemed to groan under the weight of its roof. The porch light crept across a patch of lawn and illuminated the soft mounded shapes of low shrubs, the winter-bare scaffolds of a pair of small trees that framed the house. Despite small signs of disrepair, the place struck Avtar as some exquisite confection, freshly garnished and set before him.

"We'd better stop here. My aunt Regina is home." Olivia rubbed the cold from her hands, and Avtar took them into his own and held them to warm them. "Will you be back next Saturday?" she asked.

"Tomorrow."

"No," she laughed. "Saturday."

He watched her walk off, a slender silhouette lighting up as she reached the porch, then darted up the steps. She turned back to look because she knew he would still be standing there.

He wanted to buy her a gift. He counted the box of bills under his bed, a total of ninety-seven dollars he had managed to save—a fortune by his standards. He placed a twenty in his pocket Monday morning. At the general store in Locke after his shift, a female storekeeper followed him closely as he eyed shelves full of delicate porcelain ware and jade figurines. He passed through aisles of hardware and bolts of cloth and dried goods and returned to a glass case displaying necklaces. "How much?" he asked the woman, pointing to an oval jade pendant suspended on a gold chain.

"Seven dollar," she replied. "Eighteen-carat gold, best jade," the woman explained when she saw the look of dismay on Avtar's face.

She didn't understand that he wanted to spend a little more, buy Olivia something special, something she would be proud to wear. She unlocked the case and retrieved the necklace. Gliding her fingers over the chain, she repeated, "Eighteen-carat gold."

Avtar lifted the pendant closer. It was a smooth, translucent cream-colored stone with a delicate openwork carving of two fish leaping over water and lotus plants. Curved along the top of the oval piece were two miniature dragons.

"Protection," said the woman. "Dragon, jade protection."

A bright display of silk fans, spread like a peacock's feathers, caught his eye as he pulled the bills from his wallet. Green, violet, ivory, red . . . they were all painted with the same eye for fine detail as the jade carving. He selected the scarlet one, opening and closing it repeatedly to watch as a tree spread its wide flowering branches. Behind the counter, the woman smiled the patient smile she must have had for all the fools like him who came into her store with the same desperate look in their eyes. He placed the small package in an inside pocket of his coat, thanked her, and left.

He wandered down the street to the gambling hall, wincing at the smoky haze suspended over the tables at the Dai Loy. Leandro hunched over his tiles at one of the domino tables. Avtar tapped on his shoulder and he reeled around in surprise, as if roused from a deep slumber.

"Avtar! Ready to try your luck again, eh? I knew you would be." Leandro straightened his carriage, lifting his shoulders as though they were tremendous weights uncomfortably burdening his torso.

"I had a little shopping to do." Avtar pulled up an empty chair and prepared for the ribbing he knew he was in for. "And, I like to earn my money the honest way."

Leandro bunched up in a wheeze-cough that erupted seconds later in volcanic laughter. His eyes squeezed into teary slivers as he attempted to speak. "You didn't complain too much when you had that winning lottery ticket. Got dressed up awfully nice to go see Olivia."

Avtar felt his face reddening; he loathed the seeming transparency of his barest emotions. Leandro had teased him Saturday night when he had returned to the bunkhouse early in the evening. Leandro's insinuations had struck him as distasteful, squalid at the time, and he had ignored his roommate and gone promptly to bed. I can be so serious, Avtar thought, silently chastising himself. Too serious! Leandro was another kind, of course, who assiduously avoided the kind of entanglement Avtar was headed for. He liked the company of women simply for a good time, without the emotion-wrenching agony that Avtar brought into it.

But Leandro was a decent sort who could recognize when a change of tone was in order. "Say, the foreman came by this morning," he said. "Wanted to know why you haven't cleared out of your bunk yet."

Avtar felt his spine stiffen. "What did you tell him?"

"I told him you need a few more days. You're looking for work. Asshole barged in wearing one of those ten-gallon hats. He said, 'If he don't work for Hayes and Company, he got no business bunkin' in here.'" Leandro exaggerated the vowels, mimicking the white foreman's speech.

The banker at the domino table seemed to scold Leandro in his native Zhongshan dialect.

"I'm out," Leandro replied, pushing his tiles away and rising to his feet.

Outside, the street was deserted. Only the muffled shrieks and screams of children playing indoor games came from the surrounding houses and apartments. The two men huddled under an awning, but Avtar felt his skin perspiring despite the icy breeze.

"What do I do?" he asked.

"Don't worry about it. They don't need those beds during the winter. Strip your bed every morning and throw your stuff under mine. They'll never know the difference. It's not like we pay rent for that shithole." He noticed Avtar blinking and shuffling his feet. "Look, no one's going to say anything. You worry about everything too much, Avtar. How you gonna get anywhere with that girl if you're worrying all the time?"

Leandro was right; Avtar decided to abandon the topic. "How much you win today?"

Leandro pretended not to hear him right away. He looked down the empty street as if awaiting something, someone to magically appear and absorb his attention once again. "I lost five. I came in with a ten, but that son of a bitch on the fan-tan table . . ."

"My old boss, Mr. Bingham, he might have extra work for me."

"What do you need extra work for? You're not gonna go get rich on me, are you? Hindus like you, you'll work day and night if you have to." Leandro shook his head. "Takes a lot of years of hard work to do it that way."

"Your way is better?" Avtar asked, gesturing to the Dai Loy's drab facade.

Leandro shrugged. "Don't look at me for answers. I've lived here all my life and all I got is a mother in Stockton who screams at me for never coming home." Leandro flipped his coat collar up. "You staying around?"

Avtar shook his head. "Too cold."

"Yeah. I know a place that'll keep me real warm."

Something changed in my uncle. He carried the trunks and bags of passengers on and off the boats, loaded and unloaded crates of essential goods, as his job required. He listened to the whistle of the train as it coasted into the nearby station and knew that was change, too. That the days of the boats steaming into the dock were numbered; one day they would no longer come at all. The trucks that lumbered down the river road would be replaced by larger semis routing around the levees and rivers on faster, wider highways. He stepped along the dock each day, recognizing the grain of each plank he set his foot on, though nothing felt permanent.

Perhaps my uncle would have explained it to me this way: It was simply that the stakes had changed. That in the evenings, reclining on his bunk for well-deserved rest, he no longer pulled the letters from his brother Lal from their box first. That he reached instead for the jade pendant he had slipped beneath his savings for safekeeping. He ran his fingers over its smooth edges, the scalloped rim along the top where the dragons curled their long tails. He studied the pair of fish, cut in fine relief to capture their motion as they sailed over the waves, and the serenity of the lotus blossoms. He swirled the stone in the bland overhead light, watching its brilliant opalescence reveal itself. And he rehearsed in his mind how he would present his small gift to Olivia.

Yes, the stakes had changed. It was no longer him setting off alone, impulsively, seeking adventure on the other side of the world. He had crossed the ocean, but it was only now that he felt his own world—the life of his mind and heart—expand anew. In the most rudimentary ways, he protected this new world. He stripped the sheets, blanket, and pillow from his bed each morning, stuffing them into a wooden box beneath Leandro's bed. He tucked his other belongings into a shallow locked trunk he had purchased in the general store, also stowed among Leandro's things under his bed. This ritual and the bare mattress he left behind each morning reminded him of the more permanent station he sought, that he would fight for each living day.

When he left the camp each morning, he greeted the other handful of men who had stayed on through the winter season with short, curt nods, neither friendly nor unfriendly. Each of them relied on an implicit trust. The foreman visited the camp infrequently this time of year and always with a degree of barely restrained contempt for the laborers. It was the Christmas season as well, and the attention of the Christian community was focused elsewhere.

Christmas trees twinkled with colored lights in the windows of Christian homes. Walking along the levee road, Avtar would count the windows and peer into their shadows and light and imagine the lives of those who only occasionally bothered to look out of them. He noted the paved driveways curving through verdant lawns, the dark green fringe of boxwood etching a soft line along their borders like a pattern stitched into a piece of fine cloth. An impermeable sense of order. That is what caused him to gaze so indiscreetly at these private estates. Some of the homes had massive brick chimneys, and he would smell the ashes from the simple fire ring in the dirt floor of his home in the Punjab. And he always gazed north before heading back to the camp. If he continued his solitary trek in that direction, he would reach Olivia's place, but that would take the better part of an afternoon.

Walking along the road one day, he was startled by a car that slowed as it passed him, a mud brown Chrysler with two-tone wood-paneled sides and white sidewalls and silver hubcaps polished like round mirrors. The car stopped ahead of him and a young mustached fellow popped his head out the open passenger window. The young man spoke in Punjabi. "Need a ride somewhere?"

He was unmistakably a Sikh, Avtar noted as he trotted up to the car. "I'm just going up the road." He struggled to locate the rear door handle, fumbled with it a moment before he yanked it and felt the interior latch release.

"Finding steady work in the river district?" In the front seat, another man, the driver, turned to face him fully for the first time. Avtar noted his calm demeanor, the rather delicate form of his face, but there was something focused, sharp as a razor in the man's gaze.

"So far, I've been lucky."

"How long have you been in the country?"

"Almost eight months."

The driver smiled, revealing a set of perfectly aligned teeth such as Avtar had seen only among certain astonishingly beautiful women in his native country. "You remember every day, every week the first years you are here. I did. Because I was afraid I would wake up one day in that godforsaken village back home. Fear is a powerful motivator." The man extended his hand to Avtar. "I am Mohta Singh."

"Avtar Rai."

A car passed on their left, a stream of obscenities unfurling from its windows. Only then did Avtar notice that the Chrysler had stopped in the middle of the road, its engine still idling in a low rumble. Mohta Singh made no sign that he felt obligated to move.

"I started working in this same area when I first came," he continued. "Picking pears. A view of the world from atop a ladder. Not such a bad view," he said, waggling a finger. "But I needed a better view, like the one the boss had from his Packard. He never even got out of his car when he came into the orchards. Chased the foreman out every time to check on us. Can you imagine running a place like that?"

At this stage of his life, Avtar could not imagine running much of anything other than the winch down at the dock, or the coin machines that ejected fortunes printed on slips of paper that he would save for Leandro to read to him. He felt the two men studying him carefully. "You have to get a little dust in your teeth once in awhile to remind yourself that your own ashes will be grit one day."

Mohta Singh's expression registered surprise. Avtar bristled at his own idiocy. Where had he come up with that bit of bogus wisdom? He was trying too hard to please the man. He sounded like the old pandit in his village, who, crippled by a fading memory, grasped ever harder for the truths that had eluded him in his prime.

Mohta Singh smiled again, in some forgiving way, Avtar wanted to believe. He shifted gears and pointed the car's long, rounded snout, which reminded Avtar of a Canadian moose he had seen in a photograph, ahead on the road. The sunlight streamed through the windshield. Mohta Singh's head swiveled slowly from one side to the other, from the view of the river to the rows of trees, then back to the river, as though he might miss something. The car crept along at a sluggish pace. It made Avtar think there was something extraordinarily careful about this man.

"This area has settled down quite a bit from when I lived here. No, it's not like it was in those days! Big steamboats coming through with people waving from the balconies. I still like to drive through when I get a chance. There's always a pleasant breeze coming off the water."

"We're on our way to the gurdwara in Stockton," the mustached passenger said, steering the conversation to more practical matters. "Have you been?"

'No."

"You must go! Our people come from all around. It's best to be around your own kind."

"Where are you traveling from?" Avtar asked.

"Oak Grove," the younger passenger replied. "You should go there, be with your own people. Too many bad influences around here."

They approached the gravel road leading down to the camp. The rows of square gray bunkhouses were visible through the bare trees. "Up ahead, there," Avtar said, pointing.

Mohta Singh stopped the car, once again in the middle of the road. "Don't pester the boy, Sohan. All Punjabis around here eventually find their way to Oak Grove." He turned to Avtar. "What kind of work are you doing this time of year?"

"I'm working on one of the docks. Loading, unloading, fixing boats. It's not so bad. On the river, one feels the constant movement, as if the water is carrying you someplace."

"You like the boats? I always wanted to ride the *Delta Queen* into San Francisco, but you know, it's not allowed for us. They stuff you below like a bunch of chickens. I decided if I had my own car, no one could tell me where I could or couldn't go."

"I appreciate the ride. I'll see you one day at the gurdwara."

As Avtar exited the car, Mohta Singh motioned to him with his hand. "Look for me if you need work sometime."

Avtar waved and started down the gravel road, but he stopped to watch the car accelerate slowly away. A man in no apparent hurry, who made no apologies for what was rightfully his. This is what struck Avtar about his first meeting with Mohta Singh.

The meeting unsettled him. He had whistled on his short walk into the camp after Mohta Singh left him on the road. His tongue had been untied for the first time in months. The words—the few he had uttered—had flowed with a natural ease. He felt them welling up in him now, swarming in his mouth and throat like a school of fish pooling before a dam. He had been among brothers; yes, brothers could annoy, become quarrelsome, but they remained brothers. He felt their absence keenly as soon as he pushed open the door, to find his bare bunk swaddled in sunlight.

At the counter at Lupe's restaurant, Avtar climbed onto a red bar stool and removed his wool coat and fedora and laid them on the seat next to him. The crowd was light for a Saturday, the day all the farmhands poured into the place to exchange the week's news and linger over a hearty stew or roast. Perhaps Olivia would be relieved of her duties early. He spotted the chicken-pot-pie waitress across the room, pulling the pencil clenched in her teeth to take an order. He hadn't noticed it before, but she resembled Olivia, not in manner, but in some intangible way he couldn't quite identify.

She appeared a moment later on the other side of the counter. She had already set a mug before him and, with the other hand, begun to tilt the pot before she asked, "Coffee?"

"Yes."

She slapped a menu on the counter and was off. Avtar blinked, as if she might have been merely an apparition. There was no sign of Olivia in the restaurant area. He looked over the menu, forgetting, as he often did, that he couldn't read it. He could smell the cinnamon and chili powder aroma of the restaurant from a quarter mile up the road, but his appetite vanished as he realized he might have made the journey in vain.

The waitress reappeared, heaving a crate of milk bottles onto the counter. Avtar watched as she pulled the bottles from the crate and placed them in the small refrigerator behind the counter, her back to him. Her white apron strings sagged in a loose bow at the back of her waist.

"What is your name?" Avtar asked when she turned around again.

"Regina."

The aunt! She was different from the spinsterish woman Avtar had envisioned when Olivia had spoken her name outside her house. Younger, with the bruised quality of someone to whom certain things might have happened too early. The dark bangs on her forehead bounced as she wiped the little puddles of condensation on the counter with a towel.

"Where is Olivia?"

Regina paused long enough from her duties to appraise her customer carefully. "She's home sick. She had a hundred and one fever this morning. Lupe gave her the day off."

Noticing his crestfallen look, she lifted her brow with amusement. She must be accustomed to young men inquiring about her niece, Avtar thought. He wasn't the only fool who had sat at that counter hoping Olivia would appear bearing a white coffee mug, a cup of cream, and the mere miracle of her presence.

"She's a good girl. You be careful with her." Regina held the pot menacingly between them, and Avtar thought she might pour the steamy liquid over his head.

The floorboards creaked as she huffed off to attend to new customers. He swallowed a sip of coffee, left some change on the counter, and walked out of the restaurant. He paused in the parking lot, feeling the shape of the jade pendant in his coat pocket. His fingers worked the piece of cloth he had wrapped it in. He could make out the tiny ridges in the jade, reading the story carved into the stone like a blind man reading braille. The line of gray clouds that had chased him the entire two-and-a-half-hour walk to Lupe's now blanketed the sky. Smoky tendrils unfurled from the low, dark ceiling, threatening to unleash its moisture. Pearson had warned of a storm all week, a prediction brought on by a delicate pressure building in his skull. Howard called him a walking weather station. Avtar would learn yet to trust the man's peculiar instincts.

He looked across the river at the gray-and-black patchwork of sky and landscape. He could head south along the road back to the camp, a thought more dismal to him now than the darkening sky. Or he could go north. For a few moments, he stood along the side of the road like a spider suspended along a taut web. Then he turned north. The rain would catch him before he reached Olivia's. It began to fall in long needlelike slivers and soon the river, the trees, the road were lost beneath a silvery curtain of water.

The water collected like a small moat in the brim of his hat. Several times, he tipped it to drain the water off. His feet swam in a deepening current that swirled wildly over the road before it spilled over the levee's banks. He would look like a drowned mongoose before he finally reached her.

The small lane that led down to Olivia's house was distinguishable to Avtar only by the large sycamore leaning over it. He sprinted down its slope toward the white cottage two hundred yards beyond. On the porch, he struggled from the wool coat, which was soaked through, and ran his hands over his head to flatten his mussed hair. He knew why he had come. When he didn't see her all week, he thought she would forget him. Their brief visits, he recognized, were no more than a few lines etched in the sand, which a stiff breeze might thoughtlessly blow over and erase in the interim. Then Olivia would not know where to look for him. He came each week to draw new lines in the sand.

A light went on in the house after he knocked, and he watched as a figure moved behind the lace curtain. Olivia cracked the door open, then flung it wide, tugging at Avtar's wrist to pull him inside. She was draped in a blue blanket, which made her skin look pale and her eyes dull and feverish. Before he could regret his selfish impulse to see her, she threw her arms around his shoulders. He held her at her waist and felt the fever's heat warm his own skin. He eased her onto the sofa nearby and pulled the blanket tight around her, then smoothed the damp, matted strands of dark hair away from her face. She slept a few moments, long moments, while Avtar listened as her short, shallow breaths escaped her slightly parted lips. A black iron woodstove crackled at one end of the room. The corners were anchored with heavy cabinets fashioned from thick wooden planks in the Mexican style. Behind the brown velvet sofa Olivia lay on, photographs framed in rich wood were scattered over the wall, women mostly, young and old alike with the same unflinching gaze, a dozen permutations of Olivia. A door opened onto the darkened kitchen, where a bowl of fruit sat undisturbed atop the Formica table. He absorbed all of the room's details—the smell of the fire smoldering nearby, the polished gleam of the wood floor, the blue oval braided rug beneath his feet—as though he knew then it would be the only time he would be welcomed in her home.

Olivia's eyes fluttered before they fixed on him. She seemed not to recognize him in those first seconds. What would that day be like, he wondered, when she looked at him and no longer knew who he was? She struggled to sit upright, her hair in lavish disarray about her head.

He brought her a glass of water, tipping it to her mouth so she could have a drink. "I met your aunt Regina. Scary woman."

Olivia smiled weakly. "Don't be afraid of her. My mother says I inherited Aunt Regina's temper and her fine bone structure. Not a good combination."

"She watches out for you. That's good."

"Yes. No one else is allowed to make the mistakes she has. She's made enough for the whole world, you see. So she has to look out for the whole world."

The talking weakened her once again and she rested her head on his shoulder, her body sinking firmly against his. He felt her breathing slow, then quicken again. The blanket had fallen away from her shoulders and the ribbon tie at the neck of her night-gown had loosened. Sitting there with Olivia at his side, Avtar felt an uneasiness creep through him. It shouldn't happen like this. She was ill, with fever. He should leave. Leave, he told himself, but not a single muscle in his body obeyed his thoughts. He felt himself suffocating from the clammy scent of her skin. He could hear the rainwater pouring off the porch roof, a crashing, musical sound. Olivia stirred next to him, making the small murmurs of a person waking. Her head lolled about her neck, then fell back against the sofa. She clung to him yet with her hands on his arm. Avtar pulled the pendant from his pocket.

"What! For me?"

He slipped the gold chain around her neck and watched the pendant fall against her throat. "Two fish jumping," she said as she lifted the cream-colored stone and traced her finger over the carving.

"And dragons here . . . see? For protection."

"Protection from what? You?"

"No. Aunt Regina."

Olivia pulled the blanket down around her waist; she gathered and twisted her hair and then her hands fell in her lap. The warm gold tint of her skin had returned and Avtar could hardly bear to look at her. He bent down and kissed her parched lips lightly at first, then deeply before they briefly pulled apart. The sweet, slightly ill taste of her mouth was as familiar to him as a drink of water. Olivia looked into his eyes. She put her hands on his shoulders and pulled him down against the brown velvet, where he found her mouth, kissed her neck and her breasts again and again.

The rain continued. The river rose several feet by midweek. The water turned muddy gray and churned in new, unfamiliar currents. Pearson, donned from head to foot in a black rubber rain suit, scurried over the dock, checking the moorings and scoring the fluctuating water level each day into a wooden post with a Swiss knife. The workers, Avtar, Howard, and another man, whose name was Brooks, shuffled about in the cramped boathouse, waiting for the daily boats to arrive or the weather to clear or directions from Pearson to go home. They set about cleaning the interior, restacking the shelves of bait and hooks and empty gasoline cans and dried food. The life vests and tubes were rehung on large hooks along the wall and the floor was swept and mopped. Even the latrine received a vigorous scrubbing. From the window, Avtar watched the water swell and cut along the shrinking banks. When would it let up? The skies were charcoal even at midday and the radio had reported that it was snowing heavily in the Sierra Nevada.

Even Pearson retreated from the storm at last, flinging water from himself in the doorway like a dog after a swim. "Everything's canceled today, boys. Go on home. Be lucky if the whole damn dock doesn't wash away."

Howard clung to the mop handle as Pearson disappeared into the back room, muttering to himself. A moment later, Avtar heard the radio crackling. He tossed the rag he had been using on the shelves into a bucket.

"Looks like we've got ourselves another long weekend," Howard said. He set the mop aside and fled outdoors into the rain, with Brooks behind him.

Avtar surveyed the quarters, seeking another task that might occupy his time. Perhaps he could clean the tools in the toolshed, but the mechanic guarded them as though they were bricks of gold. Those two, Howard and Brooks, had run off as if they were making a prison break.

"You still here?" Pearson looked agitated moments later as he bolted from the back room. "Go on home. When the weather breaks, we'll be back in business." He lighted a pipe, his cheeks hollowing as he sucked in his first draft of smoke.

"When?"

"I'm not a goddamn weather station. When the rain stops, you show up."

Avtar scrambled up the ramp to the road. At the camp, he pushed the bunkhouse door open, to find Leandro's bare buttocks thrusting against the young woman who lay sprawled on the mattress beneath him. The woman called out as she pulled a sheet over her hips. Her breasts swayed and shifted, then settled like plums on her small frame. Avtar turned away, the bounce of her upturned foot in the air and the soft dip of its arch still in his mind as he closed the door behind him.

Under the overhang in front of Zhang's place, he stomped the water from his boots and cursed the rain and Leandro. Behind him, the screen door creaked open and Zhang motioned him inside. It smelled of herbs and onions, but the room was spotless. Zhang ladled some soup from a kettle and set a bowl on the table for Avtar. Bits of mushroom and scallion drifted in the clear broth and Avtar sipped heartily from it. Zhang stroked his fine wispy beard as he observed his visitor. The silence was interrupted with his frequent bursts of gravelly laughter. Then he balled his fist and made a repeated pushing motion, pointing to the bunkhouse across the way where Leandro lay with the girl.

A woman's voice awoke him the following morning; Avtar thought he heard it in a dream, but when his eyes fully focused on the ceiling above and the dream of his village subsided, he heard the voice again, muffled as it traveled through the damp air. A small circle of men gathered around the dark blue sedan that was parked among the bunkhouses some thirty yards away. Avtar pulled on his boots and sprinted outside toward the car. His instincts were correct. It was Olivia, her head poking from the passenger's window; he did not recognize the woman in the driver's seat.

"There he is!" Olivia stepped out of the car, creating a considerable stir among the men. "I was asking them which one is your place."

Avtar quickly pulled her aside. "You shouldn't come here."

"But you live here."

"It's not a place for a woman to be."

Olivia thrust her chin out defiantly. "I've lived around here all my life. You don't think I've seen a camp before? Which one is yours?"

The men around the car began to mumble and gesture. Avtar firmly took her arm and led her toward the bunkhouse.

"Come on out, Pilar," Olivia called to the other young woman in the car.

A round of whistles sounded as Pilar sloshed over the muddy grounds behind Avtar and Olivia, one hand holding down the maroon half hat bouncing on her head. Inside, Olivia pulled her coat tighter over her black-and-white polka-dot dress. "Chilly in here."

He knew she wouldn't say what she was thinking: that the man who had visited her in her home lived himself in little more than a shack. He hadn't even a sheet to cover the stained mattress. Pilar remained on the steps to the door, unwilling to venture farther.

"You shouldn't come to this place," Avtar repeated, feeling desperately ashamed. He thought of the scene the day before with Leandro and that girl, who looked younger than Olivia by a few years.

"My friend Pilar and I made a plan and we wanted to invite you along." She seemed to be making a concerted effort not to look too carefully about the place, at the floorboards rotted by a leak in the ceiling or the rusted sink. "She has her family's car for the day and we're driving up to Sacramento."

"How did you find me?"

"I asked around . . . for that handsome young Hindu man." She tugged lightly at the lapels of his coat. A single look, a gesture from Olivia. He had never felt so completely commanded by the whims of another.

"And you feel better?"

"Wonderful," she said, shutting her eyes for a long second.

He washed and changed and the three of them crowded into the front seat of the car. The rain had ceased early in the morning and the trees and eaves still dripped with moisture. The water still churned in the river. Like hogs in a chute. Howard had explained the expression to him once. If the storm subsided over the region as predicted, the river would crest in the next twenty-four hours or so. Despite its threat (and Pilar's questionable driving skills), Avtar was overcome by a sense of familiarity, of belonging, at last, to a place. He knew the road stubbornly traced the path of the river and how the water's capricious, meandering way became its own. It was the same route he had taken with Leandro weeks ago, that Sunday when he had first seen Olivia at the restaurant. The road arced toward the west as they approached Courtland. A dozen cars packed the small lot in front of Lupe's. "Good business today," Avtar said. "Maybe we should leave Olivia here to help her mother." Pilar laughed and Olivia pushed his arm, then kept hold of it for the remainder of the trip. They continued north through Clarksburg and Freeport and reached West Sacramento late in the morning. They crossed the Tower Bridge over the Sacramento River into the small, bustling city that sprawled along its banks.

At a downtown diner, they sat in an enormous booth with quilted

red upholstery and ordered sandwiches and coffee. Pilar checked
her makeup in a small compact before the meal arrived and again
after their napkins lay scrunched over their empty plates. She had a
spectacular face, not incredibly beautiful, but one that drew attention to its features—large chocolate brown eyes, a longish nose set
on a slender face with the palest skin, every centimeter of it ex-
quisitely powdered and painted.

"We should visit the park. It's very beautiful. I want to show
Avtar," Olivia said. Avtar noticed the jade pendant resting below
the hollow of her throat.

"I came to shop, silly, not gaze at trees," Pilar replied. "You two
can do whatever you want." She unwrapped a stick of gum and
began chewing at a ferocious pace.

"Pilar has Spanish blood, you see. Royal, probably," Olivia teased.

"Royal, sure. That's why my father's a meat butcher in Lodi."

They emerged from the restaurant into the labyrinth of streets
crisscrossing the downtown area. The town still had an untamed quality, despite the multistory stone buildings cropping up all around. Its
legacy as a former gold rush town could still be observed in the eager
stride of its citizens.

I'm off to Hale's, Pilar shouted above the noise and activity on
the street. Men in suits and hats, newspapers tucked under their
arms, congregated with others on the street corners to discuss the
day's news. Women hurried along with Christmas packages, their
heels tapping along the sidewalks, or they shopped in the markets
for the evening's meal. The shop windows lighted up in the late afternoon with their Christmas displays . . . lights and tinsel and Santas
and angels. Olivia stopped in front of a sign in a window advertising
a big-band concert on New Year's Eve. "Look, Avtar. We could go
dancing on New Year's Eve."

Avtar was already imagining himself in a fine suit and patent-
leather shoes, making a clumsy spectacle of himself in one of those

dancing clubs. If they even allowed him inside. Olivia was fair-skinned and one could always bend the rules a little for a pretty girl. He was reluctant to agree; he had heard about brawls breaking out in those sorts of places. But Olivia was gazing at him expectantly. "Sure, we'll go," he said.

The sun broke through the clouds late in the day. The shadows fell in sharp angles over the building facades and the street. The next day he would be at the dock again and Pearson would have a long checklist on his clipboard. But he would not think about work now; he would savor this fine day. They continued walking along K Street, slowing their pace as they neared the Hales Bros. department store to join Pilar. Window displays summoned their attention again and they paused with their fingers entwined to point to lamps and chairs and bicycles propped behind the glass. One window had dozens of faceless, pale mannequin heads sporting hats of all sorts.

"Come. It's my turn to buy you a gift." Olivia pulled him into the hat shop and, after surveying the selection, set a brown felt fedora on his head. "A hat is about how you wear it."

Avtar regarded his reflection in a mirror and comically tipped the hat to one side and thrust out his chest in a ridiculous pose. "I like it," he said.

He wore the hat out of the shop. When they spotted Pilar approaching in the distance, struggling with an armful of packages, they ducked into a small alley next to the hat shop. Olivia pulled the hat low on Avtar's forehead. "Maybe Pilar will not recognize you this way."

"You always hide from your friends?"

"Only if I don't want them to find me."

They moved close against the brick wall. "Avtar." There was something lovely, something painful in the way Olivia said his name. "I wish we could go someplace, be together the way we were at my house." She took his hand in hers and pressed it against her chest. It seemed the wall fell away behind her, the cars, the street, the town, all of it. Only from a very distant place did he hear someone calling Olivia's name.

The hours spent with Olivia were a balm for the work that awaited him at the dock. He revisited their walk along the city streets in his mind as he carried lumber up and down the ramp or slapped creosote on the planks; in his mind, he spoke to her as though she were present beside him on the dock. Sometimes the sound of her voice or her laugh would float over the water and evaporate like a mist before it reached him.

The water level in the river had fallen by a few feet and Pearson was seizing the opportunity to prepare for future catastrophe. "Winter's just begun. That little storm was just a warning sign," he said, his eyelids puffy and drooping on his weary face The threat of disaster always kindled a kind of frenetic passion in him. Pearson tromped over the dock with his crew in tow, assessing some of the damage wrought by the high, fast-moving water. The free-floating dock had survived the storm in relatively decent condition; at least it hadn't broken clear of its mooring and floated four miles down-stream as it had a few years ago. He'd had to hire a tugboat to haul it back. Pearson crouched down, pointing to brackets and connec-tors that had pried loose, bolts that had sheared sections of wood into fine splinters. An end section sat twenty degrees off angle from the remainder of the dock. "Bring it back," Pearson told Avtar.

Avtar set to work removing the damaged beam from the section of dock that had torn free and sat now at a lopsided angle. The connector at one end had twisted and snapped from the cumulative pressure of the water on the wood. The job entailed replacing the beam and fastening a new connector. The most difficult part would be to reposition the dock section to align it with the others before he could secure them tightly together again. He positioned one point of the crowbar under the beam and pulled back as hard as he could. A decayed section of the wood snapped off and fell into the water. On his fourth try, he heard the nails groan as they split from the wood, and one end of the board began to loosen. He set the crowbar down and squeezed and rubbed his fingers. It was a clear, chilly morning and he'd left his gloves at the bunkhouse. He looked up toward the road and noticed a man walking along the top of the bank.

This time, Avtar recognized Bingham readily. He wore chinos and the plaid wool jacket he'd often worn at the packing plant.

"Ray," Bingham called out. He descended the ramp to the dock with long, quick strides and greeted Avtar with a stiff handshake.

"Good to see you, Mr. Bingham."

Bingham watched awhile as Avtar worked the nails from the wood with a claw hammer and wrestled the section of beam away. "We lucked out this time, didn't we? You never know what you'll get with a winter in the delta."

"Good thing it didn't float away down the river. Or no job left for me."

Ray smiled. "If you're still willing, Ray, I could use some extra help New Year's Eve. Some friends of ours have hired a boat they want to take down the river to the Ryde. We could use an extra hand. Wouldn't be much . . . loading some supplies, helping out the pilot, the guests. You interested?"

"I have plans, but . . . how much?"

Bingham squinted up at the sky. "You're a smart man, Ray. That's why I thought of you. I'll pay you a flat rate of fifty dollars for the night. That's pretty good for an evening, wouldn't you say? Oh, and the ladies usually tip pretty well."

Avtar didn't earn that much in a month. An offer like that didn't come around very often. He would speak to Olivia; he would make it up to her some way. She would understand.

The party left the final afternoon of the year from a large marina in Sacramento. The pilot, Harry, was a gruff, jowly man who had already yelled at Avtar to handle the bottles of gin and scotch and champagne more carefully. He shot his head through the cabin door regularly to curse the mechanic or the cleaning crew for not doing their jobs properly. On Harry's orders, Avtar carried the crates of sandwiches and fruit, cakes and juices and tea from the dock and set them on a cabinet below. It was a handsome boat, with polished brass fittings and its mahogany wood varnished to a rich hue. Belowdecks was a spacious cabin with sleeping quarters for four.

Mrs. Bingham made a great commotion as she stepped from the dock onto the deck of the boat, lunging at another man's arms and nearly knocking him aside. They laughed at her clumsiness as though it were a private joke; then Mrs. Bingham lifted the hem of her long sequined gown and drifted toward the cabin. "Oh, hello, Ray," she said as she passed, as though they had been long acquainted.

Avtar counted four couples who had come aboard; men in their thirties wearing pinstripes or tuxedos with bow ties, accompanied by their handsome, slightly younger wives. The women settled comfortably into their seats, ignoring the men as they took turns evaluating the features of the boat in a bid to discover who was the most knowledgeable. A fifth man, whom everyone called Hodges, had the rumpled, uncared-for appearance of a perpetual bachelor and suffered terribly at the hands of the women for arriving alone.

"New Year's Eve without a date, Hodges?" one of them asked.

Mrs. Bingham slid lower in her seat and joined the teasing. "Don't you worry, Meg. There are plenty of *unaccompanied* ladies around this place who always make sure the men enjoy themselves."

"Sallie!" another cried out.

Hodges squeezed his hat like an accordion in his hands and blushed belatedly when he got Mrs. Bingham's meaning. The depth of his embarrassment went unnoticed when the throttle of the engine starting diverted their attention. The boat glided forward on the water, the motion so smooth that Avtar thought it was the banks and the bare trees that had suddenly decided to relocate and float past them upstream.

"What do you think, Ray?" Bingham flexed his shoulders, stretching the fine black wool of his jacket as though it confined him in some way.

"Beautiful boat."

"Twenty-eight-footer. Used to be owned by a senator who filed for bankruptcy just after the war started. Two hundred twenty-five horsepower on her, but we'll take it slow and easy. Shouldn't take more than two hours till we get to the Ryde." He tinkled the ice in his glass. "Come on. Help me serve up some food."

So he had been hired as a waiter; he wasn't sure what he had expected, but it was something other than passing around trays of sandwiches and iced tea. The food and drinks disappeared as quickly as he brought them out. Except for Bingham, the guests rarely took notice of him the entire trip, reaching for one cocktail after the next as they carried on their discussions about business, sports, or wallpaper. At times, Avtar had trouble distinguishing them, except that there were women and men.

The air was brisk outside the cabin, stinging his cheeks and hands. Avtar had thought it risky to rent a boat when the rain had been so unpredictable, making travel of any sort treacherous. Bingham had called it an act of faith, and sure enough, the river reflected a cloudless blue sky. Dead branches and logs strewn along the upper banks were the only evidence of the high water that had scoured the channel only a week ago. Now the water was sluggish and mild, almost apologetically so. Except for the boat's wake, it lapped lethargically along the banks as it made its unceasing journey southward, then west, where it emptied into the bay. And the boat seemed to synchronize its own passage with the motion of the water flowing beneath it. In that moment, Avtar understood why someone like Pearson would forsake everything for a life on the water.

As they passed under the drawbridge at Walnut Grove, he could hear the sharp hum of cars driving over its metal-grate roadway. The river curved in an elbow shape before the water tower and the pink stucco of the hotel came into view. They coasted toward the small dock across the road from the hotel, where several other boats had found a berth.

The passengers filed onto the dock with considerably less energy than when they had boarded. There was talk of dinner and dancing and drinks at the bar, a forced gaiety. With her fur coat pulled up around her neck, Mrs. Bingham looked like a small captive animal.

"Harry," Bingham called to the pilot. "You and Ray keep an eye on the boat."

They climbed one by one up the narrow stairs to the road and soon their voices melded with the cries and laughter of others. Avtar surveyed the deck of the boat, which was littered with cups and saucers and glasses and used napkins. He located a bin below and began collecting the debris left by the partygoers.

Harry emerged from the cabin and stretched his heavy arms and yawned. "Gonna be a long night. I say we head up the road in awhile and get our own party started."

Avtar did not know the rules of the game, only that Bingham had asked them to watch the boat. He had already given up the dancing date with Olivia to earn the extra money and he didn't want to dodge his responsibilities. "You go ahead."

"You sure? Don't worry about them. They'll be so plastered by eight, they won't know if it's a new year or Aunt Betty's funeral they're celebrating."

Avtar carried the bin belowdecks, and when he returned, Harry was gone. He climbed the stairs to the road and watched as cars and taxis pulled up to the hotel's entrance and bellboys in black uniforms rushed forward to open car doors for their guests. It was nearly five and the building's rosy facade had faded to a deep violet. Lights twinkled behind the tall glass windows and Avtar could see bodies roving among the tables draped with white tablecloths. He crossed the road and lingered by the row of Hudsons, Chryslers, and Fords, watching the guests, people who resembled the Binghams and their friends, mill about the hotel grounds.

Mediterranean palms and yuccas accented the courtyard at the entrance. Water splashed in a circular fountain at its center. The place seemed transplanted from some exotic locale. The guests, too, had the refined carriage and aloof manner of those who are accustomed to being catered to. Inside, a band of tuxedoed musicians was setting up at one end of the large room. The brass of trumpets and horns glinted in the soft light as they were pulled from their cases. Couples jumped to the dance floor as the trumpets blared and the rest of the swing band joined them in a rousing opening number.

Avtar drew near the entrance. He listened awhile to the infectious sound, a wild, sweet cacophony harnessed by the deep notes of a stand-up bass and the staccato of drums. The smooth gliding motion of couples hand in hand, the wild jiggling antics of others on the dance floor brought a smile to his face. He searched for the

Binghams or any of their party amid the horde of people, then turned away from the windows and wandered awhile along the gravel shoulder of the road. A stream of headlights on the road signaled nightfall and it seemed the entire world had gone silent, while only the bright sounds contained within the walls of the hotel remained. It was his first New Year's Eve in America. In the Punjab, it was not until April that his father donned his saffron robes as one of the Panj Piares, commemorating the beloved first five admitted into the Sikh Khalsa in the Baisakhi Day celebration of the new year and harvest. There would be food, prayer, the sharing of karah parshad, and finally the men would convene on a hard-packed dirt court to perform the bhangara.

When he returned to the hotel, he slipped inside the front entrance. If he encountered Bingham, he would simply tell him the boat had been no trouble and Harry had gone off to find a meal. Members of the band mingled with the crowd still gathered on the dance floor. A gentleman with a broad back hunched over the piano, playing a solo. The music induced a restless, melancholy mood. Avtar spotted Sallie Bingham with her friends at one of the head tables; she was listening absentmindedly to a man he didn't recognize. Hodges lingered awkwardly by a large potted palm, but the other men in the boating party had apparently moved elsewhere.

On the river, Bingham had mentioned some of the hotel's colorful past; it had been a popular speakeasy (he'd explained that term to Avtar) and casino during Prohibition, with "lots of gals hanging around," as he put it. A secret tunnel had connected the hotel to the river. "I guess people needed to make a quick getaway now and then," he added. That atmosphere of excess still prevailed, lured patrons from miles around to experience its enduring glamour and legacy.

Avtar paced the far edge of the room, where other reluctant types had taken refuge. Overhead, ceiling fans stirred air saturated with cigar smoke and expectation. The band picked up again with "Echoes of Harlem," a Duke Ellington number he sometimes hummed along with on Leandro's radio. The muted trumpets once again lured bare-shouldered women back to their tables. He listened awhile, then moved on to the lobby, where a steady line filed up and down the stairs leading to the upper rooms. He continued down a hall to the back of the hotel, then out the French doors to a garden area. He roamed the grounds, avoiding the benches where couples lingered discreetly, eventually following a path that circled the hotel and led him once again to the front entrance. He stared through the windows where the music and dancing resumed but felt no compulsion to rejoin the exuberant crowd.

Later on the boat, he pulled a couple of blankets from one of the sleeping compartments below and returned to the deck. He would lie under the stars, alone, staring into the darkness in the first seconds of the year 1948. What remained with him now was the tinge of disappointment in Olivia's voice when she'd said, "We can do it another time." What was she doing tonight? Who was she with? She had said the restaurant would be closing early and she would make other plans.

With his earnings, he would take her to some fine place, finer than the Ryde, and he would forget the feeling he had now, the weight at the back of his neck, which kept him lying flat on the hard deck. The stars dipped lower in the sky and he imagined each of them suspended on long strings above him. Even the music had stopped now and any sounds coming from the hotel coalesced into a single drone that was absorbed by the mist rising off the water. Occasionally, he heard a fish jump in the water or the hull of a boat creak. At last, he heard not even the silence as he drifted off to sleep.

Early in the morning, he was awakened by footsteps on the deck. He rose, to find Bingham kneeling beside him. "Get up, Ray."

Avtar tossed the blanket aside, rubbing a shoulder that had stiffened. Something in Bingham's tone startled him. The faint light of a streetlamp revealed little but shadows across his face.

"You've got to do something for me. Here, take this and hold on to it until you hear from me. You remember the plan, Ray? You and Harry are taking the boat up to my place. We'll be there before daylight. Harry knows."

Still drowsy from sleep, Avtar took the parcel from Bingham's fingers. He felt the thick pad of spongy bills through the paper covering and knew even then it was money, lots of it. "Mr. Bingham—"

"Hang on to that, Ray. Wake Harry up. I'm counting on you."

Bingham was up the stairs before Avtar could tell him that he hadn't seen Harry all evening. How would the boat get up to Bingham's place if Harry didn't show up? His former boss lived in one of those great sprawling houses along the levee road, but Avtar did not know which one. Why had Bingham left the money with him? He had an idea where it had come from, but not what Bingham might've betted on. He had to find Harry; it was the only way to get the money safely back to Bingham. He tucked the parcel in his coat pocket and headed down the road.

FIFTEEN

"*A little to the left.*" *Neelam stepped* away from the ladder I was perched on to survey the line of posters covering the wall above the chalkboard. "And higher by an inch."

I adjusted the image of Guru Gobind Singh, the last in the line of the ten gurus who laid the foundations for the Sikh faith, and pushed the final tack in the wall. The guru's calm bearded face, unflinching as it met brutality and persecution, stared directly into my neck and past into the small side room of the gurdwara, urging future generations to carry the torch of the faithful, to lift their kirpans, their swords, to defend their beliefs. I had never felt so scrutinized by the gurus as when I had smoothed the paper surfaces extolling each of their virtues: Guru Tegh Bahadur seated tranquilly before the holy book, his head bathed in a white light; Guru Hargobind charging ahead on a horse, leading an army of warriors. Each portrait of sacrifice bespoke the smallness of my own trifling failures, and I eagerly jumped from the rickety metal ladder to the concrete floor, away from their powerful gaze.

Neelam uncrossed her arms, another task toward her salvation completed. We unpacked a box of kadhas, Punjabi instruction books, and stacked them neatly on the front table. It was the same edition I had learned to read and write Punjabi from, the cover sporting a boy wearing a kacha and turban, his hands joined in respectful greeting—Sat Sri Akal. The good boy. He studies when it is time to study, plays when it is time to play!

I picked up a copy and fanned through its myriad images of the good boy doing good deeds, all of it rushing by like a film reel. "I wish I'd had you as a teacher instead of old Ram Singh," I said to Neelam.

"He was frightful, wasn't he?" Neelam laughed. "With that crooked cane he shook at us whenever he became angry. No, I want my students to look forward to coming on Saturdays. Spending time in this room." She glanced around the open space, transformed from an all-purpose storage area to a spare but clean classroom with wooden tables and benches lined in orderly rows; the gurus would be pleased with her work, the souls she would spare from corruption. Neelam had thrown herself into this project like no other, though even this would become a source of concern for my mother. A recent service at the gurdwara had brought old Atta Singh scampering up the steps to the dais to deliver a scathing speech railing against the complacency of the younger generations. Why, some knew no more than the English language! Apne bache Punjabi ne bolde hai! It was a repeat performance of Ram Singh's a decade earlier. Neelam and I had tittered quietly at all the venom and rancor, but it had planted a seed in her mind. From that seed sprouted fresh ideas on ways to capture the minds and hearts of the Sikh youth.

Neelam pressed forefinger to chin. "I could teach them songs."

"Movie songs?"

"Religious songs!" She blinked her eyes indignantly, all too accustomed to my teasing about such topics. "I have a tape from those bhais from Amritsar who performed in the Bay Area last spring." She hummed softly, evidence of the multifaceted nature of her newfound devotion.

. . .

$\mathcal{A}$ sea of small heads bobbed and twisted in the classroom, small fingers scratching ears and wiping wet noses. At the front of the room, Neelam moved a pointer from one letter of the Gurmukhi alphabet to the next. *Oo-dah, aa-dah, ee-dee,* began the vowels—rounded, looping figures meant to be brought to life by quills dipped in wells of black ink, or the flourishes of brush strokes, not the hard-edged tips of pens or pencil points.

It was the second week of Neelam's summer class at the gurdwara. I had volunteered my assistance—or rather, my mother had insisted that I help Neelam with her Punjabi classes. She worried openly that the demands on my sister might be overwhelming, but privately I knew I was serving a penance of sorts for questions that remained unanswered. I was reluctant to complain, fearing the subject of marriage might resume if I refused. Though I had once envisioned a summer anticipating my fall semester away at college, I stood instead in a windowless room with twenty-six restless children of varying sizes and attention spans, listening to Neelam's patient instruction.

Next, Neelam led the students in a memorization exercise from the kadha. "The good boy rises early each morning to say his prayers." Over and over, they said the line: the repetition, the chanting, bringing the words to life, words issued from their breasts through vocal chords, mouths, tongues, lips, their sounds expelled, then returning as humble truths seeping back into them, absorbed by their skin like spilled milk onto a cloth, to form memory.

A young man in a gray tunic and white leggings appeared in the doorway. I had noticed him on previous occasions assisting the granthis and musicians with various tasks, setting up microphones before a service or ferrying messages back and forth. "Sat Sri Akal, Bibi," he said, bowing his head a little, joining his palms. "It's heartening to see all the children coming to learn about the gurus, and someone devoting their time to teach them. The granthi himself insists that you stay for langar."

Neelam flushed from the compliment.

"Jaroor ayo," he said, insisting she be sure to come.

I reluctantly accompanied Neelam to the kitchen area following class; the midday langar would surely appease a ravenous hunger sparked by two hours attending to squirming children. But it also demanded an extended display of piety, of eyes and voices lowered and chunis steadfastly secured on heads. "The widows," I whispered to Neelam as we took our plates. She cheerfully greeted the three women who worked regularly in the kitchen, as if to shrug off my insensitive comment. One of them, a short, round-faced woman in her late thirties, poured ladlefuls of dal on our plates. "It's quiet today, but next week will be the Akhand Path for Mohta Singh. Dhuniyah—people—coming and going all weekend. The grandson was just here making arrangements for food."

At the table, Neelam finished one roti with her dal, then reached for another, ripping it in half as though it were a loathsome document bearing unwelcome news. "Just when the children are hitting their stride, learning the alphabet, learning to write their names in Punjabi," she fumed. "Now comes Akhand Path for Mohta Singh. This place will be swarming next weekend."

I licked dal from my fingers, considering her suddenly prickly mood. "Maybe you should cancel class. Everyone will understand."

"Why should I? The lessons shouldn't be interrupted." She glanced behind her, pulling her chuni tight about her head. "Such an inconvenient time for everyone, with the harvests and all. They could've waited till fall or . . ." She pushed her plate away and sat steaming for a few seconds. "I want to mutha tekh again," she said, rising.

I finished my meal and found Neelam in the main hall. In front of the dais, she lowered herself to her knees and touched her forehead to the floor. Above, a granthi seated before the Guru Granth Sahib, the holy book, recited the kirtan. Neelam remained on the floor, as though entranced by the captivating power of the familiar rhythms and chants. The same young man in the gray tunic—the assistant— appeared through a side door, accompanied by another man, whose head was covered with a white ramal. The second man turned slowly from his conversation to regard the figure rising from her knees before the dais. Facing the Guru Granth Sahib, Neelam clasped her hands once more at her chest and bowed her head. It was Hari's voice, quiet and assured in that cavernous space, that struck a resonant chord within her and caused her to turn toward him. The assistant was gesturing to the front and back of the room, planning, evidently, the following week's ceremonies. Hari moved slowly toward the dais, taking small, measured steps, listening vacuously now, it seemed, to the assistant's suggestions. Were Akhand Path ceremonies not always the same, a continuous reading of the Guru Granth Sahib in remembrance of someone's birth, another's death? He stopped, swiveled, turning his back to us, as if to garner the last bit of courage required to face what inevitably stood in his path.

"Shavash!" The assistant clapped his hands once when he noticed Neelam, letting his palms rest together. "This is the lady I was just telling you about who has started a school for our young Sikhs," he said to Hari as they approached. "And her sister, I believe. Perhaps you already know one another."

"Sat Sri Akal," Neelam and I said.

Hari pulled the ramal from his head. "Actually, we're old friends. Our families have been acquainted for many years," he explained to the assistant.

Before Neelam could interject anything, the assistant launched into a fresh sermon. "This is just the sort of initiative the Sikh community needs to revitalize itself, renew its spiritual commitment. I've been here just over a year, directly from Chandigarh, but despite your fine gurdwaras, I've observed too many citizens who have abandoned the teachings of the gurus. For what? For zamin, land. For money. To drive around in these . . . these Caddy-lacs." The fine wayward hairs of his meager beard flapped in the air as he spoke. A stream of spittle foamed at the corner of his mouth.

Neelam lowered her eyes, smiling. Hari slid his hands into the pockets of his trousers. I fingered the gold thread embroidered into a leaf pattern on my sleeve.

"Tell the granthi I'll have the donation check to the gurdwara next week," Hari said.

"Shavash! I'll tell him myself," the young assistant exclaimed, his mood lightening measurably. "Your generosity allows continuing progress at our gurdwara, our community."

"Just as your grandfather would have done," Neelam said after the young man departed.

"Not exactly. My grandfather would have managed to extract something in return. He rarely did anything purely for the good of it."

"I'm sorry. I never properly expressed my condolences to you."

"It's understandable. I saw your sister just a few weeks ago, at your Uncle Avtar's." He smiled as he spoke, and Neelam was aware the smile was intended for her.

"She didn't mention it to me." She flashed her eyes at me. It had been three months since Mohta Singh passed away and Hari had moved into his grandfather's house. The day of the funeral, Neelam had sat helpless in our kitchen under my mother's surveillance, glancing furtively at her watch, or the clock on the wall. She no longer spoke of him. It was as if, like the children chanting and repeating lines from the kadha, only articulation could make a thing true. She must have counted on the laws of time and space to assure their paths would cross again. Each step she took daily moved her toward or away from him. Her faith in this was as strong as the one she invested in the gurus. And Hari? I wondered at the timing of the Akhand Path. Had he counted on the same laws? And yet it seemed no time had passed. I had never seen them standing together, speaking to each other in person. Neelam and Hari. It had been merely a story to me, its actions never visible in the flesh, only its consequences twisting the faces and hearts of those it touched.

"Your uncle and I were discussing a business venture, a land deal he's interested in," Hari continued.

"He has always been very fond of you," she said, tilting her head a little, her tone breathy.

"Your family's well? I heard you were having some difficulties." He seemed immediately reproached by Neelam's look of pain, her embarrassment that he had spoken of her miscarriage so directly. "You look well now, of course," he added quickly.

They went on like that, tethered by old secrets, a way they had of communicating, sensing things about each other. They padded off toward the entrance, barely mindful of my presence.

I lingered in the middle of the vast room, then lowered myself, kneeling on the carpet with my feet tucked behind me, never toward the dais or the Guru Granth Sahib, as I had been taught since I was a child. The granthi had concluded his afternoon of prayer and pulled the series of square silk ramals ceremoniously over the holy book. He never looked up, but languished in his purified state as he retreated into a back room. What was that like, to be guided by a single light, purged of normal, everyday concerns? Ram Singh had told us that peace and oneness in this world come from prayer and chanting the Lord's name. Could you pray for things you weren't supposed to want? What did Neelam pray for in those moments, her forehead pressed against the matted loops of teal carpet where countless others had bent forward in supplication? For serenity, the souls of her unborn children? For him? Or to be spared of all desire, which had only brought pain to her heart?

Hari cracked open the mahogany door before he departed, resting his hand against its dark polished wood. A column of light fell on the two figures. I could see Neelam's face lifted to his and her body swaying lightly with a certain exhilaration. Seconds passed, minutes. Neelam turned her head away, as if she could not bear the sight of him leaving. When she returned, she appeared serene, gratified. It had been enough, for now.

It was not a summer entirely devoted to prayer and penance. As the heat settled like a heavy blanket over the valley, an acute loneliness invaded my world. I was relieved at first to learn that Surinder was spending part of the summer with cousins in the Bay Area, but then the weeks grew long without her prickly barbs and her moods. Pritam had departed for his uncle's and my secret thrill of driving by India Bazaar for that simple sense of proximity had been snatched away. I took the time to consult the course catalog at the community college and, with a lingering sense of disappointment, registered for classes for the fall semester.

Two separate letters arrived from India one week. One announced that my grandmother in the Punjab had taken to her bed, ill with the persistent fever that would eventually take her life. The other confirmed that Ameer Singh was indeed interested in the proposed marriage after seeing a photograph of me. My mother sat awkwardly in her armchair, clutching one in each hand, the weight of one, the lightness of the other contorting her frame. The pain of the years separated from her mother, who had wept openly for weeks and privately for years after her eldest daughter departed for America, finally overwhelmed her. Still, out of sorrow was born possibility, she realized, and I overheard her in the kitchen the next morning speaking to my father about a trip to India.

My dreams and nightmares changed then, overlapping, interchanging, and consisting of this boy who had extended his hand to me from far away, Ami. Only after she had dried her tears did my mother show me his portrait. I did not argue with her just then, as her thoughts were focused on her mother's health. She explained that his schooling would take several more months to complete. When I finally looked at the picture, I saw a pair of deep-set, curious eyes and a warmth and intelligence in the face. Ami. Would that be the name I would repeat in the darkness of night? Already I felt myself tumbling down a steep cliff, unable to break the fall.

Around this time, Hardeep returned from India with a doting husband whose simple and enduring debt to her would be that she was an American citizen by birthright. Her carriage, her assured stride now was borne from blissful nights in the nuptial chambers, a lavish wardrobe of silk saris and lahengas, and the generous layer of skin-whitening foundation she smoothed on her face each morning. A cardinal red bindi pierced the space between her brows (the lips painted to match), and I sometimes felt there was an elegance and grace in the world whose essence I had yet to discover.

The children's lessons continued at the gurdwara. Stories of the gurus brought their palms to their cheeks in shock and admiration. Neelam brought in cushions the children eagerly abandoned their wood benches for, piling onto them whenever she announced it was story time. She appeared at my house early the following week, resplendent with a sapphire blue chuni framing her shoulders, somber in mood so as not to arouse any suspicion that she might cross paths with Hari. Excessive joy would only engender an equal amount of sorrow, my mother had instructed us since childhood. The Akhand Path had commenced Friday evening and would conclude late Sunday. My mother sniffled about the fact that Aunt Teji was planning to attend, a most bitter defection. Were people's memories so fleeting? The old scores applied long after the last breath departed and the souls of the dead abandoned their bodies, she insisted. Mohta Singh would confront the consequences of his questionable deeds in his next life. "I've potatoes on for aloo paratha—your favorite, Neelam," my mother said in the same breath, "if you want to hurry back for lunch."

The gurdwara filled again and marked anew Mohta Singh's passing. In the classroom, Neelam instructed the children on Guru Arjun Dev's execution, the burning sand that was poured over his bare body. Her voice faltered now and then, as though she had forgotten her place, or that the lesson itself was too unimaginably cruel for the flock of impressionable children gathered before her. She bade them goodbye one by one, adjusting a bent collar, brushing straight a twisted braid, and hurried them out the door when the class concluded.

I tidied the scattered piles of papers and kadhas, pencils that had rolled from the tables onto the floor. Neelam had released the children without her usual demand for neatness and order, forgoing her usual routine. But it was not a day for routines. She leaned by the open door, lost in thought; then suddenly, she turned. "Let's go in. Just a short while."

I followed her into the main hall, feeling dozens of eyes flash up at us as if they were all connected to a single nerve center. I searched the sea of white shirts congregated in the men's section for the face that I wanted to see, but I knew would not be there. Neelam moved on toward a small clearing amid the jumble of backs and thighs and feet that shifted around us to make room. A kirtan was beginning, the steady pounding of the dohl uniting with the singer's pure, melodious verse, music and poetry melding to reveal divine meaning. I turned around, to see Uncle Avtar conferring with Hari by the back entrance of the hall, where Hari had stood with Neelam the week before. And then I thought perhaps this would be the difficult road that lay ahead for Neelam, not that she would never see Hari again, but that she would go on seeing him like this, week after week, month after month.

Sixteen

A collar of chestnut brown hair ringed the floor beneath the chair in which one of Surinder's more prominent clients sat, ruffled, nearly slouching. Mrs. Fleming had been coming to Monique's Salon de Beauté for years, seduced by the proprietor's French accent and the exotic arsenal of beauty products purchased on the Continent by Monique herself during summer holidays. In the mirror, Surinder looked nearly cross-eyed as she leaned over the woman, carefully painting highlights into her hair. Mrs. Fleming's mouth twitched with indignity. Surinder's limp, inexperienced fingers handling her magnificent crown of hair! The salon bustled with customers, chatty, alacritous women in purple curlers, cellophane head wraps, and plastic aprons exchanging beauty tips and recipes. A secret society, it seemed, that vanished on Friday afternoons from their kitchens and hearths to infiltrate the town's beauty parlors.

I waited for Surinder to finish with Mrs. Fleming. She had been telling me about Monique's for several weeks, inviting me to visit what she called "a really classy salon." It was also her way of saying that she had forgiven me—that is, forgiven me for not forgiving her. The truth was, I missed her as well, missed our contentious way of settling matters; it had always had a clearing effect on my mind, which lately felt muddled and restless. For weeks, I had told her that my schedule at the community college didn't permit a casual visit, but I relented finally. I had expected a kind of coming to blows with her, an explosive airing of our anger with each other. It hadn't happened, and it occurred to me in slow increments that things often didn't get resolved in that manner. Gradually, you pushed the hurt away, a strenuous lifelong engagement not unlike moving a mountain. It must be what makes grown-ups look so weary and defeated much of the time, I thought. And so I took the only chair available in the salon that afternoon, one attached to a hair dryer. Beside me sat two other women with dryers rattling over their heads as they thumbed through magazines, cigarettes pressed between their fingers.

"JoEllen used to put in the most marvelous coppery highlights. It's a shame she's left," Mrs. Fleming said. Her large gray-blue eyes scanned the mirror, settling on each face reflected there, until her eyes met mine momentarily, then returned to her own pleasing visage. She looked fortyish, an altogether different fortyish than my mother looked, the kind that summoned a certain admiration when she swiveled out of her chair and clicked out of the salon in her black heels.

"Hold still, please." Surinder proceeded with the highlighting, dabbing at bangs with a small brush, ignoring the woman's obvious displeasure. "If I can impress Mrs. Fleming, Monique will keep me on at the salon for sure," she'd said the night before of her three o'clock appointment. Monique had hired her on a trial basis a month earlier, after Surinder had pleaded with her, after she'd spent much of the summer languishing in her bedroom reading beauty magazines. Her mother had mistaken her desire for solitude as a time of reflection, remorse. But Surinder had sloughed off any misgivings about running off with Pritam with remarkable ease. (And wasn't it about time for me to get over that fiasco as well? her impatient tone suggested.) Her dreams now materialized in the form of Mrs. Fleming, wife of prominent attorney Henry Fleming. They lay in the brassy shimmer of her hair caught in the sunlight, its layered waves, which would tremble ever so slightly when she turned briskly to hand her husband his evening vodka and tonic.

"JoEllen trimmed my bangs a bit more wispy," Mrs. Fleming said calmly.

"I know, Mrs. Fleming." Surinder's concentration abandoned her for a moment and she set the brush on the counter. "Trust me. When you walk out of here, you're going to look great."

Amused by Surinder's bold tone, Mrs. Fleming straightened in her chair, submitting herself willfully to Surinder's skillful hands as she twisted the last of the plastic purple curlers into the woman's hair.

"Jeeto, guess where Scottie is taking me? Scottie's my boyfriend," she said to Mrs. Fleming. "We're going to San Francisco together."

The woman beside me peered out from under her hair dryer. "Doesn't Scottie have to get permission from someone first?" I asked. Scottie was just a nickname, of course. She had confided in me one night that he was none other than Ajit Singh, a tax attorney who was married and had two adolescent daughters.

It was Mrs. Fleming's turn under the hair dryer. She swiveled around in her chair, uncrossing her shapely stockinged calves and coming toward me, all in one smooth motion. Not like a woman in a salwaar, I thought, her knees waggling well apart as she struggled from her seat. I leaped up too eagerly, offering Mrs. Fleming my place, bumping my head on the dryer, which slammed back against the wall and turned on by itself. She gave me a kind, pitying smile, then sat and adjusted the dryer over her head, as though I had performed a most thoughtful act on her behalf.

Outside in the small courtyard behind the salon, Surinder collapsed onto a cement bench and slipped off her sandals. "I only get a break when Monique returns from one of her long lunches," she complained as she massaged the soles of her feet.

"Looks like business is good. Gorees like Mrs. Fleming need more than almond oil and a comb with sturdy teeth. Do you think she'll keep coming back to you?"

"Of course. What did JoEllen do that I can't do?"

It wasn't exactly the new Surinder, but certainly one who spoke with a surge of confidence. I wanted to know more about Scottie, and how one managed the leap from running away with Pritam to ending up in a married man's arms. I couldn't imagine the two met for tea. Scottie—Ajit Singh—was a sturdy-looking man of medium height, a man with an appetite, one sensed. His wife had been ill with an undisclosed ailment for some months, but she had recovered with little more than a grayish pall and diminishing fatigue as evidence. His attentions in the interim evidently had turned elsewhere. "When will you be going to San Francisco? With Ajit Singh."

She stiffened, as if his real name conjured a reality she was not prepared to face. "Next month. He goes there on business. He promised to take me."

"But he's married. With two daughters practically our age." I paused, staring at the grayish splotches of shade cast from a flowering pear onto the brick floor, and the scattered pots of red and pink geraniums. Surinder would always find a way to make me sound sanctimonious, like her own disapproving mother, and to remind me of my inexperience. I couldn't imagine the relationship with a man perhaps in his mid-thirties. He was attractive in a roguish way, that heavy-lidded glance of his suggesting a mind preoccupied, oblivious of the topic at hand. I imagined them making love, his giant mouth consuming her slender lips (the ones she had rued inheriting from her father so many times before a mirror).

"He's been through a hard time with his wife. He told me all about it," she said, twisting a thick swatch of her hair in her finger.

"You wouldn't understand. Go ahead, marry your doctor. You haven't even shown me his picture."

"I'm not marrying him, or anyone. My mother's planning the trip to India because my grandmother's sick, probably 'dying." What I didn't dare tell Surinder was that I found myself thinking about Ameer now and then. When I lay awake at night and thought of Pritam and everything inside me hurt like a rag wrung too hard, I would turn my thoughts to Ameer. What had he wondered about me before he said yes?

"And you don't think they're going to tie you down in front of some granthi and marry you off right then and there? Jeeto, you were supposed to be the one who got away. But you're still here, aren't you?"

"What about you? Are you going to work at Monique's the rest of your life?" I pushed off the bench, away from a vague sensual scent that seemed to drip from her pores.

Surinder bent forward, slipping her slender wheat-colored feet into her sandals. She tousled her hair, pulling at the damp strands that clung to her neck from the warmth. I watched with envy as she rose from the bench, tugging at the hem of her slim, short skirt, exhibiting a new ease with her body, a new discovery of what it was meant for, even if her brow creased with a nagging tension.

"Look, don't worry about Pritam and me. He'll never look at me again. You know how Indian boys are."

So all this—Ajit Singh, the tension between us—was still about Pritam. Surinder casually flicked away a petal that had fallen on the sleeve of her sweater, seemingly unaware of the string of damage wrought by her innocent pursuits. "Pritam's back. You didn't know?" she asked. "I saw him on Fifth Street driving a black squad car. I wouldn't have recognized him, but he waved to me. He's joined the sheriff's department. He's a cop. Can you believe it?"

Pritam, a cop? The news stunned me, and then to hear it so ca-

sually from Surinder. She had invited me to the salon not to impress me with her glamorous client, but to tell me this, to witness
my reaction. How long had he been back? I had watched for him
all summer at the temple, knowing he would not attend, but seeking even the mirage of him.

"There's Monique. I'd better go in," Surinder said. Monique
stepped out into the tepid shade of the patio, pressing an unlighted
cigarette between her coral-stained lips. She had a severe quality
that tempered a fading elegance. Raven hair pulled back in a tightly
coiled bun and those pale penciled-in brows, a pair of narrow cres-
cents arched above her sad gray eyes. "Your four o'clock has arrived,"
she said to Surinder in gruff, heavily accented English.

I left without saying good-bye, darting through the metallic
haze of hair potions and sprays indoors, past the women serenely
lodged under the dome-shaped chrome hair dryers, that weekly effort that would barely elicit a comment from their husbands. In the
parking lot, a black Mercedes slowed in front of the salon. The
driver, a dark, clean-shaven man in sunglasses, craned his neck for a
glimpse inside as he passed. A gold watch glinted at his wrist. They
had met at the salon, where Surinder had taken him to the same
chair Mrs. Fleming had sat in, then begun snipping carefully at his
coarse black hair. Ajit Singh accelerated the car and, at the far end
of the lot, swerved into a shaded parking space, turned off the engine, and waited.

I settled into a full schedule of classes at the community college
that fall. My parents gladly relinquished the Chevrolet sedan to me,
an attitude that bespoke their renewed commitment to my limited
education, one that would deliver me safely into the arms of my
betrothed with the ability to converse capably about his workday at
the office.

I found my mother in the kitchen one morning polishing a new set of CorningWare she had purchased. She had sniffed enviously at the set used at a dinner party given by the Gills. The stainless-steel platters and bowls brought back from India must have suddenly seemed crude and undignified by comparison.

"Any muttis left?" I asked.

"In the tin in the cupboard," she replied, barely moving her eyes from the splendid array of dishes spread on the counter before her. The new set of CorningWare was only part of the immense pleasure my mother was reveling in that morning. "Your uncle Girpal has returned. He's promised to stay for good this time. Aunt Manjit called me yesterday." I watched as she whipped a dishcloth in quick, tight circles over a dish, then admired its lustrous finish.

"He promises that every time," I said, recalling the humiliating episode at the festival that had sent him, quickly followed by my historical display, crashing to the floor before a crowded circle of onlookers. "Well, I'm sorry for Aunt Manjit."

The dishcloth hung flaccid and rumpled in my mother's hand as she set an oval casserole dish next to the others on the counter. "How can you say such a thing? He's her husband. She must accept him back."

"Isn't he having a baby with that other woman he was living with?" And wouldn't Aunt Manjit's belly soon swell again? Embarrassed by her condition, she would hide it under layers of loose kameezes and shawls. Unable to sleep, she would stare nightly up into the stained ceiling over her bed where the rain had leaked through time and again, beseeching the gurus for a son. A woman of thirty-one years who already rubbed amla—gooseberry powder—into her scalp to replenish her thinning hair.

"Haat! That was just gossip, and you shouldn't speak of things you know nothing . . ." Her voice trailed off. "You'll understand someday when you have a husband of your own."

"I never want to understand a man like him. I don't want a husband if that's the kind of man I'll wind up with!"

"It's already written what kind of man you will marry. Nothing can be done about it." A sober expression of certitude froze on her face; it was the awful truth as she accepted it, and she expected the same blind faith from me.

"Right. Ameer Singh. That was written somewhere. Maybe I *can* do something about it—I can say no!"

"Refuse his hand and I'll leave you in the village at my brother Jogi's house. Maybe a little time there would bring you to your senses." My mother turned sharply to stack the dishes in a glass cabinet. I wondered if they would be like the blankets bought and stored in their plastic cases on the highest shelves of our closets, unused reminders that some things were best appreciated if left untouched.

I lifted two muttis from a tin, wrapped them in a napkin, and left the house. In the cool air, the skin on my face and hands smarted, as if suddenly pulled too tight. I sped off in the car, reasoning that I could elude for the moment, the day, the vast karmic net that hung aloft, not wanting to believe my mother's frequent threats and how casually she was willing to offer me into the hands of fate.

On the road, I tried to distract my mind with more immediate matters—due dates for assignments, exams. Three years earlier, the college had moved from its downtown location to a more spacious one west of town, past Stonebrook Heights, where Neelam lived, in a section where orchards were being uprooted daily to accommodate new homes with patios and pools. Past Orange Lane, just beyond the town limits, the road widened into a four-lane highway. I raced ahead in the car, telling myself that I had made the right choice by staying in Oak Grove, that the decision had been mine to make. Sometimes I imagined Jenny Holcomb crossing the grassy knolls and plazas of the Berkeley campus, rushing to her next class.

"It's your choice, ultimately," she had told me in her forceful, confident manner, disappointed that I would not be leaving with her. Not understanding that there was Neelam, fragile in her sensibilities as of late, and the complicated, demanding ways of my mother, an unceasing tide that threatened to engulf me, but which I had not found a way to turn from. I bit into a sweet masala-spiced mutti that shattered into a spray of small flakes. A guarded freedom stretched out ahead on the four-lane road, one that I intended to nurture carefully, like a weak flame.

In the school parking lot, Mani Singh, Neelam's meddlesome friend from high school, juggled a stack of books in her arm, gripping a gray vinyl attaché case in her fist as she negotiated her way through the maze of parked cars and traffic. She waited for me to catch up, looking strained yet efficient in a navy blue business suit. "Don't forget the ISA meeting today at four," she called out. "We're discussing the movie premiere." She had doggedly pursued her current position as vice president of the Indian Students Association, and I witnessed her sense of pride in this accomplishment in each clipped, purposeful step she took.

The psychology lecture focused on personality theory and the instructor spoke of its shadowy components such as the ego and the personal unconscious in a dull, anesthetized tone. All around me, desks and chairs squeaked from the relentless shifting of restless bodies. I began to think about the ISA meeting, irritated that I had promised Mani the week before that I would attend. The organization was a miniature version of the Indian-American Association, with its competing loyalties and occasional outbursts and brawls. I plodded through the school day, numbed by a succession of familiar faces and voices I had known since grade school; I longed instead for anonymity and the freedom it permitted. I arrived at the meeting as the final, climactic notes of the Indian national anthem faded and died within the speakers mounted on the wall behind the podium.

Around two dozen members, mostly male, were seated in the front rows of the small lecture room. Mani's singular devotion to the cause became partially clear in the presence of its charming, loquacious president, Vinod Singh. A portion of that charm derived from the fact that Vinod was not a local boy, or from a city or village in India, but a transplant from the fragrant asphalt landscape of Los Angeles. He prowled the front of the room clutching a microphone to his mouth, seeking suggestions for a locale to screen the upcoming movie premiere ISA was jointly sponsoring with the Indian-American Association.

"Why not try the Capri Theater?" Mani asked, interrupting him. "It's been renovated and can seat several hundred." She pursed her lips and crossed her legs when Vinod paused to acknowledge her suggestions.

A pious Karan Singh cleared his throat at the podium, tugged at his periwinkle blue tie, and renounced Indian cinema as a corruptive influence that emboldened young people to emulate the increasingly lascivious behavior displayed on the screen.

"And what are these young people doing? Holding hands?" someone replied, to laughter.

I left the meeting as a squabble over committees erupted. Vinod attempted to tame his suddenly unruly audience, running his fingers repeatedly over a nonexistent beard. In the far corner, someone had Karan Singh buckled over in a headlock for refusing to relinquish the microphone.

A student from my psychology class approached me in the parking lot, a pretty, longhaired blond boy who pretended not to realize he sat directly behind me in every lecture. We complained about the professor's dry, clinical treatment of the subject and discussed an upcoming exam before we parted. I sat in the car several moments, resolving at last to visit Neelam on the way home. On the highway, a pickup truck that looked like Uncle Avtar's blue Ford passed by, and when I glanced in the rearview mirror for a second look, I noticed a black police vehicle following about fifty yards back. The car suddenly neared the rear tailgate of the Ford, then slowed and lagged some distance behind again. I let up on the accelerator to allow it to pass ahead, but instead I saw bright red lights flashing across its roof and heard a siren sound in two quick bursts. As I turned onto a side street, the vehicle followed and stopped behind me.

Pritam emerged from the car, wearing a creaseless tan uniform and sunglasses, with his hair shorn close to his scalp.

"Serjit?" he said, bending down at the window as though surprised to see me. He leaned his elbows on the frame of the open window while his eyes searched the interior of the car. The holster carrying a Smith & Wesson revolver was slung at his hip.

"What did you pull me over for, doing forty-two in a forty-five-mile-an-hour zone?"

"Driving too slow? I haven't given any tickets for that yet."

"You're giving me a ticket?"

"Depends. Step out of the car and we can talk about it."

It's like a children's game of cops and robbers, I thought as I exited the car. I faced Pritam squarely, determined to show him that I was not intimidated by the uniform and the flimsy brass badge. "Kind of an extreme career change for you, isn't it?"

He pretended not to hear my comment. "Who was that guy you were talking to back there?" he asked.

"Where?"

"In the parking lot."

"You were watching me?" I shook my head in disbelief. "He's a guy in one of my classes. Do I need your permission now that you carry a big gun?" I could make out his hazel eyes, their serious focus behind the dark lenses of his sunglasses.

"Just curious."

"How long have you been back?"

"Three weeks. I did my training down in Stockton, but I heard they wanted an Indian cop up here. You know all the stuff that goes on."

I entertained a momentary, gratifying image of Pritam arresting my uncle Girpal. "Can I go, then?" I reached for the door handle, but he curled his fingers around my wrist in a firm grip, stopping me.

"Only if you promise to see me. Soon."

Seventeen

For a time, Pritam's name, unlike Hari's, blossomed on the tongues of the women visiting our home. They gathered over tea to share freshly molded sugary balls of pinni, discuss the complications of Rachan Kaur's gallbladder operation (the code name for a hysterectomy or an abortion), and, finally, to praise Pritam's growing sense of responsibility, his maturity, the pride he brought to our community as the first Indian police officer. There was general agreement that Pritam was just the right sort of person for the job—in touch with both the old and the modern ways. A boy raised without a father at last had found his way.

Charan Kaur boasted to one and all that her son, in fact, had been enlisted by the police department as a liaison for the Indian community. Where Pritam was concerned, however, she had more on her mind than her pride in her son's budding law-enforcement career. In a moment when we were alone together, I felt a hand grab my waist from behind me. Charan Kaur's hot, peppery breath blasted my face. "Stay away from him, and if you don't, I'll tell your mother everything. You know what will happen then."

. . .

Still, I awaited some word from him—a note, a call; a signal that showed he had returned for reasons beyond a law-enforcement career, that what had happened with Surinder no longer mattered to us. I watched the police cars that passed by on the road, and the sirens that erupted occasionally from the corners of the town began to startle me; I worried in some new, urgent way for him. At times I resented him for coming back, for this cruel trick of making me care again; all he had had to do was show up.

I mentioned none of this to Surinder, who on the phone each day anticipated her trip to San Francisco and the sights she would enjoy with Ajit Singh—Fisherman's Wharf, the Japanese Tea Garden—places she had already visited but would experience anew, shedding the final vestiges of girlhood forever as she strolled in the sea air hand in hand with her lover.

I found a note from Pritam on my windshield in the parking lot of the school one afternoon. He had scribbled an address—2452 N. Ridge—and asked if I could meet him there the following day.

I told my mother there was a study session planned for my psychology exam that afternoon following classes.

"She's meeting her boyfriend," my brother, Prem, called rather prophetically from his breakfast. He was fifteen now, with his body fleshing out to balance his oversized hands and rather prominent head. Posters of pouting blond starlets plastered the walls of his bedroom, desire apparently sanctioned, or tolerated at least, among the male offspring of the family. He tipped the bottle of syrup over his plate, drowning the single golden crescent of pancake that remained. "Look, it's true. She's blushing."

Lost in her own thoughts, my mother poured a puddle of batter onto the griddle and, in a slow hypnotic motion, smoothed it with a spoon into a circle.

I slung my book bag over my shoulder. "I have to study for a test. What about you and that Precious Sharma? She's not even a Sikh."

Prem's mouth fell open as he glanced, panic-stricken, at his distracted mother. "You're lying!" He jumped from his chair and lunged at me. But where Prem was growing in a more solid, muscular fashion, I still retained my light-footed speed, and I slipped out the door before he could reach me.

I had spent the summer helping Neelam at the gurdwara, trying to regain my mother's trust. What about now, today, my visit with Pritam, my lies to my mother? I sped over the slick streets following my classes. A light autumn rain had begun to fall. We were to meet at a place northwest of town, where the orchards gave way to scrubby low hills. I passed the wrought-iron gates of Granada Heights, a small enclave of Spanish-style homes with tile roofs and arched windows, engulfed by stately olives and citrus trees. An unfamiliar twitch started in my stomach. I thought of turning back, of Charan Kaur's blunt warning, but instead accelerated my speed down the tunnel-like road where the rows of trees on either side arched overhead, nearly touching.

The small white farmhouse appeared among the trees ahead. I turned into the dirt lane and pulled behind the house, out of view from the road. The place looked deserted. It was an old bungalow with a wide, slanting porch, probably the foreman's quarters at one time. A wooden garage and shed still housed a rusted old tractor and other farm implements. I shivered alone in the car, watching beads of water trickle down the windshield, waiting for Pritam to arrive.

A while later, he drove up in a red Dodge Charger and parked beside me. He wore his gold-rimmed sunglasses; his uniform was draped over the front seat.

"You have to work later?"

"At six."

I followed him up the back porch steps, where he reached for a key concealed inside a post.

"Who lived here?"

"Originally, the Mohans. They own three hundred acres right here. Eventually, they built a house on the other side and then the foreman and his family lived here a long time." He unlocked the door and we stepped inside.

Lace curtains, yellowed by the sun, still hung in the windows. A square wooden table sat in the center of the front room. A green upholstered chair faced a corner wall. Pritam pushed it around. "Have a seat if you like."

But I stayed by the table, my fingers skimming its cracked surface. On the drive over, I'd grown skeptical about agreeing to meet him like this. The note had mentioned a house where we could meet and talk. But we both knew why we had come. Pritam pushed a curtain aside and gazed out the front window, pretending to find something of interest out there, then turned to face me. I wanted to run into his arms; at least that was the way I had imagined it many times, wondering when I would see him again. And here he was, standing across a small sunlit room, and I couldn't move an inch. This was going to take longer than both of us had thought.

He set a paper grocery bag he was holding on the table. "I brought some soda. And M&M's. I know you like those."

"Thanks. Maybe later." I wandered toward the other rooms, two empty bedrooms, and a third with a mattress thrown on the floor, thoughtfully covered with a moss green chenille bedspread.

Pritam followed me into the room. "Jinder and the boys bring their girlfriends here sometimes. I'm sorry."

I shrugged. Where else could we meet? The motels around town were being bought up by Indians. "It's okay."

I suppose there were other times he'd looked at me that way, but

I couldn't remember them just then. He moved close; I buried my head in his chest, then lifted my mouth to meet his. A moment later, he pulled my shirt open and gently pushed me back on the mattress, then lay above me. We moved awkwardly, rolling, shifting until our bodies meshed and we could hold each other. I felt his hands tugging at my jeans and then his fingers slide toward my hips. On top of me, pushing inside, he whispered my name once.

"What did you tell your mother?" he asked me afterward.

"That I had a study session for psych. We're learning about personality formation."

"Oh," he said, impressed. "So what kind of personality am I?" I felt the strength in his arms when he pulled me closer to him. So easily, he could hurt me, or crush me. A strange thought.

"You're independent, and stubborn. But you already know that."

"It happens when you're the oldest, looking after your brothers, and your mother."

"Yes, she definitely needs looking after. She warned me the other day to stay away from you. How did she know?"

Pritam rubbed his face with both hands. "You know how she is. Don't worry about her. She found a picture of you in my room, in a drawer, that's all."

"The cop was hiding evidence? She never wants to let go of you, does she?" No wonder Ameer had come into the picture so suddenly; apparently, there were advantages to the arrangement on all ends. "I still don't understand what made you want to be a cop."

"Hard to say. I think the first time I thought about it was when I got arrested for trespassing. The officer was a young guy, like me, and he just seemed, I don't know, like he was in control of things . . . his life, I mean."

"And it feels like you're in control of things now?"

"Not exactly. But this time when the principal sees me, he's going to be afraid of me, not the other way around."

"The principal will be the least of your problems." I turned on my side, facing away from him, looking out the window. An old bird nest was perched among the boards in the eaves. "How long has this place been empty?"

"A few years," he said, stroking my back.

"Have you been here before?" I rolled over and nuzzled my face under his arm. "Never mind. Don't answer."

"I'll find another place if you want."

He didn't see me smile. He didn't hear me breathe in the oily musk scent of his skin.

Later, I watched him dress, pull on the tan slacks over his lovely long legs and then tuck the lion pendant under his white under-shirt.

"Pritam," I said, sitting up on the mattress, forgetting what I wanted to say.

He glanced down at me and stopped buttoning his shirt. "Put on a shirt or something." He turned away, as if there was a sudden need for modesty.

I crawled over the wood floor, picked up my bra and red blouse, and he watched now as I laced my arms through the straps. My underpants lay bunched next to my jeans. I reached for them, but then hesitated. I wanted to lie on the mattress with him; I wanted to feel it move beneath me again.

Eighteen

The newly renovated Capri Theater stood next to its elegant nineteenth-century counterpart, the Placer Hotel, on Placer Street. The Fremont County Women's League had undertaken the project when both buildings were slated to be razed to counter the perpetual infestation of drunks and hooligans in that section of town. The San Francisco Opera had performed a gala, scaled-back version of *La Traviata* on the opening night of the theater, attracting patrons from all over northern California. But its fortunes soon were dashed when a dance company from Mill Valley created a scandal by performing a contemporary piece nearly in the nude. It was not exactly the sort of cultural fare area residents had been clamoring for; thereafter, theater managers struggled to fill its calendar.

Its rather idle schedule notwithstanding, the managers and members of the Women's League balked when approached with the idea of hosting the West Coast premiere of *Ek Pyar*. Vinod and Mani (she in a new gray business suit and black-rimmed nonprescription glasses) pleaded that the premiere and subsequent movie dates would make Oak Grove and the Capri Theater a destination for Indians from across California. The suggestion must have horrified Mrs. Waghorn, a starchy local patron of the arts, who was president of the league. Her idea of boosting the town's economy did not entail attracting legions of turbaned and salwaar-clad men and women. But to appear diplomatic in the matter, she agreed to interview ranking members of the Indian Association. What about this altercation at the fairgrounds during a holy festival? Nika Singh, one of our community elders, nervously attempted to portray the incident as a relatively bloodless resolution to a decades-old feud between two families. Mrs. Waghorn remained unconvinced. The garrulous history of fighting at such events was well known among Oak Grove's citizens, Indian and white. Hadn't the fire department been called out recently to a wedding? *A wedding?* Nika Singh must have felt the stinging humiliation of the woman's litany of accusations. Ajit Singh was summoned as a last resort to smooth ruffled feathers; his excellent English spoken in a milky baritone was just the tonic to ease Mrs. Waghorn's fears.

The November air felt chilly and sweet as we emerged from the car down the street from the Capri Theater. The marquee was lighted up in pink and yellow neon stripes, their soft glow washing over the street and disappearing in the gray shadows. Beyond the theater was the Placer Hotel, whose crystal chandeliers, marble floors, and gold swan Jenny Holcomb had described to me in great detail once. A few drunks and derelicts, vestiges of the district's bygone raucous history, huddled in front of an abandoned bus depot. They watched with patient, weary eyes this fresh invasion of quarters that had witnessed other renaissances, however brief. They stood motionless in rumpled hats and unwashed trousers, their beards untrimmed, a warning, or a challenge perhaps, to the dark, scrubbed faces filling the street.

Lokh, humanity, streamed toward the ticket booth in front of the theater. The frosty air added to the sense of glamour—men in suit jackets and women shedding overcoats near the entrance to expose their jewel-colored silks and chiffons. The shimmer and jingle of gold bangles on wrists slender and stout, the scent of sandalwood and Old Spice added to the festive atmosphere. It was possible at times—short, passing moments—when one could feel lost, even amid this crowd of familiar bodies. We pushed ahead, my mother following with her fingers on my elbow. I could see only mouths pressed closely together, painted or plain, opening and shutting, speaking words I couldn't hear. I found Neelam at last, solemn in her bronze silk, a bronze bindi marking her forehead; she nearly ran toward us, holding me tight for a few beats longer than usual. Nearby, Ravi Bains demonstrated the cut of her gold-and-green outfit, a recent style from India with a daring mid-thigh kameez threatening to reveal the shape of her legs, and a narrow, fitted salwaar that flared at its hem. Mrs. Sidhu, ever reproachful of her advancing age, paraded by in a garish display of flame orange that would have Aunt Manjit complaining for weeks.

Surinder and I slumped in the back row of the theater, awaiting the procession of dull speeches that would surely precede the movie. The seats sloped away to the front and were rapidly filling up. From habit, our eyes roved the restless crowd, marking the places where people sat, like generals laying out a battle plan—my mother with Surinder's; Aunt Teji and Aunt Manjit a row ahead; Neelam among them, too careful to glance to the right, where Uncle Avtar and Hari sat side by side; my father, too, on the right side of the theater, the men's side, with Davinder, Uncle Girpal, and Prem and his friends—the placement of these bodies like coordinates on a map that would define our moods and actions. I suddenly remembered Pritam, his voice husky with sleep, telling me earlier over the pay phone that tonight he would be working the evening shift.

"Did I tell you? Monique's making me one of her premiere stylists," Surinder said, sounding as though she was consoling herself. "I get to charge higher rates. Build my client base. Evelyn's so mad. She's been there a year and a half."

"No more complaints from Mrs. Fleming? It's what you wanted, isn't it?"

She slurped her soft drink through a straw and seemed to consider her prospects. "Sure, a lifetime of staring into people's scalps."

"It'll be different when you open your own place."

"Look at Shanti," Surinder said, spitting the straw from her mouth. "She should wear bangs to hide that big forehead."

Moments later, when Ajit Singh bounded to the front of the screen to address the crowd, Surinder's mascaraed lashes fluttered. Silence swept over the room as a spotlight found the face of one of the Indian community's rising stars. Surinder blinked at the tears glazing her eyes, caking the black *surma* lining their rims. It had not gone well with Scottie; there had been no Fisherman's Wharf or Japanese Tea Garden. I had seen his wife in the lobby with their youngest daughter in tow, clutching the end of her royal purple sari in her other hand, luminous as she spoke with a pair of women.

The heavy red velvet curtains over the screen parted at last and a familiar newsreel in English about the Blitzkrieg in London played to an impassive audience. The movie was typical Indian cinematic fare—a boy and a girl, song and dance numbers performed in sumptuous traditional costume. Veena Kumar's pouting face loomed over us, her mouth dripping with desire whenever Ashok Apur ventured near. The gray light from the screen fell on rapt faces, faces that recognized the story, how it would begin and how it would end. When Veena tore herself virtuously away from her lover's long, demanding caresses, a distinctly frustrated breath was exhaled collectively by the audience. There was laughter when the villain mistook the private detective hiding in his closet for a lover. In the end, Ashok succumbed to Veena's powerful elixir, beat by beat, with each flagrant thrust of her hips, the ring of the little bells circling her ankles and the magic of her pencil-long fingers curling, spinning tales in the air. In these fleeting hours, moviegoers suspended the grievances, petty or large, that tormented their waking hours; my mother would forget how Hari had shamed her daughter, and Hari that Uncle Girpal had declared his mother a whore in public. It seemed a miracle of sorts.

But it wouldn't last. The tempting promises of Veena and Ashok running together over a verdant Kashmiri hillside had already begun to fade in our hearts as we filed slowly down the rows, up the aisles, and out the entrance. As the throngs poured out of the theater, crossing over the bright paisley carpet onto the pavement, the ancient feuds, some of them reverting back to circumstances in the villages of the Punjab, were quick to resurface; there were new ones to be forged that night. On the street, Sukhdev Singh—Sukhi—grandson of Jarnail Singh, had already cast his first stones, shattering the cracked windows of the old bus depot. The lights of two police cars saturated the street, whirling skyward in a tornadic spin.

Sukhi, in a gooti topknot, and a friend were pressed against the brick wall of the bus depot amid the jagged plates of broken glass. A stocky officer whose belt strained at his waist held Sukhi by his arms. Nearby, Pritam struggled to control Sukhi's friend. A large group of onlookers began to congregate in the street, a few shouting taunts at Pritam in Punjabi. Uncle Avtar, clearly troubled by the confrontation, paced the edge of the crowd, craning his neck to see over the young men, this new generation who had grown tall as trees from a steady diet of milk and meat. The rest of us could only stand by, mortified and voiceless. Jarnail Singh, a tall, imposing man in a navy turban, watched as Pritam pulled the other boy from the wall and shoved him into the police car. The large officer hurled Sukhi to the ground, throwing his knee into his back. The boy's chin grazed the concrete as Pritam applied the cuffs.

"Kutha!" Sukhi sneered at Pritam, calling him a dog in Punjabi

as he was led to the car. "Turning against your own people." Blood
oozed in little lines on his scraped chin. Pritam slammed the car
door and turned to face the accusing crowd, his face chiseled unrecognizable with anger.

Jarnail Singh stepped forward to reason with the gora officer,
who rocked implacably on his boot heels as he listened to the old
man's demands. "What's the charge?" Singh asked.

The officer leaned into Pritam as if to share a private joke, grinning as his pale eyes squeezed into slivers. The irate circle of onlookers seemed to please him; for once, these people would have to
confront one of their own wearing a badge. He had, no doubt,
been summoned to plenty of skirmishes and domestic-disturbance
calls over the years, not understanding the language, or what exactly these foreigners sought in their new lives in America. Now he
would step back, relinquish the role he had never sought in the first
place. Pritam was eager to show his partner he was the man for the
job. He laughed obligingly at the joke, then tugged at the waist of
his pants, weighed down by the revolver at his side. "Disorderly
conduct," he replied. He worked his mouth as if he were holding a
toothpick there, gazing once again into the crowd, challenging
them silently. *Look at who I am now.* Our eyes met for an instant and
he looked quickly away.

From the backseat of the police car, Sukhi's bloodied, remorse-
ful face peered nervously through the open window. Jarnail Singh's
sons restrained their father by his arms. His days of wrestling for
wagers in India long behind him, he watched helplessly as the police car sped away with his grandson.

The arrests sparked a temporary furor, with those in Jarnail
Singh's camp insisting that the police had overreacted that night,
condemning, in particular, Pritam's actions. We expected him to
represent us, not become our enemy, they cried. Others, however,
claimed it was time to face the problem posed by a certain "element,"

a new generation of unmindful sons who increasingly threatened the community with its reckless and disrespectful behavior. Pritam weathered the controversy with restraint, carrying on with his duties as his job required.

He wanted to meet at Sadie's, a doughnut shop on Jackson, where he often stopped on breaks when he was on duty. It was the final day of classes for me. I waited by a table near the window, a lukewarm cup of coffee and a croissant set before me. A glass case across the room displayed the assorted forms of Sadie's labors—the mounded crests of her banana and blueberry muffins, the O's of doughnuts frosted with maple and white icing, the swollen cambers of croissants toasted a buttery blond.

Outside, Pritam crossed the street through the late-afternoon shadows, tucking the loose ends of his shirt into his pants, his gait brisk and businesslike. He was wearing street clothes, a plaid flannel shirt under a light jacket, and jeans. I hadn't truly considered the danger of his job until I saw the blood on Sukhi's chin. I had watched him put on his uniform at the house on Ridge Road, but he seemed to be dressing for a role on some stage. And the way Pritam had laughed that night outside the theater. The anger on his face. Love, if that's what it was, couldn't change a person entirely.

An audible burst of cold air pierced the warmth indoors as he swung the glass door open. Sadie called to him as he slid onto the bench opposite me and removed his sunglasses. "Just coffee today, Sadie. Black."

From across the table, I could smell the cold on his skin and clothes. He looked both grown up and boyish with his hair cut ridiculously short, exposing the tops of his ears and his lean neck.

"Are you all right?" I asked.

Sadie set the mug of coffee between us and Pritam busied himself pouring sugar into his coffee.

"Fine. Of course. Why wouldn't I be?"

"That business at the movie. Everyone was talking about it for days."

"Nothing I can't handle. That's what they trained me for."

Yes, I thought. They had trained him well. Gone was the slouchy manner, the hesitation before he spoke. He sat with his shoulders squared and looked directly into my eyes when he spoke. He was stronger; I had noticed that when we made love.

"I've been getting some threats, that sort of thing. Nothing serious," he said, drinking his coffee in large gulps. "My mother wants me to quit. She hears I arrested a couple of Indians and wants me to give everything up. What did she think I'd be doing?"

"She's just scared for you." Charan Kaur had left the theater quickly that evening without noticing the trouble.

"It comes with the job, like I said."

"What about Sukhi? Will he be okay?"

He drained his cup of coffee, then pointed to my croissant. "You going to eat that?"

I pushed the plate toward him and watched him bite hungrily into the pastry.

"Let's get out of here," he said.

We drove to Blue Point, a ridge overlooking the river and the valley. Below, the water moved sluggishly through the channel. It would surge again with the rains and the snowmelt in spring. The town's rooftops gleamed in the afternoon sun in neat angles along the streets, and the orchards, their trees bare by late fall, spread away like a grayish brown fur over the landscape. In the distance, the soft blue-and-gold curves of the Coast Range rose up to meet the sky.

"I never think of this place as beautiful, but it is, when you get out beyond it and look over it." I rested my head against his shoulder. "We should do it more often."

"Sure, it's beautiful from here. You think because you come out here and park on a hill, it's going to make everything better? It's still the same when you go back."

I felt the muscles tensing under his shirt and I pulled back. "I've never been away from here, so I don't know what it's like to come back. What's going to happen now, Pritam?"

"I don't know. I'm learning, though—sometimes you have to go after them before they can get to you."

I had asked him once why he had decided to become a cop. Now the answer was clear: so his life could become consumed with these things—provocation, retaliation, and settling scores. Our people had been engaged in this insanity for generations; Pritam had simply found a more legitimate way to get even.

He brushed the hair from my cheek, his fingers lingering tenderly against my skin. "I like it when you wear your hair down."

"I have to clip it back before my mother sees it." It seems we were both only pretending to have found ourselves, to have gained the freedom that allowed us to be who we wanted. We were too young to know the risk that came with loving someone, to want that risk more than anything else. When I looked at him again, his hand cupped his mouth and his hazel eyes were fixed far away, past the river and the valley—those same pale eyes I could look into to see the person I thought I would always know. But I knew then: He was not thinking of me.

At home, a startling blare of horns announced the opening of the evening news broadcast on television. The living room was empty and I found my parents in the kitchen, rummaging through the papers and passports littering the table.

My mother whipped around in her chair and held up a white envelope. "March third. Your father picked up the plane tickets today. Your passport is still good from '72." It was the last trip we had planned to India, but not undertaken, because Prem had contracted chicken pox.

"The middle of the semester? I can't just leave while school is in session."

"School will wait," she said, rising from her chair. "You don't think I know what you've been up to? I warned you many times. Your father and I are giving you one chance. This boy is waiting for you." She waved the envelope in the air as if it harbored not only the plane tickets but Ameer himself.

I breezed past her, but she caught my elbow and swung me around. "If you don't do this, you are no longer our daughter. This is not your home."

I sensed a hint of relief in her voice, as though she had practiced the lines and was content now to have spoken them with such force, without breaking down. I looked at my father again, who suddenly appeared as old as his own father might've. But he didn't utter a word.

I had come home heartbroken that afternoon that I had lost Pritam to all the things I had come to loathe about Oak Grove— the feuds, the petty jealousies and competitions that strangled people's lives. In my room, I pulled the picture of Ameer from my desk drawer and fell back onto my bed. The kind eyes stared resolutely back into mine. I felt my throat begin to close shut and my body went rigid before it began to shake uncontrollably.

The streets began to choke with Christmas shoppers. Tinsel Christmas stars and angels clung to streetlamps downtown; shop windows glowed white and green with sprayed-on snow and holly. As he did each year, Prem begged my mother to set up a Christmas tree. Just a small one, she would agree finally, reluctantly. When the lights were strung and lighted, a slow smile would spread on her face, touched by an ineffable magic that no God would wish to deny her.

A ragged, cold-worn voice greeted me on the phone one evening. It was Jenny Holcomb, home from college for the December holiday. "I've only got two and a half weeks, but I'd love to see you," she said, sniffling through the receiver.

We met at Denny's, a restaurant that, for different reasons, neither of us had visited much. The seats were filled with families passing through town, soothing their travel-weary children with pancakes and milk shakes, or workers on a midday coffee break. Jenny waved to me from a gold vinyl booth, a color that drew away the warmth that normally inhabited her face. She stood and we embraced.

"I haven't been in this place since junior high," she said. She stared at the counter, the wooden bar stools lined along it, the harried waitress in a plaid apron hoisting platters of scrambled eggs and bacon, as if the scene was entirely familiar to her, though it could not have been.

I peeled my jacket off and set it on the seat beside me. "Tell me all about school."

Jenny took a deep breath. "It's hard. I mean, they've got all these brilliant kids who went to private schools all over the West. And then me," she said, pointing to herself, "from Oak Grove High." Her voice was still husky, rough from her cold. "It moves fast. We're already in second quarter."

"Sounds exciting anyway. My classes have been dull. Except for world history."

"It is exciting. It's kind of a strange time to be there. The city's trying to improve its image. They've planted trees along some of the avenues, replaced the boarded-up windows. You know, from the riots?"

We ordered coffee and muffins. The change in her dawned on me slowly. It wasn't as if one would have looked at her and not recognized her. She wore no makeup; her blond hair had darkened in streaks and clung lifelessly to her blue wool sweater. Her slender wrists rested carefully against the edge of the table, the fingers curled into her palms.

"Have you seen any old friends since you've been back?" I asked.

"A few. You!" she said, smiling, her eyes bright still against her pallid complexion. "My mom said Brian's been calling for three weeks, asking when I was coming." She scrunched her face in exasperation. "She wants to have a big party. Everything has to be that way for her . . . formal, momentous. She can't just let me be home, you know."

I didn't know, exactly. I had always ascribed a certain luxury to everything Jenny said or did. Even moments earlier, I'd found a certain glamour in her words: "It's hard. . . . It moves fast." It was vintage Jenny, forever protesting the rank and privilege so effortlessly cast her way. But that was the old Jenny, for I realized the shiny Jenny Holcomb I had known was gone, replaced, for now, by this gaunt and weary one. I poured cream in my coffee, watched it sink, then spread in concentric mocha waves to the rim of the mug.

"Hey, someone told me they saw Pritam driving a *police car* around town."

"Yes, he's a deputy in the sheriff's department." We exchanged a look of confusion, sympathy.

"He's always been decent in a different sort of way. I mean, if you dropped your pencil in class, he would pick it up for you, not kick it away like that Billy Barnes."

"He thinks it's a good step for him. Maybe it is." I buried my chin in my hand; I wasn't so sure what it meant for us.

"I know what you mean," Jenny said, steering the conversation back to herself. "I'm rethinking the whole med school thing. I haven't told my father yet." She leaned back in the booth, engulfed in a gold vinyl halo. One finger still hooked in the handle of her mug, she pressed her mouth tight, as though she might prevent the fear from spilling forth there, a fear I shared with her in that moment, for the bigness of the world.

Uncle Avtar

What had his father told him about trust? That, like an unhatched egg, one had to set it in the most careful places, tend it without smothering it. It was that final evening before his departure, when his father would not even look at him; he had, in fact, not looked at his eldest son that entire week, had cut him out of his heart, leaving it weak and misshapen. The man was not a fool; he held the fear of every aging mother and father, that he would not live to see his child again. That his two younger sons would remain behind in the village was no consolation to him. Where had all this talk come from? America!

Avtar lay on his metal bunk and stared up at the ceiling that once had been painted yellow, like the walls. An odd color for such a place. But then everything here was unfamiliar: the row of identical cells, the latrine with its unspeakable odor a mere two feet from the head of his bunk. The worst had been the first night, when they pitched him in the holding cell among the other incarcerated men. He was brought to the county jail in the early hours of New Year's Day. It was dark; he did not recognize the street or the town. The officers had treated him with a surly contempt. One of them got particularly close to his face and, with his breath reeking of beer and hot mustard, informed him that gambling was an illegal enterprise in the state of California. Then he had decided to keep quiet. The events of that day replayed in his mind dozens of times like a newsreel rewound over and over and forced upon an unwilling audience. They questioned him repeatedly about the money: Where had he been headed with that shoe box–size bulge under his jacket? Where did the money come from? He was delivering it for someone, he finally told them, but refused to divulge the name.

Leandro visited him on the third day. He wore pressed slacks and a dark wool vest, knit perhaps by his mother and donned superstitiously to ward off the kind of bad luck that had befallen his friend. He was not frightened or shocked to be at this place, only that it was Avtar he had come to visit. He was experienced at tracking down friends who had disappeared by the morning's light.

Leandro leaned against the bars. "You don't look so good."

The rudiments of a beard had begun to shadow Avtar's face. A lack of sleep and appetite gave him a withered look and he swallowed often from a perpetual thirst. He knew Leandro would not demand an explanation; he had none to offer.

"They found me with the money" was all he could say. "Bingham's money." He could not make Leandro understand because he did not understand himself. He should not have taken the money, but if he hadn't, he would not have received his wages for the day. He had his own promises to keep to others. Olivia . . . he could not think of her. Had she tried to reach him? Would she wonder why he hadn't slipped onto his customary stool at the counter today and ordered the special?

"How did you find me?" he finally asked Leandro.

"Some of Bingham's guys came around real early New Year's Day. They looked through your stuff real good. I told them I didn't know nothing, that Ingrid over in town could vouch for me." Leandro searched his pockets as if he had forgotten some item. "Can I do anything for you, Avtar?'

Avtar returned to his bunk but could not bring himself to sit. His body felt stiff, sore from these days of inactivity; his insides hurt, as though a sharp instrument had scoured them. "I need a lawyer. And one more thing. Tell her . . . tell Olivia I'll see her soon."

He dreamed of the dock and the boats and the tule marshes waving in the water that night. Which meant he slept. A banging on the bars and the officer's terse voice woke him early the next morning. A well-groomed Indian man dressed in a pinstripe suit and carrying a briefcase smiled broadly at Avtar when he lifted his head from the mattress. The streaks of gray in his hair were combed back in wavy currents. The officer cursed as he fumbled with the lock, then slid the door open. The Indian man entered the cell with a certain air of authority, tugging at the lapel of his coat to indicate that his profession sometimes required his presence in the most un-seemly of circumstances.

"Sammy Gill," he said, extending his hand to Avtar. "I'm here to secure your release at the request of Mohta Singh. He said he'd met you once?" Gill lifted his extravagantly thick brows, also pep-pered with gray.

Standing in his stocking feet, Avtar could not speak for a mo-ment. Of course he remembered the curious man who had stopped along the levee road in his wood-paneled Chrysler. How had Mohta Singh learned of his predicament so quickly? A mixture of relief and humiliation washed over Avtar like a bitter tonic. He recalled his efforts to impress the man who had struck him as worldly and shrewd; this was hardly the way to do it.

"We've already begun the paperwork at the desk for your re-lease," Gill continued. He reached into his coat for a wallet and pulled out a fifty-dollar bill. "Get yourself a ticket to Oak Grove at the bus depot. I've got some business to tend to in San Francisco, or I'd take you myself." He scribbled something on a piece of paper. "Call this number when you get into town. Don't worry about your things at the camp. They're already being collected."

At the bus depot, he bought a ticket for a 2:30 bus that would arrive in Oak Grove by five o'clock in the evening. The clerk returned his $48.50 in change. Avtar stared at the bills; was he foolish to accept money again? Hadn't the same gesture landed him in that squalid jail? If he had turned it down, he would still be sitting in his cell, listening to the groaning and cursing of the drunks who were regularly dragged in. But hadn't he felt the same compulsion when Bingham handed him the seven thousand, that he had to accept Bingham's terms and follow his instructions? What would he have lost if he had refused? At the time, his errand had seemed urgent. It had never occurred to him that he shouldn't take the money and deliver it to Bingham's house as he had requested. But as he wandered along the road that night searching for Harry, he had begun to feel uneasy, wondering how Bingham might've collected it and why he didn't transport the money himself. And then he felt the blinding spotlight of the police car flash over him in the predawn hours.

He placed the bills in his wallet; that and his clothes, fedora, and watch were the only possessions he carried with him. At a telephone inside the depot, he dialed the number at Lupe's, but no one answered. He had difficulty recalling the day and the date. Since New Year's Eve, time, for him, had collapsed; he had no palpable sense of it as he normally did. It was the fourth of January, he remembered at last, a Sunday. Perhaps Lupe's had closed for some special occasion, though he couldn't imagine it. Lupe, as Olivia herself had avowed, was an exceedingly determined woman, driven by a remote, often absent husband.

A large red bus, top-heavy from an overhead basket loaded with luggage, sputtered to the front of the depot. A handful of passengers disembarked and their bags were unloaded by the driver and a clerk he had seen inside the depot. The scene reminded Avtar of Pearson and the others at the dock, the boats that came and went. The straggly line of passengers began to disperse. Where were they coming from; where were they going? An image of a large map formed in his mind, with lines like the spokes of a wheel radiating from each place he had ever visited; the lines—all the people whose paths he had crossed—multiplied until they obliterated the spaces they moved in. He realized he had shut his eyes, perhaps was drifting off to sleep when he heard footsteps stomping toward the bench and a heavyset man in a brown uniform say, "Coming on board, son?"

The bus lurched off down the streets of shops and homes fronted with neat blocks of grass, the luggage overhead shifting whenever it turned or stopped. Outside of town, the road flanked a high levee on its right for several miles. Soon they reached the open country of green fields and oaks that were familiar to him. Eventually, the road pulled away from the river's course, heading generally to the north. Since he had arrived in America, it seemed to him, he was always heading north. At his seat near the back of the bus, he lowered the window a few inches and felt the chilly blast of air numb his cheeks. So he would meet Mohta Singh again. The idea made him anxious, given the circumstances. He was struck by the man's generosity at their first meeting. He was a man who had lived in the world, claimed a small corner of it as his own, and was therefore willing to extend an able hand to others. It was the only way Avtar could reason about Mohta Singh's swift intervention on his behalf.

They stopped along the route in small towns with the same service stations and appliance stores, their unobtrusive churches modestly adorned with steeples and crosses. The same people seemed to board the bus at each stop: mothers dragging their obstinate children, businessmen on a budget, wavy-haired, restless young men setting off for foreign adventures in the next town. He descended the bus steps at the brick bus depot in Oak Grove, located in an old section that evoked the town's beginnings. His legs restless from the long journey, he wandered along the street, passing signs announcing the upcoming centennial celebration of California's gold rush days. The broad three-story Placer Hotel stood conspicuously among the boarded-up storefronts, saloons, and boardinghouses. He tried to imagine what he had heard: the crush of people, men mostly, that flooded the region in the middle of the last century, their pockets filled with little more than a few coins and preposterous dreams. Back at the depot again, he called Mohta Singh's home and spoke with his assistant, Sohan Singh.

When the brown Chrysler rounded the corner, Avtar braced himself for an encounter with Mohta Singh, but it was Sohan Singh carefully maneuvering the car into a parking space. He motioned Avtar to the car and in his crisp, efficient manner announced that Mohta Singh was tending to business at the ranch. They drove several miles southeast of town, then turned onto a dirt road that cut through an orchard into the housing quarters.

Mohta Singh waited on the front porch of the main house, and when he spotted the car approaching, he pretended to busy himself, arranging the chairs and tables where he sat sometimes to enjoy an evening drink. Avtar felt the man watching him curiously as he crossed the lawn to the porch steps. He was not as tall as Avtar had thought, but there was an imperious quality in the set of his shoulders and jaw, the way he planted his feet.

"Come in, get warmed up," Mohta Singh said.

Inside, Avtar gazed about the living room, the honey-colored

light from the lamps striking the walls like a series of fans. He
hadn't set foot in a proper house since he had been at Olivia's. The
remnants of a fire smoldered in the brick fireplace. Bookshelves
dominated the far wall and Avtar surmised somewhat enviously
that Mohta Singh was a reader.

"I did not expect to see you so soon." Mohta Singh's amused expression caused Avtar to examine the rim of his fedora. He struggled to remain composed before his host, but then a fresh thought
consoled him: Perhaps Mohta Singh had experienced his own share
of difficulties and close calls after he emigrated.

"Sit, then. I've not had my afternoon chai." Mohta Singh
watched as his guest studied the collection of Japanese swords
mounted on the wall above the sofa and the steel blades of Sikh
kirpans reflecting the light in the room in narrow bands.

"A granthi who visited here once asked me why I keep these on
the wall rather than wearing them properly on my person. One can
never be holy enough for them, don't you find?"

"Why don't you wear them?"

"I came to this country wearing a bhag and daari." Mohta
Singh scratched at his face, where a full beard had once grown.
"But one has to be practical in this country. People sometimes con-
fuse faith with superstition."

"I wanted to find out . . . do you know what happened to
Bingham's money."

"Don't worry about that. Mr. Gill has taken care of everything."

In the kitchen, Mohta Singh prepared the tea himself. He
emerged with a tray of cups, setting it with some difficulty on the
coffee table, like a waiter still in training. "I haven't any sweets to
offer you. Carmen, my wife," he said, pointing to a photograph on
a cherry cabinet. "She learned to make all the Indian sweets—
ladoo, barfi. . . . She passed away last year."

Avtar looked away; people in photographs were like ghosts to him, though he kept one of Olivia in his wallet. The tea was over-sweetened, but he did not dare refuse the hospitality of a recently widowed man. A recently widowed man who had secured his release, he reminded himself. He swallowed several large gulps to show his appreciation. "I'm sorry about your wife."

"I'll show you about the place tomorrow," Mohta Singh said, pouring more tea in both cups. "Winter is the slow season. I don't actually need another hand, but we'll find something to keep you busy. And, by the way, your things were collected at the camp. My assistant will bring them to you."

"It wasn't much, just some letters and a little cash."

"Letters, yes. Sometimes that is all we have to keep us going."

"I want to thank you . . . for all you've done."

Mohta Singh waved both hands in the air as if Avtar spoke rubbish. "I'll see that Mr. Gill gets everything cleared up."

Later in the bunkhouse, the assistant brought the crate filled with his belongings. Avtar sorted through them: two sets of work clothes, the stack of letters from his family, ninety dollars in cash he had hidden under Leandro's bunk. Tucked among these items was the red silk fan he had never given Olivia. He slid its small wooden latch down and watched the tree's branches spread as he opened it, a childish pleasure. He wondered if she still wore the jade pendant. Two weeks had passed since he had seen her, but it felt like months. He would try to reach her by telephone again, explain it all to her. He had no idea of Bingham's intentions, but it was best for now that he stay away from Locke.

He sat on the bunk and unfolded old letters from his brother Lal. His village had receded like a distant star in his memory, just as his father had feared. But he could not forget them. Flesh was different from brick or sandstone, or the sky. He would write them about his new home, however temporary. What would he tell and what would he leave out? He was grateful that Mohta Singh had not asked him about the incident on New Year's Eve. No doubt he had heard about all kinds of youthful indiscretions from the young men who came to his door seeking seasonal or steady work.

A blurry shadow loomed over him when Avtar opened his eyes the next morning. Mohta Singh, dressed in his chinos and green cardigan for the day, tugged repeatedly at his shirtsleeve, attempting to wake him. "Avtar! Best to get an early start."

The other bunks were empty; only Ajmer, the elderly camp cook, was making a project of getting his socks on. Avtar showered in the adjacent building, then joined Mohta Singh in his car. The car was already idling, with steamy clouds of exhaust pouring from its tailpipe into the cool morning air.

"Daddy!" a young girl called from the porch. She bolted down the steps and came running toward the car, spritely as a gazelle.

"My daughter, Anna," Mohta Singh announced in a tone that was both proud and cautionary.

"Daddy," the girl said at the car window, tugging at two long pigtails. "You promised to take me to Lucy's birthday party today."

"I'll be back in time to do that. Now go inside, stay out of the sun."

The girl backed away as her father shifted gears, waving, bouncing on her ankles.

The two men spent several hours touring Mohta Singh's properties. They drove on bumpy dirt roads through the orchards along Howard Lane, where the house and camp were located. Mohta Singh explained the variety of peaches planted in sections, how they ripened in succession during the summer harvest season. A tree's fruit-bearing years were limited, he explained, and only a proper balance of instinct and diligence (and some luck with the weather) would produce a maximum yield. Several miles away, at the Fremont Road property, Mohta Singh stopped the car and they walked among the rows of trees that stretched a quarter mile in either direction. Mohta Singh tamped the ground with his shoe to check for moisture, examined the base of a trunk now and then for disease.

"All of this is yours?" Avtar asked.

"Not exactly. I am 'leasing' these acres, as my attorney puts it. A Punjabi man has to be crafty about these things. The government does not allow us to own land, as you know. But one day soon, it'll be mine. Though I have no true heir to leave it to when I'm gone. Only a daughter . . ."

In the middle of winter, there were only odd jobs to be completed on the ranch. His first week at work on the Singh ranch, he repaired ladders that were used by the pickers during harvest. One of the other hands showed him how to check for broken steps, loosening bolts, cracked or rotting wood. The bunkhouse was cleaned and the shed and mess hall repainted the same parrot green as the main house during a few rainless stretches of days.

The workers piled into the back of the pickup truck once a week, when Sohan Singh drove them into town for visits to the bank, the market, or the drugstore. Sitting in the bed of the truck with an icy wind chapping his face one afternoon, with children staring fearfully at him from the backseats of passing cars, and with his first paycheck in his pocket, Avtar spotted a navy blue Buick parked in front of a house, with a sign on its windshield that read FOR SALE—$100. The money he cashed in the bank brought his savings to $110. It was a '37 Buick Century Sport Coupe, he learned on their return trip, and if its paint was fading into a soft, velvetlike patina, the chrome grille still gleamed like a polished mirror. While Sohan Singh waited impatiently nearby, Avtar circled the vehicle three times, running his fingers over the nose of the hood and the smooth whitewalls. He climbed behind the steering wheel of the two-seater, and with the keys, he started the engine the way he had observed Mohta Singh do.

"How will you get it home?" Sohan asked. The normally humorless man managed a weak smile as he watched Avtar put his life savings into the hands of the middle-aged owner standing along the road in his undershirt.

Avtar had not considered such technicalities, but he felt emboldened in that moment as he stood before Sohan Singh. "You will come back for it with Mohta Singh."

He practiced driving each evening after work, setting off down the dirt roads through the orchards while there was still light, the roosters in panicked flight when he barely missed the chicken coop at the back of the camp a couple of times on his return in the dark. Mohta Singh accompanied him to the license bureau one day and Avtar emerged from the building marveling at the paper in his hand. Mohta Singh slapped Avtar's back with deliberate force. "You'll be driving my trucks for me this summer," he said. But it was not Mohta Singh's trucks that interested Avtar just then. On his day off, very soon, he would drive the levee roads back to Locke and find Olivia.

He composed a letter to his brother Lal that evening.

> *Dearest brother,*
>
> *If you have written me recently, the letters have not reached me, as I have changed my place of work again. On one of my walks in the river district, an Indian gentleman stopped in his car (a very fancy car) and we talked and he said I should come and work for him. I have been here since January and already I have purchased a car and obtained a license to drive it!*

Avtar paused and tossed the pen aside. He stared at the page and winced at his deteriorating penmanship. Worse, he could think of no more to write. He could not tell his family about New Year's Eve; he could not tell them about Olivia. He could not say that, even living among his fellow Punjabis, with the prospect of steady work, he missed the sound of the water in the river, its timbre changing from dawn to dusk, and Leandro's colorful tales. He could only fabricate these stories about the good fortune he had found in America. But here he was, sitting in another bunkhouse. Ajmer, the cook, was folding his clean underwear; two other men lay in their bunks studying girlie magazines, while a fourth had fallen asleep before dark.

He nearly crumpled the aerogram, but instead he reached for his pen once more.

> *How are your studies, Lal? I hope the landlord hasn't gotten*
> *the better of Father lately. Is Mohinder helping him in the*
> *fields? Please make note of my new address.*
> *Waiting for your earliest response,*
> *Your brother*
> *Avtar*

The work increased as the days grew longer. While the men were gathered in the mess hall one day, Mohta Singh warned that seven-day work-weeks lay ahead. Avtar looked up from his bowl of dal and watched his boss pace among the tables in knee-high irrigation boots. The men listened silently, with their hands resting in their laps. But Avtar did not hear as Mohta Singh divided the men into two crews and assigned their responsibilities for the days ahead. He would have to make the trip to Locke soon, Avtar realized, and his mind drifted further as he contemplated the details of his journey.

He studied the route on a map, marking the roads he would take with a pen, circling the names of towns whose names he could not read but whose relative location he could identify. The evening before his departure, he washed and polished the car while a few of the other work hands gathered around to proffer conflicting advice on soaping and rinsing techniques. He lay awake in bed for hours, imagining what he would say to Olivia.

Though he had driven into town many times, he felt a fresh exhilaration as he passed the city limits and the sheltering bounds of the surrounding orchards for the first time and entered into open country. The coupe sputtered occasionally when he accelerated after a stop, but on a long stretch of highway, the ride smoothed and quieted and he enjoyed the morning air blowing through an open window and the flow of automobiles whose drivers observed an amiable code of travel.

A right turn at a fork in the road led him to the first of the levees that crisscrossed the delta. Avtar's pulse quickened, but it was no longer the result of the pleasure a novice takes from simply driving an automobile; things had complicated considerably as the Buick crawled up the bank and followed the road along the river. He knew from his first glimpse of the water that it was more than its marshy scent, or the way the sun's path changed its hue from gray to blue to indigo; these physical qualities would endure as long as water flowed in the river. But he could no longer observe them without recalling certain events: a rainy afternoon spent at a cottage, the lottery game he'd won at the Dai Loy, or the spotlight that had illuminated his entire body as he'd walked along the road on a dark night.

His slow southward journey carried him past the stately homes of landowners and managers (one of them was Bingham's), veiled in that obscure silence and certitude that had always baffled Avtar. He slowed at the lane with the large sycamore arcing over it and through its bare branches glimpsed the white cottage beyond. He accelerated toward Lupe's; that would be the place to try first. Even on a Sunday, cars and trucks jammed the small parking area. At the entrance, Avtar readjusted the collar of his shirt under his wool jacket, then pushed the door open.

The clinking of silverware and cups settling on saucers, the baritone rumble of male conversation—all of these sounds thundered in Avtar's ears as he moved to his customary seat at the counter. But he did not sit. His eyes scanned the room and finally settled on the waitress bursting into the room with her arms balancing several platters.

Regina did not see him right away. She set the platters before her impatient customers, her bangs dancing on her forehead as she paced the floor, smiling obligingly at requests for extra gravy or a second helping of apple pie. It's the same old Regina, Avtar thought, with her slightly disheveled, frenetic manner. "Hang on. I've got a customer at the counter," she told a fourth party. Her legs seemed to lock beneath her when she recognized him.

Avtar retreated to the bar stool.

Regina set one manicured hand on the counter; the other was a fist boring into her hip. "Olivia's not here," she said, the shadow in the furrow of her brow a warning to him.

"I want to explain everything to her. It's not what you think. . . ."

"Doesn't matter what I think. Some men came by looking for you after New Year's. That's all Lupe needed to hear." She pursed her lips in an expression of scorn and pity; in the end, he was like every other man, not worth the trouble. "She sent her off to stay with an aunt in Modesto."

"Where can I find her?"

"You won't."

$\mathcal{A}$ number of years passed. Avtar moved into the pink-and-white bungalow alongside Mohta Singh's ranch house. He was number-two man in the farming operation. Sohan Singh, the longtime assistant, had departed with bitter words when Mohta Singh settled on his younger protégé as his new foreman. Avtar organized the work crews with only perfunctory orders from his boss. For him, the seasons now shifted according to the whims and demands of the land he tended.

With the immigration laws loosened, the Indian community began to flourish. Men hurried back to India and returned with Indian wives. Men who had spent years sharing space in bunk-houses moved into their own homes and hoisted young children into their arms. They began to purchase land they could rightfully call theirs. Amid this boom, Mohta Singh ensured that his own holdings would multiply—doubling, tripling his acreage to six hundred within a few years.

By then, Anna had grown up. Her hair was cut to her ears and she wore jeans rolled up to just below her knees, showing off the ankles that had strengthened from years of jumping about in her house and yard. Boys visited; they came when the house and grounds were empty. One boy, Jesse, drove her home from school sometimes. Avtar encountered the two in the back of the shed once atop a pile of canvas tarps. He had tried to slip away quietly, pre-tending not to have noticed them, but Anna had seen him.

"You won't tell my father, will you?" Anna asked in a manner that was more threatening than pleading. She seemed pleased that the young man she addressed as Uncleji had caught her in the shed with her boyfriend, her shirt undone. Avtar remained quiet when-ever Mohta Singh complained about his daughter.

Girlfriends came to the house, too; Anna had many of them, and their names would roll off her tongue in a dizzying succession: Beatrice, Isabel, Teresa, Jean, Joginder, mostly daughters of Sikh men and their Mexican wives. They would rumble down the porch steps in a whirl of skirts and petticoats and pile into cars to get a milk shake or a slice of pie in town.

But that free, rollicking manner of hers would change one day, too. In the summer after her seventeenth birthday, she grew more sullen and withdrawn, spending day after day in her room. Sometimes, Avtar would find her in the house, glued to the telephone for hours, speaking in a hushed, choked voice. The jeans were replaced by baggy slacks and oversized shirts, and one day even—Avtar had had to look twice to be certain—a salwaar kameez. There came the day when nothing could hide Anna's belly, swelling, it seemed, by the hour.

One discreet conversation at a time, the news of Anna's pregnancy spread. Mohta Singh's pride withered as his temper exploded. He thought of sending her away, but finally, he conceded, she was the only family he knew. Because he had learned to trust Avtar's counsel, he invited him frequently after dinner and the two would discuss the week's progress and plans for the days to come. Mohta Singh, in fact, came to depend on these visits as a welcome distraction from more unpleasant affairs. One evening, they were interrupted when Anna came into the living room and plunged into a chair.

Mohta Singh regarded his daughter with alarm. He struggled from his seat and approached her, keeping back several feet. "What are you crying about now? You're not feeling well?"

Anna buried her head in a cushion. "Jesse's gone away."

"Good. I never want to see that half-Mexican boy around here again."

"What are you saying?" She tossed the cushion aside and glared up at her father. Clumps of her hair clung to her wet face. "My mother—your wife—was Mexican. *I'm* half Mexican," she cried, spreading her hand over her chest.

Mohta Singh's face turned multiple shades of purple and crimson. That was different, he seemed to be thinking. Somehow, that was different. "You'll have a Sikh husband who'll show you how to behave properly. That is, if anyone will have you in this condition." He held his clenched fists at his side, as though restraining himself from striking her. Only the memory of Carmen prevented him from doing so.

But Anna had already grabbed his car keys from the table and fled out the front door to the car. Avtar listened as the motor started and the tires slid over the gravel as the car sped away.

"Come with me," Mohta Singh said. In the pickup truck, he clumsily jerked the gearshift, exasperated in a way Avtar had not witnessed before. They drove through town to the neighborhoods on the northeast side.

"Where are we going?" Avtar asked.

"Flora Mendoza left her husband many years ago. An Indian man. That boy has grown up without a father, but Anna will not be the one who pays forever for that."

He stopped the car in front of a lemon yellow house with a flat roof and a wire fence circling the lawn and flower beds.

A red-and-silver tricycle blocked the doorway and Mohta Singh kicked it aside before he knocked. The woman who opened the door recognized her visitor immediately. "Mr. Singh." She wiped her hands on an apron and invited them in.

The two men stepped inside the kitchen of the modest home. Avtar heard the retreat of children's footsteps. The room smelled warm, of a meal cooked and consumed and dish soap bubbling in the sink.

"I'm sorry to bother you so late. Where is Jesse?" Mohta Singh asked.

"I haven't seen him today." Flora peeled the striped apron from her short, wiry frame and invited them to sit.

"When does he usually come home?" Mohta Singh peeked in the adjoining room, as if the boy might be hiding brazenly there.

"Late. He works at the market."

"Working? Children are all too eager to grow up," he said, laughing a little.

The woman smiled faintly in return; that was what one did in Mohta Singh's presence, obeyed his cues and whims.

"You're sure he's not with Anna tonight?"

"He's at work," she replied without flinching.

"You make sure he never bothers my daughter again." Mohta Singh spoke with an utter calm, which made Avtar anxious. "Or I will."

Back at his home, Mohta Singh instructed Avtar to sleep on his couch in case he was needed during the night. Avtar removed his boots and socks and stretched his legs over the ends of the sofa, then curled on his side, futilely in search of a comfortable position. All night, lights flicked on and off in the house and Avtar listened to Mohta Singh move from room to room. By dawn, Anna still had not returned.

When she returned in the middle of the morning, her father did not ask her where she had been. "I prayed all night that you would come home safe," he told her before she disappeared into her room without saying a word and locked the door.

She slept for two days. Mohta Singh called for a doctor, who, following an examination, could only prescribe rest. In the many years Avtar would know Anna's father, he would never again see him quite in that state of complete bewilderment. He paced ceaselessly through the rooms, stared strangely at the items displayed on shelves and cabinets—brass figurines from his native country, ceramic knickknacks his wife had collected—as if not comprehending how they had gotten there. He once again called Avtar to his home one evening after Anna had regained her strength

Mohta Singh offered him a glass of whiskey. "Anna's visiting one of the ladies who's taken an interest in her welfare."

Avtar was relieved to see his boss in a more relaxed state, his customary sense of confidence and control restored. "I'm glad she's recovered."

"She's always been a fine girl, full of joy. People lose their way sometimes. I think losing her mother was very difficult for her. And then, of course, there haven't been many women around. To influence her in a positive way, I mean."

Avtar shifted in his seat, swirled the whiskey in his glass. He had expected to provide an update of the farming operation. But Mohta Singh showed no interest that evening in the progress of the annual pruning season or the antics of his often contentious crew. He seemed to study the grain of the floorboards, a pattern he had memorized long ago sitting in the evenings with Carmen.

"The thing is," he continued, "the thing is, my daughter needs someone she can count on. A husband." Perhaps the shock on Avtar's face caused him to lean forward a bit into a more agreeable posture. "Not just a husband, but someone I can trust. And leave everything to one day." He cut a wide swath in the air with his hand, indicating that his offer promised great advantages.

Avtar tightened his fingers around the glass; there was no question what his boss was suggesting. "I am thirty-four. Perhaps she would want someone younger." But Mohta Singh had dangled the ultimate prize before him. Not the girl. The land. What he had dreamed of long before he set foot in the fertile valley that ran like a spine the length of California. But he would be lying to himself if he claimed that he had never thought about Anna. Even with the baby growing inside her, she had a way of looking at a man, dropping her chin, her mouth forming a soft pout, as though wanting to ask some unmentionable question. "Let me think about it."

Outside, the cold autumn air hit his lungs like a brick. Even then, Avtar knew: There is no way out of this.

When Anna came onto the porch the following day and watched him unload ladders from the truck, Avtar knew Mohta Singh had spoken to her. She leaned her head against the wood post and rested a hand on her protruding stomach, looking neither angry nor pleased. A week later, they stood before a county clerk in Nevada and repeated vows that they would not part until death, and signed papers. Anna wore a simple ivory dress with a large bow that tied in the back and a white hat and gloves. On the ride back, she sat in the front seat of the Chrysler next to her new husband. Indifferent to the snow-drenched alpine peaks of the Sierra Nevada, she removed her gloves and played awhile with the radio dial, the incessant static finally earning a mild rebuke from Mohta Singh in the backseat. They dined in the evening at a fine restaurant in Sacramento and Avtar could see the pleasure in Mohta Singh's face as he pulled a stack of bills from his wallet and rewarded the smiling waiter.

Avtar's marriage to Anna was a constant process of uncovering her mysteries. He expected her to become increasingly consumed with preparations for the baby that was due in a few months. However, she rarely mentioned her condition at first, as though she was experiencing no more than a minor and temporary physical change that would soon remedy itself. He came home each evening, to find her chatting with friends about hairstyles and makeup techniques or listening to her records—Chuck Berry, the Coasters, and others.

In bed, he was never sure which Anna to expect: the one who coaxed him inside her or the one who pushed him away when she was irritable, unable to sleep. But he enjoyed tending to her diverse and unpredictable needs: preparing cool, damp towels to wrap her swollen ankles in or a glass of freshly squeezed pomegranate juice in the middle of the night. More than redemption, he felt the pleasure of caring for someone who needed him. And Anna needed him; even during a difficult mood, she would squeeze Avtar's arm so tightly, he thought his veins would burst open. Do not abandon me, she seemed to plead. Rarely, in the moments his imagination exerted its most cruel workings, he would lie next to his young wife, her black curls spread like a dark cape over the pillow, and imagine it was Olivia who carried their child inside her. But he did not dare to revel in these thoughts for long; he would turn in the bed, his back to Anna, slowly unclenching his sorrow.

The first signs of trouble in her pregnancy appeared late one night as they lay in bed. He heard Anna mumble, then moan softly.

"You're not comfortable?" he asked.

"I've had a terrible headache all day." She thrashed about the bed, trying to shift her distended, uncooperative body. "I can only sleep on my back anymore."

Avtar reached with his hand to touch the mound of her belly, hard as the rind of a melon. "Soon you'll be free of this little creature."

"Free? I'll never be free again. I'll be like one of those women at the gurdwara who never leaves the ladies' room because she's nursing or changing diapers or . . ." Anna struggled to sit up in the bed. She fluffed the pillows behind her and collapsed against them like a limp sack. "Massage my feet again."

Avtar crawled to the end of the bed and lifted one foot, pressing firmly with his fingers against the arch. "Ah," he said, inspecting the bright red nail polish on her toes, "I see you can still manage to reach your feet."

Anna kicked her leg feebly in protest. "Isabel did them."

His fingers moved to her ankles, tender and puffy, then the long, silky-firm muscles of her calves. Anna's eyes were shut tight, as though she was trying to remember nothing. Avtar felt a pinch in his chest; he suddenly wanted Anna, at the least, to remember him. "What do you want it to be, a boy or a girl?" he asked.

She opened her eyes slowly, her dark brows bunched together. "Most of the time, I don't want it to be anything."

"You'll see. It'll be different once you have it in your arms."

"You're a kind man, even if you married me only to please my father."

He found her in the kitchen the next day preparing a sandwich, when she dropped the knife, leaving a white lump of mayonnaise on the floor. She crumpled against the counter. "I feel so dizzy," she said, out of breath. She clung to him, frightened, as he led her to the sofa.

The doctor diagnosed preeclampsia and prescribed bed rest to stabilize her blood pressure. He dropped his normal jovial manner and took Anna firmly by the shoulders: "Your condition could worsen dangerously if you don't follow my instructions," he warned.

Anna protested at home; how could one stay in bed for seven weeks? Their routine would change, Avtar decided. It was near winter, when the orchards granted a brief reprieve. He brought his wife toast and eggs or hot cereal in the morning and drank his second cup of coffee while staring through kitchen windows streaked with condensation. He made midday rounds to check on a skeleton crew attacking trivial chores around the camp, then returned to the house to look after his wife. The idea of the baby was still abstract to him; when he thought of it—and Anna—he was aware mostly of an enduring responsibility, a promise he had made to her in Nevada, and to Mohta Singh.

Mohta Singh could not bear his daughter's failing condition. He was inured to the aura of illness in his home; his wife, Carmen, had lain bedridden for months with a heart condition. A subsequent visit by the doctor confirmed his fears: Anna had not improved. Her condition, in fact, had worsened and she was admitted to the hospital, where she developed abdominal pains and began to vomit. To save her, the doctor insisted, the baby would have to be delivered by Cesarean section immediately; at thirty-four weeks, it had a good chance of surviving.

In the waiting room, Avtar crouched in a blue chair, his head balanced in his hands. Mohta Singh paced the rectangular room, studying the innocuous paintings of bowls of fruit and bouquets of spring flowers. An hour and a half later, a door in the hallway swung open. The doctor, a vigorous-looking man in his fifties, paused to adjust his glasses and consult his chart before he entered the waiting room.

"Mr. Rai, your baby boy is fine. They've taken him to the nursery."

There was no congratulatory tone in the doctor's words. He allowed the two men standing before him to prepare themselves for the inevitable news. "We couldn't save Anna. I'm sorry. She had a seizure during the delivery, probably intracranial hemorrhaging. It's common in these extreme cases."

Mohta Singh had no use for such technical medical terms. "What about the boy?" he kept asking.

The doctor removed his glasses. "Mr. Singh, I don't think you understand what I just told you. Your daughter is dead."

Could one call these turns in one's life mistakes? When he held the infant boy in his arms, he could not. When those curious little eyes struggled to focus on his face, Avtar wondered about this strange journey that had made him a father now. What had brought him to this green-wallpapered room to care for his young son? Was it the money he took from Bingham? The land he now farmed alongside Mohta Singh that would be his someday? These questions troubled Avtar's exhausted mind. He tended clumsily to the baby's basic needs, holding him awkwardly when he wailed from hunger, forgetting the bottles boiling on the stove.

Mohta Singh soon brought in an experienced caretaker, Dhan Kaur, to take over the feeding and changing and washing. He grieved by retreating to the sanctuary of his office or setting off to attend unscheduled board meetings. Dhan Kaur confided to Avtar that these absences could be explained by a woman he was rumored to be seeing in the Bay Area. Mohta Singh took a passing interest in the child, at times beguiled by the face that reflected his mother's willful spirit; other times, the same face plunged him into a deep well of misery and he would not look at his grandson for days.

But Hari thrived, as if aware that a life without his mother to shield him would require an uncommon strength. By his third month, his weight had reached the normal range and Dhan Kaur surrendered the baby to Avtar's arms more willingly. He sat in the evenings with the baby on his lap. The weight, the warmth of the little body against his chest was a new comfort to him and he began to imagine the child growing; he would teach him the rhymes he'd learned as a child and how to ride a bicycle, send him to school.

Perhaps it was time to write his family again, he decided. It was time he told them about Anna and the child. He needed to tell someone, in a sense, to assure himself that all these things had truly come to pass. In his grief, his father-in-law had grown distracted and remote. By coincidence, a letter arrived from Avtar's brother: His father grew weaker and rarely left their home but for his morning walk, Lal wrote. The work on the acres they leased was left to Mohinder and him, stealing precious time from his studies. But Lal was adamant: Their father wished to see his eldest son again. Sitting in the car outside the post office in town, Avtar set the letter aside and watched the late-day shoppers and townfolk streaming back and forth along the sidewalk. He tried to imagine his father in this feeble state. He was a man who had looked old even when he was young, but he had always had the strength of a bull, the villagers said of him. He hadn't heard that voice, like someone raking stones, in over a decade.

The letter remained on his mind as he assembled his crew in the morning. The orchards had bloomed and leafed out (those brief days each spring when he marveled that the place where he toiled and sweated daily could burst alive with such beauty). Now the soil would be disked and irrigated so the fruit would grow. If the trees produced a heavy crop, the canneries would pay a decent price and perhaps a smile would light Mohta Singh's worn face once more. He dropped the crew at various sites, then carried a shovel alone into the shady orchard along Fremont Road. He started the pump in the northern quadrant, dousing his head and hair in the powerful stream of water before he set off to the point where he would break the low dam of soil and allow the water to flood into a new section of trees. It was strenuous, solitary work, which he enjoyed. The silence was like a wide, deep pail he could unburden his mind into. He shoveled at a furious pace for short spurts, then watched the water swirl around the trees until it filled the section.

He bathed as soon as he returned home in the evening and put on fresh clothes, then searched the rooms for Dhan Kaur and little Hari. He found only Mohta Singh sitting in his study, filing through papers.

"They've gone over to Bibi Rani's." Mohta Singh looked up from his papers. The room was dark, the heavy gold drapes drawn. A single lamp on the desk sent a yellow cone of light up to the ceiling. "Don't leave yet." Mohta Singh rose and opened a cabinet, where he kept his bottles of Jim Beam. "This is a dreary room. Dreary work. Accounts payable. We'll go in the living room."

Avtar took a chair across from the sofa, suddenly remembering the night he had spent there twisting and turning when Anna had run away.

Mohta Singh filled two shot glasses and handed one to Avtar.

"If the rains hold off, we're looking at a good crop this year. Better than last," Avtar said.

"Yes, the rain, the heat. Variables in the formula." Mohta Singh tilted his head back as he drained the shot glass. "You've worked for me for ten years now. Tell me honestly: Do you ever think about going out on your own?"

The abrupt question startled Avtar. He cleared his throat, sensing immediately that his boss was not speaking in theoretical terms. "Naturally, a man would think about it from time to time."

"You're a smart worker. I've watched you. You come up with new ways to solve problems. Smart workers never stay around forever. They start their own operations." Mohta Singh tugged at his chin with his fingers. "You're young, Avtar. You should remarry. Haven't you thought seriously about any of this?"

Of course I have, Avtar tried to say.

"The boy will always be here if you want to visit. But I will raise him as my own son. You understand, don't you? If you remarried and brought your wife into this house, some stranger would raise my grandson, and he'd call her Mummy." An uncomfortable silence filled the room. Finally, Mohta Singh stood, indicating he had other business to tend to. He paused as he passed Avtar on his way back to his study and set his hand on his shoulder. "To make it a little easier for you, I'll give you sixty acres on Fremont Road. The side with the gray house."

Avtar looked around the room, the house that was no longer his home. Once again, he would make a new one.

On a windy day in April, Avtar set sail again for India. As the green strip of coastline receded, he knew that there would be other chances to take, bargains to be struck. Over the years, he would wonder what terms Olivia had settled for. Unbeknownst to him, another young woman awaited deep within that other continent. She would face east toward the distant Pacific waters and pray for his safe journey. She would leave her own family behind and follow him to unfamiliar shores, bear him three boisterous sons, toil beside him on the land Mohta Singh had exchanged to claim his grandson as his own. On those nights when the moon slipped into the shadows, withholding its silver light, she would stretch her arm across his chest and hold on to him and tell him simply that the past was past.

Nineteen

Through the kitchen window, Aunt Teji spotted the square of light coming from her husband's office. Opening the metal door of the old shed, she found him at the table, fussing with the contents of an old trunk. Piles of old documents, photographs, and mementos littered the surface of the old butcher table.

She could ask him what he was looking for, yet she understood it was no single thing, but, rather, the accumulated debris of his life over the years, evident in scraps of paper and images. He would roam through his orchards the same way, grasping the furled limbs of fruit trees that scratched at his rough palms, or would scrutinize the unsuspecting faces of his sons; he witnessed a confirmation of his lived life in these physical things.

"Look here," he said, holding up her first passport, from when she had arrived in America. He squinted at the youthful image, rendered grainy and yellow under the dusky light of the single bulb overhead.

Teji smoothed the front of her kameez. She wore the purple one her husband liked, with silver stitching at the collar and sleeves.

Avtar glanced up from the photograph, softened by the vision of his wife's firm heart-shaped face swaddled in a dark shawl. "You haven't changed much, Teji. Truly."

"Change doesn't only show in the flesh." Inside her, everything had changed, many times over. When her son Juni had taken his biology course, he told her that her cells constantly divided, matured, and died in a constant process of replenishment. Don't you think I already know this, she wanted to tell him.

The lid of the old green trunk hung open like a gaping mouth, teeming with secrets. Somewhere in there, she knew, lay a photograph of Olivia; it had stopped her heart once as she sifted through the piles in the trunk. Another facet of her husband revealed. "The past is past," she would often say to comfort him.

"Is it?" he would reply. "Why do we carry it around with us like a silly old trinket we can't bear to part with? There are trees in the Sierra Nevada that were growing during Jesus' time," he said, cupping his palm toward the east. Aunt Teji did not know about such trees, only that her husband harbored an internal wound that was as private to him as it was enigmatic to her.

Here you go, Maker's Mark on the rocks." The bartender at the Loft set the glass on the polished oak bar. Hari's fingers curled around it. He swirled the amber liquid, tipped the glass toward his mouth for a sip, the ice sloshing. He watched the bartender, whose white shirtsleeves were rolled up to his elbows, plunge foggy, beer-streaked mugs into a metal sink filled with oily gray water. The place was livening up; a group of four, two couples, had taken a table behind him and ordered a pitcher of beer. A tape of Sinatra singing "Have Yourself a Merry Little Christmas" played over the speakers.

A man sitting three stools away took long, slow drags from a cigarette, as if it was oxygen. Hari thought of the oxygen tent his grandfather had lain under in the hospital before he died, the clear, quiet plastic looking as if it would smother breath rather than sustain it.

"Hey, come on, Artie, change the music. Christmas is over," the man said.

"You're Jewish, Hal," the bartender replied.

"Damn right I am." Hal glanced over at Hari, seeking a show of support, the kind of camaraderie that can instantly bud between two fellows at a bar. Hari raised his glass to him. "He's right, Artie. The Sinatra goes."

Artie filed through a stack of tapes on a ledge behind the bar. A moment later, one of the women behind him, a redhead in green sequins, began to sway and swivel to the tinny trumpet of Duke Ellington's "East St. Louis Toodle-oo."

Hari took another drink of the whiskey, which felt cool and silky on his tongue. His grandfather had trained him on Jim Beam. He had slapped two shot glasses on the kitchen table, filled them, and handed one to Hari on his eighteenth birthday. "I've made more deals thanks to ole Jim here," he said in English. Grandfather would resent the Maker's Mark. Forgetting your roots, where you came from, with that expensive stuff, he would say. No, Hari thought, I could never forget where I came from; you reminded me of it every day. The picture of his beautiful young mother, who had died as he was born, still hung with the others over the low carved cherry cabinet in the living room. Its prominent display had always felt like a horrible accusation to Hari, his grandfather's rigorous demands constantly shifting—like a variable in an equation Hari was always trying to figure out—for letting him live, his daughter die. How could he forget any of it?

The waitress, Angie Barker, was just beginning her shift, tying an apron with pockets over her short black skirt. The foil-paper tiara with HAPPY NEW YEAR carved out in glittery letters sat slightly askew on her cropped auburn hair. "Hey, Hari. Been seeing a lot of you in here lately." She tucked a small paper pad and a pencil into a pocket in her apron, pushing her chest out a little as she did so. "Not that I'm complaining." Her lips parted in a half smile.

She still wore too much eyeliner. They'd been in high school together. Suffered through physical science and, sophomore year, a hellish four weeks of square dancing in PE, a coed affair mandated by the nonstop rain that winter, which had culminated in all-night flood watches by mid-January. The two of them, humiliated beyond reason, had executed their do-si-dos and aleman de lefts with exceptional flair, he recalled.

Angie leaned on the bar, facing him. He could see the blue veins showing through the skin at her temples, her throat. He looked away; he thought he had never seen skin so pale, like candlelight.

"Staying around for the festivities? We've got prime rib on special." She slid her hand under a tray of drinks on the bar, balancing it with a practiced ease. "I'll be back in a minute."

Neelam pinched the smoldering, ashy cone of incense with her fingers. A column of silver smoke coiled upward toward the ceiling. Davinder called to her. "N, we'll be late." How to ask him to stop at gurdwara first, on the way to her mother's? He was all impatience tonight, scolding her lightly for dishes left unwashed in the sink, seizing the dishrag and soap to attack the unseemly job himself. But she would have to stop; her soul these days demanded a daily purification against the turbulence that pushed constantly in her heart. Thoughts of him: how he had looked at her by the wall in the temple, not smiling, but the pleasure of seeing her written indelibly on his face, recognizing something at her very core that no one else could, ever.

Moments later, she pushed open the tall gurdwara doors and

retraced the steps they had taken together. Davinder lingered in the back of the large hall, watching as his wife descended on her knees before the Guru Granth Sahib and pressed her forehead to the floor.

I sat by the window in my room, watching the sky grow dark. Looking through the trees, I could see cars passing with growing frequency on Fremont Road, the string of headlights piercing the charcoal gray of late evening. The world reawakening, stirring, congregating in bright rooms somewhere. I wondered, when the lights and the laughter dimmed and the sun rose in the morning, what the new year would bring.

The supper table was set with a platter of methi roti, and the chicken curry and mounds of saffron rice displayed in pearly white CorningWare. Some new movie tune had anchored in my mother's throat. She hummed as she ladled the dal into a large serving bowl. If the world beyond these walls often seemed chaotic, she at least could count on periods of respite within her own home. She loved nothing more than this simple act: the preparation of food and its sharing among those she loved beyond telling. It was that very quality of simplicity she had tried to impress upon her daughters, who seemed to want more, much more, than any worthy human being should ask for. Desire only tempted fate. Someone had told her that long ago and she had found it to be remarkably true as she settled into her midlife.

These reflections were interrupted by Neelam and Davinder's arrival. He lifted the wool coat from his wife's shoulders and announced that his prolonged afternoon nap was the cause for their tardiness.

We gathered around the table, my father in his special white going-out shirt at one end and Davinder, the sleeves of his thick brown sweater pushed to his elbows, at the other.

"Where's Teji?" My mother looked to either side of the table, as though the woman she called bhainji—sister—might have disappeared among the cabinets or behind the drapes. "I invited them. Probably held up by that brother of yours," she said to my father.

"That brother of mine is busy working on a deal that could make him a rich man," my father said.

"Ha! Rich! Teji told me he's selling a few acres with . . . with . . ." My mother's eyes darted apologetically toward Neelam, then Davinder. Neelam pushed the food on her plate back and forth with her fork.

"With Hari," I said, sounding exasperated. Everyone held their breath for a moment, then exhaled, as if someone had pricked a pin in some bloated beast, expelling its noxious gassy air.

Davinder slurped his dal. "Well, developers are paying top dollar these days. Perhaps he's smart to sell." He plunged furiously into the food, as if he had not eaten for days.

After dinner, he switched the television on to a New Year's Eve special and stretched back on the sofa, pulling Neelam close to his side. "My father was a great fan of the big bands . . . Gene Krupa, Jimmy Dorsey. He signed me up for trumpet lessons when I was nine."

"Really?" Neelam said, surprised. How little you truly knew of the person you shared your bed, your body, your life with.

She sank under the weight of his arm. The tinny rasp of the trumpets coming from the television scratched at her eardrums. Her husband's body grew still beside her and as he blinked intermittently at the screen, she slipped away from him. The sound of dishes scraping against the porcelain sink in the kitchen was silenced the moment she plunged outdoors into the pool of cold night air. But that feeling, too, would dissolve on her skin like a fine wet film evaporating into nothing. She ran across the patch of lawn, past the blocky dark shadow on her right that was her father's shop. Her feet thumped hard against the damp earth as she crossed into the orchard. She stopped amid the rows of silent trees. Her breath came in short, convulsive gasps, as though she had forgotten how to fulfill this simple primal function. Above her, the stars looked like a thousand glass beads scattered across the black sky, out of reach. She stretched her arms upward and then out, longing to feel sensation in her hollow body. Then she began to spin slowly, then faster, around and around, her face turned skyward to the flickering constellations swirling above her.

It was a routine stop. A red pickup truck had flown past, doing eighty, maybe eighty-five. Teenagers on a Friday night—New Year's Eve, no less, Pritam thought as he pulled off the shoulder of the road onto the highway in pursuit. He had not seen the gooti topknot of the boy in the passenger seat.

He sped through two stop signs before the pickup truck's tail-lights became visible, and Pritam thought it curious that the driver had not turned down a side road, in case they were chased. The distance between the two vehicles diminished rapidly as Pritam pressed hard on the accelerator. The pickup truck had slowed ahead of him. You couldn't keep up that speed forever; sooner or later, you had to slow if you wanted to stay alive. Pritam turned on the siren and the lights. The pickup wavered in its speed, accelerating and slowing, as if the driver was contemplating his next move. As he pulled close behind, Pritam noticed the passenger turning his head repeatedly to the rear, and the gooti on his head. The vehicle lurched off the road and stopped ahead of him.

There was heavy static on the radio when Pritam called for backup. He paused, checking the revolver at his side before he emerged from the car. He did not feel the night chill of the air as he approached, because his heartbeat echoed in loud thumps through his body.

"Outta the car, both of you," he said.

The boys filed out and placed their palms against the side of the truck, as Pritam asked them to do. He felt Sukhi's body trembling as he patted him down for weapons.

"I've got nothing on me, bhrava," Sukhi said. "We're not out for trouble. Just a good time."

"You won't be having a good time if you kill yourself, or someone else, driving like that."

Pritam's eyes darted down the dark road, looking for signs of the backup patrol car approaching. He was patting down the driver when Sukhi lunged for the crowbar in the truck bed and swung it once, catching him in the side and nearly knocking him over. But Pritam was stronger than Sukhi, a sluggish, lanky youth of sixteen. He tore the crowbar from Sukhi's hands, causing the boy to fall. The driver backed away from the truck, then sprinted off into a nearby orchard. A sharp pain seared Pritam's side. He tightened his grip around the metal bar as he stood over the boy, who cowered on the ground as he begged to be spared.

What he remembered most was the sound of the dense metal striking flesh and bone. A dull, unforgiving thump. Again and again, until the thing he was striking no longer flinched from his blows, but absorbed them without struggle. He could not see well. The boy had rolled off the shoulder down a short embankment, out of the powder white beam of the headlights, but not out of Pritam's reach. He felt himself bursting with rage then that the boy lay still, no longer moving, that he had to cease striking him just as that urge swelled in him most to beat back the impassive world that was closing in on him. When the backup cop finally arrived, he shined a flashlight on the boy's twisted body. "Jesus, Preet," he said before he called the ambulance.

The phone rang before dawn. I lay motionless, gravity wedging me against the sheets as the first pieces of the story filtered from the kitchen back into my room. I could almost hear the scritch of Charan Kaur's panicked voice on the other end, my mother's lilting tones as she attempted to soothe her. Pritam's mother had received the news from Jarnail Singh himself. "Your son will pay," he said, and from there on, Charan Kaur's sole charge would become warding off the threats directed at her son, the one who increasingly resembled the young husband she had married on a stormy spring day back in her village.

In the kitchen, the echo of the telephone's ring still vibrated in my ear. I filled a pot with water for tea and remembered it was New Year's Day. Looking out the window, I expected the world to look changed. The bare branches in the back orchard hung in aloof, uncaring angles, as if time itself had congealed and frozen, silent, within them. There was something irrevocable even in the water running from the tap, swirling and vanishing into the pipes below. You can't get any of it back, I thought.

My mother shuffled slowly from the cupboard to the stove, filling her cup with tea. The boy lay unconscious in the hospital, but he was expected to live, she announced. She leaned against the counter as if her legs would not support her. She would stand like that, crumpled and heavy, some nights when Aunt Manjit would call, very late, crying that her son was too young to protect her yet. The tea bitter in her mouth, my mother emptied the contents of the cup into the sink and rinsed it. She lingered at the sink, her fingers clutching its white porcelain edge. How many times had she stood there, her back bowed over vegetables to be scrubbed, or her head lifted to view fleeting pastoral images as the seasons shifted outside the window? Her weight had etched a scruffy oval patch like a scar into the green-and-white-checked linoleum.

Charan Kaur stood at our doorstep later that morning, smearing her black surma over her cheeks with her shawl. "Mera bucha," she cried. "He should've stayed at the store. I can't send him away anymore." How could this have happened to her, who held the raw destiny of so many in her grasp? My mother put an arm around her shoulder and led her into the house. Charan Kaur's hunched, fragile carriage stiffened when she noticed me standing by the kitchen door; her sea green eyes smoldered with contempt, as if I had handed her son the metal bar myself.

"He would not have done such a thing unless he was provoked," she said, raising a finger to my mother.

I got in the car later to navigate my usual routes—an aimless drive through the quiet town, which invariably carried me to places outside its limits, where the compass points of my life always seemed to lie. I passed India Bazaar on my way, then Charan Kaur's mint green ranch-style house on the edge of town. The black-and-white patrol car parked against the shaggy row of junipers along the driveway renewed my sense of dread. I imagined Pritam inside, sleeping off the late-morning hours, if one could sleep under such circumstances. I remembered what it felt like, my breasts pressed against his flat, warm chest. But the question twisted and turned like a sharp stone inside me: Who was he in those moments when he pounded Sukhi Singh's body relentlessly? I would find it difficult to face Pritam days later when he told me the boy had come after him first. But he did not tell me that he had waited many nights and days along that same road, hoping Sukhi, or someone with that same inclination for trouble, would come along and bait him.

That morning, I wound up once again at Neelam's doorstep. At the breakfast table, my mother had muttered something through a

mouthful of roti smeared with sweet chutney: It was odd that Neelam hadn't accompanied her husband to visit his aunt in San Jose.
Perhaps my sister and I needed each other's company on such a
bright and dreadful morning. Neelam's small green sedan was not
parked in its usual spot on the street. I rang the doorbell, then
knocked several times, but no one responded.

Davinder hadn't wanted to leave her behind. When Neelam
protested that morning, her whimpers muffled by the thick pile of
bedcovers she refused to easily part with, he had let her be and set
off for Sethi Mahal's for the remainder of the New Year's holiday
weekend. Neelam waved good-bye from the shadow of the doorway. The morning light flooded the car as he lifted his hand to her,
then drove off through the neighborhood, which was still slumber-
ing after the previous night's revelry. Four doors down, he would
notice the beige drapes in the Hollinghursts' living room window
sagging heavily, as though someone, in a moment of blinding joy,
had swung from them; the red Firebird parked on the lawn in front
of 4251 would also strike him as irregular. Davinder would smile
softly at these random disruptions, trusting that they would be cor-
rected by the time he returned. Awhile later, steering down Highway 80 toward San Francisco, the minuscule hope would rise in his
heart that his wife's recent malaise could only mean . . . that God,
with his unfathomable plans, at last would grant them . . .

After her husband left that morning, Neelam returned to bed
but felt a restlessness tracing through the quiet room. She threw the
covers off and sat up. A long beam of light from an east-facing
window sliced diagonally through the shadows. An acid taste of revulsion rose in her throat; she had not yet bathed, or recited her
prayers from the holy book.

She showered, then, famished, rushed into the kitchen and pulled
carrots and cream and butter from the refrigerator and raisins and
almonds and farina from a cabinet to prepare the gajjar halva her

mother had always made on special occasions. She scrubbed the carrots and then began to rub them sharply against the stainless-steel grater. Prayer would be postponed until the afternoon or evening; didn't her husband often admonish her for skipping meals in favor of honoring her spiritual duties? She scraped harder, watching the bright orange flakes accumulate in a fluffy pile, but she did not notice the bleeding on her knuckles until the blood dripped down her fingers and onto the grater and the carrots. She flexed her hand open and shut, puzzled that she felt nothing, not even an ordinary squeamish shudder brought on by the blood oozing from the cuts. Flustered, she picked up a fresh carrot and the grater and resumed her work, pausing only when a sliver of skin clung to a sharp metal point. This was what frightened her, she would tell me later—that she felt nothing at all. Nothing, not even the breath her body silently demanded. She swept the counter clean, stuffing the carrots and the grater into the garbage container, then washed her hand and wrapped it in cheesecloth.

After she wrapped her hand, she jumped into her car and drove off. It was then that our paths crossed. I saw Neelam stalled at the corner of Briggs and Tamor, as though deciding which way to turn. I would have honked and waved, but something held me back. Perhaps it was the concern in my mother's voice that morning when she told me Neelam had stayed in town. When the white sedan turned south onto Tamor, I followed it at a distance. I soon realized this was no casual weekend drive she was taking. A few miles east lay the vast property still known as the Mohta Singh Ranch. When she turned left onto Howard Lane, I knew exactly where she was going.

Neelam parked her car beside a tall, spreading deodar cedar that grew along the road. The large brick house was visible from there through the rows of bare peach trees. A red pickup truck was parked along one side of the house. Neelam waited in the car for several moments, then turned onto the gravel driveway and steered the car behind the pickup truck, where it was out of view from the road. I saw the white bandage wrapped around one hand as she knocked on the door with the other. The door opened and she slipped inside.

I drove away from there, suddenly resenting the burden of knowing what was taking place behind those walls. I maneuvered the car down the two-lane road cautiously, like someone chastised. For what? For living. Wanting. These were our terrible deeds.

Sukhi Singh was released from the hospital the following week, requiring a wheelchair, which kept him confined to the first floor of his multilevel home. His grandfather Jarnail Singh proposed an investigation of the incident and became a frequent visitor at the police station, offering boxes of cigars, cases of fine bourbon, or even money to the officers in blatant attempts to bribe them. Sheriff Snow, the newly hired eighteen-year veteran of the force in Vallejo, tolerated his demands in a bemused sort of way at first. He had burst into town with a swagger that hadn't diminished in the least in the ensuing months. The police-brutality charges struck him as absurd and he intended to protect his rookie cop, who, according to his own version of the events, had been attacked first. Finally, he warned Jarnail Singh that his continued attempts to influence the officers would land him in jail.

Gradually, the story faded in the minds of the community. A fresh scandal involving misuse of funds at the Grove Road gurdwara emerged, dominating everyone's attention. They were unsure as yet if Pritam's star had risen or sunk following the New Year's Eve incident, but they were content to withhold judgment for the time being. The occasional rumor surfaced: Pritam was baiting trouble among some of the clans, or he was soliciting protection money from others. I didn't know what to believe anymore and resisted his attempts to contact me.

I found other means to keep my mind and time occupied. At the beginning of the semester, I took an office job at a busy engineering firm. It had been awarded recently with several contracts for bridge expansions throughout the Sacramento and San Joaquin valleys. I worked afternoons mimeographing, collating, and percolating fresh pots of coffee, serving brimming cups to men in pressed suits and ties who found my cautious behavior around them curious, amusing. I would take a moment to peek around their shoulders to witness the arcs and spans of their dreams drawn boldly in fluid purple-blue across massive sheets of paper. From my desk by the front window, I would sometimes see a black patrol car pass around closing time, when the sunlight poured like water through the bare limbs of ash trees, flooding the office. It would turn the corner slowly, hesitating before it resumed the twenty-five-mile-an-hour speed posted along the street. Then I would feel that shift, a tide turning within me, pulling me back.

Twenty

I heard him call to me in a dream; or perhaps I was awake and the walls shuddered and the sound echoed my name. That's the way I remember it, just as I remember standing at my mother's vanity as she put on her gold earrings, the long, heavy ones shaped like bells, fringed at the bottom with tiny gold beads. She had tilted her chin up, an indulgent examination, an anxious appraisal (was the beauty still there—the firm, unlined face, the full lips?). I would do it, I told her. I would forget, I told myself. Forget Pritam, everything. I would trust in something new, strange, and his name was Ameer. I would go to India with her. But I knew, too, in my heart, that one never forgets. Why was my mother looking at her reflection that way, the angle of her head, her terrified mouth, a portrait of what? She turned and cupped my hands in hers. "I knew it," she said. "I knew one day you would."

The days before our departure to India were filled with a flurry of activity. We armed our medicine bag with aspirin, Pepto-Bismol, antihistamines, first-aid ointments, bandages, and laxatives. We shopped for shirts, scarves, sweaters and socks for relatives I didn't know existed. My mother rummaged through the rooms, pulling ornamental trays and vases from shelves and cabinets, rubbing the dust from them and exclaiming that no one would know they had sat unused in our house for years. These, too, were stuffed into our already-bulging suitcases, to be distributed to a thoughtful neighbor or an unexpected guest. There would be many of them, judging from past experience, because we were coming from America, and everyone in my mother's village at one time or another would pass through the doors of my grandfather's house, eager to have a look at us.

Occasionally, I would freeze amid all the commotion, reminded that someone far away was waiting for me, a notion that terrified and beguiled me all at once. How easily I had succumbed to my parents' wishes for me in the end. I could've listened to the Jenny Holcomb voice inside my head that said it was my life, but I didn't know who I was without them.

Uncle Avtar sent us off at the airport with an explicit plea to my father to visit their brother, Lal, who had finished his schooling and taken a governmental post in Chandigarh. He wasn't indifferent to my situation. When the news of my consent passed on to relatives, he had pulled me aside. "It's so sudden. Are you sure, Jeeto?" I saw the muscles clamping in his face and I slipped my hand in his. "It's all right, Chacha," I told him. As I stood behind my parents in line to board the plane, I turned back to wave at him once more, and the same distressed look plagued his face.

The plane groaned as it lifted off the ground and ascended through the layers of fog. I closed my eyes, knowing that for many, many hours there would be only water below.

In New Delhi, we hired a taxi to take us to the main railway station in the center of the city. We rode silently, mesmerized by the choked, crowded streets of Delhi, a city learning to rise once again, as it had several times in its long history, to its promised place. The driver navigated an erratic route down broad tree-lined avenues, ducking suddenly onto congested, smoke-filled side streets no wider than alleys before emerging along grand monuments of red sandstone and marble. At my mother's command, we stopped in Chandni Chowk for warm, syrupy jalebis and a mad search among the little shops to replace her worn chappals. The railway station was crowded with commuters, students, families, beggars, wandering sadhus, wearing no more than kuchas, whose detached gaze frightened me. We finally boarded the train for the long ride north to Jalandhar. Small villages, no more than clusters of mud houses, dotted the surrounding wheat and cotton fields outside of the city. My mother stared from the window of our compartment as if this were an alien land, though little had changed since her last visit. Later, an amber mist hovered above the fields as the sun set beyond. We passed through Ludhiana after dark. At the railway station in Jalandhar, we were greeted by hawkers of chai, samosas, barfi.

The slow, dusty bus ride to Satpur, my mother's village, the following morning was lengthened by an unruly passenger arguing with the driver about the route, and then a dying cow whose bloating body partially straddled the roadway. A deep, muddy ditch flanked the left-hand side of the dirt road, and though the bus had room to squeeze by, a controversy erupted as to the proper course to pursue, bringing our journey temporarily to a halt. Several men disembarked to inspect the roadway, slicing their hands in the air every which way to indicate some mode of action. My father was wiping his neck with a kerchief by this time, though the temperature outside was pleasantly cool. The condition of the cow was of paramount concern to others, who uttered words of prayer when the bus finally edged around it and sputtered off.

I fell asleep for the remainder of the journey, a half sleep where the wheezing sound of the engine, the murmur of voices, and an overwhelming smell like overripe fruit refused to release their hold of me. We reached Satpur by early afternoon. A pack of boys struggled with our suitcases along the path that wound toward the edge of the village. As we approached my grandfather's house, the smoke from the cooking fires prodded my appetite.

It was a simple one-room brick home with a small room of mud plaster added on at one side. We were greeted first by my mother's brother, my uncle Jogi, a stout man with a full black beard. His wife, Inderjit, hung back, a glint of terror in her gaze as she lifted her arms to embrace my mother. Two beds, manjas covered with mustard-colored rajais, lined one wall. On one sat my grandfather, whose hands were sealed around the top end of his wooden walking stick. He remained motionless when we entered and said little more than "So, you've returned."

My mother stared at the cement floor, which had been installed over the dirt one from her childhood. She took refuge in the arms of my grandmother, who had pulled herself upright on the other bed. Then she wept.

"Khushi," my grandmother said, taking my face in her hands as she uttered the word for happiness. "Munda?" she asked, referring to Prem, and my mother explained that we had left him behind with Neelam because of school. Her body had shrunk with the fever and her gray eyes had burrowed back into her skull. She resembled my aunt Manjit more in this emaciated state, and my mother less and less.

We pulled gifts from the suitcases: a cheap imitation-pearl necklace and matching broach my mother lifted from a case for Inderjit Auntie, and for her brother, a sweater of fine blue and black wool and black trousers with pleats. There were other bric-a-brac items my aunt unwrapped and immediately displayed on the painted wooden shelves beside the portraits and pottery and brassware. The house had struck me as bare and uninteresting when I first entered, but I also saw the pride my aunt had in keeping the house immaculate.

I followed her to the small courtyard behind the house, where the cookware was stored. She plunged her hand into the ashes from the morning's cooking fire and tossed them onto a platter, scrubbed it clean, then handed it to me. Water was too precious a commodity.

"Your fiancé, he is a handsome man?" she asked, taking another platter.

"Hahji," I replied.

"An educated man will be good for you." She wiped the platters with a cloth and poured warm dal into a brass bowl. Her chuni had fallen from her head, exposing a high, elegant forehead. There was the proud look on her face again, as though she had been meant to live a different life.

I set the bowl of dal on a low table inside. From her seat on the bed beside my grandmother, my mother was interrogating my uncle about her mother's illness.

"We've given her herbs, salves prescribed by a local woman," my uncle explained.

"But a proper doctor could diagnose her fever."

"We have no funds for a doctor in Jalandhar," my uncle replied. My grandmother lay on her side, her breathing labored. I thought of the cow dying on the road.

"Acha. I'll take her myself." There was the voluble snap of my mother's purse shutting.

A tension that had been building since our arrival only hours earlier bubbled to the surface. The letters my mother regularly wrote back to India always kindled a remorse in her by the time she sealed them. I assumed the long separation from her family accounted for her moody periods afterward. Was my uncle willing to let my grandmother perish, believing that it was simply her time? He seemed to resent my mother's intrusion, as though she had given up her rights in the matter the day she parted for America. I recognized it eventually as a natural friction between those who had managed to flee and those who had remained behind.

"Well, much to accomplish," she said, rising from the manja. I think she was glad to leave the village with my father for Jalandhar the next morning. The car was loaded with the sweets we had risen early to prepare, and my mother mentioned they would stop for a lavish basket of fruit along the way.

I spent the day with Rani, who struck me always as impossibly happy, content whether she was hauling buckets of water from the pump all morning or laundering heaps of clothes in a metal trough in the afternoons. Her long plait swung with vigor behind her as she gathered the items of clothing one by one and wrung the water from them. I had met her on my previous visit, when our brief mutual interest in making outfits from fabric remnants for her stuffed doll had bound us during a scorching, rain-filled month. Later, we sat on the stoop in front of her house and she showered me with questions about life in America. Was it true every house had a washing and drying machine? Were goree girls our age really permitted to go steady with boys? Finally, I tired of her interrogation, good-natured though it was. It was my second day in India and the excitement of our journey and arrival was quickly wearing off. I had begun to miss everything back home, the most ordinary things—my classes, a trip to the supermarket to buy milk, my bed, which cushioned my sleep with a mattress, not a woven mesh slung between posts.

My parents returned the same evening with glowing reports about the boy's family.

My mother stood in the middle of the room, commanding the attention of one and all. "A clean modern home in Gurjaipal Nagar. They have a second son, who is studying to be an engineer."

"Good people. Mr. Singh is a schoolteacher," said my father, who, in an ill-fitting kurta he had borrowed from his brother-in-law, looked the way he had the entire trip, as though he felt out of place, out of sorts.

"They have three servants," my mother emphasized. Inderjit Auntie retreated to the back room.

When she was done boasting about the family's fortunes, she turned to me. "We can arrange a meeting for you two. Ameer's parents have a restaurant in mind in Jalandhar. Then all we need is your consent to make the karmai official."

I had little time to mull it all over. What was there left to think about? my mother seemed to wonder as she paced near the doorway. I slipped outside to the courtyard behind the house to be alone. The brassware shimmered on the wood stand against the brick wall. I collapsed onto a small bench carved from a log and dropped my head in my lap. How had it come to this?

When I asked where the meeting would be held, Nani clapped her hands. She would regain her strength, she announced, if only to witness her granddaughter's engagement.

"Peking Palace," my mother replied. "Ameer will be returning from Shimla tomorrow. I almost forgot . . ." She disappeared into the back room and came out a moment later with a paper package she set on the manja and began to unwrap. It was a salwaar kameez, in sheer layers of pale coral chiffon. She held the kameez against my body. "Your size. I picked it up at Model Town in Jalandhar yesterday."

"When you marry, you can have nice things to wear, like Neelam," she had told me a few years back.

I bathed at Rani's with two buckets of water and a bar of lavender English soap I had brought with me. Rani guarded the door, watching for her grandmother, whom she privately called "Hawk Eyes." It was a small, dark room at the back of the house, with a cement floor and a crude trough that carried the water outside into the courtyard. I dressed in the coral outfit at my grandfather's house. Nani watched as my mother coiled my hair up and pinned it at the top of my head. In my reflection in Inderjit Auntie's mirror, I saw the faint outline of Neelam's face and I reeled as I thought I was becoming, in these brief days in this distant country, an altogether different Jeeto Rai.

The family assembled by the taxi stand at the west end of the village. I was pleased to see that my uncle Jogi and Inderjit Auntie had elected to join us so that a small but impressive entourage would enter the Peking Palace to greet Ameer's family. A sharp breeze picked up, carrying the scent of rain. Some of the village children who had been playing under the shade of a sissoo tree gathered around, the coming and going of an occasional bus or taxi a source of curiosity. Two little girls recognized the occasion immediately and tugged at my wrists and pulled me along to the car. "Boti, boti!" they cried. The bride. I heard an eagerness chime in their ecstatic laughter; someday that moment would arrive for them, the pinnacle of their impoverished lives. The driver flung open the doors of the taxi and we filed in one by one.

It would've taken place during the bath, I reasoned later. As I scooped a tumblerful of water from the bucket and showered my hair and skin with it, the rain on the eastern slopes of the foothills had intensified. Ameer was taking a short break from his studies and had decided to spend an extra night in Shimla with his dear friend Kirpal. Our car streamed along the narrow paved road past the irregular patchwork of green-and-brown fields toward Jalandhar. We entered the outskirts of the city by late afternoon and our pace slowed to a crawl as we encountered swarms of pedestrians and bicycles and carts overloaded with produce and wares and people crowding the walkways along the row of low, sun-bleached shops. At Model Town, I stepped from the car and smoothed my kameez, rumpled and sweaty from the drive. I checked my face and hair in a small compact I had brought with me, and when I snapped

it shut, I noticed two men rapidly approaching from the direction
of Peking Palace. Ameer's parents would not be joining us, they informed my father. Ameer had not returned from Shimla and there
were reports of a bus accident on the morning line.

I rushed to the restaurant myself and looked inside its windows,
a fading pink from the sun lowering in the sky behind me. I
cupped my eyes to shade them and peered through the glass. Patrons dining inside stared back at me, but I found the table. A vase
of yellow daisies decorated the middle of a table draped with a
crisp white cloth, where we would have sat across from each other.
Inderjit Auntie took my hand and pulled me away.

We spent the night at neighbors of Ameer, a large family that sat
up with us all night drinking tea and sending long, pitying glances
my way. My father returned to Satpur with the driver the following day to collect my grandmother. A doctor's examination had revealed no obvious malady. More tests would be required. By then,
Ameer's father had returned from Shimla with the news: On a
sharp turn in the steep hill road, the bus had skidded off the slick
pavement into a ravine swollen with water below. Only a handful
of passengers had survived.

In Satpur, I took refuge on the manja in the back room. "Let
her sleep," I heard my mother whisper to someone. As if I could. A
while later, she tiptoed into the room and saw that I lay awake, a
corner of the mustard-colored rajai clenched in my mouth.

"Jeeto," she said, putting her hand on my knee. "There is the
brother." I jumped back on the bed against the wall, my body re-
coiling from the suggestion. She never mentioned another word of
him again.

I returned to the States six days later, unengaged. An almost
widow. For a long time thereafter, I was reluctant to utter an adamant
no because it might shut a door forever, but I was also fearful at times
to say yes, for the door might open to an empty room.

Twenty-one

Seven babies were born. Balwant Kaur broke her foot trying to crawl through a window when her own daughter-in-law locked her out of the house. Nika Singh pushed Thiara Singh's pickup truck into a ditch after an argument. Neelam announced these incidents like a dispassionate newscaster on our return. But it was my news that had devastated her following our telephone call from New Delhi. She stood in our kitchen, unwrapping the cheese-cloth from the parathas; she had prepared a meal to welcome us home. It was her turn to tell me: "There'll be another time."

Our home filled once again with family. The women observed me with some curiosity, deflecting their inevitable stares toward their toes, curled in sandals, or a spot on the wall. At tea, they made small talk and carefully avoided the *k* word—karma—for I would have screamed and possibly beat my fists into the nearest one of them. "It was bad luck," announced Aunt Manjit, a woman who had experienced her share of it.

Prem helped me clear the table one evening following dinner, a rare and unexpected gesture. He stood beside me by the sink, hold-ing the plates away from his body as though repulsed by the messy results of simply eating a meal. After he had collected all the dishes, he leaned against the counter and watched me as I scrubbed each dish and utensil, then rinsed each.

"That's a lot of work," he said.

I looked up at him, for he had grown taller than I was by then, and he continued talking—about school, the Warriors-Lakers game, a sporty car he would purchase someday when he had a job. When I finished, I went to my room and he followed me, stopping at the door as if he needed another moment to figure it all out, what had happened.

I found it difficult to concentrate in my classes; after dinner, I would go quietly to my room and play the radio and sulk while I stared at my books, open to the wrong pages. I would see Ameer's body floating in the water when I shut my eyes in bed. Neelam said it was guilt, that even though I had never met him, and never would, I felt responsible on some level for his death. My parents worried about my flagging spirits, but it was my uncle who appeared one evening with a roguish smile on his face. He disappeared into my parents' bedroom for a private talk with my father, which lasted more than an hour. I found my mother more than once standing outside the door with her ear pressed to it.

The following evening, my father called me into the living room for a chat. "Sit down," he said, pointing to the blue armchair my mother normally occupied when she did her embroidery. I obeyed the earnest look in his eyes, calm and pleading, like Neelam's.

"I've been talking with your chacha. About this situation," he said haltingly. "Your chacha and I were talking. . . . Perhaps it's best if you go off to school. We need one educated person in the family. Where was it, San Francisco?" He avoided any mention of Ameer, as though my engagement had been some ill-hatched plan he regretted deeply.

"Berkeley. But it's too late to apply for next year."

"It's never too late. We'll find a way."

My mother entered one of her famous silent periods, speaking to my father only when absolutely necessary, leaving our meals on the table while she ate alone in the kitchen. Even she had been kind to me on our return from India, resisting her urge to pry into my every thought and emotion. The decision was finalized between the brothers, with little input from her. And worse, what she feared most was materializing. I would set off into the world and become something unfamiliar to her, someone she could no longer control. In my more thoughtful moments, I pleaded with her: "Mummy, don't be mad." And I understood finally that it was more than that. She feared she would never see me again, not in the same way; that a common language we shared would erode amid the books and new friends and I would become a stranger to my own mother.

Early that summer, Surinder invited me to her home. She had something to tell me that she could not divulge over the telephone. We agreed to meet over the weekend, and I wondered the rest of the week what her news might be. The lilt and crackle in her voice caused me to think it concerned a man, though I understood her involvement with Ajit Singh was long past.

Mrs. Singh greeted me at the door and guided me back through the darkened rooms in her bare feet. In her room, Surinder reclined on the rose satin bedcovers, an array of yearbooks and photo albums spread around her. The room looked small, bare. The Beatles and Disneyland posters had been removed from the west-facing walls, as though she was preparing for some new phase of her life, one that demanded more solemn pursuits.

In our embrace, I felt our bodies lock, our hair tangle together, the strength in our limbs collide as we held on to each other one

second longer. Surinder dashed to the vanity, where an eight-by-
ten photo leaned against the glass, a color photo whose weight
barely pressed on her anxious, spread fingertips. In the photograph, a young Indian man wearing a pair of gray slacks and a
blue button-down shirt with the collar open smiled openly into
the camera. One foot was set on the rungs of the stool beside him,
one hand placed on his waist, with a silver kara gleaming from his
wrist.

"Sandeep Mehta," she said, reeling at the sound of the name.
"He's an electrical engineer. He already has a position lined up
with FloTech Systems in Cupertino."

The photograph rattled in my hands. "You're getting engaged?"

"Married!" she squealed. "On November third. I'm sorry to
bring it up this way. After what happened, I mean. I didn't want to tell
you right away."

"It's all right. It's not your fault."

"He's visiting in August. We'll be house hunting in the Bay
Area. I've spoken with him on the phone and he says he wants a
place with a view of the bay."

I felt a tightening in my chest and looked into her beaming face.
She was waiting, silently begging for my approval. "It's such a surprise."

"My parents talked to me one day. They said they had heard of
someone, you know, a nephew of so-and-so's cousin . . . and I
thought, What am I waiting for?"

I looked again at the photograph; all of Surinder's hopes lay in
that young man's confident smile. How could I disapprove when I
had so recently nurtured that same faith?

"When I saw his picture, I just knew it was the right thing for
me." She squeezed my hand hard, the way she used to when she
told me she had found just the right pair of boots on sale or Pritam
had spoken to her. "I hope you'll be happy for me."

"Of course." I returned the photograph to its prominent place on the vanity. "What about beauty school, Monique's?"

"Oh, the Bay Area has some really classy salons," she said, her expression turning serious.

At home, my mother heard my footsteps in the living room. "Jeeto," she called in a serene tone. The plain white cotton shawl she always wore for prayer was draped around her shoulders: Was it for luck, or an attempt to demonstrate a kind of humbleness or purity? "So you've learned the big news. Your saheli, your friend . . ." She paused for a moment, her fingers covering her mouth, wanting to devise her plea more carefully. "You'll see. Maybe it's still too early for you, but someday your books will no longer be enough. You'll want all this." She lifted her arms as if to honor the glory of our rather dismal living room—the once-bright rose drapes, the blue damask sofas grown shabby at last from the friction of bodies shifting across their faint floral pattern over the years—then dropped them quickly like a boxer acknowledging defeat.

I began college at Berkeley that fall. Out my dormitory window, a covey of pigeons flapped about on a narrow ledge as they sunned themselves on fogless mornings; crowded buses lumbered up the avenue, dropping students, who dashed en masse across the street and onto the campus, clutching book bags and nearly forgotten jackets. I set off for classes each day, grabbing a muffin from a street vendor and sharing it with my roommate, Marie, a pale, sardonic girl from Santa Rosa who started chain-smoking the moment we left the building. Lectures on natural selection in vast halls packed with sniffling, half-dozing students, delivered by a slightly bowed professor who had survived, perhaps participated in the tumult of the previous decade. The damp, noisy nights, the whispers on the other side of the wall until dawn that left little chance to sleep, or dream. The different way boys looked at me. There were occasional weekend trips to Point Reyes National Seashore and Muir Beach piled in Lucy Boddinger's orange Volkswagen, which refused to shift into reverse, or art films at the UC Theater on University Avenue. The city streets wound in mysterious curves and angles, and if I ever felt lost, I would stop in the middle of the campus to look up past the tall gray Campanile to the green hills. If you walked up high enough, you could see all of the land sloping down toward the bay, whose deep blue waters cut in from the ocean like stout fingers. I stood in long lines at the cafeteria, saturated with the bland aroma of Swiss steak and creamed corn, cherishing my mother's promises of aloo paratha when I visited again.

And I would often think back to the time in the spring when I so easily gave myself to something I didn't really understand. I still kept Ameer's photograph in my dorm room. How easily we give ourselves to one another; we call it love. How easily it can be pulled from us, ripping our insides like a cord.

Several weeks into the fall semester, I returned to Oak Grove for the sangeet held in advance of Surinder's wedding, The women gathered on the front lawn in a ceremonial greeting line: Neelam, my mother, Aunt Teji, Aunt Manjit, and a younger new neighbor, who carried an infant on her hip. I was soon enveloped by their arms and bosoms and their sharp questions. At Surinder's house, the living room furniture was pushed back to the walls and the women gathered in a circle, like bright candles on a birthday cake. Round and round we went, our bare feet thumping the blue shag carpet, our hands clapping in rhythm or carving stories in the spice-scented air. The younger women fell away first; the older ones could go on forever, as if they, more than we, needed to forget themselves entirely. From the floor, Surinder and I watched the gidda dance, she with a fresh fascination; its festive air and steady beat contained new meanings for her. She climbed to her feet to join them again, grateful to be granted the chance she believed might already have eluded her. With her assent to marry, the women welcomed her among their ranks without question. She would be one of them now. When Aunt Teji came around and pulled me into the circle, I fell in line between her and my mother. I tried to mimic my mother's movements, their precision and strength, one hip and shoulder driving into, then away from the circle of swirling bodies. I had tried to please her once. Not just her, all of them. Now I needed to pull back, to protect something inside myself.

The wedding would take place at the Stockton gurdwara, in deference to Surinder's grandmother, who lived nearby. On a cool morning in early November, I climbed the gray steps that led to its tall, arched doorways, stopping at the top to wait for Neelam, who rustled behind me, lifting the hems of her salwaar. Standing there, I pictured myself in one of Uncle Avtar's photographs of the gurdwara showing the grandfathers, mothers, brothers, children lined along these same storied steps.

At the appointed time, Surinder appeared through a side door, shrouded in ruby red and guided by an aunt and cousin with lowered, mournful gazes. When she was led to her place beside Sandeep, I imagined for a moment that she was playacting. There was a time when we were very little when we wanted to be like our mothers, pulling silky kameezes from their hangers and pressing them against our slender bodies. Winding bright chunis about our necks and speaking in grave tones, our chins elevated. When the women released Surinder's wrists, she teetered, the balls of her bare feet rolling gently on the carpet as she sought her equilibrium. One hand emerged from her long silk veil as she lowered herself to the floor, the dark hennaed pattern painted on her skin unfurling like a net.

Afterward, the Mehtas, the groom's family, passed into the home of Surinder's grandmother in a long procession and huddled by the far wall until chairs were brought for them. The modern ranch-style house had a blue theme: cornflower blue walls and navy blue drapes and blue plaid sofa covers. Despite this conscious effort at color coordination, there were the unmistakable imprints of an Indian home: posters of a ferocious Kali charging ahead on a sprinting tiger with her spear poised for battle, multicolored embroidered throws with little mirrors sewn in them draping the sofa arms, shiny satin rajais covering the beds. "Sat Sri Akal," I said to Surinder's grandmother, a slight, elegant woman who frowned into my face until she recognized me.

I squirmed through the tight, intimate press of bodies congealed like dough in the front room, greeting this aunt or that cousin. A roar went up when someone removed the Punjabi tape and replaced it with the earsplitting beat of disco. I waved to Davinder, who was absorbed in an affable round of joking and teasing with his male friends. Charan Kaur had cornered my father at the far end of the room, seeming to relish the brief moments of his company. At the table, Aunt Manjit piled plates full of koa and samosas for her children, imploring Uncle Avtar as he passed by to keep an eye on her husband. Her daughter Lakshmi followed Neelam around the room like a lost child. It was only then that I noticed, as Neelam bent over the child to offer her a morsel of food, the loose-fitting kameez, the lavender silk puffing slightly at her waist. A moment later, she disappeared into another room.

Through the glass patio doors, I watched Pritam standing under a birch tree in the backyard, wearing a dark suit and sunglasses. Mrs. Singh had invited him at her daughter's request, albeit reluctantly. A steady trickle of men young and old shook hands with him and exchanged friendly greetings. Sukhi Singh's pronounced limp would remain a continual reminder that, even if they did not trust Pritam, they would do well to remain on good terms with him. He was no longer the boy they had shouted their grocery orders to.

I made my way to the Mehta camp, which had crowded around the bride and groom, freshly dressed in party clothes. Surinder spun around, her pink lehenga skirt twirling at her ankles.

"My best friend in the whole world," she announced, pulling me into the group. "Jeeto's going to school in Berkeley," she boasted, still clutching my hands. The women appraised me head to foot, and then, as if to break those seconds of mild tension, Sandeep stepped forward and joined his palms together in a formal greeting. "Surinder is already awaiting your first visit to our home." A hint of mischief lurked in his solemn tone and I suspected that perhaps Surinder had made a good match after all.

"I'll be there before you're unpacked," I warned them.

The crowd gradually began to disperse, with some guests leaving and others merely retiring to other rooms for a brief rest. There was a plan afoot by the younger men to decorate the bride and groom's car with flower garlands and shaving cream. I picked at the remnants of the last samosa on a platter, not realizing that the sound reverberating in my ears was only an echo in the now-empty room.

"Jeeto . . ." a familiar voice said behind me. "Shocking thing, isn't it?" Pritam remarked. "Surinder getting married like this?"

It seemed so long ago that he had run off with her. I had thought the time would never come when I could look at either of them and not think of that incident. But so much had happened since; perhaps that was life's offhand way of sparing us. "He seems like a decent guy. I think they're going to be happy together."

Pritam stood frozen in front of me, not even blinking, and I realized he was not referring to Surinder at all, but to me. The way he felt I had betrayed him. "I'm sorry for what happened."

"Everything just happened so fast," I said, dropping my chin. "I don't know . . ."

"What's school like?"

"Crazy. Very busy."

"I always knew you would go."

He scanned the room. The wedding party had gathered out-doors on the lawn and we were alone in the room for just that mo-ment. "Jeeto . . ." he said again. The vacant smile he had worn outside for his greeters had disappeared. It's me, it's still me, he seemed to plead. "Will you be coming back for the summer?" he asked.

I wiped my fingers on a used napkin. "I promised my parents I would." There was that brief moment between us, of hope—in his eyes, in my heart. But it passed, and when I looked up at him again, he seemed to search for someone else.

And then it was time for bride and groom to depart. Surinder's father began chiding his wife gently. "O-ho! She's only an hour and a half away," he said to her, sniffling copiously himself. Surinder and Sandeep emerged from the house hand in hand and stepped over the fragrant mosaic of rose petals scattered across the walkway. Mrs. Singh clasped her daughter's waist and led her to the sedan waiting by the curb. After a long embrace, Surinder turned to wave and then she was gone. It's what my father had told me once: that we mourn the birth of our daughters not because of the extraordi-nary burdens they bring to our lives, but because they leave us one day; they leave us to join their husband's families, whereas our sons remain.

We congregated by the cars along the street. The usual decisions about who would ride with whom back to Oak Grove would have to be hashed out as separate agendas surfaced among the parties. Uncle Avtar told me he had a detour in mind to test the limits of his new Lincoln sedan.

"One minute," I said to him. I had spotted the Rai boys con-vening among the crowd: Prem, standing tall, handsome in his black trousers, a blue shirt and tie; Juni, who earlier had managed the Punjabi greeting—Sat Sri Akal—to my parents now that he had made the baseball team at the community college; and Deepa squirming in a pair of stiff new loafers. "Prem," I called, dodging a pack of roaming children before I reached my brother. "Let's go back in Chacha's new car." I pulled him to the street, where Uncle Avtar waited proudly beside his shiny vehicle.

I climbed into the spacious red velour front seat beside my uncle, while Prem and Deepa tumbled into the back. It had been years since he had taken me through the river country, as he had always affectionately called it. Soon the car was bouncing westward, passing through valleys textured with broad swatches of alfalfa and plowed fields, soaring over iron drawbridges, which hummed as we crossed.

From the main bridge, we turned north along River Road. A bright orange flag fluttered ahead. Uncle Avtar slowed the car and halted beside a short, barrel-shaped man whose gloved hand held the flag's metal staff. Road construction, he said, leaning toward the car window, his mouth concealed under a furry scruff of beard.

My uncle shifted the gear to park and crossed his arms over his chest. "How long do you think?"

"Five, maybe ten," replied the road worker in his clipped, coded way of performing his duties.

"These old levee roads weren't built for cars like this," Uncle Avtar said, patting the dashboard affectionately.

The man appraised the width and breadth of the Lincoln's apple red body. "You're right there."

"This used to be the main road into the capital. Whenever the drawbridges went up, the cars backed up for half a mile." Uncle Avtar tapped his fingers on the steering wheel. "If you've got the time, get off these crazy freeways, I say. Take the back roads. See the country."

The worker, as though accustomed to chatty drivers, scratched his beard and nodded obligingly. The heat built quickly inside the car, the sun like a bright umbrella over the world. Through the open windows, I could hear bees hissing among the sparse shrubs along the road. I rested my head against the seat back, waiting for the flag to drop and the man to motion us on. To the west, a misty blue haze of clouds blowing in from the Pacific gathered over the tops of the trees, whose shadows were like smudges along the silver chain of water coursing silently southward. The minutes passed, steady creeping things. Surinder would be halfway to her new home in Redwood City by now, a split-level with a view of the bay. A new life. A husband. Tomorrow I would head back to school, my other life.

"Your saheli is gone," my uncle said, patting my shoulder as though sensing my melancholy thoughts. "You'll see her soon enough. She's just across the bay from you now."

I tried to swallow the knot caught in my throat. "It's not just that, Chacha."

"I know."

The flag dropped from its upright position and the man made a sweeping motion with it, a blurred orange line urging cars to pass on. The world was in motion again. The car accelerated slowly and my uncle swiveled his head from one side of the road to the other, not wanting to miss any of it—the sky reflected in the water, the serene lines of trees, and the grassy fields. We continued down the softly curving road and passed the warrenlike Asian communities beaded along the outer banks of the levee. My uncle pointed to a barge docked along an old packing shed, whose puckered shell of rusting corrugated metal sagged heavily. "This is where I packed pears," he said. Or: "That is where the *Mariposa* used to pick up passengers. Ladies in fancy coats, hats. The river was like a roadway then. The boats were our cars," he shouted to the boys in the backseat, who quieted for a moment, then resumed their frenetic, rumbling way of passing time.

"Hungry?" my uncle asked. A few miles ahead, he eased the car into a cramped space outside Lupe's Restaurant. The low, squat building was freshly painted cream yellow, the pattern of broad overlapping brush strokes visible at close range. Red-and-white-checked curtains framed the windows. Inside, the wooden floor slanted slightly toward the back kitchen. A couple of Filipino work hands slurped spoonfuls of posole from enormous white bowls at a table in the corner. An electric fan buzzed quietly next to them, circulating the damp, tepid air.

"I want a hamburger," Prem said as he fell heavily into the red vinyl booth next to Deepa, who nodded in agreement.

Uncle Avtar removed his fedora and slid onto the bench seat beside me. He turned frequently toward the voices coming from the kitchen, and the faces that once would have been familiar to him.

"Do you know this place, Chacha?" I asked.

He remained absorbed in the details of the room, as if trying to match them with his own memory. An old painting of a warrior with an eagle resting on his shoulder caught my uncle's eye briefly. He had intended to stop here all along, I realized; he had merely wanted company for the long ride. "It was a favorite of mine in the old days," he said, swiveling around to face the table. "They used to have a counter in that corner with a row of red bar stools."

"What's the special today?" he asked when the waitress appeared and handed out menus.

She was a young woman about my age, with a fringe of brown bangs falling into her soft green eyes. She pushed the pink eraser of her pencil against her bottom lip. "Braised beef. Comes with peas and mashed potatoes."

The waitress scribbled our orders on her paper pad as we recited them.

"I'll take the special," my uncle said, a hint of ceremony in his tone. His expression shifted when she smiled, the muscles in his face falling slack. Some years later when Hari told me his story, I understood what my uncle might have imagined when he looked so fondly at the waitress in that moment: that she might have worn red heels, a flared brown cotton skirt, and, dangling from her throat, a jade pendant. As though somewhere—harbored like a dormant secret within the young woman's skin, blood, bones—there lived still a part of Olivia.